PASSAGE
AT ARMS

Other books by Glen Cook

The Heirs of Babylon
The Swordbearer
A Matter of Time
The Dragon Never Sleeps
The Tower of Fear
Sung in Blood

Dread Empire
A Cruel Wind
(Containing *A Shadow of All
    Night Falling, October's Baby*
    and *All Darkness Met)*
A Fortress In Shadow
(Containing *The Fire in His
    Hands* and *With Mercy To-
    wards None)*
The Wrath of Kings (Containing
    Reap the East Wind and *An Ill
    Fate Marshalling)*

Starfishers
Shadowline
Starfishers
Stars' End

Darkwar
Doomstalker
Warlock
Ceremony

The Black Company
The Black Company
Shadows Linger
The White Rose
The Silver Spike
Shadow Games
Dreams of Steel
Bleak Seasons
She Is the Darkness
Water Sleeps
Soldiers Live

The Garrett Files
Sweet Silver Blues
Bitter Gold Hearts
Cold Copper Tears
Old Tin Sorrows
Dread Brass Shadows
Red Iron Nights
Deadly Quicksilver Lies
Petty Pewter Gods
Faded Steel Heat
Angry Lead Skies
Whispering Nickel Idols

**Instrumentalities of
the Night**
The Tyranny of the Night
Lord of the Silent Kingdom

GLEN COOK

PASSAGE AT ARMS

NIGHT SHADE BOOKS
SAN FRANCISCO

First Edition

ISBN: 978-1-59780-067-9

Printed In Canada

Night Shade Books
Please visit us on the web at
http://www.nightshadebooks.com

1

WELCOME ABOARD

The personnel carrier lurches through the ruins under a wounded sky. The night hangs overhead like a sadist's boot, stretching out the moment of terror before it falls. It's an indifferent brute full of violent color and spasms of light. It's an eternal moment on a long, frightening, infinite trail that loops back upon itself. I swear we've been around the track a couple of times before.

I decide that a planetary siege is like a woman undressing. Both present the most amazing wonders and astonishments the first time. Both are beautiful and deadly. Both baffle and mesmerize me, and leave me wondering, *What did I do to deserve this?*

A twist of a lip or a quick chance fragment can shatter the enchantment in one lethal second.

I look at that sky and wonder at myself. Can I really see beauty in that?

Tonight's raids are really showy.

Moments ago the defensive satellites and enemy ships were stars in barely perceptible motion. You could play guessing games as to which were which. You could pretend you were an old-time sailor trying to get a fix and not being able because your damned stars wouldn't hold still.

Now those diamond tips are loci for burning spiders' silk. The stars were lying to us all along. They were really hot-bottomed arachnids with their legs tucked in, waiting to spin their deadly nets. Gigawatt filaments of home-brew lightning come and go so swiftly that what I really see is afterimages scarred on my rods and cones.

Balls of light flare suddenly, fade more slowly. There is no way of knowing what they mean. You presume they are missiles being intercepted because neither side often penetrates the other's automated defenses. Occasional shooting stars claw the stratosphere as fragments of missile or satellite die a second death. Everything consumed in this holocaust will be replaced the moment the shooters disappear.

I try to pay attention to Westhause. He's telling me something, and to him it's important. "... instruments are rather primitive, Lieutenant. We get around on a hunch and a prayer." He snickers. It's the sound boys make after telling dirty jokes.

I'm sorry I asked. I don't even remember the question now. I just wanted to get a feel of the man who will be our astrogator. I'm getting more than I bargained for. The fifty-pfennig tour.

That's one of the tricks of telling a good story, Waldo. Before you start talking you identify the parts that are important only to you and separate them from those everybody else wants to hear. Then you *leave out* the insignificant details only you care about. You hear me thinking at you, Waldo? I suppose not. There aren't many telepaths around.

Now I understand the sly smiles that slit the faces of the others when I started with Westhause. Took them off my hook and put me on the astrogator's.

I shuffle the mental paperwork I did on the officers. Waldo Westhause. Native Canaanite. Reserve officer. Math instructor before he was called to the colors. Twenty-four. An old man to be making just his second patrol. Deftly competent in his specialty, but not well-liked. Talks too much.

He has that eager-to-please look of the unpopular kid who hangs in there, trying. He's too cheerful, smiles too much, and tells too many jokes, all of them poorly. Usually muffs the punchline.

I don't know much of this by direct observation. This is the Old Man's report.

Experienced Climber officers are taut, dour, close-mouthed sphinxes who watch everything with hooded, feline eyes. They all have a little of the cat in them, the cat that sleeps with one cracked eye. They jump at odd sounds. They're constantly grooming. They make themselves obnoxious with their passion for cool, fresh air and clean surroundings. They've been known to maim slovenly wives and indifferent hotel housekeepers.

The carrier heaves. "Damn it! I'll need my spine rebuilt if this keeps on. They can use my tailbone for baby powder now."

Some closet Torquemada had pointed at this antique, crowed, "Personnel carrier!" and ordered us aboard. The damned thing bucks, jounces, and lurches like some clanking three-legged iron stegosaurus trying to shake off lice. The dusky sorceress driving keeps looking back, her face torn by a wide ivory grin. This particular louse has chosen himself a spot to bite if she's ever stupid enough to stop.

The ride has its positive side. I don't have to listen to Westhause all the time. I can't. I can't keep tabs on the raid, either.

Why must I chase these incredible stories?

I remember a story about bullriders I did before the war. On Tregorgarth. Fool that I am, I felt compelled to live *that* whole experience, too. But then I could jump off the bull anytime I wanted.

I hear the Commander's chuckle and look his way. He's a dim, golden-haired silhouette against the moonlight. He's watching me. "They're only playing tonight," he says. "Drills, that's all. Just training drills." His laugh explodes like a thunderous fart.

Squinting doesn't help me make out his expression. In the flash and flicker it jerks like the action in an ancient kinescope, or some conjured demon unsure what form to manifest. It doesn't settle. The Teutonic shape fills with shadowed hollows. The eyes look mad. Is he playing a game? Sometimes it's hard to tell.

I survey the others, Lieutenant Yanevich and Ensign Bradley. They haven't spoken since we entered the main gate. They hang on to their seats and count the rivets in the bucking deck or recall the high points of their leaves or say prayers. There is no telling what's going on in their heads. Their faces give nothing away.

I feel strange. *I'm really doing it.* I feel alone and afraid, and fall into a baffled, what-the-hell-am-I-doing-here mood.

There is a big explosion up top. For an instant the ruins become an ink-line drawing of the bottommost floor of hell. Forests of broken brick pillars and rusty iron that present little resistance to the shock waves of the attackers' weapons. Every single one will tumble someday. Some just demand more attention.

The silent monument called Lieutenant Yanevich comes to life. "You should catch one of their big shows," he says. He cackles. It sounds forced, like a laugh given in charity to a bad joke. But maybe he's right to laugh. Maybe Climber men do have the True Vision. To them the war is one interminable shaggy-dog story. "You were too late for the latest Turbeyville Massacre."

Our driver swerves. Our right-side tracks climb a pile of rubble. We crank along at half speed, with a thirty-degree list on. A band of spacers are trudging along the same trail, lurching worse than the carrier, singing a grotesquely modified patriotic song. They are barely visible in their dress blacks. Only one man glances our way, his expression one of supreme disdain. His companions all hang on to one another, fore and aft, hand to shoulder, skipping along in a bizarre bunny hop. They could be drunken dwarfs heading for the night shift in a surreal coal mine. They all carry sacks of fruits and vegetables. They vanish into our lightless wake.

"Methinks they be a tad drunk," says Bradley, who is carrying no mean load himself.

"We looked Turbeyville over on our way here," I say, and Yanevich nods. "*I* saw enough."

The Fleet's big on-planet headquarters is buried beneath Turbeyville. It gets the best of the more serious drops.

The Commander and I had looked around while the dust was settling from the latest. The moons had been in conjunction nadir the previous night. That weakens the defense matrix, so the boys upstairs jumped through the hole with a heavy boomer drop. They replowed several square kilometers of often-turned rubble. They do it for the same reason a farmer plows a fallow field. It keeps the weeds from getting too tall.

The Commander says it was a tease strike. Just something to keep the edge on their boys and let us know our upstairs neighbors may come to stay someday.

The abandoned surface city lay immobilized in winter's tight grasp when we arrived. The iron skeletons of buildings creaked in bitter winds. All those mountains of broken brick lay beneath a rime of ice. In the moonlight they looked as though herds of migrating slugs had left their silvery trails upon them.

A handful of civilians prowled the wastes, hunting dreams of yesterday. The Old Man says the same ones come out after every raid, hoping something from the past will have worked to the surface. Poor Flying Dutchmen, trying to recapture annihilated dreams.

A billion dreams have already perished. This conflict, this furnace of doom, will consume a billion more. Maybe it feeds on them.

The carrier lurches. A track has missed its footing and we churn in a quarter-circle. Someone remarks listlessly, "We're almost there." I can't tell who. No one else cares enough to comment.

What I see over the carrier's armored flanks makes me wonder if the Old Man and I ever got out of Turbeyville. We might be *Fliegende Holländren* ourselves, pursuing that infinite path through the ruins.

The Pits are another popular target. The boys upstairs can't resist. They're the taproot of Climber Command's logistics tree, the point where the strength of Canaan coalesces for transfer to the Fleet. The Pits spew men, stores, and materiel like a full-time geyser.

All they ever reclaim is leave-bound Climber people wearing the faces of concentration camp escapees.

I was planning to do an eyewitness account of the bold defenders of mankind. The plan needs revision. I haven't encountered any of those. Climber people are scared all the time. They shy at shadows. The heroes are merely holonet fabrications. All *these* people want is to survive their next patrol. Their lives exist only within the mission's parameters. My companions have left their pasts in storage. They look no farther ahead than coming home. And they won't talk about that, for fear of jinxing it.

We've crossed some unmarked line. There's a difference in the air. The smells are changing. Hard to recognize them amid this jouncing…

Ah. That's the sea I smell. The sea and all the indignities unleashed upon it since the Pits were opened. The bay out there is the touchdown cushion for returning lifter pods. Maybe I'll be able to watch one splash in.

Now I can feel the earth tremors generated by departing lifters. They leave at ten-second intervals, 'round Canaan's twenty-two-hour and fifty-seven-minute clock. They come in varying sizes. Even the little ones are bigger than barns. They are simply gift boxes packed with goodies for the Fleet.

The Commander wants me. He's leaning toward me, wearing his mocking grin. "Three klicks to go. Think we'll make it?"

I ask if he's giving odds.

His blue eyes roll skyward. His colorless lips form a thin smile. The gentlemen of the other firm are playing with bigger firecrackers now. The flashes splatter his face, tattooing it with light and shadow.

He looks twice his chronological age. He's losing hair in front. His features are cragged and lined. It's hard to believe this came of the pink, plump cherub face I knew in Academy.

The gyrations of the brown girl's tracked rack bother him not at all. He seems to take some perverse pleasure in being slung around.

Something is going on upstairs. It makes me nervous. The aerial show is picking up. This isn't any drill. The interceptions are taking place in the troposphere now. Choirs of ground-based weapons are testing their voices. They sing in dull crackles and booms. The carrier's roar and rumble only partially drown them.

Halos of fire brand the night.

A violin-string tautness edges Yanevich's words as he observes, "Drop coming down."

Magic words. Ensign Bradley, the other new fish, sheds his harness and stands, knuckles whitening as he grips the side of the carrier. Our Torquemada wheel-woman decides this is the moment to show us what her chariot will do. Bradley plunges toward the gap left by the removal of a defective rear loading ramp. He's so startled he doesn't yelp. Westhause and I snag fists full of jumper as he lunges past.

"Are you crazy?" Westhause demands. He sounds bewildered. I know what he's feeling. I feel that way when I watch a parachute jump. Any damn fool ought to know better than that.

"I wanted to see…"

The Commander says, "Sit down, Mr. Bradley. You don't want to see so bad you get your ass retired before you start your first mission."

"Not to mention the inconvenience," Yanevich adds. "It's too late to come up with another Ship's Services Officer."

I commiserate with Bradley. I want to see, too. "How long before the dropships arrive?"

I've seen the tapes. My seat harness feels like a straitjacket. Caught on the ground, in the open. The enemy coming. A Navy man's nightmare.

They don't bother with my question. Only the enemy knows what he's doing. That adds to my unease.

Marines, Planetary Defense soldiers, Guardsmen, they can handle the exposure. They're trained for it. They know what to do when a raider bottoms her drop run. I don't. *We* don't. Navy people need windowless walls, control panels, display tanks, in order to face their perils calmly.

Even Westhause has run out of things to say. We watch the sky and wait for that first hint of ablation glow.

Turbeyville boasted a downed dropship. It was a hundred meters of Stygian lifting body half-buried in rubble. There is a stop frame I'll carry a long time. A tableau. Steam escaping the cracked hull, colored by a vermilion dawn. Very picturesque.

That boat was pushing mach 2 when her crew lost her, yet she went in virtually intact. The real damage happened inside.

I decided to shoot some interiors. One look changed my mind. The shields and inertial fields that preserved the hull juiced its occupants. Couldn't tell they had been guys pretty much like us, only a little taller and blue, with mothlike antennae instead of ears and noses. Ulantonids, from Ulant, their name for their homeworld. "Those chaps got an early out," the Commander told me. He sounded as if he envied them.

The sight left him in a thoughtful mood. After one or two false starts, he said, "Strange things happen. Patrol before last we raised a troop transport drifting in norm. One of ours. Not a thing wrong with her. Not a soul on board, either. You never know. Anything can happen."

"Looks like we'll get in ahead of them," Yanevich says.

I check the sky. I can't fathom the omens he's reading.

The surface batteries stop clearing their throats and begin singing in earnest. The Commander gives Yanevich a derisive glance. "Seems to be shit flying everywhere, First Officer."

"Make a liar out of me," the Lieutenant growls. He flings a ferocious scowl at the sky.

Eye-searing graser flashes illuminate the rusting bones of once-mighty buildings. In one surreal, black-and-white, line-on-line instant I see an image which captures the sterile essence of this war. I swing my camera up and snap the picture, but too late to nail it.

Way up there, at least three stories, balanced on an I-beam, a couple were making it. Standing up. Holding on to nothing but each other.

The Commander saw them, too. "We're on our way."

I try to glimpse his facial response. He wears the same blank mask. "Is that a non sequitur, Commander?"

"That was Chief Holtsnider," Westhause says. How the hell does he know? He's sitting facing me. The coupling was going on over his left shoulder. "Leading Energy Gunner. Certifiable maniac. Says a good-bye up there before every mission. A quick, slick patrol if he gets his nuts off. The same for her ship if she gets hers. She's a Second Class Fire Control Tech off Johnson's Climber." He gives me a sick grin. "You almost snapped a living legend of the Fleet."

Crew segregation by sex is an unpleasantry unique to the Climbers. I haven't been womanizing that much in integrated society, but I'm not looking forward to a period of enforced abstinence. There's something about having somebody else cut you off that does things to your mind.

The folks back home don't hear the disadvantages. The holonets concentrate on swaggering leave-takers and glory stuff that brings in the volunteers.

Climbers are the only Navy ship-type spacing without integrated crews. No other vessel produces pressure like a Climber. Adding the volatile complication of sex is suicidal. They found that out early.

I can understand the reasons. They don't help me like it any better.

I met Commander Johnson and her officers in Turbeyville. They taught me that, under like pressures, women are as morally destitute as the worst of men, judged by peacetime standards.

What are peacetime standards worth these days? With them and a half-dozen Conmarks you can buy a cup of genuine Old Earth coffee. Price six Conmarks without—on the black market.

The first dropship whips in along the carrier's backtrail, taking us by surprise. Her sonic wake seizes the vehicle, gives it one tremendous shake, and deafens me momentarily. Somehow the others get their hands to their ears in time. The dropper becomes a glowing deltoid moth depositing her eggs in the sea.

"There's some new lifters that'll need to be built," Westhause says. "Let's hope what we lost were Citron Fours."

My harness is suddenly a trap. Panic hits me. How can I get away if I'm strapped down?

The Commander touches me gently. His touch has a surprisingly calming effect. "Almost there. A few hundred meters."

The carrier stops almost immediately. "You're a prophet." It's a strain, trying to sound settled. That damned open sky mocks our human vulnerability, throwing down great bolts of laughter at our puniness.

A second dropper cracks overhead and leaves her greetings. A lucky ground weapon has bitten a neat round hole from her flank. She trails smoke and glowing fragments. She wobbles. I missed covering my ears again. Yanevich and Bradley help me out of the carrier.

Bradley says, "Bad shields on that one." He sounds about two kilometers away. Yanevich nods.

"Wonder if they'll *ever* get her back up." The First Watch Officer commiserates with fellow professionals.

I stumble several times clambering through the ruins. The boom must have scrambled my equilibrium.

The entrance to the Pits is well hidden. It's just another shadow among the piles, a man-sized hole leading into one of war's middens. The rubble isn't camouflage. Guards in full combat gear loaf inside, waiting to clear new debris when the last dropship finishes her run, hoping there'll be no work to do.

We trudge through the poorly lit halls of a deep subbasement. Below them lie the Pits, a mix of limestone cavern and wartime construction far beneath the old city. We have to walk down four long, dead escalators before we find one still working. The constant pounding takes its toll. A series of escalators carries us another three hundred meters into Canaan's skin.

My duffel, all my worldly possessions, is stuffed into one canvas bag. It masses exactly twenty-five kilos. I had to moan and whine and beg to get the extra ten for cameras and notebooks. The crew—including the Old Man—are allowed only fifteen.

The last escalator dumps us on a catwalk overlooking a cavern vaster than any dozen stadia.

"This is chamber six," Westhause says. "They call it the Big House. There are ten all told, and two more being excavated."

The place is aswarm with frenetic activity. There are people everywhere, although most of them are doing nothing. The majority are sleeping, despite the industrial din. Housing remains a low priority in the war effort.

"I thought Luna Command was crowded."

"Almost a million people down here. They can't get them to move to the country."

Half a hundred production and packaging lines chug along below us. Their operators work on a dozen tiers of steel grate. The cavern is one vast, insanely huge jungle gym, or perhaps the nest of a species of technological ant. The rattle, clatter, and clang are as dense as the ringing round the anvils of hell. Maybe it was in a place like this that the dwarfs of Norse mythology hammered out *their* magical weapons and armor.

Jury-rigged from salvaged machinery, ages obsolete, the plant is the least sophisticated one I've ever seen. Canaan became a fortress world by circumstance, not design. It suffered from a malady known as strategic location. It still hasn't gotten the hang of the stronghold business.

"They make small metal and plastic parts here," Westhause explains. "Machined parts, extrusion moldings, castings. Some microchip assemblies. Stuff that can't be manufactured on TerVeen."

"This way," the Commander says. "We're running late. No time for sightseeing."

The balcony enters a tunnel. The tunnel leads toward the sea, if I have my bearings. It debouches in a smaller, quieter cavern. "Red tape city," Westhause says. The natives apparently don't mind the epithet. There's a big new sign proclaiming:

WELCOME TO

RED TAPE CITY

PLEASE DO NOT

EAT THE NATIVES

There's a list of department titles, each with its pointing arrow. The Commander heads toward Outbound Personnel Processing.

Westhause says, "The caverns you didn't see are mainly warehouses, or lifter repair and assembly, or loading facilities. Have to replace our losses." He grins. Why do I get the feeling he's setting me up? "The next phase is the dangerous one. No defenses on a lifter but energy screens. Can't even dodge. Shoots out of the silo like a bullet, right to TerVeen. The other firm always takes a couple potshots."

"Then why have planetside leave? Why not stay on TerVeen?" The shuttling to and fro claims lives. It makes no military sense.

"Remember how crazy the Pregnant Dragon was? And that place was just for officers. TerVeen isn't big enough to take that from three or four squadrons. It's psychological. After a patrol people need room to wind down."

"To get rid of soul pollution?"

"You religious? You'll get along with Fisherman, sure."

"No, I'm not." Who is, these days?

The check-in procedure is pleasantly abbreviated. The woman in charge is puzzled by me. She putzes through my orders, points with her pen. I follow the others toward our launch silo where a crowd of men and women are waiting to board the lifter. The presence of officers does nothing to soften the exchange of insults and frank propositions.

The lifter is a dismal thing. One of the old, small ones. The Citron Four type Westhause wants scrubbed. The passenger compartment is starkly functional. It contains nothing but a bio-support system and a hundred acceleration cocoons, each hanging like a sausage in some weird smoking frame, or a new variety of banana that loops between stalks. I prefer couches myself, but that luxury is not to be found aboard a troop transport.

"Go-powered coffin," the Commander says. "That's what ground people call the Citron Four."

"Shitron Four," Yanevich says.

Westhause explains. Explaining seems to be his purpose in life. Or maybe I'm the only man he knows who listens, and he's cashing in while his chips are hot. "Planetary Defense gives all the cover they can, but losses still run one percent. They get their share of personnel lifters. Some months we lose more people here than on patrol."

I consider the obsolete bio-support system, glance at the fitting they implanted in my forearm back in Academy, a thousand years ago. Can this antique really keep my system cleansed and healthy?

"You and the support system make prayer look attractive."

The Commander chuckles. "The Big Man wouldn't be listening. Why should he worry about a gimp-legged war correspondent making a scat fly from one pimple on the universe's ass to another? He's got a big crapshoot going on over in the Sombrero."

"Thanks."

"You asked for it."

"One of these days I'll learn to keep my balls from overloading my brain."

For the others the launch is routine. Even the first mission people have been up this ladder before, during training. They jack in and turn off. I live out several little eternities. It doesn't get any easier when our pilot says, "We punched up through a dropship pair, boys and girls. Should have seen them tap dancing to get out of the way."

My laugh must sound crazy. A dozen nearby cocoons twist. Disembodied faces give me strange, almost compassionate looks. Then their eyes begin closing. What's happening?

The bio-support system, into which we have jacked for the journey, is slipping us mickeys. Curious. Coming in to Canaan I didn't need a thing.

My lights go out.

I have trouble understanding these people. They've reduced their language to euphemism and their lives to ritual. Their superstitions are marvelous. Their cant is unique. They are so silent and unresponsive that at first glance they appear insensitive.

The opposite is true. The peculiar nature of their service oversensitizes them. They refuse to show it. They are afraid to do so because caring opens chinks in the armor they have forged so their *selves* can survive.

The boomer drop was rough for me. I could *see* and *hear* Death on my backtrail. It was personal. Those droppers were after *me*.

Navy people seldom see the whites of enemy eyes. Line ships are toe to toe at 100,000 klicks. These men are extending the psychology of distancing.

Climbers sometimes do go in to hand-to-hand range. Close enough to blaze away with small arms if anyone wanted to step outside.

The Climber lexicon is adapted to depersonification, and to de-emotionalizing contact with the enemy. Language often substitutes for physical distance.

These people never fight the enemy. Instead, they compete with the other firm, or any of several similar euphemisms. Common euphemisms for *enemy* are the boys upstairs (when on Canaan), the gentlemen of the other firm, the traveling salesmen (I suppose because they're going from world to world knocking on our doors), and a family of related notions. Nobody gets killed here. They leave the company, do any number of variations on a theme of early retirement, or borrow Hecate's Horse. Nobody knows the etymology of the latter expression.

I'm trying to adopt the cant myself. Protective coloration. I try to be a colloquial chameleon. In a few days I'll sound like a native—and become as nervous as they do when someone speaks without circumlocution.

The Commander says the TerVeen go was a holiday junket. Like taking a ferry across a river. The gentlemen of the other firm were busy covering their dropships.

TerVeen isn't a genuine moon. It's a captive asteroid that has been pushed into a more circular orbit. It's 283 kilometers long and an average 100 in diameter. Its shape is roughly that of a fat sausage. It isn't that huge as asteroids go.

The support system wakened us when the lifter entered TerVeen's defensive umbrella. There're no viewscreens in our compartment, but I've seen tapes. The lifter will enter one of the access ports which give the little moon's surface a Swiss cheese look. The planetoid serves not only as a Climber fleet base, but also as a factory and mine. The human worms inside are devouring its substance. One great big space apple, infested at the heart.

The process began before the war. Someone had the bright idea of hollowing TerVeen and using it as an industrial habitat. When completed, it was supposed to cruise the Canaan system preying on other asteroids. One more dream down the tubes.

The address system begins hurrying us up before everyone is completely awake. I spill out of my cocoon and windmill around, banging into a half-dozen people before I grab something solid. Almost zero gravity. There's no spin on the asteroid. They didn't warn me.

I don't get a chance to complain. Yanevich tows me outside, down a ladder, and into an alcove separated from the docking bay by its own airlock. Yanevich will be our First Watch Officer. He checks names against an assignment roster as our people join us. There are a lot of obscene exchanges between our men and the ladies mustering along the way. These boys' mothers would be shocked by their sons' behavior. The mothers of the girls would disown their daughters.

I'm amazed by how young they all look. Especially the women. They shouldn't know what men are for, yet... Christ! Are they *that* young or am I getting that old?

I ask one of my questions. "Why doesn't the other firm bring in a Main Battle Fleet? It shouldn't be that hard to scrub Canaan and a couple of moons."

Yanevich ignores me. The Commander is studying faces and showing his own. Bradley is scooting around like a kid during his first day on a new playground. Westhause has the volunteer mouth again.

"They're stretched too thin trying to blitz the Inner Worlds. The guys bothering us are trainees. They hang out here a couple of months, getting blooded, before they take on the big time. When we get out there it'll be a different story. The reps on those routes are pros. There's one Squadron Leader they call the Executioner. He's the worst news since the Black Death."

I'm getting tired of Westhause's voice. It takes on a pedantic note when he knows you're listening.

"Suppose they committed that MBF? It would have to come from inside. That would stall their offensive. If we carved it up, they'd lose the initiative. And we might cut them good. Climbers get mean when they're cornered." A hint of pride has crept in here.

"Meaning they can't afford to take time out to knock us off, but they can't afford to leave us alone, either?"

The Commander scowls my way. I'm not using approved phraseology.

"Yeah. Containment. That's the name of their game."

"The holonets say we're hurting them."

"Damned right we are. We're the only reason the Inner Worlds are holding out. They're going to do something…." Westhause reddens under the Commander's stony gaze. He has become too direct, too frank, and too enthusiastic. The Commander doesn't approve of enthusiasm in the broader sense, only in enthusiasm for one's job. And there it should be a subtle, low-key competence, not a rodeo holler.

"The statistics. They're learning. Making it harder and harder. The easy days are over. The glory days. But we're still building Climbers faster than they're retiring them. New squadron gets commissioned next month."

He leaves me to go exchange greetings with a small, very dark Lieutenant. There are few non-Caucasians in our crew. That would be because so many are native Canaanites. "Ito Piniaz," Westhause says after the man departs. "Weapons Officer and Second Watch Officer. Good man. Doesn't get along well, but very competent." Just what the Old Man had to say. "Where was I?"

I hear Yanevich murmur, "Flushing the tunnel with hot air." Westhause doesn't catch his remark.

"Oh. Yeah. Time. That's what it's all about. We're all racing the hourglass of attrition."

"Jesus," the Commander mutters. "You write speeches for Fearless Fred?" I glance at him. He's pretending an intense interest in the women down the way. "Enough is enough."

"Our firm is starting to pull ahead," Westhause declares. The Commander looks dubious. We've all heard it before. High Command started seeing the light at the end of the tunnel the second week of the war. The glimmer hasn't shone my way yet.

"You guys coming? Or should we pick you up on our way home?" Only Yanevich, who is speaking, and the Commander remain. The rest of our lot have disappeared.

"Yes sir." Westhause glides into a naked shaft. It seems to plunge toward the planetoids' heart. He floats upon nothing and grabs a descending cable. He controls his duffel with his other hand. He vanishes with the down-pop of a fast prairie dog. Yanevich follows him.

"Your turn."

I take one look and say, "Not even without gravity."

The Commander grins. It's the nastiest damned grin I've ever seen. He sticks me with a straight-arm. "Grab the cable."

I stop flailing and grab. The cable jerks me down the narrow, polished tube. There isn't enough light to see much but an oily sheen as the walls speed by. The cable itself has optical fiber wound in. That sheds what little light there is.

This is a claustrophobic setting. The shaft is only slightly more than a meter in diameter.

I can just make out Yanevich below me. If I look up I can see the Commander's grin coming after me. He has rolled so he's coming along facedown. He's laughing at some hilarious joke, and I'm afraid the joke is me. He shouts, "You puke in here and I'll make you walk home from three lights out. Get ready to change cables. Damn it! Don't look at me. Watch where you're going."

I look down as Yanevich begins heaving himself along. He pumps the cable, falls free, pumps the cable again, gaining speed. He seizes the faster cable and pulls away into the darkness.

I survive the exchange through the intercession of a tapered idiot fitting. It strips my death grip from the slow cable and transfers it to the faster one. The faster cable gives me a big yank and nearly turns me facedown. Now I know why Yanevich speeded himself up.

"Damned dangerous," I shout up the shaft. The Commander grins.

From below, the First Watch Officer shouts, "Grab your balls. We'll be hauling ass in a couple minutes."

I picture myself hurtling down this tube like a too-small ball in an ancient muzzle-loader, rickety-rackety from wall to wall. I feel an intense urge to scream, but I'm not going to satisfy their sadism. I have a suspicion that's what they're waiting for. It would make their day.

I suddenly realize that getting tangled in the cable is the real danger here. Envisioning that peril helps silence the howling ape's instinctive fear of falling.

"Shift coming up."

I try to imitate Yanevich this time. My effort earns its inevitable reward: I manage to get myself turned sideways. I can't find the cable again.

"Whoa!" the Commander shouts. "Don't flail around." He shoves down on the top of my head, mashing my cap. Yanevich slides up out of the darkness and snags my right ankle. They turn me. "Get a hold. Carefully."

The real trick is to avoid getting excited. I feel cocky when we hit bottom. I've figured it out. I can keep up with the best of them. "There must be a better way."

The Commander's grin is bigger than ever. "There is. But it's no fun. All you do is climb onto a bus and ride down. And that's so boring." He indicated cars unloading passengers along a wall a hundred meters away. People and bags are floating around like drunken pigeons. Some are our men, some the women who shared our lifter.

"You prime son of a bitch."

"Now, now. You said you wanted to see it *all.*" He's still grinning. I want to crack him one and push that grin around sideways. Bet they pull this one on all the new meat. He explains that the cable system is a carryover from TerVeen's industrial days. Back then the cables carried high-speed freight capsules.

I can't pop a superior in the snot locker, so I try stomping angrily instead. The result is predictable. There is no gravity. Of course. I flail around for a handhold, which only makes matters worse. In seconds I put on an admirable combination of pitch, roll, and yaw.

"Thought you said he was a veteran," Yanevich observes laconically. Embarrassed, I get hold of myself.

"See, you haven't forgotten everything," the Commander says.

"I'll get it back. Am I in for the whole new-fish routine?"

"Not after we're aboard. There's no horseplay aboard a Climber." He's dreadfully serious. Almost comically so. There'll be no chance to get even. Grimacing, I let him tug me down so we can begin the next phase of our odyssey.

Westhause continues to explain. "What they did was drill the tunnels parallel to TerVeen's long axis. They were cutting the third one when the war started. They were supposed to mine outward from the middle when that was finished. The living quarters were tapped in back then, too. For the miners. It was all big news when I was a kid. Eventually they would've mined the thing hollow and put some spin on for gravity. They didn't make it. This tunnel became a wetdock. A Climber returns from patrol, they bring her inside for inspections and repairs. They build the new ones in the other tunnel. Some regular ships too. It has a bigger diameter."

In Navy parlance a wetdock is any place where a ship can be taken out of vacuum and surrounded by atmosphere so repair people don't have to work in suits. A wetdock allows faster, more efficient, and more reliable repairwork.

"Uhm." I'm more interested in looking than listening.

"Takes a month to run a Climber through the inspections and preventive maintenance. These guys do a right job."

Which is why the crews get so much leave between missions. They aren't permitted to make their own repairs, even when so inclined.

Westhause divines my thoughts. "We can stretch a leave if we work it right. Command always deploys the whole squadron at once. But we can come in as soon as we've used our missiles, if we have the fuel. So we get our month plus however long it takes the last ship to get home."

Within limits, I'm sure. Command wouldn't keep eleven ships out of action waiting for a twelfth making a prolonged patrol. "Incentive?"

"It helps."

The Old Man says, "Too much incentive, sometimes." For a minute it seems he's finished. Then he decides to go ahead. "Take Talmidge's Climber. Gone now. Tried to fight the hunter-killers so he could use his missiles and be first ship back. No law against it, of course." He falls silent again. Yanevich picks up the thread when it becomes obvious he'll say nothing more.

"Good encounter, too. He got three confirmed. But the rest crawled all over him. Kept him up so long half his people came back with baked brains. They set the record for staying up."

The story sounds exaggerated. I don't pursue it. They don't want to talk about it. Even Westhause observes a moment of silence.

We climb aboard an electric bus. It takes its power from a whip running on a track clinging to the tunnel wall.

"Only the finest for the heroes of the Climber Fleet," the Old Man says, taking the control seat.

The bus surges forward. I try to watch the work going on out in the big tunnel. So many ships! Most of them are not Climbers at all. Half the defense force seems to be in for repairs. A hundred workers on tethers float around every vessel. No lie-in-the-corner refugees up here. Everybody works. And the Pits keep firing away, sending up the supplies.

I think of the Lilliputians binding Gulliver, looking at all those people on lines. And of baby Kröhler's spiders playing at little trial flights around Mom. Said creature is a vaguely arachnidan beast native to New Earth. It nests and nurses its young on its back. It's warm-blooded, endoskeletal, and mammalian—a pseudo-marsupial, really—but it has a lot of legs and a magnificently extrudable whip of a tail, so the spider image sticks.

Sparks fly in mayfly swarms as people cut and weld and rivet. Machines pound out a thunderous industrial symphony. Several vessels are so far dismantled that they scarcely resemble ships. One has its belly laid open and half its skin gone. A carcass about ready for the retail butcher. What sort of creature feeds on roasts off the flanks of attack destroyers?

Gnatlike clouds of little gas-jet tugs nudge machinery and hull sections here and there. How the devil do they keep track of what they're doing? Why don't they get mixed up and start shoving destroyer parts into Climbers?

A Climber appears. It looks clean. Very little micrometeorite scoring, even. "Doesn't look like there's anything wrong with that one."

"Those are the tricky bastards," the Old Man muses. I assume he'll award me another cautionary tale. Instead, he resumes staring straight ahead, playing the vehicle's controls, leaving the talking to Westhause.

"The critical heat-sensitive stuff gets replaced after every patrol. The laser weaponry, too. Takes too long to break it down and scan each part. Somebody back down the tube will get ours. We'll get something that belonged to somebody who's on patrol already."

"Pass them around like the clap," Yanevich says.

The Old Man snorts. He doesn't approve of officers' displaying crudity in public.

Westhause says, "Everything has to be perfect."

I reflect on what I've seen of Climber people and ask myself, What about the crew? It looks like Command's attitude toward personnel is the opposite of its attitude toward ships. If they can still say their names and crawl, and don't scream too much going through the hatch, send them out again.

The bus suddenly wrenches itself off the main track. The passengers howl. The Old Man ignores them. He wants to see something. For several minutes we study a Climber with the hull number 8. The Commander stares as if trying to divine some critical secret.

Hull number 8. Eight without an alphabetical suffix, meaning she's the original Climber Number 8, not a replacement for a ship lost in action. The *Eight Ball*. I've heard some of the legends. Lucky *Eight*. Over forty missions. Nearly two hundred confirmed kills, mainly back at the beginning. Never lost a man. Any spacer in the Climbers will sell his soul to get on her crew. She's had a good run of Commanders.

Westhause whispers, "She was his first duty assignment in Climbers." I wonder if he's trying to steal her luck.

"Living on borrowed time," the Old Man declares, and slams the bus into movement. Full speed ahead now, and pedestrians be ready to jump.

The odds against a Climber's surviving forty patrols are astronomical. No pun intended. There are just too many things that can go wrong. Most don't survive a quarter that many. Only a few Climber people make their ten-mission limit. They drift from ship to ship, in accordance with billet requirements, and hope the big computer is shuffling them along a magical pathway. I think the odds would improve if the crews stayed together.

Climber duty is a guaranteed path to advancement. Survivors move up fast. There're always ships to be replaced, and new vessels need cadres.

"Isn't there a morale problem, the way people get shuffled?"

Westhause has to think about that one, as though he's familiar with emotion and morale only from textbook examples. "Some. The jobs are the same in every ship, though."

"I wouldn't like getting moved every time I made new friends."

"I suppose. It's not so bad for officers. Especially Engineers. But they only take people who can handle it. Loners."

"Sociopaths," the Commander says softly. Only I hear him. He makes a habit of commenting without elucidating.

"You're a call-up, aren't you?"

"Only to the Fleet. I volunteered for Climbers."

"How are Engineers different?" Navy is a conservative organization. Engineers don't do much engineering. They don't have engines to tinker with. Aboard line ships they still have boatswains. There's no logical continuity from old-time surface navies.

"They stay with one ship after three apprentice missions. They're all physicists. A ship always has an apprentice aboard."

"The more I hear, the more I wish I'd kept my mouth shut. This looks bleaker all the time."

"One mission? With the Old Man? With CliRon Six? Shit. A cakewalk." He's whispering. The Commander isn't supposed to hear. The set of the Old Man's shoulders says he has. "You can do it standing on your head. You're in the ace survivor squadron. We graduate more people than anybody. Hell, we'll be back groundside before the end of the month."

"Graduate?"

"Make ten. Guys make their ten with us. Hell, we're at the bay already. There she is. In the nine spot."

A whole, combat-ready Climber looks like an antique spoked automobile wheel and tire with a ten-liter cylindrical canister where the hub belongs. Its exterior is fletched with antennae, humps, bumps, tubes, turrets, and one huge globe riding high on a tall, leaning vane reminiscent of the vertical stabilizer on supersonic atmosphere craft. Every surface is anodized a Stygian black.

There are twelve Climbers in the squadron. They cling to a larger vessel like a bunch of ticks. The larger vessel looks like the frame and plumbing of a skyscraper after the walls and floors are removed. This is the mother, the command and control ship. She'll carry her chicks into the patrol sector and scatter them, then pick up any patrolling vessels that have expended their missiles and need rides home.

Though a Climber can space for half a year and few patrols last longer than a month, Command wants no range sacrificed getting to the zone, nor any stores expended. Stores are a Climber's biggest headache, her Achilles' heel. By their nature the vessels pack a lot of hardware into tightly limited space. There's little room left for crew or consumables.

"Awful lot of ornamentation," I say.

The Commander snorts. "And most of it useless. They're always tinkering. Always adding something. Always upping our dead mass and cutting our comforts. Patrols are getting shorter and shorter, aren't they? This time it's a goddamned magnetic cannon that shoots ball bearings. Just a test run, they say. Shit. Six months from now every ship in the Fleet will have one. Can't think of a damned thing more useless, can you?"

He's steamed. He hasn't said this much, in one lump, since I arrived. I'd better prod while the prodding is good. "Maybe there's a use. Might find it in the mission orders. Something new to try."

"Shit." He folds up again. I know better than to go after him. That just makes him stay closed longer.

I study the mother and Climbers. Nine slot. That one will be my home.... For how long? Quick patrol? I hope so. These men would be hard to endure over a prolonged mission.

2

CANAAN

I stepped off the courier ship, dropped my gear, looked around. "This is a world at war?"

The courier had dropped us in the middle of a grassy plain that stretched unbroken to every horizon. That vista would have scared the shit out of someone less accustomed to open spaces. I confess to mild wobblies of my own. Service people don't spend much time out of doors.

In the near distance, a vast herd of beef cattle decided we were harmless and resumed grazing. Shadowing them were a few outriders. Kick out cattle and horsemen and there'd have been no evidence that this was an inhabited world.

"Cowboys? For Christ's sake." They weren't Wild West cowboys, but not that different, either. The nature of a profession often defines its garb and gear.

The courier joined me. "Picturesque, isn't it?"

"After that ride coming in… What the hell was all the jumping about?" A courier boat has no room for observers on its bridge. I'd gone through the approach blind.

"Destroyer. Old scow." He snapped his fingers and grinned. "Shook her like that."

"How come you're such a pale shade, then?" My shipmate of the past few weeks was a black subLieutenant whose main pleasure was the witty ethnic insult. He didn't argue that one. It'd been a tight squeeze.

"They'll be along any minute. Said they were sending somebody."

"Why out here? Why not straight into Turbeyville?" He hadn't revealed his landing plan beforehand.

"We'd have got smoked. Planetary Defense doesn't waste time shitting around with Fleet couriers. They're busy covering the lifter pipe from the Pits. They don't want to hear from home anyhow." He patted the case chained to his wrist. Odd I thought, that it should be so huge.

21

Suitcase size. Big suitcase. "They'll cuss me for two weeks."

I studied the chain. "Damn. I'll have to cut your hand now."

"That isn't funny." The poor bastards. They get so they won't turn their backs on their own mothers.

The chain was long. He put the case down and sat on it. He said, "Just open them baby blues and turn yourself a slow circle, Lieutenant."

I did. The plains. The grass. The cowboys, who showed no interest in the boat.

"What do you see?"

"Not a whole lot."

"You've seen it all. Change your plans. Come on home with me."

"There's more to it than this."

"Well, sure. Trees, mountains, some busted-up cities. Big deal. Look at those bastards. Hunking around on horses. And they're the lucky ones. They don't live in caves. No boomer drops on cows."

"I fought too hard to get here. I'll see it through."

"Fool." He grinned. "Climbers, yet. Here it comes." He pointed. A skimmer wove a sinuous path across the green, a small, dark boat chopping through a breezy sea.

It rumbled up to us, downwash whipping torn grass against our legs. "Still not too late, Lieutenant. Go hide in the boat."

I smiled my holo-hero smile. "Let's go."

It's easy to grin when the fiercest monster in sight is a cow. I'd ridden the killer bulls of Tregorgarth. I was ready for anything.

The skimmer driver waved impatiently. "Not the wide-open-spaces type," the courier guessed.

We boarded. Our steed surged forward, arcing past the herd, leaving a long, dull snail track of smashed grass. Cows and cowboys watched with equally indifferent eyes. Our driver had little to say. She was the surly type. You know, "My feelings are hurt just by being here with you."

The subLieutenant stage-whispered, "You're an offworlder, they figure you're a High Command spy. They hate High Command."

"Can't blame them." Canaan had been under soft blockade for years. It made life difficult.

Back when, the other side hadn't thought Canaan worth occupation. Big mistake. It was a tough nut now. The senior officer in the region, Admiral Tannian, had assembled scattered, defeated, ragtag units for a dramatic last stand. The Ulantonids disappointed him. So he dug in and began gnawing on their supply lines. Now they are too heavily committed elsewhere to give him the squashing he wanted.

Great stuff, Fortress Canaan, High Command decided. They sent Tannian the first Climber squadron into service. He saw their potential instantly. He created his own industrial base.

You couldn't question the Admiral's energy, dedication, or tenacity. Canaan, an agricultural world sparsely settled, overnight became a feisty fortress and shipbuilding center. A loose frontier society became a tight warfare state with a solitary purpose: the construction and manning of Climbers. All Tannian demanded of the Inner Worlds was a trickle of trained personnel to cadre his locally raised legions. A bargain. High Command gladly obliged. To the sorrow of many ranking officers with ambitions or personal axes to grind.

Admiral Frederick Minh-Tannian became proconsul of Canaan's system and absolute master of humanity's last bastion in this end of space. Down the line, on the Inner Worlds, he was considered one of the great heroes of the war.

It was an hour's run to the nearest Guards' outpost. The place fit the Wild West image. Adobe walls surrounded scores of hump-backed bunkers. Most of those boasted obsolete but effective detection antennae. There were barracks for several hundred soldiers, and a dozen armed floaters.

My companion said, "I usually put down here. One company. It patrols more area than France on Old Earth. Six regular soldiers. The Captain, a Lieutenant, and four Sergeants. The rest are locals. Serve three months a year and chase cows the rest. Or dig turnips. They bring their families if they have them."

"I was wondering about the kids." It was the most unmilitary installation I'd ever seen. Looked like a way station three years into a *Völkerwanderung*. It would've given Marine sergeants apoplexy.

The Captain wasted little time on us. He spoke with the courier briefly. The courier opened that huge case and passed over a kilo canister. The Captain handed him some greasy Conmarks. They were old bills, prewar pink instead of today's lilac gray. The courier shoved them inside his tunic, grinned at me, and went outside.

"Coffee," he explained. And, "A man has to make hay while the sun shines. A local proverb."

My glimpse inside the case had shown me maybe forty more canisters.

It was an old, old game with Fleet couriers. The brass knew about it. Only their pets received courier assignment. Sometimes there were kickbacks. My companion didn't look like a man whose business was that big.

"I see."

"Sometimes tobacco, too. They don't raise it here. And chocolate, when I can make the contacts back home."

"You should've loaded the boat." I didn't resent his running luxuries. Guess I'm a laissez-faire capitalist at heart.

He grinned. "I did. Can't deal with the Captain, though. After a while one of the sergeants will notice that nobody has patrolled that part of the plain lately. He'll make the sweep himself, just to keep his hand in. And I'll find a bale of Conmarks when I get back." He hoisted his case. "This's for special people. I sell it practically at cost."

"Conmarks ought to be drying up out here."

"They're getting harder to come by. I'm not the only courier on the Canaan run." He brightened. "But, shit. There had to be billions floating around before the war. It'll come out. Just got to keep refusing military scrip."

"I wish you luck, my friend." I was thinking of a few items in my own luggage, meant to sweeten the contacts I hoped to make.

The subLieutenant kicked a floater. "Looks as good as any of them. Throw your stuff in and let's go."

We had to cross two-thirds of a continent. A quarter of the way round Canaan's southern hemisphere. I slept twice. We stopped for fuel several times. The subLieutenant kept the floater screaming all the time he was at the controls. My turns, I kept it down to a sedate 250 kph.

He wakened me once to show me a city. "They called it Mecklenburg. After some city on Old Earth. Population a hundred thousand. Biggest town for a thousand klicks."

Mecklenburg lay in ruins. Threads of campfire smoke drifted up. "Old folks with deep roots, I guess. They wouldn't pull out. They're safe now. Nothing left to blast." He kicked the floater into motion.

Later, he asked, "What's the name of that town where you want off?"

"Kent."

He punched up something on the floater's little info screen. "It's still there. Must not be much."

"I don't know. Never been there."

"Well, it can't be shit, that close to T-ville and still standing. Hell, you'd think they'd take it out just for spite."

"The way our boys do?"

"I guess." He sounded sour. "This war is a big pain in the ass."

That was the one time I didn't like my companion. He didn't say that the way the grunts and spikes do. He was pissed because the war had disturbed his social life.

I said nothing. The attitude is common among those who see little or no combat. He viewed the brush coming in as part of a gentleman's game, a passage of arms in a knight's spring jousts.

We roared into Kent in midafternoon. Kent was a sleepy village that might have been teleported whole from Old Earth's past. A few scruffy Guards represented the present. They looked like locals combining military responsibilities with their normal routine.

"You know the address, I could drop you off, Lieutenant."

"That's all right. They said ask the Guards. Somebody will pick me up. Right here is fine. Thanks for the lift."

"Suit yourself." He gave me a long look after I dropped into the unpaved street. "Lieutenant… You've got balls. *Climbers.* Good luck." He slammed the hatch and lurched away. The last I saw, he was a streak heading toward Turbeyville like a moth to flame.

Good luck, he said. Like I'd damned well need it. Well, good luck to you too, courier. May you become wealthy on the Canaan run.

That was when I started wondering if maybe I hadn't wangled my way into a *hexenkessel.*

I spoke with a Guardswoman. She made a call. Ten minutes later a woman eased a strange, rattling contraption up to me. It was a locally produced vehicle of venerable years, propelled by internal combustion. My nose couldn't decide if the fuel was alcohol or of petroleum derivation. We'd used both in the floater.

"Jump in, Lieutenant. I'm Marie. He was taking a shower, so I came. Be a nice surprise."

"Didn't they tell him I was coming?"

"He wasn't expecting you till tomorrow."

It took ten minutes to reach the house among the trees. Pines, I think they were. Imported and gene-spliced with something local so they could slide into the ecology. Marie never shut up, and never said a word that interested me. She must have decided I was a sullen, sour old fart.

My friend wasn't surprised. He ambushed me at the door, enveloped me in a huge bear hug. "Back in harness, eh? And looking good, too. See they bumped you to Lieutenant." He didn't mention my leg. He sensed that that was *verboten*.

I'm touchy about the injury. It destroyed my career.

"Boat get in early?"

"I don't know. The courier always went full out. Maybe so."

"Little private business on the side?" He grinned. He was older than I remembered him, and older than I expected. The grin took off ten years. "So let's have a drink and confound Marie with lies about Academy."

He meant what he said, and yet… There was a hollowness to his words, as though he had to strain to put them together in the acceptable forms. He acted like a man who'd been out of circulation so long he'd forgotten his social devices. I found that intriguing.

I grew more intrigued during the following few days. I was soon aware that an old friend had become a stranger, that this man only wore the weathered husk of the friend I'd known in Academy. And he realized that he had few points of congruency left with me. Those were a sad few days. We tried hard, and the harder we tried the more obvious it became.

Canaan was his homeworld. He'd requested duty there. His request had been granted, with an assignment to Climbers. He'd been home for slightly under two years, done seven Climber missions, and now had his own ship. He'd been executive officer aboard an attack destroyer before his transfer. He'd worked his way back up.

He wouldn't talk about that side of his life, and that disturbed me. He was never a talker but had always been willing to share his experiences if you asked the right questions. Now there were no right questions. He wanted to pretend that his military life didn't exist.

Just a few short years since we'd last met. And in the interim they'd peeled his skin and stuffed somebody else inside.

He and Marie fought like animals. I could detect no positive feelings between them. She'd screech and yell and throw things almost every time the both of them were out of sight. As if I had no ears. As if my not seeing kept it from being real. Sometimes the screeching lasted half the night. He didn't fight back, insofar as I could tell. I never heard his voice raised. Once, in my presence, while we walked through the pines, he muttered, "She doesn't know any better. She's just an Old Earth whore."

I asked no questions and he didn't explain. I supposed she was one of the sluts they'd grabbed early and had scattered around for the morale of the men, and had found unnecessary in a mixed-sex service. All heart, our do-good leaders. They'd dropped the women where they were.

Maybe Marie had a right to be hostile.

Three days of unpleasantness. Then, well ahead of schedule, my friend told me, "Time to go. Pick the things you want to take. We'll leave after dark. West of here it's better to travel at night." The quarreling had become too much for him. He wanted out.

He didn't admit that. He simply made his announcement. When Marie got the word, the gloves came off. She no longer kept the vitriol private.

I didn't blame him for running.

A young Guardswoman brought us a Navy floater after sundown. We boarded under Marie's fiercest barrage yet. My friend never looked back.

After we dropped the Guardswoman at her headquarters, I asked, "Why don't you throw her out? You don't owe her anything."

He didn't respond for a long time. Instead, he lit his pipe and puffed his way through. Midway, he said, "We'll pick up our First Watch Officer and a new kid. Going to start him off in Ship's Services. Academy boy. Don't get many of those anymore."

Later still, in snatches, he told me what he thought of our ship's officers. He didn't say a lot. Thumbnail sketches. He didn't want to talk about his command. He responded to my earlier question just before we collected his First Watch Officer.

"Somebody owes her. They put the hose to her. She'll never get off this rock. Might as well use my place."

What can you say to that? Call him a sucker for strays? I don't think so. I'd call it a case of one man's using otherwise unimportant resources to rectify one of this universe's countless injustices. I think that's the way he pictured it. I don't think thumbscrews would have forced him to admit it.

The First Watch Officer was Stefan Yanevich. Lieutenant. Another Canaan native. A long, lanky man with ginger hair and eyes that sometimes looked gray, sometimes pale blue. Thin, sharp features and sleepy eyes. A soft drawl when he spoke, which was seldom. He was as reticent as my friend the Commander.

He was waiting outside his quarters, alone, and looked eager to go. But there was no eagerness in the way he slung his duffel aboard.

He had long, slim fingers that moved while he gave me his biography. Twenty-five. His Academy class had been two behind ours. He'd volunteered for Canaan because it was his homeworld. This would be his sixth mission.

The Commander thought well of him. He would have his own ship next mission.

He accepted me without question. I supposed the Commander had vouched for me. He didn't seem interested in why I was here, or who I used to be. Again, I assumed the Commander had filled him in.

The Old Man said, "Next stop, the kid."

Yanevich became interested. "Met him yet? What's he like?"

"Came up last week. Squared away. Shows promise. We'll like him." There was an edge to his voice . It said it didn't matter if anyone liked the new man, but it would be a nice bonus if he turned out okay.

Ensign Bradley was as quiet as the others, but more naturally so. He wasn't hiding from anything. When he did speak, he successfully downplayed his own lack of experience. He drew both the Commander and First Watch Officer out more skillfully than I had. I pegged him as a very bright and personable young man—when he turned himself on. He wasn't a Canaanite. In an aside to me, he said, "I flipped a coin when I got my bars. Heads or tails, Fleet or Climbers. Came up heads. The Fleet." He smiled a broad, boyish smile, the kind to win a mother's love. "So I went best two out of three and three out of five. *Voila!* Here I am."

"Going to make Admiral in a year," the Old Man said.

"Might take longer than that." Bradley's grin weakened. "What I don't understand is why they sent me out here instead of to Fleet Two. Admiral Tannian is self-sufficient."

"Maybe too self-sufficient," I suggested. "Some people in Luna Command think he's too independent. He's got his own little empire out here."

The Commander glanced back. "That something you know, or just speculation?"

"Half and half."

Yanevich grunted. My friend lapsed into indifference. Later, he said, "T-ville coming up. First Watch Officer, I'll drop you and Bradley at the north gate. I'll take my friend sightseeing."

Earlier, there had been a big raid. The sky over Turbeyville had been filled with ships and missiles. I'd expressed an interest in seeing the aftermath. Once I did, I wished I'd kept my mouth shut.

Navy has two headquarters in-system. One is beneath Turbeyville. The other is buried deep inside Canaan's major moon. Canaan has two satellites, tiny TerVeen and the big moon, which has no other name. Just the moon. I was glad of a chance to poke around one headquarters before the mission.

I roamed alone. The Commander, First Watch Officer, and Ship's Services Officer were busy with what looked like make-work, preparing for the mission. I found myself more welcome among the PR-sensitive staff at Climber Command. They arranged interviews with people whose names were household words on the Inner Worlds. Real heroes of the Fleet. Men and women who'd survived their ten missions. They were a depressing bunch. I began to develop a sour outlook myself, and to wonder just how bright I'd been, asking to join a Climber patrol.

Then the Commander turned up at my room in Transient Officers' Quarters. "Our last night here. Heading for the Pits tomorrow. The rest of us are going slumming. Want to come along?"

"I don't know." I'd tried the O clubs. They were filled with dreary staff types. Their atmosphere was both boring and stultifying. There's nothing deadlier than a congregation of conscientious bureaucrats.

"We're going a different place. Private club. Climber people and guests only. The real front-line warriors." His smile was sarcastic. "Give you a chance to meet our astrogator, Westhause. Just turned up. Good man, but he talks too much."

"Why not?" I had yet to meet any Climber people but those with whom I was traveling. The others might be less taciturn.

"Called the Pregnant Dragon, for reasons lost in the trackless deserts of time." He grinned at my raised eyebrow. "Don't wear your best. Sometimes it gets rowdy."

Something came up which demanded the Commander's attention, so we arrived late. But not late enough. I should've stayed behind.

That night witnessed the destruction of a hundred cherished cities in my land of illusions.

The Dragon was up near the surface, in an old subbasement. I heard it long before I saw it, and when I saw it, I asked, "This's an Officers' Club?"

"Climber people only," Westhause said, grinning. "Down people couldn't handle it."

Four hundred people had packed themselves into a space that had served two hundred before the war. Odors hit me like a surprise fist in the face. Alcohol. Vomit. Tobacco. Urine. Drugs. All backed by mind-shattering noise. The customers had to shout to make themselves heard over the efforts of an abominable local band. Civilian waiters and waitresses cursed their ways through the press, getting groped by both sexes. I guess the tips made up for the indignities. Climber people had nothing else to do with their pay.

Athwart the doorway, lying like some fallen angel seduced by the sins of Gomorrah, was a full Commander wearing Muslim Chaplain's insignia. Smiling, he snored in a pool of vomit. Nobody seemed inclined to move or clean him. Conforming to custom, we stepped over his inert form. Not a meter beyond, two male officers were playing kissy-face huggy-bear. I'm afraid I gasped.

I mean, it does go on, but right inside the front door of the O Club?

The Commander grunted, "Hang on to your nuts. There's more fun to come." He halted two steps inside, ignoring the lovers. Fists on hips, he stared about as though springing a surprise inspection. Having glimpsed what was going on, I expected an explosion.

He threw back his head and cut loose with a great jackass bray of laughter.

And Yanevich bellowed, "Make a hole for the best goddamned Climber in the Fleet, you yellow-assed scum."

The cacophony declined maybe one decibel. People looked us over. Some waved. Some shouted. Some moved toward us. Friends, I supposed.

A tiny china doll, ethereally beautiful in makeup which exaggerated her aristocratic Manchu features, slid beneath our elbows as lithely as a weasel. A meter away she paused and, eyes sparkling, mimicked the Commander's stance.

"You're fucking full of shit, Steve," she shouted at Yanevich. "Ninety-two A's the best, and you fucking well know it."

Yanevich lunged like a bear in rut. "Shit. I didn't know you guys were in."

"Come down off your goddamned mountain once in a while, graverobber." She laughed and wriggled as he mauled her. "Can you still get it up, Donkey Dick? Or did it fall off out there in the ruins? We just got in. I could use an all-night hosing."

"We're headed out, Little Bits. Tell you what. You have any doubts, I'll stick a wad of gum on the end. You let me know when you're chewing."

I was too startled to be disgusted. A mouth like that on an Academy man?

For no sane reason whatsoever, it being none of my concern, the woman told me, "This crud has got the longest hanger I ever saw." She licked her lips. "Nice. But maybe I'll want a little variety tonight."

"Sorry." I thought she was propositioning me. I didn't want to trample Yanevich's territory.

"Variety? Mao, I'd end up chasing crabs through my beard the whole patrol." He winked at me, oblivious to my pallor and rictus of a smile. I found the girl more baffling than he. She couldn't be more than twenty. He asked, "You learn to move your ass yet?"

"No thanks to you." She told me, "This crud got my cherry. Caught me in a weak moment, way back my first night in after my first patrol. Pounded away all night, and never did tell me I was supposed to do anything besides lie there."

Surely I turned from pale ivory to infrared. Bradley was equally appalled. "Maybe they're putting us on, sir." This assault on the sensibilities had forced him to retreat into the ancient and trusted fastnesses of military ritual.

"I don't think so."

"I guess not." I thought he would lose his supper.

"I think we're seeing Climber people in their feral state, Mr. Bradley. I suspect the news people have misinformed us." I grinned at my own sarcasm.

"Yes sir." He was developing an advanced case of culture shock.

The Commander seized my elbow. "Over here. I see some seats." We marched through a fusillade of derisive remarks about our ship and squadron. Other officers, apparently from our squadron, made room for us at their table. I gutted out a barrage of introductions, doubting I'd remember anyone in the morning. Bradley suffered it with glazed eyes and limp hand.

Reality had come stampeding through the mists of myth and propaganda and had trampled us both with all the delicacy of a mastodon treading on a gnat's toe. We couldn't acknowledge it. Not till something more personal drove the lesson home.

Yanevich disappeared with his friend. I didn't understand. He didn't seem the type. He had changed at the door.

Eat, drink, and be merry?

Westhause vanished, too, before I got to learn much more than his name. Then Bradley, eyes still glazed, was spirited away by a matronly Staff Captain. "What the fuck is she doing here?" someone muttered, then plopped her face into the spilled beer on the table before her, muttering that the Dragon was a private preserve.

"Ah, let it go," someone replied. "He wasn't going to do us any good."

I withdrew into myself, drank some, and rolled the camera behind my eyes. When in shock, record. I remained only vaguely aware that the Commander was sitting out the squadron's diminution. Like me, he was a seated statue with folded arms. I tried to remember "Ozymandias." I came up with some lines about rose red cities and then couldn't decide if I had the right piece. Why "Ozymandias," anyway? I couldn't remember that, either. Must have been a reason, though. I ordered another drink.

He was observing, too, our silent, gallant Ship's Commander. Back when, that had always been his excuse for not partaking of our clique's conversational buffet.

It grew late. The mob thinned considerably. I shipped a bigger cargo than I thought. The room began to rock a little, and I to wonder if our friends upstairs had a drop on tonight. The Commander touched my elbow gently. "Eh?" At the moment that was the most intelligent thing I could say.

"Somebody you might remember." He nodded toward a tall, lean blonde doing a slow strip atop a nearby table.

I stared through misty eyes. At first I only wondered about her age. She looked older than most of the women.

"Got her own ship," the Commander said.

Fascination and horror, lust and loathing, gusted through my sodden soul. I recognized her.

She looked so *old!*

Sharon Parker. The Virgin Goddess. The Bitch Queen of Academy Battalion Tango Romeo. How I'd loved and lusted after her at a tender seventeen. How many nights had I lain with my good right hand and imagined those creamy thighs clamping me?

The memories were embarrassing. I'd been so much a fool that I'd declared my undying passion....

She'd been as cold and remote as the dark side of Old Earth's moon. She'd teased, taunted, promised forever afterward, and never had delivered. For me or anyone else, as far as I knew.

Torturing me became her pet project. I was more obvious and vulnerable than my classmates.

"No. Let it be."

Too late. The Commander waved. She recognized him. She left her little stage and came over. The Old Man kicked out an empty chair. She seemed slightly embarrassed as she settled into it. The Commander can have that effect. He seems so competent and solid, sometimes, that everyone around will feel second-rate and clumsy. I always do.

She gave me one indifferent glance while crossing the room. Just another Lieutenant. Navy is infested with Lieutenants.

"Good patrol?" the Commander asked.

"Shit. Two old tubs that belonged in a transport museum. One escort destroyer. Only one tub confirmed. One lousy baby convoy. Twelve ships. We got off our missile flight, then the hunter-killers hit us. Thought it was the Executioner for a while. Took us nine days to shake them."

"Rough?" I asked.

She shrugged, gave me another of those indifferent glances.

I watched the light dawn. She turned bright red, shed the drunken table-dancer avatar like a snake sloughs skin. For one long moment she looked like she had a hot steel splinter under her fingernail.

"You." Another moment of silence. "You've changed."

"Haven't we all?"

She wanted to run so bad I could smell it. But it was too late. She'd been seen. She'd been caught. She had to face the consequences.

I was both pleased and a little frightened. Could she value my good opinion that much?

"Civilian influence," I said. "I was out for a while. You've changed too." I wanted to bite my tongue immediately. Not only was that the wrong thing to say, it slipped out sounding bitter. My brain was on vacation. My hands had made too many connections with my mouth, carrying too many drinks.

"I heard about the accident." Bravely bearing up, that was her attitude. "You making it okay now?"

"Good enough," I lied. Twelve years of Academy had done nothing to ready me for a sudden shift to civilian life. I could have gone on, I suppose, in a desk job, buried in Luna Command, but my pride hadn't permitted it. I was Line, and by damn that was what I'd stay, or nothing. "I like the freedom. To bed when I want, up when I want. Go where I want. You know. Like that."

"Yeah. I know." She didn't believe a word.

"So. What've you been doing?"

"Climbing the ladder. Got my own ship now. Forty-seven Cee. Bravo Flight, Five Squadron. Seven patrols." I couldn't think of anything to say. After an embarrassed silence, she added, "And finding out what it's like to be on the dirty end."

The conversation lay there awhile, like a beached whale too exhausted to struggle.

"I'm sorry. For everything I did. I didn't know what I was doing. I didn't know what you could do to somebody."

"Long ago and far away. Like it happened to somebody else. All forgotten now. We were just kids."

"No."

I'd lied again. And again she'd read me. It didn't hurt as much now, but the pain was still there. There're those small places where you never grow up.

"Can we go someplace?"

The thrill again. My libido recalled antediluvian fantasies. "I don't think…"

"Just to talk. You were always the best listener in the battalion."

Yes. I'd listened a lot. To problems. Everybody had come to me. Especially Sharon.

It had been a way to be near her. Always, back then, there'd been the Plan. Move after carefully calculated move, to seduction. I hadn't found the nerve to make the most critical, daring end-game maneuvers.

There'd been nobody for me to cry on. Who confesses the confessor?

"I'll only be gone a minute." She scrambled after discarded clothing. I watched and was more baffled by her behavior than by anything else I'd seen.

"She's aged."

The Commander nodded. "It's an eight-year millennium since we graduated. Nothing left of those wide-eyed kids now. Except for you, most of them died the first year of the war."

I needed a moment to realize he meant figurative death. The lift of the alcohol had peaked long since. I was headed down the rough side.

Sharon returned trailing a belligerent Lieutenant. He was sober enough to remain civil during the introductions, drunk enough to contemplate violence when he learned she was leaving with me.

The Commander rose, scowled. The younger man backed down. The Old Man can intimidate anybody when he puts his mind to it.

The Lieutenant faded away. The Commander resumed his seat. He filled the pipe that, in deference to the rest of us, he'd ignored all evening. He was alone now.

I glanced back once. He sat there with his legs sprawled beneath the table, observing, and for an instant I sensed his loneliness.

Ours is a lonely profession. The pressures of war only exaggerate the alienation.

Sharon and I did more than talk. Of course. There was never any doubt of it. She tried to expiate the cruelties of the past. I stumbled, but managed my part.

There was really little point to it.

The dream had died. There was no magic left. Just a man and a woman, both frightened, sharing a brief communion, a feeble escape from thought.

Only I didn't escape. Not entirely. Not for one second did I forget the mission.

The incident taught me *why* there were places like the Pregnant Dragon. In liquor, drugs, sex, or self-loathing, it provided surcease from the endless fear. Fear those people knew far better than I, who knew Climbers only by what I'd read, heard, and seen on holovision.

I have this reflection on the incident. One of life's crudest pranks is to yield heart's desire only when the desire has been replaced by another. Rare is the man who recognizes and seizes the precise instant, like a perfectly ripened fruit, and enjoys it at its moment of ultimate fulfillment.

At least we parted friends.

The dawn came, and with it a message from the Commander saying it was time we moved on to the Pits. We were to lift for TerVeen in eighteen hours.

I looked at her one last time, as she slept, and I wondered, What drew me to this world where they execute dreams?

3

DEPARTURE

Our Climber is a Class IX vessel: 910 gross tonnes combat-loaded at bay of departure; 720 tonnes without crew, fuel, stores, or expendable weaponry. There are few hyper-capable vessels smaller. Deep probe and attack singleships run 500 to 600 tonnes, boasting a crew of one man.

The 910-tonne limit is an absolute. If the vessel goes over, she has to cut her contraterrene tonnage. Nine-twenty-five is the established book absolute over which Command won't permit a Climb attempt. There's a granite-hard barrier somewhere in the low 930s. Massing above it, a vessel will just sit and hum while the enemy knocks her apart.

The mass limit is why the Commander is displeased with the experimental cannon. The system, with its munitions, masses two tons. That means an equal reduction in fuel or stores. Hardware can't be touched. And Command would squeal like a hog with its balls in a vise if anyone suggested cutting missile inventory.

A Climber is a self-contained weapons system. People are aboard only because the system can't operate itself. Concessions to human needs are kept to a minimum.

You don't know what you can live without, don't know what agonizing decisions are, till you have to pick and choose what to take on patrol.

The other day, watching the Commander pack, I decided I was in for a ripe fly. One change of uniform. One kilo of tobacco, illegal. One thick, old-style book, by Gibbon. Who gives a good goddamn about the Roman Empire? One grim black revolver of equally ancient vintage, quasi-legal. A curious weapon to carry aboard a vessel with a skin little thicker than mine. Two kilos of genuine New Earth coffee, the cheap stuff, probably smuggled to Canaan by a friend on a Fleet courier. A liter of brandy, in violation of regs. Fill in the cracks and make up fifteen kilos with fresh fruit. No razor. No comb. None of the amenities expected of a civilized travel kit.

I thought his choices strange. I packed up an almost standard kit, leaving out the dinner jacket and such. He made certain my ten extra kilos were strictly cameras, stilltape, notebooks, and pencils. Pencils because they're lighter than pens.

I see all the old hands conform to the kit pattern set by the Old Man. We'll be up to our ears in fruit.

Our mother ship is one of several floating in a vast bay. The others have only a few Climbers suckered on. Each is kept stationary by a spiderweb of common rope. The ropes are the only access to the vessel. "They don't waste much on fancy hardware." Tractors and pressors would stabilize a vessel in wetdock anywhere else in the Fleet. Vast mechanical brows would provide access.

"Don't have the resources," Westhause says. "'Task-effective technological focus,'" he says, and I can hear the quotes. "They'd put oars on these damned hulks if they could figure out how to make them work. Make the scows more fuel-effective."

I want to hang back and look at the mother, to work out a nice inventory of poetic images. I've seen holoportrayals, but there's never anything like the real thing. I want to catch the flavors of watching hundreds of upright apes hand-over-handing it along with their duffel bags neatly tucked between their legs, as if they were riding very small, limp, limbless ponies. I want to capture the lack of color. Spacers in black uniform. Ships anodized black. The surface of the tunnel itself mostly a dark black-brown, with streaks of rust. The ropes are a sandy tan. Against all that darkness, in the low-level lighting, without gravity, those lines take on a flat two-dimensionality, so all of them seem equally near or far away.

The Commander beckons. "Come along, then. Too late to back out now." He's impatient to get to the ship. That doesn't jibe with his landside attitude, when he wanted nothing to do with another patrol. He's hurrying me because I'm lagging, and his custom is to be the last man to board his ship.

A mother-locked Climber can be entered only through a hatch in the "top" of its central cylinder. The hatch isn't an airlock. It'll remain sealed through the vessel's stay in vacuum. The ship's only true airlock is at its bottom. That's connected to the mother now. Surrounding it is a sucker ring through which the Climber draws its sustenance till it's released for patrol. Power and water. And oxygen. Through the hatch itself will come our meals, though not prepared. Through that hatch, too, will come our orders, moments before we're weaned.

We linger round the outside of the top hatch while reluctant enlisted men go popping through like corks too small for the neck of a bottle. Some go feet first, some head first, diving behind their duffel. The hatch is a mere half meter in diameter. The men have to scrunch their shoulders to fit. Westhause is explaining the airlock system. "The only reverse flow consists of wastes," he concludes.

"And you give that any significance you want," the Commander mutters. "Shit for shit, I say. Down the hatch, men."

"Whatever happened to your youthful enthusiasm?"

The Commander refuses the bait. He has said too much already. A wrong word falling on an unfriendly ear can flatten a career trajectory. Climber Fleet One operates on a primitive level.

Canaan is a long, long way from Luna Command. The Admiral enjoys near dictatorial powers. The proconsular setup derives logically from the communications lag between Canaan and the centers of power. It's hard to like, but even harder to refute.

Fleet personnel can wish they had a more palatable overlord.

They call the central cylinder the Can. The Can is incredibly cramped, especially in parasite mode, while attached to the mother. Then, artificial gravity runs parallel to the cylinder's axis. In operational mode, when the Climber provides its own gravity, the Can's walls become floors.

Even then there'll be very little room if everyone is awake at once.

I take one long look around and ask, "How do you keep from trampling each other?"

"Some of the men are in their hammocks all the time. Unless we're in business. Then everybody is on station."

The Can is fifteen meters in diameter and forty meters tall. Doubled pressure partitions separate it into four unequal compartments. Operations Division, the brains of the ship, occupies the topmost level. Immediately below is Weapons. The two divisions share their computation and detection capacity. The third level is Ship's Services. It's the smallest. It contains galley, toilet, primitive laundry and medical facilities, recycling sections, and most importantly, the central controls by which internal temperature is sustained. Below Ship's Services is Engineering. Engineering's main task is to make the ship go from point A to point B. Their equipment, systems, and responsibilities often overlap with Ship's Services'.

A central structural member, called the keel, runs the length of the cylinder. When the ship is in operational mode the crew will take turns sleeping in hammocks attached to it. That's something to think about. I've never tried extremely low gravity sleep. I hear that it's hard to get a good rest, and dreams become a little crazy.

In parasite mode sleeping arrangements are catch-as-catch-can, with the quickest men hanging hammocks from available cross-members, then negotiating sharing deals with slower shipmates. Some of the places hammocks get slung seem almost too small for mice.

The luxury quarters of any ship, the Ship's Commander's stateroom, here consists of a screened-off section of beam near the entry hatch. He'll share his hammock with the First Watch Officer and Chief Quartermaster. Every hammock will be shared. It takes no imagination to see the potential for havoc in that. It takes some complex shuffling to put three men in one hammock and allow each a reasonable day's ration of sleep. I suspect Command would prefer android crews who need no sleep at all.

There's little open space inside the cylinder. The curved inner hull supports most of the consoles and working stations, with little separation between them. Two meters off the hull the inner circle begins. There're a few duty stations on that level, but most of the space is occupied by the ship's nervous and circulatory systems, and those parts of her organs which don't need to be instantly accessible. With the exception of a few holes providing access to the two-meter tunnel around the keel, the central eleven meters of the Can are an impenetrable maze of piping, conduit, wiring, junctions, humming boxes of a thousand shapes and sizes, structural beams, and ductwork.

I have to ask. "How the hell can human beings work in this jungle gym?"

Westhause smiles. "Looks better on holo, doesn't it?" Clambering around like a baboon in pants, he leads me to an abbreviated astrogator's console. Flanking it are a pair of input/output consoles for the ship's main computation battery. Nudging up in front, like a calf to its mother, is the tiniest spatial display tank I've ever seen. I've seen cheap children's battle games with bigger tanks. With a perfectly straight face, Westhause reminds me, "It won't be as nasty after we go on ship's gravity."

"Any way is up when you can't get any farther down."

An argument breaks out in the keel passageway. Wanting to appear conscientious, I move toward the nearest access way.

"Never mind. They'll settle it. That's Rose and Throdahl. They're always fussing about something."

"If you say so. Where're the lockers, Waldo?"

"Lockers?" He grins. It's a mean grin. A sadist's grin. Your basic got-you-by-the-balls-and-never-going-to-let-go grin. "You *are* fresh meat, aren't you? What lockers?"

"Gear lockers." Why am I going on? I have one foot poised over an abyss now. "For personal gear." I didn't expect the comforts of Officer's Country aboard a Main Battle, but I did figure on lockers. I can't leave my cameras lying around. Too much chance they'll walk away.

"You use your hammock. Your bunkmates sleep with it."

Comes the dawn. "No wonder nobody brings anything with them."

"Just one of the luxuries they've taken away. That's why the limited modifieds, like the *Eight Ball*, are so popular. Rumor is, they've still got a shower on old Number Eight."

"And I thought we had it bad in the bombards."

"That's right. The Old Man said you were in destroyers back when. Did my original active duty there. Luxury liners compared to this. Hello, Commander."

"There's got to be a better way."

The Commander shrugs as if to say that's a matter of complete indifference to him. He smiles a thin, grim smile that seems carefully studied, the secretive smile of a Commander on top of it all and mildly amused by the antics of the children in his charge. "Nature demands her price. Board all squared away, Mr. Westhause?"

"I'm just starting my check sequence, Commander."

I take the hint. I'm in the way here. Everyone else is busy, too. The compartment is in a state of chaos. The sleeping arrangements seem fairly well settled. The men are slithering over and around one another to examine their duty stations. Despite the care the ship has received in wetdock, they want to double-check everything. It isn't that they mistrust the yardbirds' competence. They just want to *know*. Their lives depend on their equipment.

As I wander, I ponder the mystery of the Old Man. If anything, he's more taciturn, more remote, now that we've boarded the ship. He changed masks when he passed through the entry hatch. He turned on some sort of Commander's personality engineered to fit a profile of crew expectations. Strong and silent, competent and confident. Toler-ant of infractions in the personal sphere, strict regarding anything that might affect the welfare of the ship. I've seen the act before, on other ships. Never have I seen it assumed with such abruptness, such cold calculation. I hope he mellows out. I hope he doesn't exclude me from his thoughts entirely. He's half the story here.

Westhause changed, too, when the new Commander passed through his orbit. In moments he was oblivious to anything but his astrogational toys.

There must be a magic in the Climber. The Old Man and Westhause went away. First Watch Officer arrived. Lieutenant Yanevich is treating me like an old friend. Who else shifted personalities at the hatchway? Bradley? I don't know. I haven't seen him since we came aboard. I don't know any of the others.

I get out of their way in Ops by going exploring below. I don't run into anyone with the time or inclination to talk till I reach the bottom of the Can. There I meet Ambrose Diekereide, our Engineer-in-Training.

I spend an hour talking the man's speciality. He loses me after the first five minutes.

Surviving Academy requires an acquaintance with physics. I got through the courses on stubbornness and an elaborate system for memorization. I have a mind which surrounds itself with armor plate when it's faced with a physics more subtle than that imagined by Isaac Newton. I guess I really do see the fuzzy outlines of what Einstein said. Reinhardt and hypermechanics I take on faith. Despite Diekereide's heroic effort and all my pre-reading, null and Climbing will remain pure witchcraft till the day I die.

Diekereide says it's possible to look at our universe from a continuum of viewpoints. Classical. Newtonian. Einsteinian. Reinhardter. All points on the spectrum, like the central wavelength line of each color cast by a prism.

The defining parameter of the Einsteinian view is the constant c, c being the velocity of light in a vacuum.

Then along comes Reinhardt, who turns it all over by saying $2 + 2 = 4$ sometimes, and c is a constant only under certain special conditions, although those conditions obtain almost everywhere almost all the time. He conjured functions to demonstrate that gravity is the real universal integer.

Somewhere between those two views is where I start finding moss on both sides of the trees.

Diekereide tells me to imagine the universe as an orange. Okay. That's easy enough, even though my eyes tell me the universe is infinite. Hyperspace, where the Newtonian and Einsteinian rules break down, is the rind of the orange. Fine and dandy. Now friend Diekereide grips the orange like a baseball and throws the hard slider. He tells me the rind exists everywhere coequal with the universe it contains. An orange that is part rind all the way to the pips. Relates back to the curvature of space, where, if you head off on a straight line and stick with it long enough, you get back to where you started. Only, using Reinhardt's math, you can take shortcuts because in hyperspace every point touches every other point. In perfect hyperspace, which seems to be as mythical as perfect vacuum, you can travel the light years between point A and point B in no elapsed time.

Go explain me a cloud. Go out and explain me one of those great wads of wool called cumulus or cumulonimbus. Look it up in a book, how it works. Take that on faith. When I look at a cloud, I always wonder why the son of a bitch doesn't fall like a rock. Like a big hunk of iceberg, down, scrunch!

There is no pure hyper because it's polluted by leakover of time, gravity, and subnuclear matter, though the matter is not really matter in that state. Quarks and such, which aren't allowed to exist there, sit around shifting charge in zero elapsed time....

Reinhardt's hyperspace math depends on the universe's being closed and expanding. I gather that in that someday when we begin the collapse back toward the primal egg, hyperspace will undergo some sort of catastrophic reversal of polarity. Or, if Diekereide is right, the reversal will initiate the collapse.

That's why I can't get a handle on physics. Nothing is ever what it seems, and less reliably so with every passing day.

Again, gravity is the key.

One common fiction is to picture hyperspace as a negative image of the universe we see, inhabited by such woolly beasts as $-c$, contra-charged subnuclear binding energies, and anti-gravitons and anti-chronons.

Now that he has set it up, Diekereide throws the smoker up and in. He says a Climber takes it from there, in a direction "perpendicular" to hyperspace, into what is called the null.

Ain't no moss on the trees now. Ain't no trees around here. And he just kyped my compass.

In hyper $2 + 2$ doesn't equal 4. All right. My mother used to believe wilder things in order to receive communion. But…in null, e is only a second cousin of mc^2. In hyper c varies according to e in relation to a constant, m. In null even c^2 can be a negative number.

My opinion? Another triumph for the people who blessed us with $\sqrt{-1}$.

I lost my faith in God as soon as I was old enough to discern the rampant inconsistencies and contradictions in Catholic dogma. My faith in the dogma of physics went when, after having been browbeaten with the implacable laws of thermodynamics for years, I discovered the inconsistencies and contradictions involving neutron stars, black holes, hyper, and the Hell Stars. I just can't buy a package of laws that's good every day but Tuesday.

But I believe what I see and feel. I believe what works.

As a practical matter, to make the ship Climb, or go null, Engineering pumps massive energies into the Climber's torus, which is a closed hyper drive. When the energies become violent enough, hyper cannot tolerate the ship's existence. It spits the tub out like a peach pit, into a level of reality wherein nothing outside the toroid's field responds to ordinary physical law.

I'm reminded of those constructs topologists love to play with on computers. They don't try for just fourth- or fifth-dimensional constructs, they go for eighth or fifteenth. The ordinary mortal mind just can't encompass that.

Welcome to Flatland.

I'm an observer. A narrator. I should observe and report, not comment. As a commentator I tend to become flip and shallow.

Diekereide is a babbler, as mouthy as Westhause is off-ship. He meanders deeper into the forest. I hear the latest gossip about matter without fixed energy states, the new rumor about atoms with the nuclei outside. He gives me a blushing peek through the curtain at nonconcentric electron shells and light hydrogen atoms where electron and proton are separated by infinity. He whispers that matter in null has to exist in a state of excitement cubing that the same atom would have at the heart of a star. I don't ask which star. He might give individual specs.

Strange and wonderful things. I glance at the opening leading to Ship's Services and wonder if it's the same hole Alice tumbled down. I decide to keep an eye peeled for a talking rabbit with his nose in a wacky watch.

Diekereide has more secrets to share.

The more energy fed to the torus, the "higher" into null a Climber goes. Altitude represents a movement across a range of null wherein the physical constants change at a constant and predictable rate, for reasons as yet unknown.

"Oh, really?"

Diekereide is deep into his mysteries. He only catches the edge of my sarcasm. He gives me one puzzled glance. "Of course."

One of my nastier habits. If I don't understand, I tend to mock. I caution myself again: observe and report.

Jokingly I ask, "What would happen if you threw the whole thing in reverse?"

"Reverse?"

"Sure. Sucked power out of the torus. Right out of the fabric of the universe."

The man has no sense of humor. He fires up Engineering's main computer and begins pecking out questions.

"I wasn't serious. I was joking. For God's sake, I don't want to know. Tell me more about altitude."

Altitude is important. I know that from my pre-reading. Altitude helps determine how difficult a Climber is to detect. The higher she goes, the smaller her "shadow" or "cross section."

Enter the rabbit. His name is Lieutenant Varese, the Engineering Officer. He indicates that Diekereide is late for a very important date and takes over the explaining. He has a whole different style.

Our paths have never crossed before, in this life or any other. Still, Varese has decided he isn't going to like me. He sends a clear message. It won't help even if I save his life. Diekereide, on the other hand, will remain my comrade and champion simply because I nod and "Uh-huh" in the right places during his monologues.

Varese's unflattering estimate of my mental capacity is nearer the mark than his assistant's. He gives me a quick PR handout of a lecture.

He says the Effect—by which he means the Climb phenomenon—was first detected aboard overpowered singleships of the unsyncopated rotary-drive type. "The Mark Twelve fusion drive?" I ask brightly.

One sharp nod. "Without governor or Fleet synchronization." Scowl. Fool. You can't buy into the club that easily.

Pilots claimed that sudden, massive applications of power caused their drives to behave strangely, as if stalling, if you think in internal combustion terms, or temporarily flaming out, if you favor jets. Something was going on. External sensors recorded brief lapses of contact with hyper, without making concomitant brushes with norm.

Those reports came out of the first few actions of the war. The problem didn't arise earlier because in peacetime the vessels weren't subjected to such vicious treatment. There were apparent psychological effects, too. The affected pilots claimed that their surroundings became "ghostly."

Physicists immediately posited the existence of a state wherein fusion couldn't take place. The overexcited pilot would jam himself into null, his drive would cease fusing hydrogen, his ship would fall back....

Frenetic research produced the mass annihilation plant. Contraterrene hydrogen, mixing with terrene in controlled amounts, can bang out one hell of a lot of energy in any reality state.

Demand produced a CT technology almost overnight. The first combat Climber went on patrol thirteen months after the discovery of the Climb phenomenon.

End of PR statement. Thank you very much for your kind interest. Now will you please go away? We're very busy down here.

Varese doesn't use those exact words but makes his meaning perfectly clear. I don't think I'm going to like him much, either.

My second hour aboard. I've learned a valuable lesson about serving in the Climbers. Don't try to meet everybody and see everything right away. I've made myself odd man out in the hammock race.

I returned to Ops figuring I'd take whatever was left over, once everything was settled down. There isn't anything. The enlisted men are eyeing me. I don't know if it's apprehension they feel, or if my response will give them some measure of me as a man.

This ship has no Officers' Country. No Petty Officers' Quarters. No Chiefs' Quarters. The wardroom is a meter-long drop table in Ship's Services. It doubles as a cook's bench and ironing board. Everything has its round-the-clock use.

I work my way through Weapons without finding a home. Feeling foolish, I'm working my way through Ship's Services, to continuous polite negatives, when I notice Bradley watching. "Charlie, this scow is too damned egalitarian."

"I saw your problem coming, Lieutenant. Made you a place. Ship's laundry."

The ship's laundry is a sink-and-drainboard arrangement that doubles as a wash basin and sick bay operating table. Bradley has stretched an extra hammock in the clear space overhead. I up my estimate of the man. This is his first mission. He knows little more about the ship than I, yet he has identified a problem and taken corrective action.

"I won't get much sleep here." Under ship's gravity the nadir of the hammock should dip into the sink.

"Maybe not. It's the only basin aboard. But consider the bright side. You won't have to share with anyone else."

"I'm tempted to throw a tantrum. Only I think I'd get damned unpopular damned fast, throwing my commission around." A couple of Bradley's men are watching me with stony faces, waiting for my reaction.

"True." He's begun whispering. "The Old Man says seeing how much the new officers will take is their favorite sport."

"You and me against the universe, then. Thanks. If there's a next time, I'll know better than to play tourist."

"It's your time outside the Service, I guess. Dulled your instincts. I caught on right away."

He's skirting the edge of a painful subject. I beat the wolf down and reply, "The instincts better come back fast. I don't want to be the poor relation at the feast forever."

The watchers are gone. I've passed the first test.

"The Old Man says first impressions are critical. Half of us are outsiders."

"We'll all know each other better than we want before this's over."

"Hey, Lieutenant," someone shouts through the hatch to Weapons. "The Old Man wants you on the Oh-one."

O-1. That's Operations. O-2 is Weapons. And so forth.

I dump my gear into my hammock and hand-over-hand up hooks welded to the keel. When we shift to operational mode, they will become hangers for slinging hammocks and stowing duffel bags.

Getting through the hatches is miserable in parasite mode, even under minimal gravity. The hatches are against the hull, not near the keel. You have to monkey over on bars welded to the overhead. They'll become a ladder to the keel when the vessel goes operational.

Once at the hatch I have to hoist myself through, then repeat the process getting to Operations.

"The man who designed this monster ought to be impaled."

"An oft-heard suggestion," Yanevich says. "But the son of a bitch has gone over to the other firm."

"What?"

He smiles at my expression. "That's why we're all so gung ho. Didn't you know? We can't lay hands on the bastard till we win the war. Only then we'll have to fight over who gets to do what to him first. You want your shot, you'd better put in your paperwork now. Just don't count on too much being left when your chit comes up."

"There's got to be a better setup."

"No doubt. Actually, it's a computer design. They say the programmers forgot to tell the idiot box there'd be people aboard."

"The Commander sent for me."

"Not a command performance. Just so you can watch departure if you want. We're moving now." He nods toward the cabin. "The Old Man is up there. Here. Take my screen. It's on forward camera. This'll do as your duty and battle station for now."

"Not much to see." The bearing and tilt on the camera tell me nothing. Forward. It should be staring at the wall of the wetdock. Instead, the screen shows me an arc of darkness and only a small amount of wall. The lighting seems brilliant by contrast with the darkness.

High on the wall, at the edge of the black arc, a tiny figure in EVA gear is semaphoring its arms. I wonder what the hell he or she is up to. I'll probably never know. One of the mysteries of TerVeen.

A martial salvo from French horns blares through the compartment. The Old Man shouts, "Turn that crap down!" The march dwindles till it's barely audible.

Damn! How imperceptive can one man be? We're moving out. We're under way already. Must have been for quite a while. That creeping arc of darkness is naked space. The mother is crawling out of TerVeen's backassward alimentary canal. "They didn't waste any time."

"Excuse me, sir?" The man on my left offers a questioning look. A Tachyon-Detection Specialist, I see.

"Thinking out loud. Wondering what the devil I'm doing here." I catch the strains of the horns. "Outward Bound," I realize. I've never heard them sung, but I hear some idiot has put words to an ancient march, retitled it, and made it the official Climber battle hymn. Full of eagerness to be at the enemy. A nitwit's delight.

Someone in the inner circle reads my mind and breaks into song. "Outward Bound," all right. I recognize the version I heard being sung by bunny hoppers in the ruins. From somewhere else an authoritative voice says, "Stow it, Rose." This isn't a voice I recognize.

Someone I haven't yet met.

I close my eyes and try to imagine our departure as it would appear to an observer stationed on the wall of the great tunnel. The Climber people come hustling in, hours after the mother crew has begun its preparations. They swarm. Soon the mother reports all Climbers manned and all hatches sealed and tested. Her people scamper over her body, releasing the holding stays, being careful not to snap them. Winches on the tunnel walls reel them in.

Small space tugs drift out from pockets in the walls and grapple magnetically to pushing spars extending beyond the mother's clinging children.

Behind them, way behind them, a massive set of doors grinds closed. From the observer's viewpoint they're coming together like teeth in Brobdingnagian jaws. They meet with a subaudible thud that shakes the asteroid.

Now another set of doors closes over the first. They snuggle right up tight against the others, but they're coming in from left and right. Very little tunnel atmosphere will leak past them. Redundancy in all things is an axiom of military technology.

There are several vessels caught in the bay with the departing mother. They have to cease outside work and button up. Their crews are cursing the departing ship for interrupting their routine. In a few days others will be cursing them.

Now the great chamber fills with groans and whines. Huge vacuum pumps are sucking the atmosphere from the tunnel. A lot will be lost anyway, but every tonne saved is a tonne that won't have to be lifted from Canaan.

The noise of the compressors changes and dwindles as the gas pressure falls. Out in the middle of the tunnel, the tugs slow the evacuation process by using little puffs of compressed gas to move the mother up to final departure position.

Now a pair of big doors in front of the mother begins sliding away into the rock of the asteroid. These are the inner doors, the redundant doors, and they are much thicker that those that have closed behind her. Great titanium slabs, they're fifty meters thick. The doors they back up are even thicker. They're supposed to withstand the worst that can be thrown against them during a surprise attack. If they were breached, the air pressure in the 280 klicks of tunnel would blow ships and people out like pellets out of a scattergun.

The inner doors are open. The outer jaws follow. The observer can peer down a kilometer of tunnel at a round black disk in which diamonds sparkle. Some seem to be winking and moving around, like fireflies. The tugs puff in earnest. The mother's motion becomes perceptible.

A great long beast with donuts stuck to her flanks, moving slowly, slowly, while "Outward Bound" rings in the observer's ears. Great stuff. Dramatic stuff. The opening shots for a holo-show about the deathless heroes of Climber Fleet One. The mother's norm-thrusters begin to glow. Just warming up. She won't light off till there's no chance her nasty wake will blast back at her tunnelmates.

The tugs are puffing furiously now. If the observer were to step aboard one, he would hear a constant roar, feel the rumble coming right up through the deckplates into his body. Mother ship's velocity is up to thirty centimeters per second.

Thirty cps? Why, that's hardly a kilometer per hour. This ship can race from star to star in a few hundred thousand blinks of an eye.

The tugs stop thrusting except when the mother's main astrogational computers signal that she's drifting off the centerline of the tunnel. A little puff here, a little one there, and she keeps sliding along, very, very slowly. They'll play "Outward Bound" a dozen times before her nose breaks the final ragged circle and peeps cautiously into her native element. Groundhog coming up for a look around.

The tugs let go. They have thrusters on both ends. They simply throw it into reverse and scamper back up the tunnel like a pack of fugitive mice. The big doors begin to close.

The mother slides on into the night, like an infant entering the world. She hasn't actually put weigh on but has taken it off. She's coming out the rear end of TerVeen, relative to the asteroid's orbit around Canaan. The difference in orbital velocities is small, but soon she'll drift off the line of TerVeen's orbit.

Before she does, word will come from Control telling her the great doors are sealed. Her thrusters will come to life, burning against the night, blazing off the dull, knobby surface of TerVeen. She'll gain velocity. And up along her flanks will gather the lean black shapes of her friends, the attack destroyers. The French horns may toot a final hurrah for those who'll never return.

Outward bound.

What am I doing here? The arc of darkness has devoured the last of the light. And there're creatures hidden in it, somewhere, eager to end my tale.

"No sweat, sir," my neighbor informs me. "Getting to the patrol zone is a milk run. They haven't hit a mother yet."

That record doesn't impress me. There's a first time for everything, and my luck hasn't been hot for several years. The butterflies stampeding in my stomach are trying to tell me something.

"The Lord is with us, sir. Recall the psalm, if you will. 'Though I walk through the valley of the shadow of death, I will fear no evil.'"

At the moment I could use a comforting rod and staff. Anything. A little superstition doesn't hurt once in a while does it? "Huh?"

"*Meow?*"

Something is rubbing against my shins. I push back from the console.... "Oh, shit. What the fuck? A goddamned cat?"

I'm surprised at myself. I must be more on edge than I'm willing to admit. I don't usually have a garbage mouth.

"That's Fleet Admiral Minh-Tannian," my neighbor says. "Pureblood, registered alley cat. A pedigree a millimeter long." He smiles so I'll know that he's joking. The smile is useful. He has a flat delivery.

An enlisted man with Chief's stripes leans on the back of my seat, considering the cat. I've never seen a more scabrous beast. The Chief offers his hand. "Felipe Nicastro, sir. Chief Quartermaster. Welcome aboard. Your four-legged friend usually answers to Fred, or Fearless Fred. Named after our glorious leader, of course. Those yardbirds take good care of you, Fred?" Nicastro glances round the compartment. "Old Fearless himself should be up on squadron net by now. Throdahl? Anything from the Great Balloon?"

Throdahl is the Climber's radio operator. At the moment he's pressing a tiny headphone to his left ear. "His carrier is open, Chief. Any second."

The Commander calls out, "Log it, Throdahl. Give the Lieutenant a couple minutes for flavor, then shit-can it. Except for the Recorder."

I glance up at the Chief. He's hanging on my reaction. "Not much formality here, Chief. Does it affect discipline?"

"Our competitors pack guns. That's discipline enough."

I make a mental note: Query the Commander re his order. Ignoring the Admiral won't set well in some quarters. The Mission Recorder remembers everything, be it a command decision or simple whisper of discontent.

My exterior view gives way to the craggy, photogenic visage of Fleet Admiral Frederick Minh-Tannian, Navy's proconsul on Canaan.

"You probably see more of this nitwit on the Inner Worlds than we do out here." Glancing up, I see Nicastro has given way to Lieutenant Yanevich. The Chief has stepped to one side. "He's a glory hound."

"A gasbag too," Nicastro declares. He's needling me subtly. Maybe he thinks I report direct to the Admiral.

Hardly. At the moment, faced by my first mission, after weeks of having heard how bad it is out there, the last thing I'll have is a rousing attack of patriotism. I'm too busy being scared.

Tannian is speaking. I don't bother listening to more than a few snatches. "… implacable resistance… Remorselessly onward… Until the death, jaws locked in the throat of the enemy… Bold and courageous warriors yielding your final gram of courage…"

Such is the stuff of the Admiral's speech. Such is the stuff of his worldview. Some pep talk. He could bore the last erg of fight out of the home team before the biggest game of the year. Didn't he ever serve in a fighting ship? Nobody wants to hear that shit.

I can't help growling, "Sounds like he thinks we're a destroyer squadron off to shoot up a Sangaree raidstation."

"Cruisers." Yanevich grins. "He came up in cruisers."

Before Throdahl abbreviates that football rally of a speech, I become as derisive as any of my companions. It's catching. The Admiral *asks* for it. It's painfully clear that he doesn't understand fighting men at all. There's something very definitely wrong when even the career officers hold their supreme commander in total contempt.

Yanevich is worse than the enlisted men. He seems to think Tannian is making a direct assault on his intelligence. He has several crude suggestions for the Admiral, all involving donut-shaped titanium suppositories.

Nobody seems to care that the Mission Recorder will remember what they say.

Only one man listens to Tannian. I pick him out instantly. He's the one nodding in all the right places, and looking mildly dismayed by his shipmates.

"Chief?" I point.

"Gonsalvo Carmon. Operations Electronic Technician. Fourth Mission. Bronwen. They skragged it at the beginning of the war. He's a crusader."

"Oh." They're worse than the Tannians. The Tannians are just blowing hot air. The crusaders mean it. They can get you killed, trying to do the things the Tannians just talk about.

"Gentlemen, please," the Commander shouts into the catcalls and obscene suggestions. "Please remember your dignity. Please remember that this is Navy, and Navy demands respect for senior officers." The compartment descends into nervous silence. There could be some black marks coming up. "Besides, the old fartbag means well."

Redoubled howling.

"Don't you worry about the Recorder?" I asked the First Watch Officer.

"Why? There's a war on. Unless we take a ride on Hecate's Horse and they recover the Recorder, the scanners only check our operational statistics. Missiles expended versus shipping destroyed. Tactics, successful and unsuccessful. You can't tell one voice from another on that cheap tape anyway. Unless you want to take voiceprints. The scanners are old Climber people anyway. They know what's going on out here."

"Oh." Nevertheless, I reprimand myself for having participated in the mockery. My position is precarious. I dare not antagonize anyone for fear I'll dry up my sources.

My screen blanks. Nicastro murmurs, "Look at that! He screwed up his channel changes."

Instead of space, my screen is showing us the most beautiful black woman I've ever seen. The Chief says, "I'll straighten him out."

"Don't bother. I don't mind looking at this. I don't mind at all."

It's obvious that she and the radioman are very close friends. Embarrassingly close. Even while I'm considering swearing off Nordic blondes, I'm beginning to fidget. Voyeurism's never been my cup of tea.

"Hey, Monte," one of the computermen shouts. "Tell her to save some of that for me."

Only then does Throdahl realize that he has fed his intership personal to every screen.

"Shove it, Rose." The beautiful lady vanishes. I suppose it's the situation, being on the edge of peril, that makes me overreact. I know I'm going to mourn and remember this vision forever. I'm going to fall asleep thinking about her. Hell, maybe I'll try to meet her when we get back. Assuming we get back.

We have to. This Climber is invulnerable. I'm aboard. They can't dust a Climber carrying a correspondent. Yes. I'll be seeing you, lady.

Some of the others are adopting the same plan. It's the nature of the moment, surely. I've seen it before, on other ships. Soon there'll be no further talk of tomorrow, and very little thought of it. Life will become moment to moment. The Climber will contain the whole universe. Big plans for the future will extend no farther than work to be accomplished during the next off-watch period.

The cat lands in my lap. Startling as his presence was, I forgot him. "Uh. Hello, Fred." I'm not on good terms with cats. Generally we contrive to ignore one another. I scratch the top of his head, then around his ears. He seems satisfied. "What do you think?" I ask him.

These clowns have broken a whole volume of regs by installing an animal aboard. How did they manage it? In one of the duffel bags?

What's cat hair doing to the atmosphere system?

A cat is a small thing. But getting him from Canaan into TerVeen, then into the ship, would require a substantial conspiracy.

"All is forgiven, I see." That's the Commander's uniquely calm and toneless voice. Turning, I see him balanced among the cross-members, clinging like a spider monkey. He has his cap pushed way back on the crown of his head. His hair sticks out like pieces of broken straw. He looks younger and happier now that he's here, now that the unknowns have been removed from his life. His smile seems gentle, almost feminine. There's a playful humor in his eyes.

"What do you mean?"

"That was Fred's mass share you took for your extra gear. There won't be any goodies for him this patrol." He waves one hand. I wonder why I've never noticed how long and delicate his fingers are. Piano-player fingers. Artist's fingers. Definitely not the thick sausages of a professional warrior. "No matter. Fred is a master of the innovative scrounge. He'll get fat while the rest of us turn into pus-colored scarecrows."

I've seen tapes of "victorious heroes" returning from successful patrols. The Caucasians were, indeed, pus-colored and ragged. Even the darker spacers had a washed-out look.

The Old Man must be in on the plot. He drifts away before I can ask any questions. So I'll ask Yanevich. But the First Watch Officer has vanished, too. Along the way and partly up the curve of the hull, Westhause is engrossed in the subtleties of his Dead Reckoning system, murmuring to it as if it needs endearments now so it will perform well later. Is he seducing the equipment?

Everyone is preoccupied. Except the Chief Quartermaster.

Nicastro is a small, lean, dark man, mid-twenties going on fifty. This will be his last patrol. Daring fate and superstition, he married during his leave. He now looks like he regrets his temerity. His jitters are showing. The short-timer shakes, they call them. They say it takes a rock of a man to get through the tenth mission without cracking a little.

"Chief, tell me about Fred." How does the animal survive? This plainly isn't his first mission. The old hands act like he's part of the crew.

Has some genius cobbled together a feline combat suit and taught him to go to it when the alarm sounds?

Nicastro turns his small, dark eyes my way. They're slightly crazy eyes, eyes that look back on too many patrols. "He comes with the ship. He's got seniority. Nobody knows how he got here anymore. This's his fourteenth patrol. Won't take a groundside billet. Hides out whenever we pull in. Hangs in there smiting them hip and thigh, just like his namesake says. Please keep an eye on the screen, sir. We're not redundant in the Climbers. You're the only visual watch right now."

Nicastro's answer doesn't satisfy me, but I suspect it's the best I'll get. For a while. I still have to prove myself. I have to show these men that I can pull my weight, that I can take the heat. I'm supernumerary. That means there'll be just a little less for everyone else. I take up space, generate heat, consume food. Worse, I'm an outsider. One of those damned fools who fill the holonets with utter shit.

There won't be much joy in this for me. Let's hope that it'll be a short, showy mission.

I'll handle my shipboard duties. You don't forget the training. What worries me is that I may have lost my edge. I may have gotten fat. I may no longer have the self-discipline needed to endure the hardships.

"After-drag scoops clear," one of the nonrated men reports. He's repeating information coming from the mother ship. Nobody really cares. But we need to know where we are should we have to jump off the mother. A few minutes later, the same man reports, "Released from tug control. Stand by for point-one gee acceleration."

Nicastro gestures. I glance up. He points. Inertia will drag us in that direction. I nod. I'd forgotten our attitude on the mother. There'll be a little sideways drag.

"Quartermaster, sound general quarters when acceleration commences." The First Watch Officer has returned. Nicastro changes position slightly and speaks to one of the men.

I punch commands to my camera mount, scanning surrounding space. The mother is clear of TerVeen. A bright half-moon is slowly dwindling behind her. She's no longer safe. We've entered the battle zone. We have to be ready. The gentlemen of the other firm could show at any time.

The relay talker begins chattering continuously. "Planetary Defense standing by. Red Flotilla on station. Screen Romeo Tango Sierra, axis two niner seven relative, fifteen degrees zenith."

Somewhere, someone is typing madly, entering the information into a computer terminal. I'm startled because the keys make noise. They must be mechanical. On the big ships, terminals don't have keys, just a lettered, pressure-sensitive surface that records the lightest touch of a finger.

Keeping one eye on TerVeen, I beckon Yanevich. He ambles over wearing a slight smirk, as if he's sure I'll ask an especially stupid question. "Where're the suit lockers?" I've realized that I haven't been fitted. What've they done, taken something off the rack for me?

"Don't worry about it."

"But I'll need one for GQ."

He grins. "Just stay put."

In a slight panic, "What about the suit?"

He lays a finger alongside his chin in mock thoughtfulness. It's a strong, square chin. A recruiting-poster chin. It doesn't go with his narrow face and string-bean body. It makes him look bottom-heavy. His face has a sort of dull look in repose. "Suits. Let's see. I think Mr. Varese might have a few EVA jobs down in Engineering."

"No suits? My God…" They snuck one through on me. Never have I heard of going into action without the extra protection of suits. I glare at the hull. Six millimeters of stressed titanium alloy between me and the big dark. Two more millimeters of spray-on polyflex foam there to fill any micrometeorite punctures, plus a little insulation. All that inside the metal. And no suits.

"Surprise!" Yanevich crows. "You know how much a suit masses?"

That's incredible. What can they possibly be thinking at Command? No suits. It indicates an appalling lack of concern for the men.

There's a hand on my shoulder. I look up into Chief Nicastro's weak smile. "Welcome to the Climbers, sir."

No suits? One breach in the hull and we're done. Welcome to the Climbers indeed!

Some quick impressions.

Officers: generally cool. Those I traveled with cool to medium-friendly. Of the others, only subLieutenant Diekereide has shown any warmth. Not too much resentment, considering. I suppose most of it has been transferred to the Admiral. They assume my presence is Tannian's idea. Only the Commander has any inkling of how hard I fought to get aboard. I wonder if he has an inkling of how sorry I am already?

Crew: so far neutral to cool, with the possible exception of Chief Nicastro.

Of the others, only the tachyon man has spoken to me. I'll have to be patient. Even in the Line the men are wary of new officers. This go they have three to break in.

This is Diekereide's third patrol, but his first with this Climber. They shuffle hell out of Engineers before they give them their own ship. Then they become part of the power plant. The subLieutenant strikes me as the type eager to be friends with everybody—at least till he settles in. He comes on a little too strong. I presume he's a solid Engineer. He wouldn't be here otherwise. The propaganda is right in one respect. Climber people are the best of the best, the Fleet elite.

However competent he may be, I can't picture Diekereide's becoming a good officer in the leadership sense. Maybe that goes with his territory.

It took no genius to discover that Lieutenant Varese isn't popular. I didn't have to observe his men behind his back to guess it. He's the perpetual fussbudget, never satisfied with anyone's work. He can't keep his mouth shut when that's the wisest course. And if he has a choice of a positive and a negative comment, he'll choose the latter every time.

I've only had glimpses of Lieutenant Piniaz. He's somewhat like Varese, though quieter, yet more belligerent and bitter. There's a huge chip on his shoulder. I understand he came up through the ranks.

Bradley appears to be standard Academy product. He's self-sufficient, competent, and confident. He's efficient and soft-spoken. He seems to have won his men already. He'll get ahead if he survives his ten missions.

He's a child today. In two years he'll be a clone of the Commander.

There'll be lines in his face. He'll have hollow eyes. He'll look ten years older than he is. And his men will have complete confidence in him, and none at all in Command. They'll follow him in a strike on the gates of hell, confident the Old Man can pull it off. And they'll curse the idiots who formulated the mission all the while.

I've had little real opportunity to gauge the enlisted men. Here in Operations the outstanding characters seem to be Junghaus (the tachyon man, commonly called Fisherman), Carmon (occasionally called the Patriot), Rose, Throdahl, and Chief Nicastro. They're all old hands, and they've all spaced with the Commander before.

Rose and Throdahl are prototypical noncoms. Struck from the original mold, designed by Sargon I. They have one-track minds. They seem to know nothing but sex. Their banter, though probably old at the time of the fall of Nineveh, has its entertaining moments.

Carmon is a silent patriot, thank heaven. He doesn't irritate us with speeches. He reminds me of a lizard quietly awaiting the approach of prey. He has that patient, "the day is going to come" air. His intensity makes the others nervous.

As advertised, Fisherman is the resident evangelist. Every ship has one. It seems to be an unofficial billet, generated by some need in the group subconscious. I was surprised to find one on a vessel this small. Ours is a Christian, with a definite charismatic bent.

Since we have a Preacher, it seems likely we'll also have a Loan Shark, a Moonshiner, a Peddler (the man who always has something to sell, and who can get you anything you want), a Bookmaker, a Thief, and a Gritch. The latter is the man everyone loves to hate, and the most important character in any small, closed social system. A closed group always seems to create one. He becomes a walking catharsis, a small-time Jesus who involuntarily takes our sins upon himself.

He's always that one man who's a little more different, a little more strange. The body politic alienates and hates him, and as a consequence everyone else gets along a little better.

Chief Nicastro may be our coward, simply by circumstance. He's scared to death of this mission. I suspect it would be that way for any man making his final patrol. I have a touch of it myself. When there's nothing but another mission ahead, a man can look forward to nothing but another mission. He knows better than to plan the rest of his life. The short-time shakes set in during the magical final run. There's a chance there might be a tomorrow. You don't want to jinx it by thinking about it. And you can't help thinking.

There are seven more men in Ops: Laramie, Berberian, Brown, Scarlatella, Canzoneri, Picraux, and Zia. They're less obvious, less flamboyant, less loud, either by nature or because this is their first patrol aboard the Climber.

"Got to piss, better do it now," Yanevich says. "Compartment hatches seal at GQ."

The hatches are massive, one on each side of the double intercompartmental bulkhead. They'll keep a breach from claiming the entire ship. Each compartment is its own lifeboat. The Can is held together by explosive bolts. We can blow the four sections out of the hole in the donut if we have to.

I want to ask about that. Has anyone ever actually tried it? Is there any point? I can't see it. Again the First Watch Officer has disappeared before I can formulate my questions.

How do they cut the keel? The keel is a single piece of steel running the height of the Can. Some way has to exist to sever it between compartments. And how do we drift apart? There has to be a thruster to drive the compartments away from the doomed donut.

I can see that, I think. There's a big, wide lump around the keel in the bulkhead facing Weapons. A lot of tubing runs into it from small tanks slung around the compartment. Conduit too. Must be a small chemical thruster, just enough to kick the compartment away. Five or ten seconds of burn time, just a pittance of delta-v...

The Tachyon-Detection Technician volunteers, "I was in Sixty-seven Dee." His attitude says that means something. Maybe it does to veteran Climber people. It rings no bells with me. Maybe if he told me her Commander's name ... A few successful patrols can make a Commander famous. The Old Man is one of the current crop. No one knows from hull numbers. A ship has to be big and have a name before it becomes famous. I'd barely heard of the *Eight Ball* before reaching TerVeen. But I know *Carolingian* and *Marseilles* and *Honan* well, and all they ever did was get skragged. Dramatically, of course. Very damned dramatically, with the holonets beating the drums all the while.

Fisherman wants priming. He's like a brand-new acquaintance who hands you a holo of the kids, then, embarrassed by his own temerity, bites his lips and awaits your comment. "What happened?"

"Not that great a story, I guess." He manages to look both sorry he's spoken and mildly disappointed in me. Sixty-seven Dee must be one of the legends of the Fleet.

"I don't know. I haven't heard it."

Junghaus doesn't look old enough to be a veteran. He can't be more than nineteen. Just a pimply faced, confused kid who looks two sizes too small for his uniform. Yet he has four little red mission stars tattooed on the back of his left hand, over the knuckles at the roots of each finger. "Catch a fistful of stars…" They'll creep along the next rank of knuckles now. A barbarous custom that's scrupulously observed. One of the superstitions.

Half the crew is under twenty. They're the influx from Canaan. The older men are Regulars from the Fleet.

The Old Man calls this the Children's War. He seems to have forgotten his history. Most of them are.

Fisherman thinks it over and shrugs. "We lost hull integrity in Engineering. We weren't even in action. Just running a routine drill. Lost everybody in the compartment. Couldn't get through to seal the breach. All the suits were stored there. Regulations. The rest of us had to gut out twenty-two days before we were picked up. The first two weeks weren't that bad. Then the stored power started to go…."

A shadow crosses his almost cherubic face. He doesn't want to remember, and can't help it. His effort to stay here with me produces a visible strain.

"Engineering supposedly has better protection. Guess that's where you can get killed the quickest."

He startles me, using the word killed. He looks calm enough, but that betrays his turmoil. He's talking about *the* traumatic experience of his life.

I try to envision the terror, inexorably fading into hopeless resignation, aboard a vessel that's lost power and drives. Those who survived the initial disaster would depend entirely on outside intervention. And Climber paths seldom cross.

Give Command this: They try to find out why when a vessel stops reporting.

"You didn't blow the bolts?" I'm curious about those bolts. They're a facet of the ship wholly new to me, a nifty little surprise that must have all its secrets exposed.

"Blow them? Out there? Why? They can find a ship. They usually know where to look. But a section… They almost never find them. You don't break up unless the ship is going to blow." His final sentence has the ring of an Eleventh Commandment.

"But with the power dwindling and all that unmonitored CT hanging there…"

"The E-system functioned. We made it. Don't think we didn't argue about separating." He's becoming defensive. I'd better change my style. You can't grill them. You have to get them to volunteer. "Really, you can't separate unless you know they'll pick you up right away. Only Ship's Services can last more than a few days after separation."

"That's what I call gutting it out." How did they take the pressure? With nothing to do but watch the power levels fall and bet on when the magnetics would go. "I don't think I could handle it."

"Acceleration in ten seconds," the relay speaker tells us. "Nine. Eight…"

The acceleration alarm yammers. Everything is supposed to be secure. Don't want anything rocketing around, smacking people. The hatch to Weapons clunks shut. Yanevich gets down on his stomach to examine the seal.

The Old Man glares at the compartment clock. It says we're nineteen hours and forty-seven minutes into Mission Day One. Down on Canaan, at the Pits, it's the heart of night again. I search with my camera, and there's the world, immense and glorious, and very much like every other human world. Lots of blue and lots of cloud, with the boundaries between land and sea hard to discern from here. How high is TerVeen? Not so high the planet has stopped being down. I could ask, but I really don't care. I'm headed the other way, and an unpleasant little voice keeps reminding me that a third of all missions end in the patrol zone.

"Where're the plug-ups?" the Commander demands. "Damn it, where the hell are the plug-ups?"

"Oh." The man doing the relay talking hits a switch. Little gas-filled plastic balls swarm into the compartment. They range from golf-ball to tennis-ball size.

"Enough. Enough," Nicastro growls. "We've got to be able to see."

A new man, I decide. He's heard about the Commander. He's too anxious to look good. He's concentrating too much. Doing his job one part at a time, with such thoroughness that he muffs the whole.

The plug-ups will drift aimlessly throughout the patrol, and will soon fade into the background environment. No one will think about them unless the hull is breached. Then our lives could depend on them. They'll rush to the hole, carried by the escaping atmosphere. If the breach is small, they'll break trying to get through. A quick-setting, oxygen-sensitive goo coats their insides.

The cat scrambles after the nearest ball. He bats it around. It survives his attentions. He pretends a towering indifference. He's a master of that talent of the feline breed, of adopting a regal dignity in the face of failure, just in case somebody is watching.

Breaches too big for the plug-ups probably wouldn't matter. We would be dead before we noticed them.

Satisfied with the hatch, Yanevich rises and leans past me to thumb a switch. "Ship's Services, First Watch Officer. Commence conversion to patrol atmosphere."

The ship is filled with the TerVeen mixture, which is nominal planetary. Ship's atmosphere will be pure oxygen at twenty percent of normal pressure. That reduces hull stress and potential leakage and eliminates useless mass. Low-pressure oxygen is standard Fleet atmosphere.

The convenience has its drawbacks. Care to avoid fires is needed.

That madman, the Commander, brought a pipe and tobacco. Will he actually smoke? That's against regs. But so is a ship's cat.

"Radar, you have anyone from the other firm?"

"Nothing immediate, sir."

That's a relief. I won't get my head kicked in during the next five minutes.

Why does Yanevich bother? In parasite mode the vessel's only usable weapon is that silly magnetic cannon.

Out of nowhere, Junghaus says, "The Lord carried us through. He stands by the Faithful." It takes me a moment to realize that he's returned to our earlier conversation.

A trial shot, I suppose. To see how I react. It'll build to full-scale proselytization if I don't stop it now. "Maybe. But it seems to be he spends a lot of time buddying up with the other team."

"That's 'cause they've got the aged whiskey," someone hoots. Junghaus stiffens. I glance around, can't identify the culprit. I didn't realize that our voices carried that well.

It's very quiet in here! The equipment makes almost no noise.

Junghaus persists. I guess that's why they call him Fisherman.

It seems like forever since I've encountered a practicing Christian. They just don't make them anymore. The race has no need for its old superstitions out here. New faiths are still in formative stages.

"We're being tried in the crucible, sir. Those who are found wanting will perish."

That same voice says, "And the Lord saith unto him, verily, I shall tax you sorely, and tear you a new asshole."

Nicastro snaps, "Can the chatter."

Was Fisherman a believer before his toe-to-toe with death? I doubt it. I can't ask. The directive to silence includes myself, though the Chief would never be so insubordinate as to tell an officer to shut up.

"Increasing acceleration to point-two gee in two minutes."

"Contact, by relay from tender Combat Information, desig Bogey One, bearing one four zero right azimuth, altitude twelve degrees nadir, range point-five-four million kilometers. Closing. Course..."

Here we go. The beginning of the death dance. They've spotted us. They'll throw everything but the proverbial sink. They don't like Climbers.

I missed something while trying not to panic. From the talker's information Yanevich has deduced, "It's just a picket boat. She's staying out of our way. Carmon, warm the display tank."

I sneer at that toy. On the Empire Class Main Battles they have them bigger than our Ops compartment. And they have more than one. For a thrill, in null grav, you can dive in and swim among the stars. If you don't mind standing Commander's Mast and doing a few weeks' extra duty.

TerVeen slips past the terminator. Canaan is barely visible. No evidence of human occupation. Surprising how much effort it takes to make human works visible from space, considering them with the eyeball alone.

I adjust the camera angle. Now I see nothing but stars and a fragment of mother-ship frame almost indistinguishable in the darkness. Doubling the magnification, I set a visual search pattern. I catch a remote, traveling sparkle. "Watch Officer."

Yanevich leans over my shoulder. "One of ours. Putting on inherent velocity. Probably going to check something out."

I continue searching and become engrossed in the view. A while later I realize I'm daydreaming. We've moved up to point-four gees acceleration. Someone has a magician's touch. His compensations have prevented inertia from vectoring any weird gravity orientations.

We have three bogeys numbered and identified. Chief Nicastro tells me, "They don't bother us before we clear the Planetary Defense umbrella."

The thin screen surrounding the planet will have sucked round our way, to help give us a running start.

From planetside it looked like the gentlemen of the other firm were everywhere. But a sky view from a surface point makes only a tiny slice of pie. A slice studied only when it is occupied. In space the picture becomes much more vast.

The minuteness of an artifact in space is such that you would think that searches might as well be conducted by rolling dice. Chance and luck become absurdly important. Intelligence and planning become secondary.

Still, Command knows whence the enemy comes, and whither he is bound. A sharp watch on the fat space sausage between those points helps narrow the odds. Climbers patrol the likeliest hunting grounds.

The passing legion of verbal reports fades, becoming so much background noise, no more noticed than the ubiquitous plug-ups. I shift my attention from the chatter to the chatterers. I can't always see them, either because they've gone around the curve or because they roam. Fisherman. Monte Throdahl. Gonsalvo Carmon, who is almost worshipful as he nurtures the display tank. N'Gaio Rose and his Chief, a computerman named Canzoneri who has a diabolical look. Westhause remains fixated on his Dead Reckoning gear. The men I can't see are Isadore Laramie, Louis Picraux, Miche Berberian, Melvin Brown, Jr. (he gets insistent about that Jr.), Lubomir Scarlatella, and Haddon Zia. I don't know all their rates and tasks yet. I catch what I can when I hear it mentioned.

The men I can see are serious and attentive, though they don't resemble the heroes Admiral Tannian has created in the media. They sneer at the part, though I think they'd play it to the hilt given leave on a world where they're not well known.

Looks like I've got it made. Nothing to do but watch a screen. And damned sure nothing is going to happen on it before some other system yells first. Everybody else is doing two jobs at once. While the Climber is being taken for a ride.

An hour after departure we reach point-five gee acceleration. The compensator finally muffs his adjustment. The universe tilts slightly and stays askew for two hours. The Old Man doesn't bother complaining. They don't notice it down in Engineering because they're closer to the gravity generators in the mother.

Yanevich's prowling brings him within range. "Why are we holding hyper?" Seems to me a quick getaway is in order.

"Waiting for the other firm. They have ships in hyper waiting to ambush us. We won't take till they drop and show us their inherent velocities and vectors. Can't just go charging off, you know. Got to give them the slip. If we don't, they'll dog us to Fuel Point and all hell will break loose."

I crane and look at the display tank. The mother is the focus there. Neither side looks inclined to start anything.

Each is hoping the other will screw up.

Reminds me of my short career as an amateur boxer. What was that kid's name? Kenny something. They shoved us in the ring and said have at it. We circled and feinted, feinted and circled, and never did throw a real punch. Not chicken, either one of us. Just cautious, waiting for the other guy to commit, to reach and leave an opening. Coach got peeved and sarcastic. We danced while he bad-mouthed our conservative style.

We didn't let him get to us. We circled and waited. Then our turn in the ring was up. They never put us in again.

The next two kids were Coach's type. Gloves flying everywhere. *Whup! Whup! Whup!* Pure offense, and the winner is the last man twitching. Your basic kamikaze. Blood, spit, and snot all over the ring. Coach had to cut it off before somebody got creamed.

Coach Tannian stays out of the way while a squadron is departing. He's a mixer but has learned to appreciate the conservative approach. There *are* times when footwork is more important than punch.

While the butterflies float, the mother keeps increasing her rate of acceleration. The relay talker says, "Coming up on time Lima Kilo Zero."

"What does that mean?"

Yanevich is passing. "The point when we hit fifty klicks per second relative to TerVeen. When we throw a rock in the pond to see which way the frogs jump. We're following a basal plan preprogrammed after an analysis of everything that's been done before." He pats my shoulder. "Things are going to start happening."

The clock indicates that Mission Day One is drawing to a close. I suppose I've earned my pay. I've stayed awake all the way round the clock, and then some.

"Bogey Niner accelerating."

We've got nine of them now? My eyes may be open, but my brain has been sleeping.

I watch the tank instead of trying to follow the ascensions, declinations, azimuths, and relative velocities and range rates the talker chirrups. The nearest enemy vessel, which has been tagging along slightly to relative nadir, has begun hauling ass, pushing four gravities, apparently intent on coming abreast of us at the same declination.

"They do their analyses, too," Yanevich says.

His remark becomes clear when a new green blip materializes in the tank. A pair of little green arrows part from it and course toward the point where bogey Nine would've been had she not accelerated. The friendly blip winks out again. Little red arrows were racing toward it from the repositioned enemy.

"That was a Climber from Training Group. Seems he was expected."

The two missile flights begin seeking targets. Briefly, they chase one another like puppies chasing their tails. Then their dull brains realize that that isn't their mission. They fling apart, searching again. The greenies locate the bogey, surge toward her.

She takes hyper, dances a hundred thousand klicks sunward, and ceases worrying about missiles. She begins crawling up on the mother's opposite quarter.

"A victory of sorts," Yanevich observes. "Made them stand back for a minute."

By evading rather than risking engaging the Climber's missiles, our pursuer has complicated her inherent velocity vector with respect to her quarry. We can take hyper now and shake her easily. Unfortunately, she has a lot of friends.

The enemy missiles head our way. We're the biggest moving target visible. The mother's energy batteries splatter them.

This is a complex game, played in all the accessible dimensions and levels of reality. The Training Climbers give the home team an edge. Each of their appearances scrapes another hunter off the mother's trail, making her escorts more formidable against any attack.

"We're almost clear," Yanevich says. "Won't be long before we do a few false hyper takes to see what shakes."

The first of those comes up a half-hour later. It lasts only four seconds. The mother jumps a scant four light-seconds. Her pursuers try to stay with her, but time lags taking and dropping hyper distort their formation. While they're trying to adjust, the mother skips twice more, in a random program generated beforehand and made available to our escort.

They're not dummies over there. They react quickly and well. They have one grand advantage over us. They have instantaneous interstellar communications gear, or instel. All their ships are equipped. We only have a handful scattered throughout the Fleet. Our normal communications are limited to the velocity of light.

Yanevich says, "Now a test fly to see if they've been holding anything back. And they are. They always are."

This time there's a half-hour interval between the take and drop hyper alarms. In the interim the opposition throws in a pair of singleships. They bust in out of deep space almost too fast for detection. For a few seconds a lot of firepower flashes around. No one gets hurt. The singleships bounce off the escort screen.

"Now a lot of stutter steps and mixing so they lose track of which ship is which. We hope." The mother's maneuvers have gained her a margin in which she can commence grander maneuvers.

Alarms jangle almost continuously while the flotilla mixes its trails. I await the final maneuver, which I assume will be a flower, with every ship screaming off in a different direction, getting gone before the other firm decides which to chase.

I guess right. "What now?"

"We have lead time now," Yanevich assures me. "Next stop, Fuel Point."

4

FIRST CLIMB

Christ, am I blown out. Seems like a week since I got any sleep. A couple catnaps since I left Sharon… Let's don't even think about that. An incident. Best forgotten. Sordid. And already looking good in retrospect.

The sleeplessness wouldn't be bad if it weren't for the stress. Enemy ships out there… Maybe we see them and maybe we don't. No wonder these men are lunatics.

We're in hyper now. I have to get some sleep while I can. If I don't sleep before Fuel Point I'll go hyper-bent when we go norm and the pressure comes on again.

The others aren't doing badly. But they're accustomed to it. Most of them have been here before.

Damn! Why did I pick such a crazy way to make a living?

A dull day is about done. Just finished a second bout with my hammock. Sleeping there is worse than I expected. Someone is going on or coming off watch all the time. And every man of them just *has* to stop to use the sink. If they aren't washing themselves or their socks, they're using the damned thing as a urinal.

This flying donut has only one head. Bradley says there were three in the original design. One low-grav and two universal-gravity stools. That last two went the way of the shower. Eliminated in favor of increased weaponry mass.

The lines form before watch change. The men going on watch want to take care of their business because they'll have no chance later. Those who need to squat line up outside the Admiral's stateroom. The others just hose into the sink and spritz with a flash of water. Sometimes it takes a half-hour to get them all by.

Then it's time for a repeat performance from the retiring watch. That's good for another half-hour. And all the while they're jostling and cursing one another, banging me around, and digging into their

67

endless inventories of crude jokes and improbable anecdotes.

I'd hate to wash anything in that sink. The odor alone keeps me awake.

I've been looking for a better home. And have concluded that said place doesn't exist, though I should be admired for my persistence. Like the men looking for the eido.

Eido. I thought the word came from eidolon when first I heard it. Ghost. Specter. Spook. Someone you don't see, slipping around behind you, watching over your shoulder. But no, it comes from eidetic, as in eidetic memory.

Crews have a game with which they begin each patrol. An intellectual recreation caused by, I suspect, a grave error in Psych Bureau thinking. In extended hard times the eido might become a more abused scapegoat than the creature I call the gritch.

The eido is a human Mission Recorder, a crewman with a hypnotically augmented memory. He's supposed to see, hear, and remember everything, including the emotional impact of events. He's always one of the first-timers, supposedly because that maximizes objectivity.

This is a facet of Climber life they don't mention on the networks. A puzzling facet. When first I heard of the eido, I thought him a pointless redundancy. Then I began to wonder. He's a tool of Psych Bureau, not Climber Command. The Mission Recorder works for Command. The distinction is critical. Psych looks out for the men. The differences between Bureau and Command often become a wide, fiery chasm.

Psych is the only power in the universe able to overrule the Admiral, it seems.

Command's task is to turn the war around. Psych is supposed to put the right people in the right places so the job gets done efficiently. More importantly, Psych is supposed to minimize the damage done people's minds.

The point of the hunt here is to spot the eido so you know when to hold your tongue. You don't tell anyone else when you find him. You just stand back and grin when somebody says something that might haunt him later.

Now I understand the crew's coolness. It'll be a pain getting them to open up. I'm a prime suspect.

I've been running with the pack in hopes I can show them that I'm not the head spy. My work would be hard enough without the eido crap. Navy men are paranoid about having their secret thoughts fall into Psych Bureau's hands. Out here they're equally paranoid about their illustrious supreme commander.

A while ago I asked the First Watch Officer if he knew some way I could make the men more comfortable. He grinned that savage, sneering grin of his and said, "You sure the eido knows what he is?"

Hell of a man, friend Yanevich. Always knows the right thing to say to send you howling off into the swamps of your mind, hunting the million-word answer to his dozen-word question.

Fuel Point is a big patch of nothing in untenanted space within a tetrahedron of stars, the nearest of which is four light-years away. A look through my video screen shows me nothing familiar, though I know we aren't more than ten lights out of Canaan. Captured, I could reveal nothing.

"Has anyone ever been captured? In space?"

"I never heard about anybody," Fisherman replies. "Go ask the Patriot. He keeps up on that stuff."

Carmon says, "I don't know, Lieutenant. Not that I've heard of, anyway. Have we ever captured any of them?"

Well, yes, we have. But I can't tell him so. I'm not supposed to know myself.

A continuous shudder runs through the ship, transmitted from the mother. She has a lot of velocity to shed before we match courses for fueling. Throdahl has an open carrier feed into the Operations address speaker. Occasionally we hear chatter from someone aboard the mother, trying to contact the vessels we're to meet.

Junghaus looks concerned. "Maybe they didn't get away."

Last word we had, the tanker was dodging after an accidental brush with an enemy singleship. "Maybe they called the heavies in time." He seems genuinely stricken.

"Then we'll just have to go back."

"No we won't. We'll stay here till they send another tanker."

Aha! comes the light.

"Got you on the upside, *Achernar*," a remote voice says. "Tone it and decline. *Metis*, over."

Fisherman visibly relaxes. "That's the tug. Guess we were sending off the band. There's so much security stuff sometimes, there's mixups in stuff like wavelengths."

Or that might be the competition talking, trying to lull us with that idea.

That suspicion apparently occurred to no one else. Everybody is cheerful now. In a moment, Throdahl has, "*Achernar, Achernar,* this is *Subic Bay. Starsong.* Go Mickey. Lincoln tau theta Beijing Bohrs. Over."

"Why not *shibboleth?*" I murmur.

"*Subic, Subic,* this is *Achernar.* Blue light. Go gamma gamma high wind. London Heisenberg. Over."

"The sweet nothing of young love," Yanevich says over my shoulder. "We found the right people."

"Why a Titan tug? What's to move around out here?"

"Ice. They built a hunk as big as the Admiral's head, years ago. *Metis* will slice off a few chunks and feed them to the mother. She'll melt and distill it and top our tanks."

"What about heavy water? Thought it had to be all light hydrogen."

"Molecular sorters. The mother will take the heavy stuff home to make warheads."

"*Subic* is the tanker?"

"Uhm. A few hours and you can help pray us through fueling."

Antimatter is why we're fueling out here. There'll be one hell of a bang if anything goes wrong. And the CT does come from somewhere else. Somewhere very secret. Nor would it make much sense to run it in through the fleet blockading Canaan.

"You think Climber duty sounds hairy?" Yanevich says. "Dead is the only way they'll get me on a CT tanker. Those are some crazy people."

I think about it. He's right. Sitting on a couple hundred thousand tonnes of antimatter gas, knowing a microsecond's failure in the containment system will kill you...

"I guess somebody has to do it," he says.

The tanker must have done some heavy dodging. Our relative velocities are all wrong. It'll take several hours to lay the ships in a common groove. I suppose I should scribble some notes while I'm waiting.

The Old Man, First Watch Officer, and several others are with me in the wardroom. This is our third supper. The Commander tries to conduct that one meal as if we were aboard a civilized ship. It's difficult. The fold-down table is painfully cramped. I keep banging elbows with Lieutenant Piniaz.

The Old Man asks, "How are you sleeping?"

"This's no pleasure spa on The Big Rock Candy Mountain. But I'm coping. Barely. Damn!" Piniaz has his elbow in action

The Weapons Officer is a remarkably tiny and skinny man, Old Earther, as dark and shiny as a polished ebony idol. He calls a city named Luanda home. I've never heard of it.

This little spider of a man scaled the enlisted ranks in corvettes. He volunteered for Climbers when they offered him a Limited Duty Officer's commission. At twenty-nine he is the oldest man aboard. Unfortunately, he isn't the paternal sort.

Both Ensign Bradley and his leading cook, a piratical rating named Kriegshauser, hover over the conclave, listening. Here's where the secrets will fall, they reckon. They'll rake them in like autumn leaves. If the cook hears anything, it'll be all over the ship in an hour.

· "Maybe not a spa." The Commander grins. His grin today is a ghost of that of days ago.

He's playing to his audience. He does a lot of that. Like he's firmly convinced that the Commander is a rigidly defined dramatic role, subject to very limited interpretation by its players. He suspects that he's been miscast, perhaps. His specific audience seems to be Kriegshauser. "But I think a few people are pushing. This old hulk hasn't seen so much sock-washing and ball-scrubbing since we ran into Meryem Assad's Climber on patrol."

Kriegshauser adopts the blandest, most innocent of faces. He pours us each a touch of the Commander's coffee. I begin to understand.

"Could be you're a good influence, though. They could be worried about their image. But I doubt it. Kriegshauser hasn't changed his underwear since he's been in the Climbers, let alone washed it." The Old Man doesn't check the cook's reaction.

"He'd better do something about the chow if he's worried about his image," I say. "I'd be doing it a favor calling it reconstituted shit."

"That you would. That you would. And you wouldn't hurt any feelings, either."

The stuff *is* terrible. Tubes of goo and boxes of powder yield the base ingredients. Kriegshauser and whomever gets stuck as helper of the day mix the stuff with water and a little oil of vitriol. Climber people are unanimous. They insist it looks and smells like crap, but probably lacks the flavor.

It's chock full of vitamins, minerals, and amino acids, though. Everything the human body needs to run well. Only the soul has been left out.

Too much mass, of course. There's no constituter, as on the big ships. Now I understand all those duffel bags filled with fruits and vegetables.

I've been worrying about roughage. After the accident I went through a prolonged diet-freak period. I still worry sometimes. Roughage is important.

In the old Climbers there were fresh stores. The reefers and freezers went when they increased the missile complement to its present level.

The Commander bites into an apple. His eyes smile over top it.

The only thing to like here is the reconstituted fruit juice. Plenty of concentrates. Plenty of water. The crew likes to mix them. Bug juice, they call the result. Sometimes it looks it.

Water is in long supply. It serves as fuel, atmosphere reserve, emergency heat sink, and primary dietary ingredient. It keeps the belly full, the house warm or cool, the air breathable, and the fusion chamber purring.

"Permission to jettison waste," Bradley asks in a transparent effort to attract the Commander's attention. If the Ensign has a weakness, it's this wanting to be noticed by superiors. I look round to see who'll explain what he's talking about. He does the honors himself.

"After the water is salvaged, our wastes, including the carbon from the air, get compressed and jettisoned. No room for fancy recycling gear."

"Hang on to it," the Old Man says. He turns to me. "Can't you picture it? The mother plowing along in norm surrounded by a cloud of shit canisters." He smiles, munches his apple. Just when I give up on hearing the rest, he says, "A million years from now an alien civilization will find one. It'll be the biggest puzzle in their xenoarcheological museum. I can see them putting in fifty thousand creature hours trying to figure out its religious significance."

"Religious significance? Is that a private joke?"

The Old Man waves his apple core at the First Watch Officer. Yanevich says, "He's laughing at me. I help poke around the pre-human sites on leave."

The Commander says, "They're old, and nonhuman, and Mr. Yanevich's friends have an explanation for everything there. Unless you ask the wrong question. If they tell you something had ritual or magical significance, they're really saying they don't know what it is. That's the way those guys work."

My surprise must be obvious. Yanevich wears one of his delighted smiles when he looks at me. People are infinite puzzles. You put together piece after piece after piece, and you still have hunks that just don't fit.

The battle alarm shrieks.

It makes a *bong-bong-bong* sound not especially irritating in itself. But you respond as if someone has dragged their nails across a blackboard, then fired a starter's pistol beside your ear.

The wardroom explodes. I'm a little out of practice, a little slow. I try to make up the difference with enthusiasm as I pursue the more able men upward. I happen to glance down as I reach the hatch to Weapons.

The Commander is staring at a watch and grinning.

"A drill. A goddamned drill right in the middle of supper. You sadistic bastard."

The gimp leg betrays me. The Ops-Weapons hatch slams before I get to it. So there I hang, a great embarrassed fruit dangling from the compartment ceiling.

"Come down here," Piniaz says in a too-gentle tone. "You can't reach your station in time, I'll put your dead ass to work. Take that goddamned magnetic cannon board. Haesler. Energy board."

Crafty little Ito. He covers his most useless weapon with a spare body, then shifts Leading Spacer Johannes Haesler to the system he's supposed to be learning anyway.

The all clear comes in five minutes. Piniaz turns the compartment over to his Chief Gunner, Holtsnider. I follow him to the wardroom.

"Your buddy ain't too nimble," he growls at the Old Man. His attitude toward the Commander is one millimeter short of insolent. The Commander tolerates it. I don't know why. Anyone else would find himself hamstrung.

"He'll loosen up." He smiles his thin, shipboard smile.

I grab a squeezie of orange juice and start nursing. Kriegshauser puts the drinks up in "baby bottles" because parasite gravity is too treacherous for normal cups. It varies according to some formula known only to the Engineering gang aboard the mother. Once Diekereide and I were playing chess when the pieces just up and roamed away.

"Damned drills," I say, feeling no real rancor. "I forgot about that crap. Never did get used to them. Your mind says they're necessary. Your gut keeps saying bullshit."

"A bitching spacer is a happy spacer," the Commander observes.

"You'll find me a very happy-type fellow, then." I try to laugh. It doesn't come off. Piniaz's snake-eyed stare makes me nervous.

The next drill comes while I'm asleep.

They put off fueling again, so I decided to grab some hammock time. No go. Wearing nothing but shorts, I give it my best go. And barely make it to Weapons. Shaking his head like a disappointed track coach, Piniaz points to the cannon board. He doesn't say a word. Neither do I. I'm the only man aboard sleeping outside the compartment containing my duty station. Isn't that excuse enough? No. You don't make excuses in Navy. Not if you don't want a crybaby reputation. "Hello, board. Looks like we're going to be friends."

The show of good humor is just that. A show. I rumble. I fume. I try hard to remember that I vowed that if I blew up, it wouldn't be over something beyond my control, or because of conditions I accepted beforehand. I'll gut it out. If my leg makes it harder for me, I'll just try harder. My companions are gutting something out, too.

The other breed of sleep disturbance has ceased. I guess Kriegshauser passed the word.

This crew has a strong respect for the Commander. That's how it's supposed to be, and here it works well. It encompasses the new men as well as those who have served with him before. I suspect it has to do with survival. The Old Man brings his Climber home. That, more than anything else in this universe, impresses the men.

I've begun to note quirks. Fisherman, who is hyped on Christianity, brought tracts in his fifteen kilos. Chief Nicastro gets furious if anyone passes him to the left. Better you ask him to drop what he's doing and let you by. Kriegshauser never removes his lucky underwear.

The Commander himself has a rigid ritual for rising and departing his quarters. Faithfully observed, I suppose, it guarantees the Climber another day of existence.

He wakens at exactly 0500 ship's time, which is TerVeen standard, which in turn is Turbeyville and moon time. Kriegshauser's helper has a squeezie of juice and another of coffee waiting. He passes them through the curtains. At 0515 the Commander emerges. He says, "Good morning, gentlemen. Another glorious day." It's customary for the watch to respond, "Amen." The Commander then descends to Ship's Services and the Admiral's stateroom, which is never occupied. He washes up. He accepts another squeezie of coffee from the cook, along with whatever is on the breakfast menu. He then makes his way back to Ops and his quarters, where he secures his copy of Gibbon, ousts the Watch Officer from his seat, and reads till precisely 0615, when the morning reports come in, fifteen minutes before they're technically due. Following morning reports, he goes over the previous day's decklog, then the quartermaster's notebook. At 0630 he lifts his eyes and surveys his kingdom. He nods once, abruptly, as if to say we villeins have pleased him.

Remarkably, the men give a collective sigh. It begins with those who can see the Old Man and spreads around the Can and into the inner circle. Our day is officially begun.

We keep our rendezvous with the CT tanker our fourth day out of TerVeen.

We begin by undertaking the long, arduous process of rigging for operational mode. A lot of the hardware, including my little nest, has to be realigned for the new gravity.

As senior vessel, by right of having survived sixteen patrols, our ship will fuel first. To do so we'll stand off the mother a thousand kilometers. If there's a screwup, only we, the tanker, and anyone else nursing will blow. Several ships will fuel at the same time.

The reorientation for operational mode is complete. I have fed myself and cleared my bowels. We'll go to action stations before fueling, so I saunter on up to Ops and cunningly occupy my seat before the exterior screen. That's a difficult task now, what with the gravity still aligned parasite. Crafty operator that I am, I'm going to be on time.

The Old Man ambles by. "You won't see much from here. Go on down to Engineering."

I like the idea. I love to observe from the heart of the action. But that means wasting the on-time coup. "I'd just get in their way."

"Mr. Varese says there's room."

"Really?" I can't picture Varese making room for me, or inviting me down. We haven't warmed toward one another. This thing sounds arranged.

"Go on down." His tone is a little more forceful.

Varese is waiting at the Engineering hatchway. He wears a smile that's painted on. "Good morning, sir. Glad to have you. We'll give you the best show we can. I do want to ask you to help by staying in the background." He talks like that most of the time, like he's dying to keep his temper, and still I get the feeling he *did* invite me, that I'm not here entirely at the Commander's insistence. Varese doesn't want me underfoot, yet wants me to watch his crowd in action. A quaint character. A proud papa. "This's a good place here, sir. The view will be somewhat limited, but it's the best we can provide."

His strained affability and politeness is more disconcerting than his usual hostility.

The seat is a good eight meters around the curve from the center of action. Still, I could be trying to follow the fueling from Ops.

"Take notes if you like, but save your questions till we finish. Don't move around. There'll be some hairy moments. We can't be distracted."

"Of course." I'm no moron, Varese. I know this will be delicate.

The anti-hydrogen has to be transferred without losing an atom. The tiniest whiff might pit or scar the Climber's CT globe. Even if the tank weren't breached, the risk of its being weakened is so feared we would have to return to TerVeen for repairs. Command has geniuses creating new miseries to inflict on crews who make that sort of mistake.

Varese will command the Climber during fueling maneuvers. He's closer to the action, knows best what needs doing.

We commence our approach before the general alarm. Varese opens communications with Ops.

"Range one thousand meters," Ops reports. That sounds like Leading Spacer Picraux speaking. "Range rate one meter per second. Activating spotter lights. Secondary conn stand by to assume control."

Varese responds, "Secondary conn, aye." He surveys the idiot lights on a long board, points to one of his men. Engineering's one viewscreen lights up. Outside, directed by Fire Control, searchlights are probing the tanker. She's too close for a good overall view. She's a huge vessel. Her flanks show luminescence in coded patches.

Our computers guide the approach with a precision no human can match They have us in a groove that's exact to a millimeter. And every man here is sweating, holding a hand poised should Varese order manual control. No spacer ever completely trusts a computer.

"Range, five hundred meters." That's the First Watch Officer. "Range rate one meter per second. Secondary conn assume control."

"Secondary conn, aye. This is Mr. Varese. I have the conn." He lifts a spring-hinged safety bar, trips three safety switches. Diekereide repeats the process on his own board. Varese inserts a key into a lock on a dramatically oversized red switch handle.

All that redundancy says even the ship's designers respected the hazards of CT fueling.

The computers, communing with their tanker kin, ease the Climber into position beneath a vast, pendent flying saucer of a tank.

"Second Engineer. Commence internal magnetic test sequence."

"Aye, sir." Diekereide bends over his board like an old, old man trying to make out fine print. "Shahpazian. Activate first test mode." He begins a litany which includes primary, secondary, and emergency tubes; elbows; valves; junctions; skins; generators; control circuits; and display functions. Most involve shaped magnetic fields like those containing the plasma in a fusion chamber. I note that this system is also triply redundant.

"Activate second test mode." The litany begins anew. This time Diekereide counterchecks the test circuitry itself.

Meanwhile, Lieutenant Varese satisfies himself that his Climber had adopted the most advantageous attitude in relation to the tanker. "Stand by the locking bars," he orders, speaking to someone aboard the other vessel. "Extend number one."

I lean forward as much as I dare, trying to see the viewscreen better.

A bright orange bar slides out of the tanker's hull like a stallion's prang, gently touches the Climber's globe. Varese studies his side displays, gives a series of orders which move us less than a centimeter. The locking bar suddenly extends a bit more, penetrating its locking receptacle. "Number one locked. Extend number two."

There're three bars. They'll hold the Climber immobile with respect to the tanker.

"Maser probe. Minimum intensity," Varese says. In seconds his boards show a half-dozen green lights. "Maser probe. Intermediate intensity." More green. The pathway for an invisible pipeline is being created.

Varese double-checks his board. There'll be no redundancy in the ship-to-ship. "Bring your probe up to maximum. Mr. Diekereide, how do you look?"

"All go here, sir. Ready to flood." He returns to his ongoing checklists.

"Stand by."

"Aye, sir. Shahpazian. Arm the hazard circuits."

"*Achernar, Subic Bay*, we have a go on one. I say again, we have a go on one," Varese says. "*Subic*, standing by for your mark."

"*Subic,* aye," a tinny voice replies. "Clear from *Achernar.* Thirty seconds. Counting."

The flashing lights have me hypnotized. I stop taking notes. There's little enough to record. Too much takes place out of sight.

"Thirteen seconds and holding."

"What?" The hypnosis ends. Holding? Why? I stifle a surge of panic. Print data rush across the viewscreen. It says another Climber is maneuvering nearby, approaching another tank. *Achernar* wants her a little farther along before letting the tanker nurse us.

"Thirteen seconds and counting." Then, "... one. Zero."

"I have pressure on the outer main coupling," Diekereide says.

"Very well," Varese replies. "She looks good. Open her up. Commence fueling."

"Opening outer main valve. I have pressure on number two main valve. Opening number two main valve. I have pressure at primary tank receiving valve."

"We're looking good." Varese moves across the compartment, toward me. "This's a tricky spot. His first time doing it himself. Got a good go, so I'll leave him to it." He grasps a cross-member and stands beside me, watching his apprentice.

"He has to bleed it in a few moles at a time to begin. To annihilate any terrene matter inside the tank. No such thing as a perfect vacuum. It'll be hotter than hell in there for a few minutes."

"You travel with the tank open?" That hadn't occurred to me.

He nods. "Space is the best evacuator. Another reason we fuel so far from anywhere. Not much interstellar hydrogen around here. Comparatively speaking."

I try guessing how much energy might be blasting around the tank's interior. Hopeless. I don't have the vaguest notion of the hydrogen density in this region.

Diekereide opens the final valve. We all tense, waiting for something to go boom.

The tanker constricts her internal tank field. Diekereide bombards the compartment with a barrage of pressure reports. And then it's over. Almost anticlimactically, it seems. I was so tense, waiting for something to screw up, that I feel let down that it hasn't.

Disengagement reverses the fueling process. The only tricky part involves venting the CT gas still in the ship-to-ship coupling.

The cycle, from Varese's assumption of the conn till he yields it again, takes a little over two hours. When we finish, he and Diekereide shake hands. Varese says, "*Very* good show, men. The best I've ever seen." He must mean it, so seldom does he have anything positive to say.

"We were lucky," Diekereide tells me. "Usually takes three or four tries to get a go. The Old Man will be pleased."

The Engineers commence operational routine. I don't pay much attention. Diekereide has launched one of his long-winded and rambling explanations. "When it comes time to Climb," he says, after telling me things I already know about the tank atop the vane and the magnetics which prevent the CT from coming in contact with the ship, "we bleed the CT into the fusor, along with the normal hydrogen flow. Instead of fusing, we annihilate, then shunt the energy into the torus instead of the linear drives."

I don't pay much attention. The way to listen to Diekereide is through a mental filter. Let most of the chatter slide, yet catch the gems.

"There isn't any way to beat the fogging. It's because the ship is separated from the universe. If you can't stand it, stay out of null."

He's describing the subjective effects of Climb. When a vessel goes up, its crew experiences a growing insubstantiality in surroundings. From outside, the vessel becomes detectable only as an apparent minuscule black hole. There's a continuing debate over whether this is a real black hole or just something that looks and acts like one. It has moments when it violates the tenets of both Einsteinian and Reinhardter physics.

In essence, a ship in Climb can't be seen from outside, which is valuable in battle. Unfortunately, said ship can't see, either. Astrogation in Climb is tricky work. Which explains Westhause's ardent affair with his Dead Reckoning tracer.

In null you have no referents, but you can maneuver. Even if you do nothing, you retain your norm inherent velocity and whatever weigh you put on in hyper. It vectors. You have to keep close track unless you don't mind coming down inside a star.

"That's really no problem, though," Diekereide says. "Unless you're operating in a crowded system, you won't come down in the middle of anything. The statistical odds are incredible. Build yourself a dome on a one-kilometer radius. Paint the inside black. Have a buddy take a blackened pfennig and stick it on the dome somewhere while the lights are out. Then put on a blindfold, pick up a target rifle, and try to hit the coin. Your odds are better than ours of hitting a star by accident. The real danger is heat."

Every machine, even the human machine, generates waste heat. In norm and hyper ships shed excess heat automatically, by leakage through their skins, and, especially in Climbers, through cooling vanes. Our biggest such vane supports the CT tank. There are others on both the can and torus. The vessel has lots of lumps and bumps warting its basic can and donut profile.

In null we can't vent a calorie. There's no place for the heat to go.

Heat is the bane of the Climbers, and not just because of the comfort factor. Virtually all computation and control systems rely on liquid helium superconductors. The helium has to remain at temperatures approaching absolute zero.

One way to cripple a Climber is to keep on her so tight she has to stay up. If she stays long enough, she'll cook herself. Forcing that is the principal function of the other firm's hunter-killer squadrons.

We aren't as unpredictable and evasive as the holonetnews would have people believe.

That little black hole, that little shadow we cast on hyper and norm, can kill us. "A pseudo-Hawking Hole," Diekereide says. "Named after the man who posited substellar black holes."

A Climber's shadow is minuscule but still distorts space. If someone comes close enough, with equipment sensitive enough, he can locate it.

"There're three ways to hammer on a Climber in null," Diekereide says. He holds up three fingers, then folds one down. "First, and most effective in theory, and the most expensive, would be to send a drone Climber up to collide with your target and blow its CT. That's no problem right now. The other firm doesn't have Climbers. Let's hope the war ends before they figure them out."

"Oh, yes." My tone is sufficiently sarcastic to raise an eyebrow.

"The other ways sound more difficult, and probably are, but they're what the other team has to work with. Their favorite is to concentrate high-wattage shortwave energy on our pseudo-Hawking. Doesn't physically hurt us, naturally. But every photon that impacts on our shadow adds to our heat problem and shortens the time we have to shake them. They use fusion bombs the same way, but that's a waste of destructive capacity. Your pseudo-Hawking's cross section won't intersect a trillionth of the energy. But they'll do it if they want you bad enough.

"One thing they did, till we got wise, was to maneuver our shadow into their fusors. That puts a lot of heat in fast. But if you know what they're doing, you can maneuver and destabilize their magnetic bottle. They've given that up."

The other method of attack is plain physical battery.

A pseudo-Hawking point is so tiny it can slip between molecules. It doesn't leave the other firm much room to obtain leverage. But they've found their ways, usually using graviton beams from multiple angles. A Climber suffers every shock as the coherent graviton beams slam her Hawking point a centimeter this way or that.

"I went through one of those my first patrol," Diekereide says. "It was like being inside a steel drum while somebody pounded on it with a club. It's more frightening than damaging. They have so little cross section to work with. If it gets too bad, you go a little higher and cut your cross section. It's a game of cat-and-mouse. Every time out they try some new tactic or weapon. They say we have a few of our own in the cooker. A missile we can launch from null. A device we can run down from null to vent heat while we stay up."

"And a magnetic cannon?"

He snorts derisively. "I've got to admit, that's the only new gismo we've actually seen. What use the thing is, is beyond me."

"Ambrose, I'm getting a feeling about it. Nobody sees any use for it. Command isn't so thick they'd stick something on just because the Admiral's nephew thought it up." That theory has gone the rounds. Strange tales crop up to explain anything Command doesn't see fit to illuminate. "Maybe it's some special, one-shot thing. Special mission."

"Think so? The Old Man say something?"

"No. And he wouldn't if he knew anything, which he doesn't. Orders haven't come through yet."

"Anybody tell you how Tarkenton took out one of their Main Battles during the siege at Carmody? That was in the *Eight Ball.* Her third mission."

Climber Fleet Tannian has developed a plethora of legends about famous patrols and Commanders. Tarkenton's story is one of the big ones. His kill came during the war's darkest hour. It threw the enemy fleet into total confusion. The ship he skragged was control for the entire Carmody operation.

Those were the glory days, the easy days. Tarkenton is still alive. He commands Climber Fleet Two, far in toward the Inner Worlds. I saw him once, shortly after his appointment. He's a lean, hollow-eyed man who travels with a guard of ghosts.

There're a thousand stories, and I'm sure I'll hear them all. Diekereide dearly loves to talk.

One he tells is about the Executioner. The Executioner is the other team's best. He commands a pack of hunter-killer specialists. They operate more like bounty hunters than an escort squadron.

"We don't have to worry about him. They sent him to take on Tarkenton's Fleet six months ago."

You have to admire a man who makes a name for himself in destroyers. Destroyer people do the most thankless, unnoticed work there is.

I return to Ops after action stations secures. I want to see what the Old Man does with his fueling luck. Diekereide made a good guess. He wants to shake down his new hands and get the feel of the refitted ship.

"Not bad when you can walk around, is it?" Yanevich asks as I amble in.

"No. But the mode can be confusing. We'll go parasite again just when I get the hang of it."

He winks. "So it goes. So it goes. Have a seat." He offers the viewscreen chair.

I don't refuse. My leg is aching and I want a better look at *Subic Bay*. I didn't see much of her from below. I switch to augmented infrared and skip from camera to camera.

The image, when I find it, has a spectral look, which isn't unusual with infrared.

"That a new-type tanker? Or is the augmentation screwed up?"

The only tanker I ever saw consisted of a long rectangular girderwork with a perpendicular squashed-egg CT tank on either end. A flying dumbbell. Drives were at the ends of crossbars athwartships amidship, turning the dumbbell into a giant jack. Crew's quarters were inside the arms.

Subic Bay's main structure is similar, but she's twice that other vessel's length. She has lesser dumbbells crosswise at either end, giving her four tanks instead of two. The thwartships crossbars are longer. They mount heavier drives and probably provide roomier quarters.

Two Climbers are nursing. A third is maneuvering into position. I suppose the naked tank is the one we used.

"First one of these I've seen myself," Yanevich says. "The new *Kiel* class. They're trying to speed things up. Put more Climbers into action and get more missions per ship. Which means they have to get more

CT to Fuel Point faster."

"How about safety? Seems like doubling the handling capacity would cube the chance of disaster."

"Never lost a tanker yet." He grins at my sour expression. "Those people are *careful*. They *know* they're sitting on a live volcano. You think our OC was bad? You should see those people. They stay out a year at a time. When they cut loose, they cut loose." He glanced at the screen wistfully. "But they do have mixed crews."

The absence of comrades of a more delicate persuasion is having its effect. Conversations have grown less impersonal and professional. Throdahl is entertaining the watch with an intimate account of his relationship with the black radiowoman. His friend Rose is playing straight man. It's obvious they're old story-swappers.

Throughout, Fisherman stares at his displays and pretends deafness. His particular faith has a strong fundamentalist bent.

From the shadowed jungle gym of the inner circle, Laramie calls, "Wouldn't it be a candy game if we ran into a she-ship out? Link locks, and holiday routine for the crews." He giggles. When he laughs, Laramie sounds like a nine-year-old girl being tickled.

"Yeah," someone muses. "Wouldn't it be straight dusty, making it in null grav?"

Rose has a story about it. His is as unlikely as all such tales. Nobody believes a word, of course. Convincing the listener isn't their object. The someone again mentions how he'd like to try it in free-fall.

Someone else says, "You want to try it, go down and see Hardwick."

The old hands snigger.

Nicastro pauses between me and Fisherman. "So soon you forget, Spook. Your playmate isn't with us this go." I'm surprised. The Chief doesn't usually join the game. He pats Fisherman's shoulder. "Good board, Junghaus."

Good board? Either he has something in detection or he doesn't. Good and bad have nothing to do with tachyon gear, only the operator's skill at interpreting what he sees. When he has no contacts, he can do nothing but watch green lights and a blank screen. Only when yellow shows does he have to pay attention.

Then it dawns. Fisherman is short on confidence. He needs reassurance. His faith is one attempt to bolster it.

"How did Laramie get the name Spook?"

The Chief says, "Earned it in boot camp, I hear. Because he has a talent for becoming invisible when there's work to do. Buckets got his name because he has the chamberpot detail when we Climb. A reward the Old Man gives people who get on his nerves. The men below can explain their names better than I can."

Nicknames intrigue me. How is it some people attract them, some repel them? There were people in our battalion who always had one. Subject to momentary change. Some I never did know by a given name. On the other hand, I've never had one myself. I worried about it when I was younger. Didn't they like me?

I suppose I lack color.

Yet Rose and Throdahl are colorful enough. Throdahl's "Thro" is the only thing I've heard used on either of them. It's curious.

Rose is telling a new tale. This one from his recent leave. "We're cruising this road south of T-ville, see, and here's this bitch, maybe sixteen, just shaking along. Kicking up dust. Javitts spots her and says, 'I'm going to pick this up.' She ain't even hiking. Like maybe she's headed for the next cabbage patch. Javitts wheels over, asks her does she want a ride. She fish-eyes us maybe half a minute, says okay. You never seen a mover like Javitts. Ten minutes, man, I shit you not, he talks her into stopping by the barracks while we shift to Class A's. Soon as he gets there, he calls this other bitch to say we're going to maybe be a little late. All the time we're driving, he's talking shit. Now it's my turn while he's on the horn. I'm thinking, what do you do to follow his act? I don't have to worry. She starts talking first. Man, you wouldn't believe it."

"Not from you," Throdahl says. "You got shit coming out your ears. But you're going to tell it anyway, so get it over with. We can't stand the suspense."

"One of these days, Thro. Pow! You know that? Wham! I got my right hand registered. Know what's wrong with you? You got no couth, Thro. Damn right I'm going to tell it. Get some class."

"What about the slut?'

"You got less couth than Thro, Barbarian. What she does is, she turns to me and says, 'You know, I started fucking when I was eleven.' I shit you not. Just like that. Straight off the bulkhead, and wearing the shit-eatingest smile you ever seen. Dusted me. Only thing I could think to say was, 'You should be pretty good, then.' And she said she is, and started telling me about all the guys she screwed and how they all told her she was the best they ever had."

"Get into her?"

"Fucking well right. Let me tell it…."

"Hey," one of the inner circle calls down. "You pick her up on Heyrdahl Road? She have a big Caesarean scar?" That's Laramie again.

"Yeah. So?" Rose sounds a little defensive.

"He ain't lying, guys. That's the slut that gave me the clap last time we were in."

General laughter. Catcalls.

"You get that certain feeling when you piss?" Throdahl asks and hoots at his own comedic triumph.

"Knowing him," Laramie shouts, "he better start worrying about spitting."

The First Watch Officer leans past me and punches the general alarm button.

The Commander descends from his eyrie in seconds, surveys the silent compartment. He smiles when he sees me at my station.

He thumbs a switch on the shipwide comm. "This's the Ship's Commander. I have the conn. Stand by for maneuvering exercises. Department heads, report."

Each reports his men on station and ready.

"Engineer, what's your influential status?"

"Go, Commander."

"Astrogator, are you clear?"

"Clear, Commander."

I glance at Westhause's back. He seems as embarrassed as Fisherman. Curious. He was no prude at the Pregnant Dragon.

"Engineering, take hyper at my mark. Stand by. Execute."

For an instant the ship's interior seems to spin and twist away into a geometric surreality.

"Departments heads, report."

Again all bailiwicks report a go.

"Mr. Westhause, program me a ten-minute Inoko Loop."

The maneuver is a four-dimensional figure eight. Jokester astrogators call it a Moebius trip. This one will return the ship to her starting point in the stated time.

Aboard normal warships the Bridge Engineer would relay the astrogator's program to his own department. Here the astrogator and Chief Quartermaster handle the data relay.

"Ready, Commander."

"Execute."

There's no sensation of motion. Momentum has no detectable effect inside an influential field. There's no evidence of movement inside the display tank, either. Westhause has chosen a small, slow, lazy, tight loop involving very little relative motion.

The man is deft, quick, and certain. He's a first-rate astrogator. It's nice to know I'm flying with an expert.

The Climber completes the loop. The Commander polls department heads again, drops hyper, conducts yet another poll. Everything is go-go-go.

He has Westhause program an hour's loop with secondary loops built in. Again the results are satisfactory.

There's but one test left. A Climb.

A terrible cold hand seizes me as the Commander begins the count-down. We're in hyper again. For a few minutes I'm wholly convinced that we're going to die. Then there's a conviction that nothing can happen to this Climber. I'm aboard. Nothing can happen to me. Then the premonition of doom returns. Back and forth, a ball pounded by emotional racquets.

Worrying, I miss the antimatter ignition sequence. My first hint of how far matters have progressed is the Commander's "Take her up."

There's no mistaking the groan of the Climb alarm. Tannian's PR people have saturated the media with it.

"Annihilation stabilized," Engineering reports.

"Take her to ten Bev," the Commander orders.

"Ten Bev, aye, sir."

My companions suddenly acquire an ectoplasmic insubstantiality. They seem to glow from within. And the scene has become black and white. It's like looking into a big holo cube with its color module out. Gone are the flashing green, amber, and red lights. Gone are the colors of the nonuniform clothing the men all wear. Gone are the color-codings of piping, wiring, and conduit.

It's a spooky scene, these surroundings. Almost an argument for Fisherman's beliefs.

The glow in the men has nothing to do with life-force or souls. The hardware glows too. Even the atmosphere sparkles. During one of his lectures Diekereide told me we'd be sensing the energies binding subatomic particles when we saw the glow.

I can also discern the big darkness beyond the ship's hull. That's the spookiest part. A big black nothing without stars, trying to push its way in. A black dragon keeping mouth and eyes closed till it's close enough to gobble these fools who dare enter its lair.

I admit that I was warned. I didn't believe. The warning was useless. I'm scared shitless.

"Systems check," the Commander says. "Department heads report."

All departments are go. TerVeen treated the ship well.

"Take her up to twenty Bev."

I mutter, "Holy shit." I'm drowning in my own sweat, and with no better excuse than fear. Internal temperature hasn't risen a tenth of a degree. My animal brain snarls. The heat converters are secured. The accumulators for the energy weapons haven't been discharged. Fuel Point might be attacked. We could be caught with our endurance limited….

The Commander won't discharge a weapon here, fool. That would be a dead giveaway. A subtle treason. The signature of an energy weapon lasts forever, though it flees the scene at the velocity of light. It can be backtracked to its point of origin.

I'm not the only one sweating before the drill ends. Fisherman, too, is soaked and twitching. Will he settle down? Will the pressure of combat be too much for him?

"Astrogator. Let's see your ten-minute Inoko again."

I stare at a lifeless screen and wonder how Bradley's troops put up with Climb. Their only clues to current events are the alarms. They're shut off from both the universe outside and the rest of the ship. Theirs is a tiny world isolated within our slightly larger universe.

"Loop completed, Commander."

"Very well. Take her down to twenty-five Bev."

"Twenty-five Bev, aye, sir."

Twenty-five? I must have missed us going up. How high were we?

"Ship's Services, commence dehumidification."

The rarefied atmosphere is near saturation. The simple thermometer near the compartment clock says real temperature increase has been but 3.7 degrees. I remind myself that in battle, crews routinely endure temperatures approaching eighty degrees.

The Commander eases us back into hyper, shifts to fusion power, then drops to norm. "Vent heat," he orders.

A midnight woods-whisper trickles through the ship. Ship's Services is circulating atmosphere through the radiator vanes. In minutes the air feels chilly.

"Mr. Westhause, return to the tender. Mr. Yanevich, rig for parasite mode. Department heads. Meeting in the wardroom as soon as the ship is secure."

I invite myself to the conference. As far as the Commander is concerned, I have access to everything but his classified material. None of the others asks me to leave, though Piniaz obviously resents my presence.

Performance in null is the subject. Everyone agrees. The ship is ready. Crew and intangibles remain the question marks.

"I want music piped into the basement," Lieutenant Varese says.

"We went through this last patrol," Yanevich replies.

"We'll keep going through it. I stick by my arguments. It'll help morale."

"And generate heat."

"So secure it in Climb."

"No point discussing it this trip," the Old Man says. "We don't have the tapes."

Varese slaps the table, glares at the First Watch Officer. "Why the hell not?" His voice cracks.

"We had to reduce mass to accommodate eighty-two kilos of writer. The library had to go."

"Everything?"

"All but the study materials. Maybe that'll speed up the cross-rate training."

I shrink from Varese's venomous glare. I'm at the head of his shit list for sure.

"I'll get something from the mother," Yanevich offers. "We've used most of the personal mass."

Varese isn't to be mollified. He wants to fight. "No music?"

"Sorry."

"A magnetic cannon *and* a goddamned useless extra body. Fucking shitheaded Command."

"Mister Varese," the Commander says. The Lieutenant shifts his glare to his taut, pallid hands.

"How about personnel?" I ask, shoving my fingers into the dragon's mouth. "Fisherman... Junghaus looked like he might crack under pressure."

"So did you," Yanevich says.

Psych Bureau screens to the nth degree, but no test is perfect. People get past. They change under stress. There's no follow-up testing of people assigned to Climber duty.

Four men make the observation list. Junghaus isn't one of them. I am.

My ego has big bruises.

I *am* an unknown quantity. I haven't had Climber training. I haven't been through the Psych test battery. I would've made the list had I gone through the exercises like a rock.

Chief Nicastro makes the list because this is his last patrol, because he got married, because he'll want so badly to make it home. The stress on him will be severe.

The others are enlisted first patrollers who showed spooky. Jon Baake and Fehrenbach Cinderella. They're Piniaz's men. He made his own judgments, so it's possible they were considered by harsher standards. Piniaz is a perfectionist.

The nascent hostility between Varese and myself receives no mention. We're like flint and steel, that man and I. He flat doesn't like me. We'll strike sparks no matter what I do to avoid it.

The Old Man detains me when the meeting breaks up. He stares into nothing till I grow nervous, fearing he may be worried enough to leave me aboard the mother when the ship commences her patrol. Finally, "What do you think?"

"It isn't like the holo shows it."

"You've said that before. You've also said there's got to be a better way." He smiles that pale smile.

"It's true."

"Nothing is like it is on holo."

"I know that. I just didn't expect it to be this different."

He slides away somewhere behind his eyes. Has he returned to Canaan? What is it? Marie? Navy as a whole? Something unrelated? He isn't the sort to lay his soul out on a dissecting table. He's a human singularity. You have to figure him out by inference and his effect on the orbits of others.

"I'm going to put you in Weapons for a while. Don't mind Piniaz. He's a good man. Just playing an Old Earther role. Learn the magnetic cannon. You were good at ballistics." He fiddles with his pipe, acting as if he wants to light up. I haven't seen him smoke since we came aboard. In fact, this is the first I've seen that nasty little instrument since then. "And do some of your famous observing."

"What am I looking for? Personal problems? Like Junghaus?"

"Don't worry about Fisherman. He'll be all right. He's found his way to cope. Ito is the man worrying me. Something's eating him. Something more than usual."

"You just said…"

"I know. It's the Commander's prerogative to contradict himself."

"There's always something eating Old Earthers. They're born with chips on their shoulders. What about Varese? I'm scared to turn my back on him."

"Bah! Nothing to worry about. He's a culture nut. A pseudo. Wants to enlighten his philistines. He goes through the same routine every patrol. He'll come out of it after we make contact."

"And you?"

"Eh?"

"I thought maybe something was bothering you."

"Me? No. All systems go. Raring to get into competition."

His face belies his words. I'll watch him closer than Piniaz. He's my friend…. Is that why he wants me out of Ops?

5

ON PATROL

It's a twelve-day passage to the squadron's patrol sector. As the days drift away, the men become quieter and more reserved. They have a crude, seldom reliable formula. A day's travel outward bound translates to three days' travel coming back. We've been aboard the Climber seventeen days.

Fifty-one days to go? That seems unlikely. Few patrols last more than a month. There's so much enemy traffic.... Hell, we could run into a convoy tomorrow, scramble, clear our missile elevators, and be home before the mother.

Eventless travel leaves a lot of free time, despite the depressing frequency of drills. I'm spending a lot of time with Chief Energy Gunner Holtsnider. He of girder-clinging fame. He's refreshing my knowledge of ballistic gunnery.

"This's your basic GFCS Mark Forty-six system," he tells me. I guess this is the fifth time we've been through this. "You got your basic Mark Thirty gun order converter, and your basic gyros, stabile element, tracking, and drive motor units. Straight off a corvette secondary mount. You just got your minor modifications, what they call your One-A conversions, for spherical projectiles."

Yeah? Those are killing me. My poor senile brain keeps harking futilely after my Academy gunnery training.

Half the problem is my sneaking suspicion that the Chief is learning while I am, staying a few pages ahead in the crisp new manual.

"Now, off your radar, and your neutrino and tachyon detectors if you have to, and even your visuals if it comes to that, and your transitting missiles in norm, you get your B, your R, your dR, your Zs, your dE, and your dBs. You feed them all to your Mark Thirty-two. Then you get your Gf...."

I keep getting lost in the symbols. I can't remember which is relative motion in line of sight, angular elevation rate, angular bearing rate, gravity correction, relativity correction, light velocity lag time….

"And send your *RdBs over V* and your *RdE over V* to your Mark Thirty…."

I could strangle the man. He has a too-ample store of that most essential of instructor's virtues: patience. I don't. I never had enough. Many a project and study have I abandoned for lack of patience to follow through.

"… which brings your *B prime gr* and *E prime g* to your cannon train and elevation pump motors." For all his patience, the Chief is ready to give me up.

"Cheer up, Chief. We could be trying to program a twenty-meter air burst in tandem quad with the co-battery in nadir."

"You did time in the bombards?"

"Second Gunnery Officer on *Falconier*. Before this." I tap the bad leg. "Thought everybody knew."

"I was in *Howitzer* before I cross-rated Energy."

We exchanged reminiscences about the difficulties of putting unguided projectiles onto surface targets from orbit. Tandem quads are the worst. Two (or more) vessels each fire four projectiles, over each pole and round each equatorial horizon, so that they all arrive on target simultaneously. Theory says the ground position can't duck it all because it's coming from everywhere at once.

The bombards, or planetary assault artillery ships, are a poor man's way of softening ground defenses. A way which, in my opinion, is a little insane and a whole lot optimistic. Budget people find the system attractive. It's cheap. A sophisticated missile delivering the same payload costs a hundred times as much.

Once a world's orbital defenses are reduced, bombards are supposed to blast away, creating neutralized drop zones for the Fleet Marines. The main weapon is a 50-cm magnetic cannon. It launches concussion projectiles of the "smart" type. The bomb packs a hell of a wallop but has to be on target to do its job.

Bombard tactics were theoretical till the war. I was involved in just one live operation, against a base used by commerce raiders. I did most of my shooting in practice.

The system was worthless. In practice on planetary ranges we found the ballistic ranges so long, and so plagued by variables, that precision bombardment proved impossible. My First Gunnery Officer claimed we couldn't hit a continent using "dumb" projectiles.

The other firm uses bombards, too. For harassment. For accuracy they rely on dropships, or use a missile barrage.

"Ever shoot the range at Kincaid?" Holtsnider asks.

"That's where I screwed up the leg." Kincaid is a Mars-sized hunk of rock in Sol System's cometary halo. Its orbit is perpendicular to the ecliptic. It's so far out Sol is just another star.

"I wondered. Didn't think it would be polite to ask."

"Doesn't bother me anymore," I lie. "Except when I remember that it was my own fault."

Holtsnider says nothing. He just looks expectant.

I have mixed feelings about telling the tale. The man shouldn't give a damn, and probably doesn't want me to bore him with the whole dreary story. On the other hand, there's a pressure within me. I want to cry on somebody's shoulder.

"Remember the Munitions Scandals? With the Mod Twelve Phosphors for the Fifties?"

"Bribes to government quality-control inspectors."

"Yes. Flaking in the ablation shields. Normal routine was to blow a cleaning wad every twentieth shot during prolonged firing. With the Jenkins projectiles we were getting flakes instead of dust. We had orders from topside to use them up practicing. The Old Man had us blowing a wad after every shot."

"Royal pain in the ass, what?"

"In the kneecap, actually." It's easy to recall the frustration, the aggravation, and the sudden agony. They're with me still. "We'd been at it watch and watch for three days. Trick shooting. Everything but over the shoulder with mirrors. We were all tired and pissed. I made the mistake. I blew the tube without making sure my trainee had opened the outer door."

"Recoil."

"In spades. Those outer doors can take a lot more pressure than the inner ones. So the inner door blew back while I was climbing up to reset for live ammo."

Holtsnider nods sympathetically. "Saw a guy lose his fingers that way. Our magnetics went out. We had a live time shell in the tube. He tried to blow it like it was a wad. Worked, too. But the inner door locks snapped. Lost two-thirds of our atmosphere before we got the outer door sealed." He glances at my leg. "Medics had him good as new in a couple months."

"Wasn't my day, Chief. We were alone out there. Nearest medship was in orbit at Luna Command. And the reason we were screwing around out there in the first place was because our number two hyper generator was down.

"The medship hypered in fast, but by the time she arrived my knee was beyond salvation—more through the agency of an overzealous medical corpsman than from the initial injury.

"*Falconier* was so old she wasn't fit for training Reserves anymore, which's what we were doing."

Funny. This sharing of an unpleasant past is loosening me up. I'm more relaxed. My mind works better. I feel the old data coming back. "Chief, let's try it from the top."

I haven't spent all my time in Weapons. I've tried, with limited success, to visit with each crewman. Other than the officers I met on Canaan, only Holtsnider, Junghaus, and Diekereide have cooperated. Varese's Engineers barely remain civil. The men in Ship's Services tolerate me only because they have to live with me. I hear they've convinced themselves that I'm the dreaded eido. My sessions with Holtsnider have eased the situation in Weapons. But only in Ops do I have much chance to ask questions.

The Ops gang considers itself the ship's elite. That pretense demands more empathy with the problems of another "intellectual."

I'm worried. Seventeen days gone, and no headway made. I still don't know half the names. Climber missions don't last long once the ship reaches its patrol zone. It's in, make a couple of attacks, and get out fast. The other firm is sending so much traffic through that quick contact is inevitable.

Westhause says it takes about a week to get home once the missiles are gone. Meaning I can't count on more than another ten days to find my story.

I mention it to the Commander during a lonely lunch in the ward-room. The others are preparing the shift to operational mode. I figure he has similar problems acclimating new men each patrol.

"One thing to remember. No matter how much alike they act, they're all different. When you get to the bottom line, the only thing they have in common is that they stand on their hind legs. You have to find the right approach for each man. You have to be a different person to every one."

"I can see that. From your viewpoint…"

"You and me, we're crippled by our jobs. What have they got to judge you by? The news nosies they've seen on holo. You have to break that image."

I nod. Those people are the pushiest, most obnoxious ever spawned. I understand their Tartar style, but I don't like it and don't want to be lumped with them.

"Guess my best chance is a long patrol."

The Old Man doesn't say anything. His face speaks for him. He's ready to go home now.

A Climber is, I'm convinced, our most primitive warship. Cheap, quickly built, and highly cost-effective if the combat statistics are valid. Balancing the statistics against the reality of Climber life, I develop a conviction that High Command considers our ships as expendable as the missiles they carry.

We're almost ready. The tension began building yesterday. We're tottering at the brink. This fly, deep into the patrol zone, is sandpapering nerve ends. It's about to climax. Action and death may be no more than an hour away.

As senior ship, even though we don't carry the squadron flag, we rate first separation. This is a tradition of Tannian's Fleet. To the proven survivors go the small perks. Will the head start be worth anything in the long run?

Suddenly, we're beyond the moment of peak tension. The sealed orders have come through. The mother is about to drop hyper. We'll be operational soon.

The Old Man's face is stiff and pale when he leaves his stateroom. His upper lip is lifted to the right in a faint sneer. He gathers Westhause, the First Watch Officer, our two Ops Chief Petty Officers, and myself. He whispers, "It doesn't look good. Figure on being out a while. It's beacon to beacon. Observation patrol. We start at Beacon Nineteen, Mr. Westhause. I'll give you the progression data after I've gone over it myself."

Well. I may get time to break the ice after all. Running beacon to beacon means there's been no enemy contact for a while. If they're out there, they're slipping through unnoticed. Because nothing is happening, the squadron will roam carefully programmed patterns till a contact occurs.

I begin to comprehend the significance of our being on our own.

We'll be out of contact completely, unless we touch the rare instelled beacon. No comforting mother ship under our feet. No pretty ladies in a sister ship to taunt and tease when Throdahl isn't using the radio more professionally. Alone! And without the slightest notion how near we are others of our kind.

This could get rough, emotionally. These men aren't the sort I'd choose as cellmates.

Some three hundred observation/support beacons are scattered around Climber Fleet One's operations zone. On beacon-to-beacon patrol a Climber pursues a semirandom progression, making a rendezvous each twelve hours. Ours is to be an observation patrol initially, meaning we're supposed to watch, not shoot.

The Commander shuffles order flimsies. "I'll tell you what we're looking for when I get this crap straight."

"What're observation pauses?" I ask the First Watch Officer. The Old Man says we have to program several into our beacon progression.

"Just go norm to see who did what last week."

"I don't follow."

"Okay. If we're not looking for something specific, we'll make equally spaced pauses. Say each four hours. If Command *is* looking for something, we'll drop hyper at exact times in specified places. Usually that means double-checking a kill. Ours or theirs."

"I see."

The beacons are refitted hulks. They form a vast irregular three-dimensional grid. When a Climber makes rendezvous, it discharges its Mission Recorder. In turn the beacon plays back any important news left by previous callers. The progress of a patrolling squadron is calculated so no news *should* be more than twenty-four hours old. It doesn't work that well in practice, though.

One in twenty beacons is instel-equipped, communing continuously with beacons elsewhere and with Climber Command. Supposedly, a vessel can receive emergency directives within a day and news from another squadron in two. On the scale of this war, that should be fast enough.

Sometimes it does work, when the human factor doesn't intrude too much.

The other firm occasionally stumbles onto a beacon and sets an ambush. The beacons are manned but have small crews and few weapons.

Climbers approach them carefully.

Fortune has smiled on us in a small way. The competition hasn't broken our computer key codes. If ever they do, Climber Fleet Tannian is in the soup. One beacon captured and emptied of information would destroy us all.

The other firm wastes no time hunting beacons. It takes monumental luck to find one. Space is *big*.

We're operational now. Past our first beacon.

Operational. Operational. I make an incantation of it, to exorcise my fear. Instead it has the opposite effect.

The web between the beacons. The spider's game. The vastness of space can neither be described nor overstated. When there's no known contact the Climber's hunt becomes analogous to catching mites with a spider's web as loosely woven as a deep-sea fishing seine. There are too many gaps, and they're too big. Though Command keeps the holes moving, ships still slip through unnoticed. Climbers often vanish without trace.

After we leave the beacon the Commander repeats all the tests made at Fuel Point. We commence our patrol in earnest.

I watch a Climber die. Twice. Our first two observation pauses bracket the event. We drop hyper, allow the light of it to overtake us, then jump out and let the wave catch us again. Like traveling in time.

There's little but a long, brilliant flash each time, like a small nova. The spectrum lines indicate massive CT-terrene annihilation. Ops compartment remains quiet for a long time. Laramie finally asks, "Who was it, Commander?"

"They didn't tell me. They never tell me..." He stops. His role doesn't permit bitterness before the men.

"Forty-eight souls," Fisherman muses. "I wonder how many were saved?"

"Probably none," I say.

"Probably not. It's sad. Not many believers anymore, Lieutenant. Like me, they have to meet Him, and Death, face to face before they'll be born again."

"It's not an age of faith."

For four hours men not otherwise occupied help maul the data, searching for a hint that the other firm precipitated the Climber's doom.

Nothing turns up. It looks like a CT leak.

Climber Command will add our data to other reports and let it stew in the big computer.

"It doesn't much matter anymore," Yanevich says. "She blew three months ago. The way they bracketed us, they were rechecking something they already knew. Glad we didn't have to take a closer look."

"There wouldn't be anything to see."

"Not this time. Sometimes there is. They don't all blow. Ours or theirs."

I feel cold breath blowing down the back of my neck. Firsthand studies of a gunned-out hulk aren't my notion of fun.

There's nothing going on in this entire universe. Beacon after beacon, there's nothing but bored, insulting greetings from squadron mates who were in before us. Decked out in his sardonic smile, the Old Man suggests the other team has taken a month's vacation.

He doesn't like the quiet. His eyes get narrower and more worried every day. His reaction isn't unique. Even the first-mission men are nervous.

First real news from outside. Climber Fleet Two says a huge, homebound convoy is gathering at Thompson's World, the other team's main springboard for operations against the Inner Worlds. Second Fleet hasn't had one contact during the forty-eight hours covered by their report.

Neither have we.

"Them guys must be taking the year off," Nicastro says. Today he's Acting Second Watch Officer, in Piniaz's stead. Weapons is having trouble with the graser.

I'm exhausted. I hung around past my own watch to observe Piniaz in command. Guess it'll have to wait. The hell with it. Where's my hammock?

Climber Fleet Two reports a brush with hunter-killers way in toward the Inner Worlds. Nothing came of it. Even the opposition's baseworlds are quiet.

This patrol zone is dead. We're caught in a nightmare, hunting ghosts. You don't *want* action, but you don't crave staying on patrol, either. You start feeling you're a space-going Flying Dutchman.

Beacon after beacon slides by. Always the news is the same. No contact.

Once a day the Commander takes the ship up for an hour, to keep the feel of Climb. We spend the rest of our time cruising at economical low-hyper translation velocities. Occasionally we piddle along in norm, making lazy inherent velocity corrections against our next beacon approach. There isn't much to do.

The men amuse themselves with card games and catch-the-eido, and weave endless and increasingly improbable variations in their exchanges on their favorite subject. To judge by their anecdotes, Throdahl and Rose have lived remarkably active lives during their brief careers. I expect they're doing some creative borrowing from stories heard elsewhere. They have their images to maintain.

I'm making some contact with the men now. Through no artifice of my own. They're bored. I'm the only novelty left unexplored.

The days become weeks, and the weeks pile into a month. Thirty-two days in the patrol zone. Thirty-two days without a contact anywhere. There are three squadrons out here now, and the newly commissioned unit is on its way. Another of the old squadrons will be leaving TerVeen soon. It'll be crowded.

No contact. This promises to become the longest dry spell in recent history.

The drills never cease. The Old Man *always* sounds the alarm at an inconvenient time. Then he stands back to watch the ants scurry. That's the only time we see his sickly smile.

Hell. They're breaks in the boredom.

This is oppressive. I haven't made a note in two weeks. If it weren't for guilt, I'd forget my project.

I think this is our forty-third day in the patrol zone. Nobody keeps track anymore. What the hell does it matter? The ship is our whole universe now. It's always day in here and always night outside.

If I really wanted to know, I could check the quartermaster's notebook. I could even find out what day of the week it is.

I'm saving that for hard times, for the day when I need a really big adventure to get me going.

We're a hairy bunch now. We look like the leavings of a prehistoric war band. Only Fisherman has bucked the trend and is keeping some order about his person. The only smooth faces I see belong to the youngest of the young.

The Engineers express their dissatisfaction by refusing to comb their hair. I'm the only man who takes regular sponge baths. Part my fault, I suppose. I spend a lot of time in my hammock. And I won't share my soap, which is the only bar aboard.

Curiously, these filthy beasts spend most of their free time scrubbing every accessible surface with a solution that clears the sinuses in seconds. Our paintwork gleams. It's a paradox.

One point of luck. No lice or fleas have turned up. I expected herds of crab lice, acquired from hygienically lax girlfriends.

Fearless Fred is sulking. He's the most bored creature aboard. No one has seen him for days. But he's around, and in a foul mood. He expresses his displeasure by leaving odiferous little loaves everywhere. He's as moody as the Commander.

Something is bothering the Old Man. Something of which this patrol is just part. It began before the mission, before I found him at Marie's.

He's no longer my friend of Academy days.

I did expect to find him weathered by the Service, changed by the war. War *has* to change a man. Combat is an intense experience. Comparing him to other classmates I've encountered recently, I can see how radical the changes are. Even Sharon wasn't this much transformed. The Sharon of the Pregnant Dragon always existed inside the other Sharon.

A few of the changes are predictable. An increased tendency toward withdrawal, toward self-containment, toward gloominess. Those were always part of him. Pressure and age would exaggerate them. No, the real change is the stratum of bitterness he conceals behind the standard changes.

He was never a bitter person. Contrarily, there was a playful, almost elfin streak behind his reserve. A little alcohol or a lot of coaxing could summon it forth.

Something has slain the elf.

Somehow, somewhere, while we were out of touch, he took one hell of an emotional beating. He got himself destroyed, and all the king's horses...

It's not a career problem. He's very successful by Navy standards. Twenty-six and already a full Commander. He's up for brevet Captain. He may get his first Admiral's star before he turns thirty.

It's something internal. He's lost a battle to something that's part of him. Something he hates and fears more than any enemy. He now despises himself for his own weakness.

He doesn't talk about it. He won't. And yet I think he wants to. He wants to lay it out for someone who knew him before his surrender. Someone not now close, yet someone who might know him well enough to show him the path back home.

I admit I was surprised that my request for assignment to his Climber went through. There were a hundred hurdles to surmount. The biggest, I expected, would be getting the Ship's Commander's okay. What Commander wants an extra, useless body aboard? But the affirmative came back like a ricochet. Now I know why, I think. He wants a favor for a favor.

The Commander's moods are a ship's moods. The men mirror their god-captain. He's aware of that and must live the role every minute. This's been the iron law of ships since the Phoenician mariners went down to the sea.

The role makes the Old Man's problem that much more desperate. He's tearing himself apart trying to keep his command from going sour. And he thinks he's failing.

So now he can't open up at all.

I now dread the future for more than the usual reasons. This is a miserably long patrol. And it's demonstrated repeatedly that the best Climber crew, highly motivated and well-officered, can start disintegrating.

More than once the Commander tracked me down and asked me to accompany him to the wardroom.

He makes a ritual of our visit. First he gives Kriegshauser a carefully measured bit of coffee. Just enough for two cups. There's been no regularly brewed real coffee since we learned we'd be on beacon-to-beacon patrol. What we call coffee, and brew daily, is made with a caffeine-rich Canaan bush-twig that has a vague coffee taste. That's what the Commander drinks during his morning ritual. After yielding his treasure, the Old Man stares into infinity and sucks the stem of his fireless pipe. He hasn't smoked in an age. The old hands say he won't till he decides to attack.

"You're going to chew that stem through."

He peers at the pipe as if surprised to find it in his hand. He turns it this way and that, studying the bowl. Finally, he takes a tiny folding knife and scrapes a fleck off the meerschaum. He then plunges it into a pocket already bulging with pens, pencils, markers, a computer stylus, a hand calculator, and his personal notebook. I'd love to see his notes. Maybe he writes revelations to himself.

He has his ritual question. "Well, what do you think so far?"

What's to think? "I'm an observer. The fourth estate's eido." My response is a ritual, too. I can never think of anything flip, or anything to start him talking. We drift through these things, waiting for a change.

"Remarkable crew?" Today is going to be a little different.

"A few individuals. Not as a whole. I've seen them all before. A ship produces specific characters the way the body produces specialized cells."

"You have to get through the hide. Get inside, to the meat and bones."

"I don't think I'm that good." I'm not. I keep seeing the masks they want me to see, not the faces in hiding. I may have been exposed too long now. An immunological process may be taking place. Something of the sort happens in every closed group. After jostling and jousting, the pieces of the jigsaw fall into place. People adjust, get along. And they stop being objective about one another.

The Old Man says, "Hmm." He's developing that sound into a vocabulary with the inflectional range of Chinese. This "hmm" means "do go on."

"We've got people who want to be something the ship has no niche for. Take Carmon. He believes his propaganda image. He wants to be Tannian's Horatio at the bridge. The rest of us won't let him."

"One right guess. Carmon aside, did you find anybody who gives a rat's ass about the war?"

Have I stumbled onto something? They *are* volunteers…. This is as near an expression of doubt as I'll ever hear from the Commander.

I'm too eager to pursue it. My sharp glance spooks him.

"What did you think of Marie?"

I think the relationship is symptomatic of a deeper problem. But I won't say that. "She was under a strain. An unexpected guest. You about to leave…" There're things a man doesn't do. One of mine: Never say anything bad about a friend's mate.

"She won't be there when we get back."

I knew that before we left.

Well, it isn't the realization of his own mortality that has gotten to him. This isn't the odds-closing-in blues that plagues Climber Commanders. If I look closely, I can catch glimpses of the *it can't happen to me* of our age group.

Is it the realization of his own fallibility? Suppose last patrol he made a grotesque error and got away with it through dumb luck? The kind of man he is, that would bother him bad because forty-seven men might have gone out with him.

Maybe. But that's more the kind of thing that would break a Piniaz. The Old Man never claimed to be perfect. Just close to it.

"She'll be gone when I get home." His eyes are long ago and far away. He has had these thoughts before. "She won't leave a note, either."

"You really think so?" I nearly missed the cues telling me to ask.

Marie isn't his problem. A problem, and a symptom, but not *the* problem.

"Just a feeling, say. You saw how we got along. Cats and dogs. Only reason we stayed together was we didn't have anywhere to go. Not that didn't look worse."

"In a way."

"What?"

"Hell probably offers a sense of security to the damned."

"Yes. I suppose." He draws his pipe from his pocket, examines its bowl. "You know Climber Fleet One hasn't ever had a deserter? Could be."

For a moment I envision the man as an old-time sea captain, master on a windjammer, standing a lonely, nighted weather-deck, staring at moon-frosted wavetops while a cold breeze fingers his strawlike hair and beard. The sea is obsidian. The wake churns and boils. It glimmers with bio-luminescence.

"For what distant, heathen port be we bound, o'er what enchanted sea?"

He glances up, startled. "What was that?"

"An image that came to me. Remember the poem game?" We played it in Academy, round robin. It was popular during the middle class years, when we were discovering new dimensions faster than we could assimilate them. The themes, then, were mostly prurient.

"My turn to come up with a line, you mean. All right." He ponders. While he does so, Kriegshauser delivers the coffee.

"Zanzibar? Hadramaut? The Ivory Coast? Or far Trincomalee?"

"That stinks. It's not a line, it's a laundry list."

"Seemed to fit yours. I never was much good at that, was I?" He puts his pipe away and sips coffee. Under ship's gravity we can drink from cups if we like. A small touchstone with another reality. "I'm a warrior, not a poet."

"Ah?"

"'Ah?' You sound like a Psych Officer."

Whatever its nature, his bugbear won't reveal itself this time. Not without inspired coaxing from me. And I have no idea how to bait my hook.

I think I know how a detective hunting a psychopathic killer must feel. He knows the man is out there, killing because he wants to be caught, yet the very irrationality of the killer makes him impossible to track....

Can his problem be this role he lives? This total warrior performance? Is there a poet screaming to get out of the Commander? A conflict between the role's demands and the nature of the actor who has to meet them?

I don't think so. He's the quintessential warrior, as far as I can see.

He chose me because I'm not part of the gang. And maybe now he's hiding from me for the same reason.

"You slated for Command College?" I ask, shifting my ground. If he hasn't made the list, that might take him by the balls. Passing an officer over amounts to declaring he's reached his level of incompetence. No one gets pushed out, especially now, but the promotions do end.

"Yes. Probably won't get there before this fuss is over. I'm slated for the squadron next two missions, then Staff at Climber Command. Won't get off Canaan for at least two years. Then back to the Fleet, probably. Either a destroyer squadron or number two in a flotilla. No time for war college these days. All on-the-job training."

A weak possibility lurks here. Upward mobility threatened by war's master spirit: Sudden Death.

"Why did you volunteer?"

"For Climbers? I didn't."

"Eh? You said..."

"Only on paper. I asked for Canaan. Talk to the officers our age. A lot of them are here on 'strong recommendation' from above. What amounted to verbal orders. They're making it simple. The Climbers are the only thing we have that works. They need officers to operate them. So, no Climber time, no promotion. You have an unprofessional attitude if you don't respond to the needs of the Service." A bilious glow of bitterness seeping through here.

He drains half his cup, asks, "Why the hell would I ask for *this?* The chances of me getting my ass blown to ions are running five to one against me. Do I look fucking stupid?"

He recalls his role. His gaze darts to Kriegshauser, who may have overheard.

"What about rapid advancement? Glory? Because Canaan is your home?"

"That's shit for the troops and officers coming up. Navy is my home."

My stare must be a little too sharp. He changes the subject. "Strange patrol. Too quiet. I don't like it."

"Think they're up to something?"

He shrugs. "They're always up to something. But there are quiet periods. Statistical anomalies, I guess. They're out there somewhere, slipping through. Maybe they've found a pattern to our patrols. We don't really run random. Human weakness. We have to have order of some kind. If they analyze contacts, sometimes they figure a safe route. We change things. The hunting is good for a while. Then, too, Command wastes a lot of time taking second and third looks at things."

There's bitterness whenever he mentions Command. Have I uncovered a theme? Disenchantment? He wouldn't be the first. Not by thousands.

There's no describing the shock, even despair, that clamps down on you after you've spent a childhood in Academy, preparing for a career, when the Service doesn't remotely resemble classroom expectations. It's worse when you find nothing to believe in, or live, or love. And to be a good soldier you have to live it, to believe your work has worth and purpose, and you have to like doing it.

There's more going on in the Climber than I thought. It's happening beneath the surface. In the hearts and minds of men, as the cliché goes.

I'm sipping coffee with the Commander when the alarm screams.

"Another fucking drill?" The things have worn my temper to frayed ends. Three, four times a day. And the only time that bitching horn howls is when I have something better to do.

The Commander's pallor, as he plunges toward the hatch, is answer enough. This time is for real.

For real. I make Ops before the hatch closes, barely a limp behind the Old Man.

It *is* easier in operational mode.

Yanevich and Nicastro crowd Fisherman. I wriggle into the viewscreen seat. The Commander elbows up to the tachyon detector.

"Ready to Climb, First Watch Officer?"

"Ready, Commander. Engineering is ready for annihilation shift."

I hunch down, lean till I can peek between arms and elbows. The tachyon detector's screen is alive for the first time since we lost touch with the mother. It shows a tiny, intense, sideways *V* at three o'clock, which trails an almost flat ventral progression wave. The dorsal is boomerang-shaped. A dozen cloudy feathers of varying length lie between the two.

"One of ours," I remark. "Battle Class cruiser. Probably Mediterranean subClass. *Salamis* or *Lepanto*. Maybe *Alexandria*, if she's finished refitting."

Four pairs of eyes drill holes into my skull. Too wary to ask, both men are thinking, "What the hell do you know?"

Chief Canzoneri calls out, "Commander, I've got an ID on the emission pattern. Friendly. Cruiser. Battle Class. Mediterranean subClass. *Salamis* or *Alexandria*. We'll have to move closer if you want a positive for the log. We need a finer reading in the epsilon."

"Never mind. Command can decide who it was." He continues staring holes through me. Some of the men look at me as if they've just noted my presence. "Mr. Yanevich. We'll take her up for a minute. No point them wasting time chasing us."

Making a Climb is a simple way of saying friend.

Back in the wardroom, the Old Man demands, "How did you do that?"

Why not play a little? They're always playing with me. "What?"

"ID that cruiser."

I was surprised when they stared but was more amazed that Fisherman bothered with the alarm. "The display. Any good operator can read progression lines. I saw a lot of the Mediterraneans, back when."

"Junghaus is good. I've never seen him do anything like that."

"Battle Class ships have unique tails. Usually you look at the feathers. But Battle Class has a severe arch in the dorsal line. The Meds have a top line longer than the bottom. From there it's just arithmetic. There're only three Meds out here. I can't remember the feathers or I would've told you which one. I didn't do any magic."

"I don't think Fisherman could've done it. He's good, but he doesn't worry about details. He'll argue Bible trivia from now till doomsday, but can't always tell a Main Battle from a Titan tug. Maybe he doesn't care."

"I thought that was the point of having an operator and a screen."

"In Climbers we only need to know if something's out there. Junghaus is just cruising till he gets his ticket to the Promised Land."

"That's a harsh judgment."

"The man gets on my nerves…. But they all do. They're like children. You've got to watch them every minute. You've got to wipe their noses and kiss their bruises…. Sorry. Maybe we should've had a longer leave. Or a different one."

Fearless Fred wanders in. This is the first I've seen him this week. He one-eyes us, chooses my lap.

"Remember Ivan the Terrible?" I ask, scratching the cat's head and ears.

"That idiot Marine unarmed combat instructor? I hope he's getting his ass kicked from pole to pole on some outback…."

"No. The other one. The cat we had in kindergarten."

"Kindergarten? I don't remember that far back." After a moment, "The mascot. The cat that had puppies."

"Kittens."

"Whatever. Yeah. I remember."

First year in Academy. Kindergarten year. You were still human enough and child enough to rate a few live cuddly toys. Ivan the Terrible was our mascot, and less reputable than Fearless. All bones and battle scars after countless years of a litter every four months. The best that could be said for her was that she loved us kids as much as we loved her, and brought her offspring marching proudly in as soon as they could stumble. She died beneath the wheels of a runaway electric scooter, leaving battalions of descendants behind. I think her death was the first traumatic experience of the Commander's young life.

It was my biggest disappointment for years. That one shrieking moment unmasked the cruel indifference of my universe. Thereafter it was all downhill from innocence. Nothing surprised or hurt me for a long time. Nor the Commander, that I saw, though we eventually suffered worse on an adult value scale.

"I remember," the Commander says again. "Fearless, there was a lady of your own stripe."

"Bad joke."

Fred cracks an eyelid. He considers the Commander. He yawns.

"But he don't care," I say.

"That's the problem. Nobody cares. We're out here getting our asses blown off, and nobody cares. Not the people we're protecting, not Navy, not the other firm, not even ourselves most of the time." He stares at the cat for half a minute. "We're just going through the motions, getting it over so we can go on leave again."

He's getting at purpose again, obliquely. I felt the same way during my first active-duty tour. They hammered and hammered and hammered at us in Academy, then sent us out where nobody had a sense of mission. Where no one gave a damn. All anyone wanted was to make grade and get the retirement points in. They did only what they had to do, and not a minim more. And denied any responsibility for doing more.

Admiral Tannian, for all his shortcomings, has striven to correct that in his bailiwick. He may be going about it the wrong way, but… were the Commander suddenly deposited on one of the Inner Worlds, he'd find himself a genuine, certified hero. Tannian has made *those* people care.

Even the smoothest Climberman, though, would abrade the edge off his welcome. Like a pair of dress boots worn through a rough campaign, even Academy's finest lose their polish in Tannian's war.

"Don't scratch. It'll cause sores."

I find myself digging through my beard again. Is that a double-entendre? "Too late now. I've got them already. The damned thing won't stop itching."

"See Vossbrink. He'll give you some ointment."

"What I want is a razor." Mine disappeared under mysterious circumstances. In a ship without hiding places it's managed to stay disappeared.

"Candy ass." The Commander uses his thin, forced smile. "Want to ruin our scurrilous image? You might start a fad."

"Wouldn't hurt, would it?" The atmosphere system never quite catches up with the stench of a crew unbathed for weeks, and of farts, for which there are interdepartmental olympiads. Hell, I didn't find those funny in Academy, when we were ten. Sour grapes, maybe. I was a second-rate athlete even in that obscene event.

Urine smells constantly emanate from the chamberpots we use when sealed hatches deny us access to the Admiral's stateroom.

Each compartment has its own auxiliary air scrubber. These people won't use them just to ease my stomach. "Feh!" I give my nose a stylish pinch.

"Wait a few months. Till we can't stop the mold anymore."

"Mold? What mold?"

"You'll see, if this goes on much longer. First time they make us stay up very long." What looked like a drift toward good humor ends as that thought hits the table. The ship will stay out as long as it takes.

"Enough piddling around. Got to write up the war log. Been letting it slide because there's nothing to say. Shitheaded Command. Want you to write twice as much, saying why, whenever there's nothing happening. Someday I'll tell them."

I've glimpsed that log. Its terse summations make our days prime candidates for expungement from the pages of history.

The minimum to get by. From bottom to top.

I clump after the Old Man and consequently reach Operations in time for a playback of the news received last beacon rendezvous.

Johnson's Climber preceded ours in. The girls left love notes.

"How the hell did they know we were behind them?" I ask.

"Computers," Yanevich says, amused. "With enough entries you can determine the patrol pattern. It's never completely random."

"Oh." I've watched Rose and Canzoneri play the game when they have nothing else to run. They also try to identify the eido. It's just time-killing. The eido is as anonymous as ever.

They're making a huge project of trying to predict first contact. To hedge the pool. They run a fresh program every beacon call, buy more pool slips, and are convinced they're going to make a killing. The pot keeps growing as the weeks roll along. There're several thousand Con-marks in it already.

The compartment grows deadly still. Reverently, Throdahl says, "Here it comes."

"... convoy in zone Twelve Echo making the line for Thompson's System. Ten and six. Am in pursuit. Eighty-four Dee."

I estimate quickly. We aren't that far away. We could get there if we hauled ass. Must be an important convoy, too. Six escorts for ten lo-gistical hulls is a heavy ratio, unless they're battle units coincidentally moving up. The other firm likes to kill two birds with one stone.

The orders don't come. Climber Command won't abandon patrol routine to get something going. Yanevich tries to raise my spirits by telling me, "We'll get our shot. Maybe sooner than you really want."

The Commander shouts down. "I'm going to give him a chance to work off his boredom, Mr. Yanevich. Gunnery exercises next observation break. We'll see what he can do with his toy."

Now I know why Bradley has been hoarding waste canisters. They'll make nice targets.

Always something strange going on here. And no one explains anything till it's my turn in the barrel.

The Old Man is no help. For no reason I can fathom, he keeps every ship's order ultra top clam till the last second. What point security out here? The only rationale I can see is, he wants the crew ready for anything.

He is, probably, following Command directives. Logic never has much to do with security procedure.

Do those clowns think our competitors have an agent aboard?

Not bloody likely. There's a limit to the power of disguise.

Gunnery exercises are little more than gun error trials. Everything but the final firing order is handled by computer. A dull go. No sport. But a break in an otherwise oppressively monotonous routine. The Energy Gunners spear their targets on second shot. I batter mine to shrapnel with my third short burst. The range, however, isn't extreme.

Later, I suppose, there'll be exercises on full manual, or with limited computer assistance, simulating various states of battle damage.

I do find a constant error in gun train or gun train order. I enter a correction constant. So much for another exciting day.

Curious that gunnery exercises weren't scheduled till this late in the patrol. Did the Commander know there would be no action? The man nearest me is an Energy Fire Control Technician named Kuyrath. I ask him, "How come the Old Man put this off so long?"

"Typical crap, probably. Command probably sent us out knowing we wouldn't run into anything. Just for the hell of it. Just to have us jacking around. And you wonder why morale stinks?"

He has a lot more to say. None of it compliments Command. He hasn't a bad word for the Commander. But now I'm wolfing off along a new spoor.

I've decided that I've been overlooking an inexplicable undercurrent of confidence among the more experienced men. As if they knew no action was imminent. If gunnery exercises are a signal, that should change. We shall see.

The changes comes, and sooner than any of us expect. With the possible exception of Climber Command.

The word is waiting at the next beacon, which is the contact-control for our present patrol sector.

There won't be time for manual gunnery exercises.

6

FIRST CONTACT

Pushing hell out of two months now. Same old zigzag. One step back, two forward. But…

Our baseline has twisted around. We're headed toward Canaan now. More or less. Westhause figures about twelve years to get there at our present rate of approach. We're not taking it in one big rush.

We're turned around. That's the point. Something has happened. We have hunting orders. At last.

Like everything else about this patrol, they make no sense.

Command has targeted us a vessel crippled more than a year ago. She's been rediscovered, running in norm. Must be a crafty bunch, to have kept their heads down this long.

The Old Man doesn't like it. He keeps mumbling, "Coup de grâce," and, "Why waste the time? The poor bastards deserve better." I've never seen him so sour.

None of the others are excited, either.

I'm nervous as hell. It's been a long time.

Yanevich says it could get complicated. The target is running for the hunter-killer base we called Rathgeber before the other firm took it away. She is pushing point-four *c*. That'll mean some fancy maneuvering when we engage her.

And some trick shooting. That's a lot of inherent velocity. We haven't the time or fuel to match it. "What are they doing for fuel?" I ask.

"Ramscooping, probably," Yanevich says. "They may have tankers dumping hydrogen ahead of her."

Still, she must have been fat to start. Maybe she's a tanker herself. "Why the hell didn't they abandon her? Or, if she's that important, why didn't a repair ship come fix her generators?"

Yanevich shrugs. "Maybe they got a lot of pressure from our people back then. Maybe running in norm was their only option."

Our first chore will be to relocate the ship. Those aren't dummies running the other team. They'll know she's been spotted. She'll be running a jagged course.

First we'll run a search pattern surrounding a baseline drawn from the target's last known position to her suspected destination. During the search, Piniaz will decide how to tackle a vessel traveling almost too fast to track. Point-four c in norm. That's smoking.

The obvious tactic is to drop hyper ahead and shove a missile flight down her throat. Hitting the tiny, necessary relative motion window would be a trick, though. The target is moving too fast to hit from even a slight angle. Knowing that, she'll be running a constantly changing course.

Shooting down the throat means shooting blind. The target is moving too fast. (That's an endless refrain, like a song with only one-line lyrics.) She'll run over us if we take time to aim. The Fire Control system needs a quarter-second, after detection, to lock and fire. In that split second our target will traverse more than thirty thousand kilometers.

"You're right," I say. "They aren't dummies. I don't see how we can stop them. I suppose Command says we can't waste missiles."

Yanevich smiles. "You're thinking Climber now. Damned right. Never waste a missile on a cripple." More seriously, "We couldn't use one. No time to target and program in norm, not enough computation capacity to compute simultaneity close enough to plop one into their laps from hyper. Tannian should send minelayers. Seed the target path."

"Why're we bothering?"

"Because Fearless Fred told us to. Why do we bother with any of this shit? Don't ask why. Why doesn't matter in the Climbers."

How sour he is lately. He's saying the things the Commander is thinking. He'll have to learn to control himself if he wants to become a Ship's Commander.

"It doesn't matter anywhere else, either, Steve. You're supposed to do your job and trust your superiors."

"What the hell? Anything beats what we've been doing. It's something to mess with till a convoy shows."

Later, while the First Watch Officer confers with Mr. Westhause, Fisherman says, "I hope they make it, sir."

"Hmm? Why's that?"

"Just seems right. That their efforts be rewarded. Like it says in the Bible... but the Lord's will, will be done."

Curious. Compassion for the enemy...

I find it a widespread attitude, though the men all say they'll do their jobs. Even Carmon shows no hatred or hysteria, just respect and a hint of an anachronistic chivalry.

The gentlemen of the other firm aren't wholly real, of course. Making them real, believable, and sinister, has been a problem for our captains and propaganda kings. The men can't get worked up about someone they have never seen. It's hard to interact emotionally with an electronic shadow in a display tank.

It's like fighting specters who take on flesh only for those inescapably in their clutches. Only on our lost worlds do our people actually see their conquerors.

It's hard to hate them, too, because they practice none of the common excesses of war. We never hear atrocity stories. There have been no pointless massacres. They avoid civilian casualties. They don't use nuclears inside atmosphere. They simply operate as a vast, efficient, and effective disarmament machine. From the beginning their sole purpose has been to neutralize, not to subjugate or destroy.

We're baffled, naturally.

Confederation won't be as charitable, if ever the tide turns. We play tougher, though we've stuck to the tacit rules so far.

The Commander and Mr. Westhause comp a program that will drop us on the target's last known position. Nicastro keeps nagging the computermen for a search program. Mr. Yanevich flutters hither and yon, mothering everyone.

The First Watch Officer's role is constricted this patrol. Under normal circumstances he plays a prick of the first water, a rigid disciplinarian, a book-thumper, and becomes the focus for the crew's antipathy toward authority. The Commander remains aloof, and when needed goes round with a warm word or unexpectedly friendly gesture. His role is that of father figure without the usual disciplinary unpleasantness. Most Commanders cultivate quirks which make them appear more human than their First Watch Officers. Our Old Man lugs that huge black revolver and chews his pipe. Occasionally he hauls the weapon out to sight in on targets only he can see.

In private he admits that success as a Ship's Commander reflects success as a character actor.

The men know that, too. This shit has been going on since the Phoenicians. It works anyway. It's a big conspiracy. The Commander tries to make them believe and they work hard at believing. They want to be fooled and comforted.

There are no supporting fictions for the commander. He stands alone. He can't take Admiral Tannian seriously.

Mr. Yanevich is heir apparent to the loneliness, which is why he has a softened image this patrol. This is his chrysalis mission. He came aboard remembered as a martinet. He'll emerge remembered as a wacky, lovable butterfly.

"How many ships are going with us, Steve?"

Yanevich shrugs. "Maybe we'll find out next beacon."

"What I figured. Any reason I can't go see what they're doing below?" I want to see how the prospect of action has affected other departments.

Weapons should be the most altered. It's been the most bored. The triggermen have nothing to do but sit and wait. And wait. And wait.

Everyone else is here simply to give them their moments at their firing keys.

They're excited. Piniaz has undergone a renewal of spirit. He actually welcomes my visit. "I was going to look you up," he says, wearing a smile he can't control. "We've been running cost-effectiveness programs."

I glance at Chief Holtsnider. The Chief nods pleasantly. Piniaz says, "We may try your cannon." He babbles on about accuracy probabilities, cumulative ion stress in the lasers, and so forth.

There's no tension in Weapons. Every mug brandishes a smile. How simple we've become. Just the prospect of change has us behaving as if we'll be home tomorrow night.

One of the gunnery trainees, Tuchol Manolakos, asks me, "Can you imagine what one of those bearings would do, sir?"

"Ricochet off their meteor shunt. The velocity they're making, with their ramscoop funneling, they're running with screens up and shunts on all the time. Detection-activation circuitry would be too slow."

"Yeah. Didn't think of that."

"Have to screen against hard radiation, too."

"Yeah."

I wonder if they're moving fast enough to see a starbow. Certainly there'll be gorgeous violet and red shifts fore and aft. Rectification of Doppler will consume most of their enhancement capacity.

The faces round me go grim. "What is it? What did I say?"

"I didn't consider the screens," Piniaz grumbles.

"Better consider the subjective time differential, too," I suggest.

"I thought of that. Ain't much, but it's to our advantage."

"And the Doppler on your energy beams?"

"Considered. Damned toy cannon."

"You could still try. If we're close enough to shoot, they'll shoot back. If they're armed. They'll have to break screens to do it."

"Put a two-centimeter ball into a ten-centimeter shield gap with a point-four-second endurance on a target moving at point-four *cee*? From how far away? Shit. Shit and more shit. Why're we chasing these clowns, anyway? They aren't exactly what you'd call a major threat to the universe. Ain't there a goddamned *convoy* somewhere?"

"Guess the Admiral thinks it would be a propaganda coup."

"Shit." Piniaz's vocabulary is suffering. "It'll just piss them off over there. You don't keep kicking a guy when he's out of it. They'll start kicking back."

"I'll tell old Fred next time we take tea together." I don't know what it is about Piniaz. He can aggravate a stone just by standing beside it.

My antipathy is, in part, prejudice against his origins. I know it, and probably am overcompensating. Piniaz's dark little features are tight. He can guess my thoughts. "You do that. And tell him from me... Never mind."

The eido hasn't been fingered.

Piniaz didn't reach his present status by letting Outworlders get his goat. He knows how to play the game.

It's a game in which the Outworlds' elite have rigged the rules, though not quite enough to keep him from beating them on their own terms.

I respect the man despite disliking him. More than I respect my own kind. My people aren't brought up being told they're the dregs of the human race.

Still... Old Earthers have an infuriating habit of blaming the mother-world's problems on the rest of us. And they're disgustingly consistent in their refusal to help themselves. We Outworlders are expected to carry them simply because Old Earth *is* the motherworld.

We all have prejudices. Piniaz should resent me less than the others. I make an attempt to control mine.

Varese tells Old Earther stories in Piniaz's presence. His favorite goes, "You hear about the Old Earther who comes home from the Social Insurance office and finds his woman in bed with another man?"

Someone will say, "No."

"He runs to the closet, grabs his Teng Hua, points it at his own head. His woman starts laughing at him. He yells, 'What's so funny, bitch? You're next.'"

There are several false assumptions in the story. There are in all Old Earther jokes. Welfare status. Extreme stupidity. Promiscuity. Universal possession of a Teng Hua hand laser. And so on.

Varese makes me ashamed of my breed when he does that.

After touring the ship I evict Fearless from my hammock. It's become the cat's favorite loafing place. He isn't often disturbed.

I can't sleep. The prospect of action doesn't excite me anymore. All I want is to go home. I'm tired of the Climbers. I'm sorry I had the idea. Please, can I take it back? No? Damn.

Sleep sneaks up on me eventually. I have my best nap since coming aboard, a solid twelve hours that end only because Fearless starts a flamenco on my chest.

"You're getting goddamned bold, cat."

The animal places chin on paws four centimeters from my face. He closes his good eye. The warmth of him, the quick patter of his heart, leak through my grimy shirt.

"You'd better not have fleas."

Fearless twitches disdainfully, resumes his snooze.

I don't know why I've been selected main friend for the patrol. I can put up with cats, but comprehend them no better than women. This one lives like a prince. He has forty-nine lackeys keeping his castle for him.

I scratch his ears. He rewards me with a gravelly purr and a few gentle nips at my finger.

The shrill cry of the general alarm shatters our interlude.

I make Ops with time to spare, wondering how I slept through the alarm when we dropped hyper.

I didn't. The story I get is, Westhause was whipping the ship through complex search loops as he approached the new operational area. Fishermen got something on screen.

I didn't expect such quick results.

Glancing over Junghaus's shoulder, I see that we have not lucked onto our quarry.

Of course not. The target would generate no tachyon distur-bances running in norm. "One of ours?" I slide into the First Watch Officer's seat.

Fisherman smiles. Yanevich grins. The Commander says, "Very good. Which one?"

I shrug. "A Climber, but I've only seen textbook plates. They just show the basics."

"Johnson's. That teensy lump on the arch of the fourth feather."

I glance at Westhause. He's pounding program keys like a mad organist.

Climbers have no instel. Smart operators communicate, in pidgin at close ranges, with behavior and the detection gear.

I give the Old Man a look.

"No hanky-panky, sir. Wouldn't think of it. There's a war on, you know. That's serious business."

Yanevich whispers, "We'll drop hyper and trade search patterns. Two of us working will find where she isn't real quick."

"How can we learn anything without going norm?"

He looks at me oddly. "We're norm now. Hadn't you noticed? We've been norm one minute in five for the last six hours. We're not up to the mark yet, but we thought we'd get the routine pat. Haven't you been paying attention?"

"The alarms…" Better keep my mouth shut. I slept through one of my watches.

"Jesus. You think I'm going to bang that mother all year long? Screw the regulations. People have to sleep. Speaking of which—where were you on the eight to twelve?"

What can I say? There's no excuse.

"Not to worry, Mr. Better-Late-Than-Never. The Recorder hears the alarm. That's good enough for us." Yanevich manages the grin the Commander can't quite produce. "You learn these little tricks. The Recorder remembers what we want it to remember. They know what's going on at Mission Review. They've been out here, too. As long as it doesn't endanger the ship, and doesn't leave out anything important, they let it slide. Got to be flexible. That's what they told us in Academy, wasn't it?"

"Maybe. This isn't the Navy I knew."

"Yeah?"

"I thought wartime would get the regs pushed harder."

"You're in the Climbers now." He laughs. "What's it matter? Long as we don't buy you a seat on Hecate's Horse? At least you got some sleep." His smile grows thin. "I'll get that back. Stand watch and stand again till you catch up."

It's not as bad as I expected. Piniaz is the sort of watch officer who stays out of the way. He makes his presence felt only when he joins Chief Nicastro in making sure Westhause's preprogrammed jumps are putting the ship into the right places in the search pattern. The astrogator can't be on the job all the time, though he does sleep less than anyone else.

Yanevich's shipboard title is a misnomer this patrol. The Commander himself has taken the first watch. Yanevich really has the second. Piniaz has the third. In Line ships the Astrogation Officer normally stands the third watch. In Climbers that usually falls to the Ship's Services Officer. The Commander is kept free.

The Old Man thinks our Ensign too green. In the quiet passages, though, he brings Bradley in for a watch. He hands it to me at times, too. Sometimes Diekereide takes a turn—"just in case." The Commander has even dragged Varese in on rare occasion. One of an officer's unwritten duties is to learn everything possible. It may save your ship someday.

Watch schedules don't mean much aboard a Climber, except to officers, who assume four-hour chunks of responsibility. The men come and go. In Ops Chiefs Nicastro and Canzoneri just make sure that the critical stations are manned. In Weapons Chiefs Bath and Holtsnider do the same.

In Engineering, where they stand six on and six off and most of the stations must be continuously manned, life is more structured.

Our first program, beginning at the target's last known position, yields nothing. Westhause develops another while we wait for Johnson. It's a waste of time. Johnson got a sniff of neutrino emissions.

The news subtly alters everyone. Within minutes the men are near their combat stations again. The banter fades to an occasional obscene remark, either too loud or too forced.

Boredom is dead. The men have a sharper edge than past appearance would suggest. The Commander has done his job well.

Westhause exchanges professional chatter with his colleague aboard the other Climber. The Old Man and First Watch Officer hover close.

Two hours later. We begin quartering the region where Johnson got her neutrino readings. She dances with us, our two radii of detection barely overlapping.

I'm alert and interested, though not in my screen. I want to catch every nuance in each man's stance, movement, expression. I want to see the subtle alterations in speech patterns that betray emotion.

The Commander demonstrates the most marked change. It's a matter of intensity. Some internal switch has closed. Suddenly, he has a truly commanding presence. The men respond without words being spoken. Their eyes flick to him, then back to their work.

The Climber has come alive. The shark has caught the smell of blood.

This new Commander is the man I came to Canaan to see, the man who was usurped by a bitter, unfathomable stranger sailing without a compass. The doubts and fears and alum-flavored self-despite have been set aside.

He has his effect on me, too. My nerves settle. He will get us through.

What's happening inside his head? Has he set it all aside and let duty take control? His thinking remains impenetrable even during his most open moments. For all I know, he's scared shitless.

The new search program has both ships covering a tiny chunk of space in one-minute hyper translations, and closing the communications gap each half-hour.

During the first half-hour we get a dozen neutrino readings.

"Intensity?" the Commander demands after the last.

"High, Commander."

"Direction? Estimated course line?" This is tricky business here. Like cutting the beam of a handflash at a kilometer, at an angle, in a microsecond, and trying to guess where the flash is and where it's heading if it's moving.

Rose and Canzoneri curse and mutter incantations over their thinking devil. The devil puts numbers into the Chief's mouth.

"Put it in the tank," the Old Man orders.

The display tank flickers to a slight adjustment. It gives a skewed view, with the Climber at one boundary. The ship casts a thin cone of red shadow across the tank.

"Got her within twenty degrees of arc," Canzoneri says. A thin black pencil stroke lances down the heart of the red cone. "Baseline within three degrees of Rathgeber."

"Range?"

"Indeterminate." Of course. We'd have to know what kind of ship she is to guess her distance from the intensity of her neutrino output here.

"Very well. Mr. Westhause, let's see what the Squadron Leader has."

The net is closing. Johnson's data should pull it tighter.

Time drags. I fidget. Two hunting Climbers leave a lot of tachyon traces. Those people hear us coming. They'll be on their toes. Right now they're filing their teeth and calling their big brothers.

The Commander grins as if reading my thoughts. "Don't worry. Our team is sending in the best we have."

"Waiting gracefully isn't one of my virtues."

The others are more patient. They've been schooled for this. As I should know by now, 99 percent of Climber duty consists of waiting.

Can they keep their edge till contact?

Johnson has enough data. We narrow the hunting zone to the size of a backyard garden. Time to go kick the rabbit out of the lettuce patch.

We jump knowing we'll meet the other firm within hours.

We drop hot on the trail. The neutrino gear sings and pops. We can't be more than a few light-hours behind. Westhause and his co-conspirator confer only briefly. The computers commune. We translate again.

We almost bracket her this time. On infrared I can pick out the long, wild rapier of ions blowing behind her. Even on max enhancement I can get no image of the ship. She has her black warpaint on and is moving too damned fast.

"Jesus God in a canoe!" Berberian murmurs. "Commander! Check the size of this blip."

The target is millions of kilometers away already.

"Commander, she's started a turn," Berberian adds.

At her velocity it'll be a vast, lazy arc, and the best evasive maneuver available—especially if she keeps it irregular. There's no way we can keep her in radar range for more than a few seconds.

"Chasing after wind, eh?" The Commander is whispering to Fisherman. I barely catch it. The TD operator nods. The Old Man notes my interest. "Silly pastime, eh?"

"We'll need luck. Or they'll have to do something stupid."

"They won't. They don't anymore. We've taught them too well."

"Here she comes!"

Startled, I look round wildly, then glare at my screen. Westhause has translated us into the fugitive's path. For an instant I catch a glimmer that must be Johnson firing.

"That the Squadron Leader?"

"It is," the Commander replies. "She'll attack. We'll observe."

"Commander!" Chief Canzoneri shouts. "That's no logistic hull. That's a goddamned Leviathan Main Battle."

Bright spider's silk spins across the black satin backdrop from spinnerets on the black widow that is Johnson's Climber. I stare, enthralled, though it lasts but an instant. We skip again. For a moment I forget to roll my visual tapes.

Skip-fire-skip-fire-skip-fire. How can we do any damage this way? Maybe we're just getting her measure.... Canzoneri says the Squadron Leader is tickling her round her bows. I'll have to take his word for it.

A nova takes life at the lase-fire's source.

The next few minutes get lost. My stomach falls out from under me. My mind goes numb. Somebody is groaning. I don't know if it's me or someone else.

Throdahl is saying, over and over, "Oh, shit. Oh, holy fuck. Brenda." His voice is soft, his words are quick. He speaks without inflection.

Fisherman begins a prayer. "Lord, have mercy on their souls." It fades into an unintelligible mumble. A moment later I realize he means the people aboard the Main Battle.

The huge warship whips off into the big dark while we remain mesmerized by our sister's destruction. How the hell did they manage that?

"Canzoneri. That was on camera. Give me an analysis."

"Aye, Commander." The Chief keys the tape from my screen to his. In a minute, "A missile. Radar transparent. I still have some numbers to run."

He figures it in minutes. The other firm outcalculated us, pure and simple. They knew where we were coming out. Where we had to come out to make the down-the-throat shot. They put missiles out there. Johnson probably never knew what hit her. They didn't take a poke at us because we were running in a trailing position.

"*They* aren't worried about conserving armaments," Yanevich growls.

"A Leviathan doesn't have to," I snap back.

Leviathan is Navy's label for the enemy's biggest and meanest warship. We don't know what they call them. We have nothing comparable. They carry crews of twenty thousand, bristle with weapons, and are fleets unto themselves. They can remain in deep space indefinitely.

Our Empire Class Main Battle carries seven thousand people, is eighteen hundred meters long, and masses a fifth as much.

Now it's pretend time. We all make believe our loss doesn't hurt, doesn't make us hungry for blood. We shut one another out and concentrate on our work.

I didn't meet any of Johnson's women. Still, my revenge lust runs deep, startling me. I can't banish the face of Throdahl's sepia beauty. All thought of practical difficulties yields to the gale of unreason.

It doesn't matter that we came here looking for trouble. It doesn't matter that the Leviathan outguns us a thousand to one. It doesn't matter that her velocity is so ridiculous. I don't even worry about her being able to call for help while we can't. I want to attack.

"Commander, there's a drop in her neutrino emissions."

"Chief Canzoneri. What's she doing?"

Thirty seconds pass. "Looks like she's putting out a full missile screen. So she can drift along inside."

The Commander leans till his forehead almost touches the astrogator's. "Very well." He doesn't seem surprised. He whispers with Westhause.

What are they planning? We can't get near them now. We can't put a missile in, except from hyper.

Fisherman calls, "Commander, I'm getting a continuous diffuse tachyon response."

Everyone understands. The Leviathan is having a little chat with hunter-killer headquarters at Rathgeber. Help is coming. She'll stay in contact. Fisherman is catching leakage from an instel link.

Only Nicastro has anything to say. "That tears it. All we can do is haul ass. The bastards are going to get away with it. Command will have to send the heavies."

I seem to be the only one who hears him. The others keep watching the Old Man.

Nicastro has the shakes. He's perspiring heavily. He wants out of this deathtrap.

The Commander thumbs a comm key. "Engineering, this is the Commander. Indefinite Climb alert. Emergency Climb at any time. Mr. Varese, prepare an analysis of your drive synch. Send me the graphs when you're ready. Understood?"

"Understood, Commander."

Nicastro wilts. The others sit a little straighter. Carmon grins. The Old Man hasn't quit. He's got an angle. He's going to have a try.

Fisherman mumbles something incantatory, probably to benefit the souls of the gentlemen of the other firm. He has a faith in the Old Man almost equaling his faith in Christ.

Westhause makes a merry chase of it, stuttering in and out of hyper in little flicks almost too quick to sense. His chase baffles me. Hours pass. Still he dances round the Leviathan and her deadly brood. Not once does he hold norm long enough for a missile to target.

The quarry's tactics compel her simply to coast, watch, and wait for help.

"How far is Rathgeber?" I ask Fisherman.

He shrugs. I look for someone who can tell me. The Commander, First Watch Officer, and astrogator are all busy. So are the computer and radar people.

I become more baffled. It's obvious that we can do nothing. Nothing is what we're doing. Loathsome as it seems, Nicastro's suggestion is the only viable course.

So why is everyone busy? Will the Commander get even by ambushing the first destroyer?

That wouldn't please Command. Engaging escorts is considered a waste of kill capability. That's supposed to be employed against the logistic hulls moving men and materiel toward the Inner Worlds, or against the big warships making it difficult for Navy to stand its ground.

The computer keeps humming. Rose and Canzoneri push hard, though they seem unsure what the Commander wants. Every sensor strains to accumulate more data on the Leviathan.

The Commander breaks his conference long enough to tell Carmon, "Erase the tank display."

Wide-eyed, Carmon does as he's told. This is a big departure from procedure. It leaves us flying blind. There's no other way to bring all the information in a single accessible picture.

"What the hell are they doing?"

Fisherman shrugs.

The Old Man tells Carmon, "Ready for a computer feed."

"Aye, sir."

Rose and Canzoneri pound out silent rhythms on their keyboards. The tank begins to build us a composite of the Leviathan, first using the data from the identification files, then modifying from the current harvest. If reinforcements give us time, the portrayal will reveal every wound, every hull scratch, every potential blind spot.

It looks something like a moth with folded wings and grasshopper eyes. Those wings are two hundred meters thick. Their backs provide a landing platform where smaller warships can be tended by the Leviathan's regiments of technicians. A few hulks are piggybacking now. Presumably, more casualties from the same action.

Twelve long, quiet, maddening hours pass. I wonder what they're thinking over there, watching us stick like we're hooked on a short rod, maybe looking confident, maybe like we're just waiting for the rest of the gang to show. They have to be running their computers ragged trying to figure our angle, trying to find the soft spot we noticed, trying to dream up a way to pry us out of our safe spot.

The men lean into it for the first few hours, figuring the Old Man does have an angle. They slacken with time. Soon they're squabbling and grumbling. They're tired and beginning to think the Commander's effort is just for show.

Eventually the display tank contains an exact replica of our target, hitchhikers and all.

I have no inkling of the insane scheme hatching from the half-rotten egg in the mare's nest of the Commander's mind. Only a pale Westhause and shaky Yanevich are privy to The Plan.

The Old Man breaks away from the astrogator and climbs to his cabin.

His departure is a signal for discontent to be voiced. Only Fisherman, Yanevich, Westhause, and I have nothing to say. And Nicastro, who's too unpopular to hazard an opinion. Tempers have frayed to a point where neither the eido, Recorder, nor Commander himself constitutes a force sufficient to keep the lid on.

Too much momentum developed all that time screwing around? Just pent-up frustration building since we lost Johnson? I get a fat ration of fighting stares simply because I'm a friend of the Old Man.

In a less disciplined service this moment would be the first step toward mutiny.

The Commander returns, resumes his post beside Westhause. With studied casualness he produces the infamous pipe and loads it. Little dragon's tongues of blue smoke soon curl between his teeth, drift through his beard.

The old hands fall silent. They apply themselves to their work. He's given a signal.

"All hands listen up. This's the Ship's Commander. We're about to engage. Weapons, discharge your power accumulators. Ship's Services, vent heat and stand by on converters. I want internal temperature down to ten degrees. Engineering, I remind you that you're on standby for Emergency Climb."

He puffs his pipe and surveys the Operations crew. They avoid his gaze.

He's going up. Why? The hunter-killers haven't shown. They shouldn't for a while yet. Rathgeber is a long fly.

"Initiate your program, Mr. Westhause."

The ship ceases its endless hop, skip, and jump. A flurry of orders and their echoes fly. Weapons discharges accumulators. Ship's Services lowers internal temperature till I wish I'd brought a sweater. We make a brief hyper fly.

"Right down our throat!" Berberian shrieks. "Missiles..."

"Radar! Compose yourself."

"Aye, sir. Commander, missiles bearing..."

The collision alarm shrieks. Those missiles are close! That alarm is never heard except during drills.

"Emergency Climb," the Old Man orders, immune to the near-panic around him. "Take her to twenty-five Bev. All hands, be prepared for sudden maneuvers."

I haven't the slightest idea what's happening. I don the safety harness I'm supposed to wear whenever I'm on station. It seems a wise course.

The Commander gets a firm grip on a frame and thwartships brace. His pipe is clenched in his teeth, belching a noxious fog.

The Climber trembles as a missile detonates near her Hawking point. Internal temperature rises a degree.

"That was close," Fisherman murmurs. "Very close." He's pale. His hands are shaking. Moisture covers his face.

"Stand by," the Commander says.

The ship lurches as if punted by some footballer god. Metal squeals against metal. Plug-ups skitter like maddened butterflies. A barrage of loose articles slams around the compartment. A plastic telltale crystal pops off my board, smacks me over the eye, then whistles off to dance with the rest of the debris.

Internal temperature screams up forty degrees in a matter of seconds. The change is so sudden and severe that several men collapse. The converters groan under the load and begin bringing it down.

Coolly, Westhause keeps moving ship.

"Take us down!" the Commander bellows. "Take us the hell down."

Five men are unconscious in Ops. Another dozen have collapsed elsewhere. The ship is in danger.

The Commander shuffles men to the critical stations.

A thermometer near me shows mercury well into the red zone. The converters alone won't get it down in time to prevent shock to the supercold systems. Venting heat externally is our only option.

The Climber goes down with sickening swiftness.

"Vent heat!" the Commander thunders. "Goddamnit, Bradley! Anybody down there. Move!"

Red lights on every board are howling because the superconductors are warming.

Fuck the superconductors. Cool *me* off…. I never thought of heat as physically painful. But this… My head throbs. My body feels greasy. I've sweat so much I have a calf cramp. It takes all my concentration to keep my eyes on my screen.

Stars appear. "Oh!" A comet of fire spills across them, splashing the track of the Main Battle with blinding death. Glowing fragments pinwheel around the main glory, obscuring and overshadowing the background lights. She's millions of kilometers away and still the brightest object in the heavens.

The fire begins to fade.

I check my cameras. Hurrah! I turned them on.

A thought wanders through the aches and pains. That has to be the aftermath of a fusion chamber eruption. How did the Commander manage it?

The compartment cools quickly. As it does I come out of my universe of agony. My horizons expand. I discover the Commander snapping an endless series of questions into the inboard comm. The first I register is, "How long till you get it stabilized?"

I prod Fisherman. "What's happening?" The kid seems not to have noticed the heat.

"Sounds like we've got an oscillation in our CT magnetics," he croaks. His body took it well, but his soul is in bad shape. He's got the morning-after shudders. His face is the color of a snake's belly. He and I and the Commander seem to be the only Ops people able to do any useful work. I drag out of my seat and try to lend a hand at something more important than visual scan.

It occurs to me that Fisherman is scared not because of the Climb, nor because of the danger of a CT leak. He's locked into his own mad dread of another entombment aboard a crippled ship. This one the other firm would find first.

He's of little use on the tachyon board, so I point him toward Rose's station and tell him to get a gradient on the supercoolers for the superconductor system. That'll keep him too busy to think.

The temperature is dropping faster. The scrubbers and blowers are throbbing, pulling the moisture out and moving the air around. Most of my discomfort is gone.

Worry about Fisherman diverts my own impulse to panic. Having put him on the compute board, and having started Westhause's board on automatic recall, I make the rounds of the men. That's the most important job left. The Commander is handling everything else.

They say my behavior is common to Climber people. They worry about their shipmates before themselves. I've heard it called the unit/family response.

Yanevich is first to revive. I divert him with questions. He answers one, "We're the legion of the damned. All we've got is each other. And a universal contempt for Command types who sentence us to death by putting us in Climbers. I'm all right now. Let me go. Got work to do."

I still don't know what happened. They don't want to bother explaining…. It hits me. The Commander spent all that time refining his calculations so he could run our Hawking point through the Leviathan's fusor. Sure. No wonder we got rattled around. Our full mass hit their magnetic bottle at point-four c.

Amazing. And we hit it first try.

And came near killing ourselves, too.

The Commander's was a superb move. As a surprise tactic. On any other grounds it was sheer idiocy. Would he have tried it again had he missed first shot?

Probably not. Even the old hands don't have the nerve to go into that with their eyes open.

Later, over an emergency cup of coffee, I ask the Commander, "Would you have taken a second crack?"

He slides off the subject. "You took it pretty good. Didn't think you were that tough."

"Maybe I'm used to more heat."

He slugs his coffee back and leaves without saying another word.

New tension grips the ship. She can't Climb till Varese gets his magnetic containment systems stabilized. The hunter-killers are closing in.

Fisherman is the center of attention. His board remains pleasingly silent.

Dead in space. Seven hours. Varese hasn't reestablished the balance among several hundred minuscule current loads in the CT containment fields. The field control superconductor circuitry suffered localized overheating.

Time drags—except when I calculate how long it's been since the Leviathan yelled for help. Then it seems time is screaming past.

We're still at general quarters. The friends of our retired friends could turn up any minute. They've had long enough to get a fast attack destroyer from Rathgeber here and back again.

The honeybuckets are getting the best of the atmosphere systems.

I'm scared. Goddamned scared. It's bloody murder, sitting here unable to do a thing.

The Commander keeps growling at Varese. How long? I can't hear the reply, but it's noncommittal. The Old Man tells Piniaz to charge accumulators. He's getting ready for a shoot-out in norm.

Damn! If I weren't keeping notes, keeping somewhat occupied, I'd scream. Or do like Nicastro. The Chief runs around like an antsy old lady, driving everyone crazy with his fussing.

I'm continually amazed by how these men take their cue from the Commander's slightest action or remark. Already they're steeling themselves for hard times to come. You can see it in the way they stand or sit. I'm getting a little better feel for the Old Man.

While the screws are tightening he doesn't dare scratch at the wrong instant.

A lot of pressure would come down on a man who became too conscious of that.

It's easier for a Ship's Commander aboard a normal ship. He has his quarters. He isn't on display all the time.

As tired as we are, we won't make much of a showing if the other firm catches up.

Varese still reports unsatisfactory stabilization after twelve hours. That's a lot of getaway time lost. Suddenly, Fisherman shouts, "Commander, I have a tachyon pattern."

I lean and check his screen before the crowd thickens. The pattern is alien. Definitely alien. I've seen nothing like it before. The Commander orders, "Power down to minimum, Mr. Varese."

The Climber drifts in the track of the destroyed warship. Her neutrino emissions are a candle in the conflagration of the wake.

Running is pointless. The other firm can detect us if we can detect them. The hyper translation ratios of their hunter-killers exceed those of our Climbers. Swiftness is the critical element in destroyer design.

We can't run. The Commander won't go up till the magnetics are stable. So we'll pretend we're not here.

The odor in Ops grows thicker. Tempers grow shorter. Only Fisherman, preoccupied with his board and prayers, maintains his equanimity.

He is, I suspect, secretly delighted at the prospect of a quick out. Here's a chance for an early encounter with his God. Hey! Big guy in the sky! How about disappointing the silly sack of shit?

The hunters skip here and there, watching and listening. Sometimes they charge right past us, keeping Fisherman's detector chirping like a crickets' convention.

"At least eight of them," he says, after they've been rooting around for three hours. "They look hungry."

"That's a lot of firepower just to keep a second-rate writer from getting a story."

The joke falls flat. He says, "Not much else for them to do, sir. No convoys to watch."

The hunters are stubborn and crafty. One destroyer, doing mini-jumps along the course of the Main Battle, skips right over us. Pure luck saves us being detected. Another, creeping round in norm, gives herself away only because she hasn't powered down enough to conceal her neutrino emissions adequately. Like us, she's running with sensors passive. Active radar would nail us in an instant.

The hours roll on. Men fall asleep at their posts. Neither the Commander nor the First Watch Officer protests.

Each time I begin to relax, thinking they've moved on, another of their ships whips into detection. I can't sleep through that.

"How come they keep on?" I wonder out loud. "You'd think they knew we're here. That they want to spook us."

"Could be," Yanevich says. "The Leviathan might have gotten some boats away, too. They could be looking for survivors."

Not bloody likely. Not at those velocities.

Yanevich and the Commander are spending more and more time with Westhause. Their faces reflect a deepening concern. The Leviathan's wake is dispersing. It won't mask us much longer. Canzoneri keeps coming and going. The computers must've noticed something else.

I stop the First Watch Officer during one of his forays into my part of the compartment. "What's up? Why the long faces?"

"They're going to get a fix pretty quick. They've been taking readings on our neutrino emissions from before we went silent. Their computers will figure it out. We'll have them in our pockets."

"Damn. Should have known. The ripples never settle in this pond, do they?"

"Nope. They just keep going till they get mixed in with other ripples."

"So what's to do?"

"We run first time it looks good. They know we're around. There's no way we're going to bluff them, even if they can't computer-fix us. They'll keep quartering till they get a radar contact."

"Stubborn bastards. How'd they catch on?"

"Who knows? Maybe the Leviathan had an observation drone in her missile screen. Or an escort we didn't spot. Anything. How doesn't matter."

Fifteen minutes later we have one of those rare moments when there's nothing in detection.

"Power up," the Commander orders. "Engineering, stand by for hyper and Climb." Varese has the magnetics close to stable. Looks like the Old Man is willing to take a chance.

"Case like this," Fisherman says, "it's better to Climb first, then run. Unless they've got somebody doggo right on top of us, they won't get a track on our Hawking point."

"We'll make a hell of a racket getting started. And draw a hell of a crowd of mourners if Mr. Varese doesn't have the magnetics right."

"Yes sir." He isn't especially worried.

There's a rush to the honeypots. We may stay strapped in for hours.

How much longer can I stand their stink?

"Discharge accumulators. Vent heat. Secure all Class Two systems," the Commander orders. Acknowledgments and action-completed reports come back as quickly. People are anxious to leave. "Mr. Varese. How do your magnetics look?"

I don't hear the response. That's not reassuring.

"Commander, I have a tachyon pattern," Fisherman says.

"Very well. Engineering, shift to annihilation."

The feathers on Fisherman's screen are faint but nearly vertical. Their foreshortening is extreme. The dorsal and ventral lines are almost invisible. The hunter is coming right at us.

The Commander says, "Take hyper. Max acceleration. Mr. Westhause, make a course of two seven zero at thirty degrees declination." His voice is calm, as if this is just another drill.

The Climber stutters, moves out. The compartment lights dim momentarily. The hasty shift in power is touchy but successful. The Climb alarm tramples the Commander's line. Afterward, he adds, "Mr. Westhause, make your course two four zero at twenty-five degrees declination."

"Type two fool 'em, sir," Fisherman explains. "Show them a course they can fix and hope they think you'll swing way off it in Climb. We'll make a little change instead, and stay up a long time. They're supposed to look everywhere but where we're at."

"Supposed to?"

"We hope. They're not stupid, sir. They've been at it as long as we have."

My companions grow hazy. The screens and display tank die. The nothing of null peers in through the hull.

We've pulled our hole in after us. We're safe. For the moment.

For the moment. The destroyer has yelled "Contact!" Her friends are closing in. Their combined computation capacity is producing predictions of our behavior already.

Despite Fisherman's prophecy, I'm startled when the Commander doesn't go down after the customary hour. All those drills... wake up, monkey! This is for real. There're people out there who want to kill you.

The air is raunchy. Interior temperature has climbed a half-dozen degrees. The Old Man's only response is to have Bradley release a little fresh oxygen, then blow the atmosphere through the outer fuel tanks.

They've been allowed to freeze. Supercold ice makes a nice sink for waste heat.

It isn't a ploy which Command approves. Climbers aren't engineered for it. Our air is rich with human effluvia. It'll contaminate the water as it melts.

Operational people don't care. Heat is the bigger problem. They willingly strain the filters with contaminants.

It takes only five hours for that water to match interior temperature. The ship is generating too much heat.

The Commander lets temperature approach the red line. We're sweltering. The superconductors flash warnings, but they do so long before any actual danger.

The air feels thick enough to slice.

The Commander orders heat converters and atmosphere scrubbers activated at hour nine in Climb. From then on, in my humble opinion, it's all downhill.

The machines which hold temperatures down and keep the air breathable are efficient and effective, but are powerful heat generators themselves.

This heat isn't the sudden, shocking heat we experienced when the Main Battle died. This is a creeping heat. It comes on as inexorably as old age. Weariness doesn't help when one is battling its debilitating effect.

The Climb endurance record is fourteen hours thirty-one minutes and some-odd seconds, established by Talmidge's Climber. Talmidge commanded one of the early craft. It carried less equipment, fewer personnel, and entered Climb under ideal pre-Climb conditions.

Sitting here in stinking wet clothing, sucking a squeezie, unable to leave my station, I wonder if the Old Man is shooting for the record.

By hour eleven I'm toying with the notion of a one-man mutiny. The Commander's voice breaks through the mist clouding my mind. What's this? Hey! He's counting down to an emergency heat drop....

We'll plunge into norm, vent heat briefly, then get back up and see what our detection systems have to say about the habitability of this neck of the night.

"Isn't he a little too cautious?" I croak at Fisherman. The TD operator is barely sweating. "They can't have stayed with us this long."

"We'll see."

From the corner of my eye, while I'm watching the lances of the energy weapons discharging the accumulators, I see the weak *V* on Fisherman's screen.

"Contact, Commander. Fading."

"Very well. He'll be back. Mr. Westhause, we're making for Beacon One Nine One. Get out of here before he fixes our course. Drop us again as soon as we're beyond detection."

The emergency venting procedure lasted forty seconds. Each second bought about one more minute of Climb time.

Two hours roll past sluggishly. The Commander takes us down again. He's kept the ship up on pure guts. Throdahl, Berberian, and Laramie have gone slack in their harnesses. Salt tabs and juice only help so much.

This can't be doing our health much good.

It seems the more experienced men should handle the hardships easier. Not necessarily true. Nicastro is the next to go. Is it the cumulative effect of ten missions? Tension? The physical wear of hustling round seeing to everyone else?

Nicastro isn't quiet about going, either. He screams as sudden cramps tear at his legs and stomach. My nerves won't stand much of this.

I suspect the Commander wanted to stay up longer. Losing both his quartermasters changes his mind.

"Mr. Yanevich, work on Laramie and the Chief. Use stimulants if you have to. Junghaus, keep a wary eye."

"Aye, Commander." This time five minutes pass before he announces a contact.

"We're gaining on them," Yanevich tells me as he massages Nicastro's calves. There's barely room to lay the Chief out on the deck grating. The First Watch Officer grins like a fool. "Better get some salt into him." He shouts into the inner circle, "We have any calcium pills in the medkit?"

"Sorry, sir."

"Shit."

Westhause whips the Climber off at a wild angle. He asks, "Commander, you want to change beacons? They could get a baseline…."

"No. Keep heading for One Nine One."

Despite a temperature fit for making raisins, I'm shivering. Internal is down twenty degrees and falling. Humidity is a sudden ten percent.

"What are you fucking smirking about?" I snarl at Yanevich. And, "Shit! I'm getting as foul-mouthed as the rest of you. Anyway, seems to me that if the bastards can hang on this good, they'll run us down. How the hell do they do it, anyhow?"

Nicastro groans, tries to throw Yanevich off. The Commander helps hold him down.

"They've got a giant think-box at Rathgeber. Instel linked to all their hunters. Human brains cyborged in for subjectives. And nothing else for it to do. By now they know what ship this is, who's commanding, and how long we've been out. They've made an art of it. The head honcho at Rathgeber is sharp. And he gets better all the time."

"So why didn't we stay put and let them chase their computer projections?"

"Because that's the oldest trick of all. We would've come down in somebody's lap. See, our main problem is, we're outnumbered. They can follow up a lot of projections. They're probably working the top forty from that last contact."

"And we're not going to do anything about it?" Why is he so cheerful? That irritates me more than the other firm's stubbornness.

"Of course not. We don't get paid to slug it out with destroyers. We beat up on transports."

Next time down we vent heat completely, dispose of accumulated wastes, and take hyper before the opposition shows. We've shaken them. The Old Man says it was an easy routine. I find the assertion dubious.

I race for my hammock the instant he lets us off battle stations. The men who had difficulty getting through Climb are supposed to have first shot, but this time I'm taking advantage of my supernumerary status and my commission. I've had it. I can be a candy ass once in a while.

More than one man curses me for having my ass in the sink. I tell them what they can do with their personal hygiene.

No one has gone out of his way for me.

The last I see of the Commander, he's standing at a stiff parade rest, staring into the empty display tank.

Our destination proves to be an instel-equipped beacon. The Recorder busies itself reporting the Leviathan affair. It's a time of relaxation, a time of realization.

We still have our missiles.

7

ORDERS

The patrol is getting to me. I've been rude to or belligerent with almost everybody today. I have a lot of fear and nervous energy pressure-bottled inside me.

I'm not the only Sam Sullen. I see fewer smiles, hear fewer jokes. The tone of the crew is quieter. There's an unmentioned but obvious increase in tension between individuals. There'll be a fight before long. Something has to act as a valve to relieve pressure.

I'll hang around Ops till it happens. I don't want to be part of the process. The Old Man's inhibiting effect makes Ops the safest place to be.

Piniaz has the watch when I arrive. The Commander is on hand. Command has responded to our report. Finally.

"The sons of bitches," Piniaz growls.

The Commander hands me a message flimsy. It's a congratulatory message. Over Tannian's chop.

"Not one goddamned word about Johnson," Piniaz mutters. "The brass-bottomed bastards. Be the same fucking thing when we get ours. Some sad sack of shit will move us to the inactive file, wait a goddamned year, then send the regret-to-informs."

Nicastro gives Piniaz a poisonous look. His hands are shaking and white.

"Goddamned printout form letter, that's what they send. Full of Tannian's bullshit about valiant warriors making the supreme sacrifice. Jesus. Talk about insensitive."

I get in the way as the Chief lets fly. Startled, he pulls the punch. I tap him back and ask, "How are they hanging, Chief?" He settles into an embarrassed calm.

Piniaz missed the swing, but catches enough of the postmortem to understand. He cans the bitching.

Too many eyes missed nothing. Word gets around.

Maybe this will give me my breakthrough. One ordinary occurrence, entirely unplanned. After all that time trying to engineer something.

The Commander is first to mention the incident. In private, of course. "Happened to notice something odd this morning," he says, between sips of coffee brewed to spice another of our sparring sessions.

"Uhm? I doubt it."

"Doubt what?"

"That you *happened* to do anything. You choreograph your breathing."

He permits himself a weak, weary, sardonic smile. "You handled that pretty good. Could have caused trouble. Ito would've insisted on his prerogatives." He goes to work on his pipe. "You always were good at that. Guess I'll have to chew the Chief." He finds whatever it is that displeases him about the pipe's bowl, returns the instrument to his pocket.

"Sometimes a patrol goes sour after a fight. Just gets hairier. Like moral gangrene. Between officer and enlisted is bad. Turns the crew into armed camps." He reaches for the pipe, realizes he's fiddled it half to death already. "You bought some time. Maybe the Chief will take a look at himself now." After a pause, "Guess I'll tell department heads to lean on the big-mouths."

I can imagine the potential for disaster. A blow struck relieves pressure but plants a seed. Establishes a precedent. We need some sort of distraction. Pity there's no room anywhere for athletics.

"You might suggest that Mr. Piniaz be less abrasive."

His eyebrows rise.

"I know. He just said what we're all thinking. It's not *what* he said. It's the way he said it. It's the way he says everything."

Still he says nothing.

"Damn it, the man doesn't have to keep proving he's as good as everybody else. We know it. That Old Earther shoulder chip is going to get his head twisted."

"Could be me doing it, too. I'm tired of it. But what can you do? People will be what they are. They have to learn the hard way."

He's been leading me along. I figure it's time to punch back. "And you? What's your chip? What's eating you?"

His face darkens like an old house with the lights going out. He gulps his coffee, leaves without answering. I don't think to call after him.

Kriegshauser materializes immediately, ostensibly to clean up.

But he has something on his mind. He makes a production of the simple task.

I've barely tasted my coffee. "You drink this stuff, Kriegshauser? Want the rest? Go ahead. Sit down." I'm sure he gets his sips off each batch. Real coffee is too great a temptation.

"Thank you, sir. Yes sir. I will."

I wait, unsure how to draw him out. Like everyone else aboard this mobile asylum, the real Kriegshauser is well hidden.

He finds his nerve. "I've got a problem, Lieutenant."

"Yes?"

Kriegshauser chomps his lower lip. "Sex problem, sir."

"Ah?" It's hard to disbelieve the claim that he never bathes nor changes his underwear. His personal mass must consist entirely of deodorant and cologne. He reeks.

"This's my fifth patrol on this ship."

I nod. I know that much.

"They won't let me off. I've put in."

What does that have to do with boy-girl? Maybe nothing. Few of us are direct.

"There's this other guy that's been on, too…." It gushes. "Been trying to get me to make it. Putting on pressure. Kept my requests from going through. That's why I don't wash. It's not for luck, like the guys think. Anyway, he's got me against the wall."

"How so?"

"There was this girl, see? Leave before last. Said she was eighteen. Well, she wasn't. And she was a runaway."

So? I think. The universe festers with unhappy people. Too many of them are children.

"She was using me to get at her parents."

"Uhn?" That happens. Far too often.

"I found out last leave, when I tried to look her up. Her parents are big in Command. And they're out for blood. The kid jobbed me, but they think I did her. When they caught up with her, she was too far gone for an abortion."

"You sure it was you?" That's a reasonable question considering the situation on Canaan. Anger darkens his face. I change the subject. He cares about the girl. "This other party found out?"

"Yes sir. And if I don't come across, he passes the word on me."

Sexual harassment? Here? It's hard to credit. "Why tell me? I could be the eido. I could put it in my book. Or I could pass the word myself. Don't officers always stick together?"

"Got to talk to somebody. And you don't finger people."

Wish I was as sure of me as he is.

An advice columnist I'm not. As bad as I've screwed up my own life, I'd be a positive peril counseling anyone else. "Is he bluffing?"

"No sir. He's tried petty shit before. Did it to my friend Landtroop."

"How about you just tell him you'll kick the shit out of him if he don't back off?"

"I'd be bluffing."

I nod. That's understandable. We're military and at war. And the thought of personal violence is repellent. An act like Nicastro's occurs only under stress. People are schooled from childhood to contain their animal violence. Society does a fine job. Then we take the kids and make them warriors. We're a curiously contrary breed of ape.

"The damage would be done already, wouldn't it?"

"I suppose. But what would happen if he did talk? We're talking staff-type parents, aren't we?" Staff people are in a position to exact agonizing bureaucratic revenges.

"I don't want to find out, sir. I just want to get my ten, get laid in between, and get the hell out when I can. Maybe move to a training billet."

Few Climber people expect to survive the war. Most suspect they're playing for the losing team anyway. All they want to do is survive.

This is a strange kind of war. No end in sight. No out till it's over, unless you're torn up so bad you're good for nothing but dog food or sitting by the window at the veteran's hospital. None of that hope for tomorrow which usually animates the young. It's a war of despair.

"That's what you stand to lose. What about him?"

"Huh?"

"It can't be all one way. Isn't he vulnerable too?" I feel like an ass, playing games with people's lives. But I asked for it. I made a deal with Mephistopheles. You can't be selective about getting into lives. I want to know and understand the crew. The cook is one of them. There'll be no understanding him without dealing with his problem. Otherwise he'll remain a simple human curiosity, a bundle of odd quirks.

"Not that I know of, sir."

"Let's backtrack. How did he find out about the girl?"

"I don't know, sir."

"Who'd you tell?"

"Just Landtroop and Vossbrink, sir."

"Landtroop? You mentioned him before."

"Kurt Landtroop. He was here last patrol. Went cadre. We spent our leaves together."

"The three of you?"

"Yes sir. What're you getting at, sir?"

"You talked to Voss? Ask him if he told anybody?"

"Why, sir?"

"If you only told two people, one of them told somebody else. I'd guess Landtroop. You said he was under the same pressure. You should make sure." He's being intentionally dense. Doesn't want to involve his friends, doesn't want to risk his faith in them. Maybe he figures he'll lose his best friend if he questions Vossbrink. A very insecure young man. "You need to isolate the leak. It could give you a handle. Get back to me after you talk to Voss. I'll think on it meantime."

"All right, sir." He isn't pleased. He wants miracles. He wants me to push a magic button and make everything right. It's a nasty little habit we humans have, wanting an easy way out. "Thanks for the coffee, sir."

"You're welcome." It would help if he could give me a name. I could corner the predator and threaten him with my book. Power of the press, what? But Kriegshauser won't reveal it. I don't have to ask to know that. The fear in him is obvious.

There could be a second side, too. We humans, even when we try, tend to tint the facts. Kriegshauser might be doing more than tinting.

My proposed book is a for-instance. I want to be objective. I plan to be objective. Of course. But how objective can I be? I saw little of Command and wasn't impressed by what I did see. I identify with the fighting men too much already. I'm too much tempted to ignore the reasons why they have to endure this hell....

I snort in self-mockery. I'm a powerful man. One reason these people won't open up is that they're afraid of what I'll do to them in print. So I'm a species of eido after all.

The occasional threat might have amazing results.

Yanevich says that clown Tannian has ballyhooed my presence since I boarded the Climber. He's promised all Confederation a report from inside, the true story of the everyday life of heroes. His PR people are good. Half the population will be waiting breathlessly. Oh, ye mighty megaConmarks, gather ye in mine account....

I think Fearless Fred is going to be pissed. I think he assumes I'll follow the Party line.

Can I really do it straight? I really am afraid I won't give the broader picture that shows *why* Command does things that make the men in the trenches furious.

My real coup, arranging participation in a Climber mission, didn't reside in getting the Admiral to agree. The man is publicity-mad. No, it was getting the predators senior to Tannian to guarantee not to interfere with what I write. I conned them. They think I have to show the warts or the public won't believe.

Maybe the coup isn't that great, though. Maybe they outsmarted me. Tannian's foes are legion, and bitter. A lot of them reside in Luna Command. The guarantees could be a ploy to discredit the popular hero.

I haven't found anything *but* warts. So many warts that an imp voice keeps telling me to hedge my bets, to be sure I get past not only Tannian but that coterie of Admirals eager to defame him.

After talking to Kriegshauser, I clamber into my hammock. It's been an exhausting few days.

The loss of Johnson's Climber finally rips through the shroud of more immediate concerns. I replay the entire incident, looking for something we might have done differently. And end up shedding tears.

I give up trying to force the gates of slumber and go looking for the cat. Fearless confesses this confessor. He's awfully patient with me.

He remains as elusive as the eido.

Despite the long, enforced proximity of the patrol, I've begun feeling lonely. I've begun detecting traces of the same internal desolation on other faces.

I'm not unique in remembering our sisters. The long, leave-me-alone faces are everywhere. It's a quiet ship today.

Our ship and Johnson's had an unofficial relationship for a long time, a romance that was a metal wedding, a family understanding. The two hunted and played together through a dozen patrols and leaves, beginning long before anyone in either crew came aboard. In the Climbers that makes an ancient tradition.

I find myself asking a bulkhead, "Do Climbers mate for life?" Will we, like some great, goofy bird, now go hunting our own demise? Have we become a rogue bachelor?

An inattentive part of me notes that the bulkhead has grown a layer of feltlike fur, like blue-green moleskin. I touch it. My finger leaves a track. I wander off, forgetting it.

In Engineering I find a surly Varese supervising two men cleaning the guts of a junction box with what smells like carbolic. "What's up?"

"Fucking mold."

I recall the moleskin wall. "Ah?" I don't see anything here.

In Weapons half the off-watch are scrubbing and polishing. The carbolic smell is overpowering. Here the fur is everywhere, on every painted surface. It has a black-green tinge. The paler green paint seems to be the mold's favorite snack.

"How the hell does it get in here?" I ask Holtsnider. "Seems it'd be wiped out going through TerVeen."

"They've tried everything, sir. Just no way to get every spore. It comes in with crew, food, and equipment."

Well. A distraction. Instead of pining about dead women, I can research mold.

It's an Old Earth strain that has adapted to Canaan, becoming a vigorous, fecund beast in the transition. Left unchecked, it can pit metal and foul atmosphere with its odor and spores. Though more nuisance than threat, it becomes dangerous if it reaches sensitive printed circuitry. The heat and humidity of Climb encourage explosive growth. Climber people hate it with an unreasoning passion. They invest it with a symbolic value I don't understand.

"Who won the pool?" I ask as I enter Ops, still having found no sign of Fearless.

Blank faces turn my way. These men are busy with mold and mourning, too.

Laramie catches on. "Baake, in Weapons. The little shithead."

Rose nods glumly, head bobbing on a pull-string. He says, "He only bought one goddamned slip. To get us to quit bothering him. Ain't that a bite in the ass?"

"Better get him to teach you his system," Yanevich suggests, with a heaviness that implies this scene has been played before. "You only need one when it's the right one."

"Useless goddamned electric moron." Rose kicks the main computer. "You screwed me out of a month's pay, you know that? What the fuck good are you if you can't figure out..."

Laramie and Throdahl bait him halfheartedly. Others join in. They start to show some spirit.

It's a distraction, the cut-low game. Not an amusement anymore. They go at it viciously, but no tempers flare. They're too drained to get mad.

Throdahl's comm gear *pings* gently. The games die. Work stops. Everyone stares at the radioman.

We're lying dead in space beside the instelled beacon. The rest of the squadron is parsecs away. We assume that we'll be ordered to catch up.

Command has other ideas. Only now does Fisherman tell me we've been awaiting special orders.

That little *ping* brings the Commander swinging down from his cabin, an ape in a metal jungle. "Code book," he calls ahead. Chief Nicastro produces the key he wears on a chain around his neck. He opens a small locker. The closure is symbolic. The box is hardly more than foil. A screwdriver could break it open.

The Chief takes out a looseleaf book and pack of color-coded plastic cards banded with magnetic stripes.

"Card four, Chief," the Commander says after a glance at the pattern on Throdahl's screen. He slides the card into a slot. Throdahl thumbs through the code book. He uses a grease pencil to decode on the screen itself.

Only the initial and final groups translate: COMMANDER'S EYES ONLY and ACKNOWLEDGE.

Muttering, the Old Man scribbles the text groups in his notebook, clambers back to his hideout. Shortly, a thunderous, "Jesus fucking Christ with a wooden leg!" rips through the compartment. Pale faces turn upward. "Throdahl, send the acknowledge. Mr. Yanevich, tell Mr. Varese to establish a lock connect with the beacon."

The beacon begins feeding a sector status update while he's talking. Our chase, kill, and escape has kept us out of the biggest Climber operation of the war.

The convoy that took so long to gather at Thompson's System is on the move. Second Fleet pecked at it and let it get away. In his grandiose way, Tannian has declared that none of those empty hulls will survive his attentions. One hundred twelve and one twenty are the estimates. Thirty-four Climbers are in the hunt. Every ship in three squadrons. Except ours and Johnson's.

"Shee-it," Nicastro says softly. "That's one hell of a big iron herd." His eyes are wide and frightened.

"Bet that escort figure goes up fast," Yanevich says.

"Hell. With that many Climbers they should take the escort first."

"Smells like a trap to me," I say. "With bait Tannian couldn't resist."

The fighting hasn't yet begun. Our brethren are still maneuvering into attack positions.

At first I think the Commander is upset because he's been ordered into the cauldron, too. Wrong. The sense of that is too clear. Instead, our orders are bizarre.

The Old Man explains over coffee, in the wardroom, with all officers present.

"Gentlemen, we've been chosen—because of our superb record!—to initiate a new era of Climber warfare." There's an ironic cast to his smile. He taps a flimsy. "Don't look at me. I didn't make it up. I'm just telling you what it says here. We're supposed to take advantage of the brawl back yonder." He jerks his head as if in a specific direction.

He doesn't pass the message around. He holds to the eyes-only rule. "A hint or two here that they had this planned all along. It's why we were off chasing that Leviathan. Johnson was supposed to go in with us."

"For Christ's sake," I mutter. "What the hell is it?"

He smiles that grim shipboard smile. "We're going to scrub the Rathgeber installations. Right when the other team needs them most."

Puzzled silence. Makes a strange strategic sense. With Rathgeber's backing the hunter-killers will have a field day, finding thirty-four Climbers in one small sector.

"Didn't we just get out of there?" I ask, more to break the silence than because I want to know.

"Sure. We were a couple of days away. Still are, on another leg of a triangle." He muses, "Rathgeber. Named for Eustaces Rathgeber, fourteenth President of Commonweal Presidium. Brought Old Earth into Confederation. Only moon of Lambda Vesta One, a super-Jovian, sole planet of Lambda Vesta." He smiles weakly.

"Been doing my homework. For what it's worth, the base started out as a research station. Navy took over when the research outfit lost its grant. The other firm picked it up during their first sweep."

The wardroom echoes, "But..." like a single-stroke engine having trouble getting started. The Commander ignores us.

"We'll hyper in to just outside detection limits. That and the other intelligence data we'll need will be assembled aboard the beacon. They have a printer. Then we Climb and move in. We go down, tear the place apart, and run like hell."

"What the fuck kind of idiot scheme is that?" Piniaz demands. "Rathgeber? We use our missiles up, we won't have anything to shoot back with while we're getting away. Hell, they've got fifty hunters ported there."

"Sixty-four."

"So how the hell do we get out?"

No one questions our ability to get in, or to smash the base. It's not a plum ripe for picking. I've been there. It's tough.

"Maybe Command doesn't care about that," Yanevich says.

"Nobody will be home but base personnel," the Commander counters. "This convoy operation will draw them off. Tannian isn't stupid. He figures it's a trap. So we give them what they want, then scrub Rathgeber so they can't take advantage. Hell, everybody's always saying it'd be a rabbit shoot out here if it weren't for Rathgeber."

It makes sense. The strategic sort of sense, where a chess player sacrifices a pawn to take a bishop. Rathgeber's loss would hurt the other team bad, just as we'd be bad hurt if Canaan went.

The Old Man continues, "I think the Admiral is counting on us to pull the escort off the convoy."

"Hitting them with rabbit punches," Bradley mumbles. He and I lean against a bulkhead, staring down at the in-group. "Threaten here, threaten there, make them drop their game plan."

"Right out of the book."

He shrugs.

The Old Man says, "Our problem will be ground and orbital defenses. Intelligence is supposed to give us what we need, but how good will the data be? Those clowns can't figure what side of their ass goes in back. Anybody ever been to Rathgeber?"

I wave a reluctant finger. "Yeah. A two-day stopover six years ago. I can't tell you much."

"What about defenses? You were gunnery."

"They'll have beefed them up."

"You look them over? How's their reaction time? They won't have messed with detection and fire control."

"What do I know?"

"What size launch window can we expect? Can we do it in one pass? Will we have to keep bouncing up and down?'

"I spent my time getting snockered. What I saw looked standard. Human decision factor. You'll get seven seconds for your first pass. After that you only get the time it takes them to aim."

"Very unprofessional. You should've anticipated. Isn't that what they taught us? Never mind. I forgive you."

I stare at the Commander. Why has he accepted a mission he doesn't like? He has the right to refuse.

No one suggests that.

They bitch about Command's insane strategies but always go along.

"Mr. Westhause, program the fly. We'll take hyper as soon as all the data comes through." He steeples his fingers before his face. "Till tomorrow, gentlemen. Bring some thoughts. I want to be in and out before this convoy thing blows up. Our friends are counting on us."

I smile grimly. He really hopes we get an extended leave out of this.

Is Marie in his thoughts? He hasn't mentioned her for a long time.

Wonder what she did after we left. By now she must think we're done. Our squadron is overdue. Command knows we're alive, but they don't keep civilians posted.

Varese keeps fidgeting. He decides to tell us what's on his mind. "We've been out a long time, Commander. We're way down on hydrogen and CT."

"Mr. Westhause, see if there's a water beacon on our way."

We haven't spent much time under pursuit, but a daily Climb routine draws steadily on our CT. Normal hydrogen is less of a problem. Some beacons maintain water tanks for in-patrol refueling.

That's the Engineer mentality surfacing. It compels them to start having seizures when fuel stores reach a certain level of depletion. The disease is peculiar to the breed. They've got to have that fat margin. In the bombards they got antsy when down by 10 percent. At 20 percent they kept everyone awake dragging their fingernails over the commander's door.

They want that margin "in case of emergency."

Varese is less excitable than most Engineers.

"We won't need much CT after we shake loose," the Commander muses. "We'll burn what's left going home anyway. We can pick up more water anytime."

Once a Climber concludes active patrol, she remains on annihilation till she has just enough left to sneak in to Canaan. Venting excess is too dangerous, especially near TerVeen.

A Climber is most vulnerable before CT fueling and after final CT consumption. Those are the times when she needs big brothers and sisters to look out for her. She's just another warship then. A puny, fragile, lightly armed, slow, and easily destroyed warship. Vulnerability is why she has a mother take her out to Fuel Point.

Climbers aren't sluggers. They're guerrillas. In the open they're easy meat.

Lieutenant Varese takes no reassurance from the Commander's confidence. Engineers never do. A wide streak of pessimism is a must in the profession.

"Any more questions?"

There are. No one cares to broach them.

The Commander allows us to board the beacon. I go through the hatch just to see how those people live.

Holy shit! Fresh faces! Clean faces. Well-fed, smiling faces, with welcomes for the heroes of the universe. Gleaming, apple-cheeked babies. But no women, damn it.

We look like prisoners lately released from a medieval dungeon. Sallow, gaunt, filthy, wild of hair and eye, a little tentative and timid.

Damn! There really are other people….

Right now, the first few minutes, while we're staring at the beacon crew, I feel a fresh wind blowing on our morale. It's a cool gale driving away a poisonous smog. Some of the men grin, shake hands, clap backs.

There's a shower! Rumor says there's a shower! These boys must live like maharajahs. Crafty old me, I disguise myself as a great spacedog and con one of the lads into showing me the way. I'm first man there. Hot needles nibble and sting my crusty skin. I bellow tuneless refrains, luxuriate in the warmth, the massagelike effect.

"Hurry up in there, goddamnit! Sir."

Shouldn't be a pig, should I? There's a line out there now. "One minute." Grinning, I thunder out the "Outward Bound." Several men threaten to make it a shower I'll remember the rest of a very short life.

They have sinks, too. Several of them. Men line up there too, shaving. Don't think I will, though. I'm used to mine now. Completes the spacedog disguise.

Tarjan Zntoins, a Missileman, begins hopping about in a parody of an old-time sailor's hornpipe while his compartment mates honk and hoot, using their hands as instrumental accompaniment.

Not bad. Not bad at all.

The beacon is a one-time Star Line freighter. Big mother. Only the quarters are in use these days. The crew of nine have been out here four months. They're eager for fresh faces, too. Their long vigil is lonely, though never as harrowing as ours. Their tachyon man tells me he's been in beacons since the beginning. He's had only two contacts in all that time.

They're overdue for relief. Three months is their usual stint. A converted luxury liner makes regular rounds, changing crews each three months. Something is happening, though. Command has withdrawn the liner.

They're hungry for news. What's going on? How come they've been extended? Poor bastards. In continuous contact with Command and kept constantly ignorant. I tell them I don't know a thing.

Great guys, these people. They put on a spread. A meal fit for a king. Command didn't skip the luxuries here.

The mess decks are small. We wolf our feast in shifts, dallying and stalling while our successors curse us for farting around.

One last trip to the can. Isn't this great? No waiting. I take another look at my beard. I look like a real space pirate. Like Eric the Red, or somebody. I give it a big trim, to a nice point beneath my chin. There. Gives me the look of a pale devil. The girls will love it.

"Attention. Climber personnel. Return to your ship. Please return to your ship."

The holiday is over. "Up yours, Nicastro," I mutter.

On my way I stop by the beacon's vegetable crate of an office, liberate a half ream of clean paper. I'm tired of keeping notes on scraps.

Command's intelligence is astonishingly detailed. Tannian has had this raid in his trick bag a long time. The man is a little brighter than his detractors admit.

The orbital data for Rathgeber have been redefined to the microsecond and millimeter, finer than we need or can handle. We could make a setdown in null, using the data.

The defense intelligence looks just as good. Surface holo charts, which can be fed to the display tank, detail scores of active and passive systems, revealing their fields of fire and kill ranges. The companion fire control grids look as though they were lifted from Rathgeber's Combat Information Center. Alterations to the original Navy installation are carefully and prominently noted.

"We must have a guy on the inside," Piniaz chortles. He's delighted with the information.

"Bastards probably gundecked the whole thing," Yanevich counters. "Made it look solid so idiots like us would go in with smiles on our clocks."

"I doubt it," I say. "I mean, Tannian only looks like a prick of the first water. He'll throw lives around like poker chips, but I don't see him wasting many."

"For once we agree," Piniaz says. "This was put together right. And saved for the right time."

Yanevich won't flee the field. "Yeah? Wonder what the big brain had to say about our chances of getting out. Bet you won't find that in there anywhere."

I say, "Only thing I question is the need for the raid. And why they're sending a Climber."

Sourly, Yanevich says, "Fishing for propaganda points inside Navy. It's a job for the heavies."

"Regular units couldn't get past the orbital defenses," Piniaz snaps. "And maybe we don't know everything. Could be some other reason, too."

The Commander says, "Maybe it's occurred to them that this's a classic way to get rid of an embarrassment." He drives one hand into a shirt grown ragged with continuous wear, pauses momentarily. One eye narrows as he looks at me. A what-the-hell crosses his face. "Friend of mine slipped this into the intelligence dispatch." He throws out a piece of flimsy.

Yanevich snatches it. "Shee-it!" He flips it to Piniaz. Ito reads it, gives me an unreadable look, passes it on. It finally meanders around to me.

It's a typical Command press release, describing the Main Battle encounter. That the vessel we destroyed was crippled isn't mentioned. Neither is the loss of Johnson's Climber. The only outright untruths are improbable patriotic quotes attributed to my companions….

And to me. In fact, the whole damned thing is supposed to be my report from the front! "I'll kick that asshole right in the cocksucker!"

My juice squeezie ricochets off a bulkhead. "He can't do that to me!"

"Nice throw," Yanevich observes. "Smooth. No break in your wrist."

According to the release, I filed a report running, thematically, "Shoulder to shoulder... Heedless of the death screaming round them... United in their implacable will to exact retribution from the destroyers of Bronwen and plunderers of Sierra..."

"Shit. 'Shoulder to shoulder' is the only true thing here. Should've said asshole to elbow. Screaming? In vacuum? Where the hell is Bronwen? I never heard of it. And Sierra is such a nothing we didn't bother defending it."

Grinning, Yanevich intones, "'Driven by the justice of their cause...'"

Piniaz titters. "'Inspired by the memories of the slavery these vermin impose... Every man a hero...' Hey. You're one hell of a writer."

"Sure. When butterflies give milk."

"You saying I ain't a hero? I'll sue, you slanderer. I can prove it. Says so right here. If the Admiral says it, it's got to be true."

I can't take any more. I fling the flimsy at Bradley. "Here, Charlie. More toilet paper."

That goddamned Tannian. Just when I was starting to defend him. Issuing press releases over my name.

It's a kick in the head, that's what. I don't mind having my name spread all over Confederation. That'll help the book when it comes out. But I want the words by which I'm known to be my own.

I can cut my own wrists just fine, Admiral. Don't give me any help.

Maybe Johnson's fate and Command's failure to acknowledge it are making me a little touchy. I don't know. But these cockamamie reports have got to stop.

I suppose it's time to follow through on a project that's hung around the back of my mind for a month. From here on in I'll keep duplicate notes and have somebody smuggle them out. Let's see. Somebody to get them off the ship. Somebody to carry them down to Canaan. Maybe my friend the courier to carry them back to Luna Command...

First I have to survive this Rathgeber raid.

Right now, judging by this release, my assurances that I'll be allowed to write what I want are worth the paper they're written on.

The bastards. I'm going to pound it to them.

"Don't get your balls in an uproar," Varese sneers. "If you complain, they'll just look surprised and say it's what you'd've written if you'd really filed a report."

He's probably right.

The Commander agrees. "It would've come out the same. They've probably been publishing under your by-line since we left. You being out here is too good not to turn into a circus."

Yanevich says, "Wouldn't be surprised if they had an actor who does live holo reports."

"I'll give them reports. I'll write a bomb that'll blow the asses off those charlatans." I'm mad, yes, but I have only myself to blame. I should've seen this coming. I had enough clues. It was these dreadfully false-sounding releases that brought me snooping in the first place.

"Now, now," the Commander says. He grins a real old-time grin. "Just think what you'll have to say about the Rathgeber raid."

"I can't wait."

"They might not mention it," Yanevich says. "They haven't admitted losing the base."

"Little thing like consistency won't slow them down." The Old Man turns my way. "The spooky thing is, Tannian believes the shit he puts out. He keeps it up in private. He lives in a whole different universe. I'm going to get us through this. Whatever it takes. I want you to tell the real story."

"That would be nice." The anger is going. "Trouble is, people have been served bullshit so long they might not believe the truth."

Piniaz, Varese, and Bradley fidget. Westhause looks bored. They don't give a damn what the public believes. All that interests them is staying alive long enough to get out.

Do Yanevich or the Commander care? This may be a game of spit and roast with me playing the suckling pig.

"I divided the data into packets," the Commander says. On cue, Chief Nicastro appears with several folders. "Take yours. After we finish our hyper approach, I plan to order holiday routine. Be a meeting then. Bring your questions."

Holiday routine? Sounds like a mistake. Too many men getting too much time to think.

One man got too much time. Me. I ease into the wardroom in a near-panic.

I have this feeling that I've just moved to the one slot on death row. I've quit duplicating notes almost before starting. Why bother?

"Mr. Yanevich?"

"All go in Ops, Commander."

"Mr. Westhause?"

"Concur, Commander. Penetration program ready to run."

It better be. He calculated it often enough, trying to reduce the chance of error. He's good, this Westhause. Does that make me confident? Hell no. *Something* will go wrong. Murphy's law.

Chief Nicastro agrees. And the Chief doesn't suffer in silence till the Commander has him aside.

"Mr. Piniaz?"

"Go, Commander, though I'm getting minor stress indicators from the graser. They'll get four missiles, the accumulator banks, and whatever your friend can throw with his popgun."

I've been directed to operate the magnetic cannon. The Commander wants to hit them as hard as he can. The missiles will be targeted on Rathgeber's ship-handling facilities. The energy weapons are supposed to take out detection and communications facilities. The rest of the base is mine.

I've chosen the tower at the hydrolysis station as my first target. On follow-up passes I'll snipe at the solar power panel banks.

The Commander is contemplating three missile passes. None should last long enough for us to be targeted.

Why bother with the cannon? Even perfect shooting on my part will contribute little. The other firm can jury-rig some means of extracting hydrogen from water. The solar panels are there only as an emergency backup for the base fusion plant.

"Mr. Bradley?"

"Ship's Services go, Commander." He's cool. He doesn't understand what we're jumping into.

"Mr. Varese?"

"Commander, I'm damned short on fuel. If we have to..." He wilts before a basilisk glare. "Go in Engineering, Commander."

Does the Old Man have some special interest in this assignment? He looks willing to sacrifice ship and crew to prove Tannian incompetent.

Yet the only real fault of the plan is that this isn't a traditional Climber mission. Precedent is, perhaps, too important in Navy.

"You ready to go?" the Commander asks me.

"Of course not." My grin hurts. "Let me off at the next corner."

He frowns. This is no time for whimsy. "I'll go over it again. Down to fifty meters in null, over Base Central. Four seconds in norm. Missiles launch at one-second intervals. Cameras rolling. Energy weapons on continuous discharge. Same for the cannon. Then twelve minutes of Climb. That'll require fast target evaluation.

"Positional maneuvers in null will conform to lunar motion. We'll go norm again at the same point. Two seconds. Four missiles at half-second intervals. Energy weapons and cannon.

"Then thirty minutes in null for comprehensive evaluation and selection of final targets. We'll take an attack position suited to neutralizing the most important facilities remaining. Two seconds for the final salvo. Half-second intervals again. We'll then climb and evaluate.

"If the computer recommends it, we'll continue attacking with energy weapons. If not, we move out. I estimate our maximum attack window at two hours… If we're to escape the hunter-killers.

"Gentlemen, the actual attack looks like an exercise. I don't see how they can stop us. Getting away will be the problem. Questions?"

Again, scores are left unasked. Sometimes you'd rather not know.

"All right. Have the men take care of their business. We begin in a half-hour." He catches my arm as I start to go. "Don't miss a thing on this one. If we luck through… I want it all on the record."

"If? It's an exercise, remember?"

"The easy ones never are. Murphy's law operates on the inverse-square principle." He grins.

"I can't follow anything from the cannon board."

"I had Carmon bug Engineering and Ops for you. A plug for each pointy little ear. You'll hear everything. Have the men fill in any blanks later."

"Whatever you say." Resigned, I collect notebook and recorder and get in line outside the Admiral's stateroom. The place is drawing a crowd. There're all the usual cracks about taking a number, selling tickets, and using someone's pocket.

I finish with time to spare, so I visit Kriegshauser, who looks in need of encouragement, and Fearless. All the activity has the cat edgy. He knows its meaning. He's not fond of Climb. I even grab a few seconds with Fisherman. "I'm no good at praying. Say one for me, will you?"

"Ability has nothing to do with it, sir. He hears every prayer. Just accept Christ as your Savior and…" The alarm cuts him short.

The cannon board control chair seems harder than usual. I set out my notekeeping materials, start writing. My hand shakes too much. I concentrate on getting Carmon's talking earplugs into place. The hyper alarm sounds before I finish. I see Holtsnider looking my way, smiling nervously. I wave in pure bravado.

Climb alarm.

It's begun. We're on our way. I feel cold. Very cold. My pores are twisted into tight little knots. I'm shivering. Air temperature is down, but not that much.

It begins, as always, with waiting. The seconds grind slowly away. At hour two Westhause takes us down just long enough to make sure he won't have to fine-tune his approach. Rathgeber's sun is the brightest star.

There's nothing to do but think.

Are they keeping a close watch out there? Did they see us drop?

Just sitting here waiting for the walls to cave in. We're in the final leg of our approach. I have the cannon pre-aimed. I've gone through the numbers four times, just to have something to do.

Nothing is happening anywhere. The bugs are a waste. Except for occasional muffled remarks from the First Watch Officer or Commander, Ops could pass as a tomb. From Engineering there's nothing but Varese's occasional remark to Diekereide bemoaning the fuel situation. And, of course, the endless, repetitive, ritualistic status reports. Those I tune out automatically.

It's no different in Weapons, though it was livelier while they were arming, testing, and programming the first missile flight. The tests have been rerun and the programming double-checked. Done to death for something to do.

Just like an exercise. As the Commander promised.

So why are we all scared shitless?

"Five minutes." Nicastro is doing the time-scoring. His voice betrays as much humanity as that of a talking computer.

We must be close. Within a few kilometers of our point of appearance. We're playing mouse in the walls of the universe, looking for the perfect hole to the inside. A mouse armed to his cute little teeth.

It seems incredible that the other firm won't know anything till we start shooting. All my instincts say they'll be waiting with a megaton of death in each hand.

God, this waiting is shitty. The fear thoughts, the what ifs, keep chasing one another round my head like a litter of kittens playing tag. My palms are cold and wet. I keep moving slowly and carefully so as not to do anything clumsy. I don't want the others to see how shaky I am.

They don't look scared. Just professional, businesslike. Inside, though, they probably feel the way I do. I don't see how it can be helped. We're great pretenders, we warriors.

Shit. Almost time. God, get me through this one and I'll...

I'll what?

8

RATHGEBER

"Five. Four. Three. Two. One…"

My targeting screen comes to life. The cracking tower lies dead center amid the aiming rings. Sunlight washes a typical lunar landscape, all black and white and sharp-edged shadows on the bones of a world that died young.

"Away One," Piniaz sings. "Away Two."

A missile's exhaust scars the view on my screen. I hit my triggering key.

A lance of emerald hell, startling against the monochromatic background, slices a corner from the screen. It sweeps on continuous discharge, vaporizing rock and exposed plant. There's chatter in Engineering as they compensate for the surge of power being drained from the accumulator banks.

"Christ!" comes through from Ops at the same instant. "The bastard is right on top of us!"

"What?"

"Away Three," Piniaz chants. "Away Four. Klarich, what the hell is wrong here?"

A sewing machine stitches a line of black holes up the cracking tower an instant before my screen goes white with the violence of the first missile. It blanks. The bulkheads ghost.

Four seconds. It seemed much longer. Everything happened so slowly….

"Twelve minutes," Nicastro intones. "Commence target evaluation and selection."

We're safe now. Outside, lunar rock is boiling and fusing into man-made obsidian.

The Commander says, "Mr. Piniaz, reprogram one missile for above-surface pursuit. Berberian will give you the data. We had an incoming destroyer at eight o'clock."

Piniaz has problems of his own. "Commander, we've got a jam in the elevator on Launch Three. Looks like the lead dolly kicked back and knocked the mid dolly out of line. The Seven missile is against the well wall. Programming and command circuits have safety-locked."

"Can you clear it?"

"Not remote. I'll have to send some people out. Which target do you want dropped?"

"Forget the destroyer. We'll take our chances."

I slam my fist against my board. If we survive two more passes, we'll still have two missiles aboard.

The screen starts sending up target data. I sigh. Things look a little better. Indications are we got Rathgeber's comm center. They can't call for help. And the destroyer, which may have been crippled, was the only warship around.

I'm obsessed with going home. Home? Canaan isn't home. My personal universe has shrunk to the hell of the Climber and the promised land of Canaan. Canaan. What a choice of names. Whoever selected it must have been prescient. Odd. I consider myself a rational man. How can I make of the baseworld a near-deity?

Does this happen to all Climber people?

I think so. My shipmates seldom speak of other worlds. They don't mention Canaan that much, and then only in a New Jerusalem context. The quirks of the human mind are fascinating.

I see why they go crazy planetside. That business at the Pregnant Dragon wasn't *for tomorrow we die.* People were proving they were alive, that they had survived a brush with an incredibly hostile environment.

So. I'll have to adapt my behavioral models. I'll have to see where and how each man fits this new scheme. And the Commander? Is he a man for whom no proofs carry sufficient conviction? Is he a prisoner in a solipsistic universe?

"Sixty seconds," the good Chief says. Christ, twelve minutes go fast. I'm not ready for another plunge into the *hexenkessel.*

Alarm! I start, scattering notes. "Away Five."

I begin shooting immediately. I can't see the purpose, but any action holds the fear at bay. The movement of a finger makes work for body and brain for a fractional slice of time.

"Away Eight."

Climb alarm. "Thirty minutes. Commence target evaluation and selection."

"Magic numbers," I murmur. Seven and Eleven are the missiles that can't be launched.

"Eh?" My nearest neighbor gives me a puzzled look and headshake. The men think my brain was pickled by civilian life.

The bugs don't give me a thing. Engineering is a graveyard peopled by specters reciting rosaries to Fusion and Annihilation. In Ops, Yanevich observes that the destroyer weathered the first pass and was trying to run. The Commander's silence says this is no news to him. Nicastro ticks time in colorless tones.

Tension mounts faster than the temperature. Third time counts for all.

I amuse myself by nibbling tidbits of target evaluation data. Seven fusion warheads can do a hell of a lot of damage.

Molten rock and metal and people are quickening into concave black glass lenses. A billion days hence, perhaps, some eldritch descendant of a creature now wallowing mindlessly in a swamp will gaze on that lunar acne and wonder what the hell it means.

I wonder myself. What's the point?

Well, we can honestly say we didn't start this one.

Right now, with death a-stalk, the only question that matters is, How do we stay alive? The rest is foam on the beer.

The universe is very narrow, here in Rathgeber's shadow. It's a long, lonely hallway through which even close friends can do little to ease one another's passage.

Again the ship lies panting in the embrace of that cold-hearted mistress of Climber warfare, Waiting. Months of waiting. Climaxed by what? Eight scattered seconds of action. Damned minuscule flecks of meat in a huge, hard sandwich of time.

Almost indigestible.

My butt is driving me crazy. I can't count the times I've stayed seated longer, but those times I had the option of moving. Getting up could become an obsession. Got to move. Got to do something. Anything...

Nicastro's countdown grows louder and louder. The ass-agony vanishes. Death is a bigger pain. I have a sudden, absolute conviction of my own mortality.

The orbitals will have their guns out. That hunter-killer will be ready. She'll be laying back, a big iron bushwhacker eager for a dry-gulching.

Unless we were damned lucky and skragged her instel wave guides, she'll have howled for her packmates. They'll come whooping to avenge the base. We'll pull pressure off the squadrons stalking the convoy. I should be pleased with such success. But I can't get excited about the gospel according to St. Tannian.

The destroyers will be hours getting here. They'll be way too late to help Rathgeber. But I know they'll catch our trail. The way my life goes, it can't happen any other way.

Must be getting old. They say pessimism is a disease of the aged.

Here we go!

Missiles away. Energy weapons blazing. My little cannon sowing its seeds. There isn't much to see. The same old bleached bones of an aborted worldlet acned by ground zeros. The silhouettes of startled beings in spacesuits. They'll remain forever in my memory, taking one futile step toward cover.

Ghostdom returns with a ship-wide shudder.

"Commander." Varese is speaking. Softly, metallically. "A low-intensity beam brushed us on the upper torus, at plates twenty-four and twenty-five. Damage appears minimal."

"Very well. Keep an eye on it."

Damned well better. Let's not buy any trouble we could avoid with a little attention to detail.

I secure the cannon board, then bestow a negative blessing on our illustrious Admiral. His madman's game put us in this predicament. Being a pawn on a galactic chessboard wasn't what I had in mind when I asked on. The rewards are too small, except in pain and doubt.

"Secure from general quarters," the Commander orders. "One hour, gentlemen."

I exchange glances with Piniaz. This is an unprecedented breach of Climb procedure. The crew is supposed to remain at battle stations any time the ship is in Climb.

No one argues. We all need to move around, to interrupt tension with frivolous activity.

Yet work goes on. I'm the one man free to stray far from my station. I duck into Ops when the hatches open.

Fisherman hasn't moved, though in Climb he and his station are useless. Yanevich, more the butterfly than usual, flutters round the compartment. Westhause and the Commander hug the astrogation consoles. Already they're trying to outguess the hounds.

Rose, Throdahl, and Laramie have a tricorner game of *When I get back to Canaan* going. It ignores the fact that we have missiles aboard. They're banking on the elevator damage's being irreparable. The names, addresses, and special talents of loose women volley around, often accompanied by the hull numbers of the ships of the men who have primary claim to them.

Chief Nicastro is staying out of the way, imitating a statue. He moves just once that I see, to thumb a switch and announce, "Forty-five minutes."

I want desperately to badger the Old Man. Will he go norm and clear the elevator right away? Will he run as far and fast as he can? I can think of arguments for both courses.

He has no time to waste on me.

Time has turned its coat. It's gone over to the other firm. It's become their standard-bearer, almost. Whatever the Old Man decides, he has to do it quick. The death hounds are slavering toward Rathgeber.

No one has time for me. If they're not on station, they're busy scrubbing mold. They're losing themselves in ritual. I'll try Ship's Services and Engineering.

Same story. The Commander's ploy hasn't worked. After a moment of release, the men have grown tense again, retreating into themselves. Even Diekereide is stone-silent.

Trudging back, I note a lump in my hammock. "Where you been, fat boy?"

Fearless opens his eye, yawns, meows softly. I scratch his head listlessly. His purr has no heart in it either. "Going to be hard times," I tell him. He's getting lean. He's been on short rations lately.

Fearless is in one of his lonely moods. So am I. I'm a little hurt. They're shutting me out. We share a silent commiseration, the cat and I. My thoughts, when not lusting after hammock, wolf after other worlds, other times, other companions. I'm very sorry that I'm here.

The reporter, the observer, ideally, remains neutral and detached. However, I've altered the experiment simply by being here. I've tried to be both remote and intimate, both Climber man and reporter. I've failed. My shipmates, so young, came to Navy with near-virgin pasts. Trying to mirror their innocence, I've kept my own past fairly private.

And so I've been hiding from myself as well.

There with the cat, waiting and wishing I could sleep, I rediscover my once-had-beens and should-have-dones, the tortoise shell of pain and past all men drag with them forever.

A dam cracks. It begins as a leak…. I understand why so many mouths are sealed.

This ship is filled with a conviction of imminent death, tainted with only the slightest uncertainty.

Maybe now… Maybe in a few hours. The condemned man wants to order his life and explain everything. To, perhaps, make someone understand.

These men are just reaching their conclusions of condemnation. Maybe, now, I'll learn more than I ever wanted to know.

The conviction has hold of the Commander, I'm sure, though he hides it well. His face is more pale, his smile more strained, his primary expression the one you see before the body goes into the coffin.

This is a ship manned by zombies, by corpses going through life-motions while awaiting cremation. We died the moment that destroyer sent her call.

We know she did. Fisherman caught the leakover of an instel link during second attack.

Nicastro is listless because his revelation came early.

"Five minutes."

"Take care, Fearless." I'm sure we won't meet again. "Make yourself a home here." I ease him back into the hammock.

A syrupy silence has swamped Weapons. The gunners have had time to mourn themselves.

They don't seem afraid. Just resigned or apathetic. I suppose that's because they've been waiting for so long. Why panic in the face of the inevitable?

Fear is a function of hope. The bigger the hope, the greater the fear. There's no fear where hope doesn't exist. I park myself in Ops.

The general alarm sounds briefly.

"This's the Commander. We're going norm to clear a jammed missile elevator. EVA is required. All compartments will remain prepared for extended Climb. Mr. Piniaz, sustain your accumulators at minimum charge. Mr. Bradley, maintain internal temperature at the lowest tolerable level. Scrub atmosphere. Empty and clean all auxiliary human waste receptacles. Distribute combat rations for three days. Mr. Varese,

Mr. Piniaz, select your working parties. Suit them and brief them. Mr. Westhause, take us down when they're ready."

We go norm in the depths of an interstellar abyss. The nearest star flames three light-years distant. The universe is an inkwell with a handful of light motes populating its walls. It's a forceful reminder of the vastness of existence, of just how far beyond the Climber's walls other realities lie.

The constraints of concerted activity nibble away at the pandemic gloom. Embers of hope and fear begin to glow. My belief in my immortality revives. The big goal, survival, looks more and more attainable as the little problems come to successful conclusions.

When you think about it, how would God Himself find us amid all this nothing?

There isn't much for me to do. Visual watch is a waste of time. Fisherman will spot any traffic long before I could. To kill time I help Buckets with the honeypots. A minor morale builder. Having finished, I feel a sense of accomplishment. It segues over into the bigger picture. I get this feeling of having yanked old Death's beard with impunity.

The Seven missile is solidly wedged. A riser arm has to be removed from the lift linkage before the missile can be manhandled into proper alignment. The riser arm and related hardware then have to be reinstalled. Only afterward can the missile be elevated into the firing rack in the launch bay.

Piniaz wants to replace the entire riser assembly with another taken from the number two elevator. He's afraid the arm is warped and will jam again when he tries to elevate the Eleven missile.

"Negative," the Commander says to the proposal. "We're pushing our luck now. We can't stay put long enough. Use the old arm. How long for that?"

"Five hours," Chief Holtsnider says from Launch Three. The Chief doesn't belong out there. That's Missileman's work. Piniaz disagrees. He wants his best man on the job. He says Chief Missileman Bath doesn't have enough EVA experience.

"My ass, five hours. You've got two. Get done or walk home. Mr. Varese, your men just volunteered to help Chief Holtsnider. Two hours."

Varese had Gentemann and Kinder out examining the torus plates touched by the other firm's beam. They're in the lock, coming back. They do colorful things with the language when Varese tells them to turn around. I use my camera to watch them glide out the safety lines to Launch Three.

Kinder and Gentemann are Canaanites. They have homes and families. It doesn't seem right to risk them. Gentemann is a sensible choice, though. He's the ship's Machinist.

They realign the Seven missile in forty minutes. Eleven isn't jammed. It lifts to ready without difficulty. Holtsnider studies the riser arm. He says it should lift if it's properly adjusted.

"Commander!"

Fisherman's shout rocks the ship.

Junghaus has been distracted by the working party. He hasn't been watching his screen.

"Goddamned! That mother's really coming!" Throdahl yelps.

"Varese!" the Commander shouts. "CT shift. Mr. Westhause, all departments, stand by for Emergency Climb."

"Commander..." Varese protests. Five men are outside. Their chances are grim if they slip out of the field or the ship stays up long.

"Now, Lieutenant." I can't tell if he's growling at Varese or Westhause. The astrogator is the sick color of old ivory piano keys.

Fisherman's screen looks bad.

"Right down our throats. Couldn't miss us if they were blind." The Old Man has done his sums. He's balancing five lives against forty-four. The men won't like it but they'll live long enough to bitch. "Shitty fucking luck."

That damned ship is going to land in our pocket. Fisherman, where the hell was your mind? Why the shit didn't you have your buzzer on?

The frightened questions from the working party end abruptly when we hit hyper. Radio is useless here. Nor is there anything when we flash into the ghost abode. The men remain silent. They exchange guarded glances.

Holtsnider comes through on the intercom links used by inspection personnel in wetdock. A quick thinker, the Chief. His voice is calm. It has a relaxing effect.

"Operations, working party. Commander, how long will we stay in Climb?" Fear underlies Holtsnider's words, but he's in control. He's a good soldier. He sticks to his job and lets a narrow focus see him through the tight places.

"Give me that," the Commander says softly. "I'll cut it as short as I can, Chief. We've been jumped by a singleship. We'll drop back when we have her going into her turn. Be ready to come in. How're you doing out there?"

"I think we lost Haesler, Commander. He was clowning on tether. The rest of us are in the launch bay."

Poor Haesler. Floating free nine lights from nowhere. The ship gone. Must be scared shitless right now.

"How's your oxygen, Chief?"

"Manolakos is down to a half-hour. We can share if we have to. Say an hour."

"Good enough. Hang on." Mutedly, "Mr. Westhause, go norm as soon as your numbers show her going away."

"Fourteen minutes, Commander."

"We go norm in mikes fourteen, Chief," the Old Man repeats for Holtsnider's benefit. "We won't have a big window. Start Manolakos in now. Safety line him with the man next shortest on oxygen. The rest of you double-check that Eleven bird. Then start in too. Don't waste time. We're borrowing it now. We'll have to do some fancy dancing to pick up Haesler and dodge this singleship, too."

"Understood, Commander. I'll keep this line open."

"Balls!" Picraux growls, punching a cross-member. I can't tell if he's cursing the situation or commending Chief Holtsnider.

I've never heard of anyone's going outside in Climb. "Anyone tried this before?" I ask Yanevich.

"Never heard of it."

No one knows how far beyond the ship's skin the effect extends. It might slice the universe off a millimeter away. Anyone who leaves that launch bay stands a chance of joining Haesler.

Manolakos and Kinder are convinced that will happen.

Everyone overhears Holtsnider's half of the argument. The protests of his men are too muted to make out. They're communicating by touching helmets.

The discussion is bitter, embarrassing; and, I suspect, each of my shipmates is wondering if he'd have the guts to try it.

One of them breaks down. We hear him crying, begging.

"Holtsnider," the Commander snaps, "tell those men to move out. Tell them they have to do it this way or they don't have a chance at all."

"Aye, Commander." The Chief's tone makes it clear he doesn't like this any better than his men do. Moments later, "They're off, sir. Gentemann, get up there and make sure the bird's nose stays level when I start the lift cycle. Commander, looks like Seven jammed because the riser arm hydraulics didn't equalize. If it looks like the nose won't stay with the tail, we'll balance with the hand crank."

"Very well."

Once the handful of novels have been read, the drama tapes have been run to death in the display tank, the music tapes have been played to boredom, once the lies have all been told and the card games have faded for lack of a playable deck, Climber people turn to studying their vessels. To what we call cross-rate training, the study of specialties other than their own. Gentemann is an old hand. He can help the Chief without complicated instructions.

I've browsed a few Missileman's manuals myself. (Like most writers, I spend a lot of time avoiding anything that smacks of writing.) I could manage Gentemann's task myself. Not that I'd want to.

The mechanical drama continues. Concern for Kinder and Mano-lakos overshadows the inexorable march of time.

"One minute." Nicastro's voice shows some life. This is waking him up.

"Eleven's ready, Commander. She tests go all the way. We're coming in."

"Good, Chief. Hang on where you are. We're going norm. Scramble when we do."

"Aye, Commander."

The alarms play their cacophonous symphony strictly by the book.

"Mr. Varese, stand by the airlock." That has to be the most needless instruction I've heard all mission. Half the engineering gang will be there waiting. "Throdahl, you ready to fix on Haesler's beeper?"

"Ready, Commander."

We drop.

Holtsnider comes through on radio. "Commander, I don't see any suit lights. Have they reached the lock?" The lock, at the bottom of the Can, can't be seen from the torus.

"Over there, Chief," Gentemann says.

"Shit. Commander, they fell loose. They're drifting pretty fast. Okay. They've spotted us."

"Lights on," the Commander snaps.

Kinder's voice whispers, "There she is, Tuchol. Yo! I see you! I'm bringing us in on my jets."

Manolakos is babbling.

"Kinder, this's the Commander. What's the matter with Manolakos?"

"Just panic, sir. He's calming down."

"You see Haesler's lights? Anybody?"

"Not…"

Fisherman interjects an "Oh, goddamn!" startling everyone. "Commander, I've got another one. Coming in from two seven zero relative at forty degrees high. Destroyer."

"Berberian?"

"Singleship in norm, Commander. Tracking."

"She's coming in, Commander," Fisherman says. "We're fixed."

"Time?"

"Five or six minutes to red zone, Commander. In the yellow now." Red zone: optimum firing configuration. Yellow zone: acceptable firing configuration.

"Damned instel link with the singleship," Yanevich growls.

The Old Man thunders, "Holtsnider, get your ass in here *now!*"

"Commander, I've fixed Haesler's beeper," Throdahl says. "Nineteen klicks out, straight past Manolakos and Kinder."

"Commander, the destroyer is launching missiles," Fisherman says. "Double pairs. Multiple track."

"Time. Canzoneri."

Weapons has the missiles boarded but can do nothing to stop them. They're coming in hyper, will drop at the last second. The way a Climber beats that is maneuver. We can't maneuver. We're no Main Battle. We carry no interceptors. All the Commander can do now is Climb.

Piniaz orders the accumulators discharged again. He does so on his own authority. The Commander doesn't rebuke him.

"Throdahl, get on the twenty-one band and put a tight beam on that singleship," the Commander says. "Stand by for Climb, Mr. Westhause. Mr. Varese, do you have anyone up to the lock yet?"

"Negative, Commander."

A murmur runs through the ship. Men releasing held breath. The situation is tighter than I suspected. Looks like the Old Man is going to tell the other firm he has to leave people behind.

There's no policy, no agreement, but in those rare instances where something like this happens the other team usually honors the lifesaving signals—if they're heard over the tactical chatter. They're even kind enough to relay the names of prisoners taken.

Our side isn't always that polite.

"Holtsnider, where are you?"

"Coming up on the lock, Commander. Five meters more. I have Kinder and Manolakos with me."

"Damn it, man…."

"What's happening?" Kinder demands. He's been holding up. Panic now edges his voice. Manolakos is babbling again.

Chief Canzoneri says, "Commander, we're running out of time. We won't clear the fireballs if we don't go soon."

"Mr. Varese, get those men in here!"

Westhause has more guts than seems credible. He holds Climb till the last millisecond. A schoolteacher!

And still we go up without the Chief or Machinist, without Kinder or Manolakos or Haesler.

The walls mist. And Varese sighs, "Oh, shit. I can see Holtsnider…. He's trying to turn the wheel…. He's gone. Just seemed to fall off."

He falls, with Gentemann, Kinder, and Manolakos, into multiple fireballs. The ship bucks, rattles, and warms appreciably. They're shooting straight over there.

Pale faces surround me. Four men have reached the end of the line. Maybe Haesler was lucky.

"Think they'll count us out?" Westhause asks.

"Organics in the spectrum?" Yanevich counters. "I doubt it. Not enough metals."

"Evasive program, Mr. Westhause," the Commander snaps. "Take her up to fifty Bev." His voice is tightly controlled. He's become a survival computer dedicated to bringing the rest of us through.

His face is waxy. His hands are shaking. He won't meet my eye. This is the first he's ever lost a man.

"Too old a trick, waiting till the last second," Yanevich says. His voice sounds hollow. He's talking just to be doing something. "They won't buy it anymore."

"I wasn't trying to sell anything, Steve. I was trying to save four men." Westhause too is shaken.

The Climber bucks again. And again. The plug-ups skitter around. Odds and ends fall. Gravity acts crazy for a second. "Damn!" somebody says. "She's got us figured close. Damned close."

"See what I mean?" That's Yanevich. I can't tell who he's talking to. Maybe the Commander.

The Old Man isn't one to abandon a tactic because it's familiar.

Nor will he not take advantage of the inevitable loss of men. He'll try anything once, because it might work, and do his crying later. In this situation his inclination is to sit tight and hope the destroyer thinks she got us.

First move in a larger strategy.

The Climber rocks again. The lights wink. So much for fakery. Someone snarls, "It's that damned singleship. She's got a fix on our point."

So it begins. The run after the Main Battle was never this hairy.

I have a feeling it'll get hairier.

My expression must be grim. Seeing it, Yanevich smiles weakly. "Wait till his family comes to the feast. That's when we separate the men from the boys." He chuckles evilly, forcedly. He's as scared as I am.

This kind of action is part of every Climber mission. You'd think the old hands would get used to it. They don't. Even the Old Man shows the strain.

The hammering continues.

The Ship's Commander aboard the hunter-killer will have tactical control now. He'll be nudging countless brethren into position throughout the spatial globe defined by our estimated range in Climb. Their strategy will be to jump us when we try to vent heat, forcing us to Climb before we can shed it. Thus, the globe they have to patrol can be reduced, densifying their operation. And reducing our chance of venting much heat next time we go down.

And round and round and round again, till the Commander is faced with a choice of abandoning Climb or broiling.

When they can't pull the noose that tight, they try to force a Climber to exhaust her CT fuel. That takes patience. Unfortunately, they have patience to spare.

"Looks like the fun is over," I tell Yanevich.

"Yeah. Damned Tannian. Just *had* to go after Rathgeber."

"Stand by, Weapons," the Commander orders. "Get your accumulators on the line."

"What the hell?" Even the first Watch Officer seems puzzled. "We're barely getting warm."

"Junghaus, Berberian, I want a course, range, and velocity on that destroyer instantly. Take her down, Mr. Westhause."

The walls solidify.

We shed our heat in seconds, amid probing beams.

"Take hyper." The destroyer is closing fast.

Mr. Piniaz discharged his weapons in her direction just to be doing something.

"Four missiles, Commander," Berberian says. He adds the data the Old Man ordered before going down.

"The singleship?"

"Dead in space in norm, Commander."

"Good. Maybe he's collecting Haesler. He'll be out of it awhile. Junghaus. Anything else in detection?"

"Negative, Commander."

"All right, Mr. Westhause. Take her up. Twenty-five Bev. Weapons, Ship's Services, I want all heat shunted to the accumulators. Chief Canzoneri, see if you have enough data to predict that destroyer."

"Course and speed, Commander. Want to guess which way and how tight she'll turn?"

The Old Man stares into the distance for a moment. "Take it as standard. Looks like he's following standard procedure, doesn't it? Mr. Westhause, when you have the data, put us down on her tail. As soon as Mr. Piniaz has a charge on the accumulators."

"Sir?"

"Baiting her. She's gotten off twelve missiles already." The Climber shakes. Fearless states a yowling opinion from somewhere round the far side of the compartment. "She only carries twenty."

Is the man abetting Tannian's mad strategies? If he keeps kicking up dust he's going to draw a crowd. We've got to get hiking.

Piniaz murmurs, into an open comm, "Or twenty-four, or twenty-eight, depending on her weapons system. What the hell is he doing? She'll still outgun us when her missiles are gone."

"Mr. Piniaz." Icicles dangle from the Commander's words.

Let's not count missiles before they're hatched. Whatever they have, they'll use them intelligently. I don't like this. My stomach is surging up round my Adam's apple. We should be running, not dancing.

But the Commander is in command. His job—and curse, perhaps—is to make decisions.

"Ready, Commander," Westhause says.

"Take her down."

We drop almost too close for the destroyer to see, in a perfect trailing position, which presents her with an impossible fire configuration.

"No imagination," the Commander mutters. "Fire!"

The Energy Gunners drain the accumulators.

The opposing Commander skips into hyper before we more than tickle his tail. He sends return greetings by way of another missile spread.

Through the chatter of Fisherman, Rose, Berberian, Westhause, and others, comes the Commander's, "That'll give him something to think about."

Ah. I see his strategy. Little dog turning on big dog. Maybe we'll startle them into a mistake that'll give us a chance to break completely free.

An hour dancing with the hunter-killer. They're disconcerted over there. We've spent no more than five minutes in Climb. Our ability to vanish gives us a slight advantage in maneuverability. The singleship has lost track of our Hawking point. We can duck their missiles, appear unexpectedly.

The hunter-killer has quit wasting missiles. It's now a beamer duel.

"Hit!" Piniaz cries, in a mix of glee and amazement. "We hurt her that time." This is his second victory cry. Our horsefly game has paid off, viewed strictly as a one-on-one.

"She's gone hyper," Junghaus says. "Not putting weigh on. Looks like drive anomalies."

"Coward," the Commander jeers. He's won the round. They're staying in hyper, where we can't reach them without using a missile. A missile they can, no doubt, dodge or intercept. Climbers make their easy kills because they appear out of nowhere, making their missile launches before the other team can react.

The petty triumph feels good. We made monkeys out of them. But behind the good feeling there's the worry about the destroyer's sisters. They'll be forming their shell around our sphere of range.

"Commander, singleship is putting on headway."

"Ach! Getting too busy around here."

"She's launched, Commander."

"Climb, Westhause! Emergency Climb!"

The Climber shakes as if she's in the jaws of an angry giant hound. What a shot! Dead on our Hawking point. Only my safety harness keeps me in my seat. The ship feels like she's spinning.

One missile. That's all a singleship carries. She won't be hitting us again. Let's hope we break away before she gets a good lock on our point. Don't want her dogging us forever.

I catch a glimpse of my face in the dead visual screen. I'm grinning like a halfwit.

"Take her down, Mr. Westhause. To hyper. Junghaus, check that destroyer."

Seconds pass. Fisherman says, "Still no weigh on, Commander. Drive anomalies are worse."

"Very well. What do you think, First Watch Officer? Did we damage her generators?"

"Possibly, Commander."

"Easy meat, eh? Make a launch pass, Mr. Westhause."

We make the run, coming in from behind, but the Old Man doesn't give the order to launch. The destroyer wriggles, but not well enough to get away. She doesn't shoot back. Out of missiles. Damaged. Easy meat indeed.

"Take us out of here, Mr. Westhause."

Victory enough, Commander? Just let them know you could've taken them?

He pauses behind me. "That's for Haesler. They'll understand."

Piniaz's comm line is still open. The gunners all grumble about the lost chance to avenge their Chief. The Old Man scowls but says nothing. Must be a malfunction in the switch down there.

"Make for that star now, Mr. Westhause." Throughout the action, between maneuvers, the Commander and astrogator have been eyeing a sun with what seems an unhealthy lust. Why get in there where the mass of a solar system will complicate our escape plan?

Another case of my not knowing what the hell is going on.

The star is an eleven-hour fly. In Climb. Blind. With internal temperature rising every minute. It passes in silence, with crew taking turns sleeping on station. Piniaz and Varese get little sleep. They wrestle with the agonizing chore of redistributing the work of the men we lost.

I'll take on some of Piniaz's slack, though I'd rather stay in Ops. That's where the action is. I assume a post at the missile board while an energy-rated Missileman moves over to cover for Holtsnider. Covering Missiles shouldn't be difficult with only the one launch bay armed. The control position for Launches One and Four can be abandoned.

Varese ameliorates his shortage by using Diekereide and commandeering Vossbrink from Ship's Services. Bradley can cope without Voss.

Westhause again demonstrates what a fine astrogator he is. He brings us down so near the star that it appears as a vast, fiery plane with no perceptible horizon curvature. And he manages to arrive with an inherent velocity requiring only minimal angular adjustment to put us into stable orbit.

How does he manage so well with a computation system scarcely more sophisticated than an abacus?

The roar of the star should mask the Climber's neutrino emissions and confuse all but the closest and most powerful radars. I'm told orbiting or slingshotting off a singularity is even more effective.

"Vent heat."

It'll be slow going this close to so mighty a nuclear furnace. Typhoons of energy pound our black hull.

"Fire into the star," Piniaz tells his gunners. "We don't want them seeing beams flashing around."

Slow work indeed. After a time, I ask Piniaz, "Will continuous firing strain the converters?"

"Some. More likely to cause trouble in the weapons themselves, though."

Another in an apparently endless string of situations I don't like. "How long before the other firm figures what we've done?"

"They'll be checking stars soon," Piniaz admits. "The trick isn't new. One of the Old Man's favorites, in fact. We once star-skipped all the way home. He'll bounce us to another one as soon as Westhause has his numbers."

"Where'd you serve before you came into Climbers?" I ask, hoping to profit from a talkative mood.

Piniaz gives me a queer look and dummies up. So much for that. The man is as self-contained as the Commander, and less interested in coming out.

Next star-stop is an eight-hour fly. The troops again nap on stations. Westhause slides us into another gem of an orbit. I think we'll make it. The Commander has forced the enemy to enlarge his search sphere. He can no longer adequately monitor it. Visiting Ops, I suggest something of the sort to Yanevich.

He raises one eyebrow, smiles mockingly. "Shows what you know. Those people are pros. They know who we are. They know the Commander. They know our fuel margins." He nods. "Yeah. We've got a good chance. A damned fine chance, with Rathgeber gone. We've gotten out of tighter places."

Doesn't look that tight to me. Been no contact for over twenty hours.

The crew haven't used the hours well. To a man they're on the edge of exhaustion. They need to rest, to really relax, in order to bury the ghosts of those we left behind....

Some of the old hands are eyeing me oddly. Hope they're not thinking I'm a Jonah....Convince yourself, Lieutenant. Would those men be alive if you hadn't elbowed your way aboard? Would Johnson's Climber still be part of the patrol?

A man could go mad worrying about crap like that.

9

PURSUIT

We keep chipping away at the mission duration record. Yanevich says the longest was around ninety days. He doesn't remember the exact figure.

Memory gets tricky out here. It adapts to the demands of Climber service. For instance, the men we lost—I can't remember their faces.

I knew none but Chief Holtsnider very well, and he not as well as I'd like. I can make a list of physical characteristics, but his face won't come.

It takes an effort to mourn them.

The lack of feeling seems common enough. We're under pressure.

We've found ourselves an uninhabited star-covert. It has planets and moons and a full complement of asteroidal debris. A fine place to get lost. And just as fine a place for the opposition to have installed a low-profile detection probe, a passive observer as easily detected as our own beacons.

This guilt I have, about not hurting enough for those we lost, isn't an alien feeling. I used to feel the same way at funerals. Maybe it's a result of the socialization process. I just don't hurt.

Our grief and anger didn't last long after Johnson's girls mounted Hecate's Horse, either. Maybe this pocket society has no room for them.

Piniaz has shifted me to the gamma radiation laser. The weapon has a beam that can punch through the stoutest shielding when properly target-maintained. It's a notoriously unstable weapon, and this unit is no exception. It's been acting up for weeks.

The first indication came when it produced barely discernible anomalies in the power-pull readings. The draw varied despite a constant output wattage. The tendency of the input curve was upward, which meant we were putting more and more energy into waste wavelengths.

That doesn't cripple the weapon as a device for shedding heat, but it does bode ill for its future as a weapon.

That's but one of a score of problems plaguing the ship. Mold that can't be beaten. Stench that seems to have penetrated the metal itself. One system after another getting crankier and crankier. In most cases we'll have to make do. We carry few spare parts, and not many are available at beacons. Main lighting has begun to decay. The men are spending more and more time on corrective maintenance.

Stores, too, are getting short.

It's scary, watching a ship come apart around you.

It's even spookier, watching a crew disintegrate. This one is definitely headed downhill. We've reached the point where Command's policy of having men bounced from ship to ship is paying negative dividends. They don't have that extra gram of spirit given by devotion to a standing team.

That's critical when you're down to the bitter end and barely hanging on.

I say, "Mr. Piniaz, I have trouble here. Output wattage oscillating."

Piniaz studies the board sourly. "Shit. Guess we're lucky it held up this long." He rings Ops. "Commander, we've developed a major stress oscillation in our gamma gas cartridges."

"How bad?"

"It won't last more than ten minutes if we keep using it." To me, Piniaz remarks, "I've been saying we should be using crystal cassette lasers since I got here. Will they listen to me? Absolutely not. They just tell me crystals burn out too fast and they don't want to waste the mass-room needed to haul spares."

"Wait one while I get some numbers, Mr. Piniaz."

"Standing by, Commander."

"No replacement cartridges?" I ask. "In the bombards we could change units in five minutes. Like *click-click*."

Piniaz shakes his head. "Not here. Not in the Climbers. You have to go outside to get at the cartridges. But Command's main argument is that we're never in action long enough to need spares."

"But this star business…"

He shrugs. "What can you do?"

The Commander says, "Mr. Piniaz, go ahead and use it, but only when Mr. Bradley needs it to sustain internal temperature."

Piniaz snorts. "Heavier load on the others."

I listened with one ear while the Old Man talked it over with Yane-vich. My bugs steal everybody's privacy. They decided the weapon was wasted, that the ship has to move to a cooler hiding place. Fine with me. Having all that incandescent fury under my feet is doing nothing for my nerves.

Westhause is calculating a passage to the surface of a small moon. Its gravity shouldn't put undue stress on the ship's structure.

Varese, too, overhears the comm exchange. He reasons out the consequences. "Commander, Engineering Officer. May I remind you that we're low on CT fuel?"

"You may, Lieutenant. You may also rest assured that I'll take it into consideration." There's a touch of sarcasm in his tone. He has no love for Varese.

My guess is we have no more than thirty hours Climb time left. That's a tight margin if we haven't been lucky with our sun-hopping.

Are they still after us? It's been a long time since the raid. A long time since contact. Maybe they've overcome their emotional response and gone back to guarding their convoy.

What's going on out there? We've had no news, made no beacon connections. The biggest operation of the war… Being out of touch leaves me feeling like my last homeline has been cut.

Has the raid given Tannian's wolves the edge they need? Have they panicked the logistic hulls? Once a convoy scatters, no number of late-showing escorts can protect all the vessels. Climbers can stalk the ponderous freighters with virtual impunity. Some will get through only because our people won't have time to get them all.

Uhm. If the convoy has scattered, the other firm might feel obligated to keep after their most responsible foe. They know this ship of old. Her record is long and bloody. She's hurt them. Her survival, after what she's done, might be an intolerable threat.

I'm caught in the trap of circular thinking that lies waiting for men with time on their hands and an invisible uncertain enemy on their trail. I want to shriek. I want to demand certain knowledge. Even bad news would be welcome at this juncture. Just make it certain news.

Varese and the Commander, during the computation of the fly to our new hiding place, have a rousing battle over the level of our CT fuel. Finally, against his better judgment, the Old Man says he'll make the passage without Climbing.

"Goddamn!" Piniaz explodes as an illumination tube above his sta-

tion fails. "Damned shoddy Outworlds trash…" He excoriates quality-control work on Canaan, insisting nothing like this would happen
with an Old Earth product. He's vicious and bitter. The men tuck their
heads against their shoulders and weather the storm.

He has a point, though his claim for Old Earth manufactures is spe-
cious. The human race seems incapable of overcoming human nature.
Just do the minimum to get by.

With one weapon all but out and the others likely to degrade, our
ability to shed heat is crippled. We can't rely on radiator vanes alone
if the pursuit closes in.

Teeter-totter, teeter-totter. Each time the situation shows promise, something ugly raises its head. Lately, it seems, life is a Jurassic
swamp.

Sometimes things go from bad to worse without any intervening
cause for optimism.

The Commander was right, Lieutenant Varese wrong. We should have
made the transfer fly in Climb, and fuel levels be damned.

We fall foul of the other firm's new tactical intelligence system.
They've been seeding tiny, instelled probes near stars to catch sun-
skippers. If the unit detects a Climber's tachyon spray, it sends one
tiny instel bleep.

The sharks, who have been casting about in confusion, turn their
noses toward the scent of blood.

Fisherman gets a trace when the squirt goes out. "Commander, I've
got something strange here. A millisecond trace."

"Play it back." A moment later, "Play it again. Make anything of it,
First Watch Officer?"

"Never seen anything like it."

"Junghaus, you're the expert."

"Sorry, sir. I don't know. Never had anything like that in E-school.
Maybe it's natural." There are natural tachyon sources. Some Hawking Holes are known to produce them in much the same fashion as a
pulsar generates its beam.

"Maybe you should ask the writer," Yanevich suggests.

"No point. Wasn't a ship, was it? That's what matters."

"Maybe a Climber going up? Looks a little like that."

"Shouldn't be anybody in the neighborhood. Keep an eye on it,
Junghaus."

In ignorant bliss we settle gently into the soft dust of a lunar crater bottom, cycle down to minimum power, and prepare to possum for a few days. Sooner or later the other firm will go after livelier game. If they haven't already.

The Old Man says, "Old Musgrave used a trick like this when he was in the *Eight Ball.*"

"Uhm?" The coffee is gone. Even the ersatz. We do our fencing over juice glasses now.

For several minutes he doesn't say anything more. Then, "Found himself a little moon with a big hollow spot inside. Don't ask me how. Used to duck in there, go norm, and power down. Drove the other firm crazy for a while."

"What happened?"

"Went to the well too often. One day he showed up and that moon was a gravel cloud with a half-dozen destroyers inside."

"They didn't get him?"

"Not that time. Not in the *Eight Ball.*" He swallows some juice, chews his pipe. "He was a wily old trapdoor spider. He'd sit in there for a week sometimes, then jump out and get himself a red star. He took out more destroyers than any two men since." Silence again.

"End of story?"

"Yep."

"What's the point?"

He shrugs. "You can't keep doing the same thing?"

They're crafty. They do nothing for hours. They make sure they have plenty of muscle before they move. We have twelve hours to loaf and get fat thinking we have it made.

Fisherman says, "Got something here, Commander." He sounds puzzled.

I've been pestering Rose, trying to unravel a few strands of a misty personality. Without success. It's Yanevich's watch. He attends Junghaus.

"Playback." We study it. "Same as before?"

"Not quite, sir. Lasted longer."

"Curious." Yanevich looks at me. I shrug. "Same point of origin?"

"Very close, sir."

"Keep watching." We go on about our business.

I go try to get Canzoneri to tell me about Rose.

Five minutes later Fisherman says, "Contact, Mr. Yanevich."

We swarm round. No doubt what this is. An enemy ship. Two minutes of fast calculation extrapolates her course. "No problem," Yanevich says. "She's just checking the star."

She gets in a sudden hurry to go somewhere. I sigh in relief. That was close.

Two hours later there's another one. She hurries to join the first, which is now skipping around crazily the other side of the sun. Yanevich frowns thoughtfully but doesn't sound the alarm.

"They act like they're after somebody," he says. "Junghaus, you sure you haven't had any Climber traces?"

"No sir. Just those two bleeps."

"You think somebody heard us come out of the sun and went up from norm?"

Fisherman shrugs. I say, "Those sprays don't look anything like a ship."

"I don't like it," Chief Nicastro says. "There's a crowd gathering. We ought to sneak out before somebody trips over us."

"How?" Westhause snaps. For the first time in months he doesn't have more work than he can handle. The lack has him edgy.

"We'll get you home to momma, Phil," Canzoneri promises.

Laramie calls, "That's what he's afraid of, Chief. He's had time to think it over."

I smile. Someone still has a sense of humor.

"Laramie..." Nicastro starts into the inner circle, thinks better of it, wheels on the First Watch Officer. "At least go standby on annihilation, sir."

The neutrino detector starts stuttering, *clickety-clack, clickety-clack*, like a typewriter under the ministrations of a cautious two-fingered typist.

"Missiles detonating." Nicastro says it with a force suggesting he's just confirmed a suspicion the rest of us are too dull to comprehend.

"I've got another one," Fisherman announces.

"Picraux, wake the Commander."

Nicastro nods glumly. This one will whip past less than a million kilometers out. The Chief would die happy if she blew us to ions.

More typewriter noise. It dies a little as Brown reduces the neutrino detector's sensitivity.

"They're really putting it on somebody."

"Here comes number four," I say, catching the first ghostly feather before Fisherman does.

"Carmon, better activate the tank." Yanevich pokes me with a finger. "Pass the word to Mr. Piniaz to wake everybody up. Picraux. While you're up there, shake everybody out."

When it's no drill and there's time, general quarters can be handled in a civilized manner.

Brown reduces the detector's sensitivity again.

"Another one," Fisherman says.

"Any pattern yet, Carmon?"

"Not warm yet, sir."

"Move it, man. Engineering, stand by to shift to annihilation."

The Commander swings down through the jungle gym. "What have you got, First Watch Officer?" He's so calm that I, lingering near the Weapons hatch, get a flutter in the stomach. The cooler he is, the more grave the situation. He's always been that way.

"Looks like we're camped in the middle of the other firm's company picnic."

The Commander listens impassively while Yanevich brings him up to date. "Junghaus, roll that second sighting at your slowest tape speed. On the First Watch Officer's screen. Loop it."

"What're we looking for?" Yanevich asks.

"Code groupings."

The typist is a fast learner. His *clickety-clack* has become a fast rattle. Brown cuts the sensitivity again.

"Poor bastards have had it," Rose says. "Their point is taking everything but the sink. Must not be able to move."

Better they than me, I think, the stomach flutters threatening to mature into panic. And, hey, what does the Old Man mean, code groupings?

"We ought to haul ass while we have the chance," Nicastro grumbles, trying his luck with the Commander.

"Two more," Fisherman announces.

"Three," I say, leaning over his shoulder. "Here's a big one over here."

The Commander turns. "Carmon?"

The display tank sparkles to life.

"Damn! Brown. Turn that thing all the way back up."

Clickety-clack nearly deafens us.

Floating red jewels appear where none ought to be, telling a tale none of us want to hear. We've been englobed. The trans-solar show is a distraction.

"Oh, shit!" someone says, almost reverently.

They aren't certain of our whereabouts. The moon is well off center of their globe.

"Commander." Chief Canzoneri beckons. The Old Man goes to look over his shoulder. After a moment, he grunts.

He says, "They're beating the piss out of an asteroid. Must be nice to have missiles to waste." He strolls toward Fisherman, his face almost beatific. "Fooled us, didn't they?" he tells me. "Wasted a few missiles and locked the door while we sat here grinning."

The distant firing ends.

The Old Man stares steadily at the craft Fisherman has in detection.

Yanevich mumbles, "They reckon we've got it figured up now and didn't panic." There's agony in his eyes when he meets Nicastro's gaze.

Varese, you prick. I could choke you.

The swiftest reaction would've done us no good. They've had half a day to tighten the net. What the hell can we do?

I don't like being scared.

The Old Man takes a pen from his pocket. He taps the end against his teeth, then against one of the feathers on Fisherman's screen. "It's him."

Fisherman stares dumbly. He grows more and more pallid. Sweat beads on his upper lip. He murmurs, "The Executioner."

"Uhm. Back from his holiday with Second Fleet. I'll take the conn, Mr. Yanevich."

"Commander has the conn." Yanevich doesn't conceal his relief.

I want to say something, to ask something. I can't. My gaze is fixed on that tachyon spray. The Executioner. The other firm's big man. Their number one life-taker. They want us bad.

The Old Man grins at me. "Relax. He's not infallible. Beat him patrol before last. And Johnson, she had the hex sign on him."

I feel awfully cold. I'm shivering.

"Engineering, bring CT systems to full readiness."

This is a state of readiness midway between standby and actual shifting. It's seldom used because it's such a strain on personnel. Apparently the Commander does appreciate the fuel problem.

"All hands. Take care of your personals," he says. "General quarters shortly." He sounds like a father calming a three-year-old with nightmares.

I'm so nervous my bladder and bowels *won't* evacuate. I stand staring at the display tank. A dozen rubies inhabit it now. Flight would be suicidal. Amazing that they'd devote so much strength to one Climber.

We have to stay put and outfox them.

Outfox the Executioner? His reputation is justified. He can't help but find us....

"Mr. Westhause, bring up the data for Tau and Omicron."

"Got it already, Commander."

"Good. Program for Tau with just enough hyper to give it away. Once we're up, zag toward Omicron, then put us back inside this rock."

"It's mostly water ice, Commander, with a little surface dust. There seems to be a real rock surface several thousand meters down, though."

"Whatever. I trust you've resolved its orbitals? Can you hold us deep enough to shield the point?"

"I think so, sir."

"Can you or can't you?"

"I can, sir. I will. Might have to run high Bevs to get the cross section down so we don't take core heat if we go deep."

"This rock isn't that big. But keep gravity in mind. Don't let it upset your calculations."

"Maybe we shouldn't go down more than a couple klicks. Just deep enough to escape their weaponry."

"Can you hold it that fine?"

"I did on Rathgeber. Finer."

"On Rathgeber you had a century's worth of orbital data. Go down twenty-five. Hell. Make it fifty, just to be safe. They might try to blast us out."

They're doing this out loud to let the men know there's a plan. It's an act. I try not to listen. It doesn't sound like much. I check the time. Still got a chance to piss before strap-in.

The alarm sounds. "To your stations. They've found us. Missiles incoming. Prepare for Climb. Lift off, Mr. Westhause."

The lighting fades to near extinction as the drives go from minimum to maximum power.

"Vent heat, max," Yanevich orders.

Back in Weapons now, I commence firing. My unit survives, though not without protest. The air gets colder and colder. The hyper alarm howls. I push my bug plugs into my ears.

"Secure the gravity system, Mr. Bradley," the Commander orders. "Secure all visibility lighting."

What? We're going through this in the dark? I feel the caress of panic. Blind panic. That's a joke.

"Climb."

The visibility lights aren't necessary. The glow of Climb, complemented by the luminescence of the idiot lights, provides adequate illumination. So. A little more Climb endurance won.

The Commander shuts down systems till it seems nothing but the Climb system remains on-line. Internal temperature is so low frost forms on nonradiant surfaces and men exhale fog into their clasped hands.

The first salvo arrives and delivers enough applied cross-sectional kinetic energy to rattle bones and brains. I gasp for breath, fight a lost bug back into my right ear.

Down in the basement Varese is frenetically trying to catch up on a million little tasks he let slide during ready. The last hint of refinement has fled him. His cussing isn't inventive, just strong enough to crisp the paint off every surface within three kilometers.

The Commander continues securing systems. Even all detectors and radios, which, normally, would be maintained at a warm idle.

Piniaz taps my shoulder. "Shut her down," he says. "Then go kill the cannon." His dark face makes him hard to read. As if catching my thoughts, he whispers, "I think he's going a little far. We ought to be ready to slash and bite if we have to do down."

"Yeah." It'll take time to bring everything back to ready. Frightened, I close the systems down.

Up in Ops Yanevich and the Old Man are running and rerunning Fisherman's tapes, assembling the details of a cautionary message to the rest of the Fleet.

Six hours. For every second of them the Climber has whispered and stirred in response to forces acting on her Hawking point. Twice the Commander has ordered us deeper into the moon. We're down nearly three hundred kilometers. We're running a hundred Bev, the most I've ever seen, giving our point a diameter smaller than that of a hydrogen atom. We're gulping CT fuel....

Yet we're being buffeted. Continuously. I don't know what they're doing up there, but... the whole surface has to be boiling, throwing trillions of tons of lunar matter into space.

The buffeting gradually increases. "Take her down another hundred kilometers, Mr. Westhause."

I didn't pay much attention to the moon when I had a chance. Is it big enough to have a molten core? Are we trapped between fires? Does the Executioner have the firepower to tear the moon apart?

Waiting. Thinking. Always the fear. What if they blast away till there's nowhere left to go?

God. They must have brought a Leviathan. Nothing else has so much firepower.

Suppose they destabilize the moon's orbit? The Commander and Westhause are betting on its stability. What if the moon can't take it and breaks up? What if? What if? Will there be any warning when it sours? Or will internal temperature just shoot up too fast for us to react?

Maybe they're punching their missiles deep by throwing them in in hyper. Their sudden materialization and explosion would crack the mantle to gravel—except that that massed energy weapon fire will have turned it to a sea of lava. The water ice, surely, has boiled off into space by now.

Why are they so damned determined to skin this particular cat? I never did anything to them.

It's stopped. Suddenly, like a light switch being thrown. What the hell? God. I thought it would drive me insane. Alewel did lose his cool for a minute, holding his head and screaming, "Make it stop! Make it stop!" Piniaz had to sedate him.

Silence. Stretching out. Getting spooky. Stretching, stretching. Becoming worse than the bombardment.

Have they gone away? Are they laying back, waiting for us to come down?

The Executioner, they say, is a master of psychological warfare.

I unbuckle and venture to the honeypot. Sacrifice made, I prowl the confines of the compartment, trying to calm myself.

Piniaz endures my footsteps for five minutes before snapping, "Sit down. You're generating heat."

"Shit, man. That seat's getting hard. And wet."

"Tough. Sit. You're in the Climbers now, Lieutenant."

My restlessness isn't unique. This silence is a rich growth medium for the jitters. Nobody looks anybody else in the eye.

Ten hours. Somebody in Ops is whimpering. Curious. We've been up this long before. Why is this time harder to endure? Because the Executioner is out there? They use a sedative to quiet the whimperer.

The Commander's methodical madness has proven effective. Internal temperature increase is lagging well behind the normal curve despite the fact that we haven't much fuel to use as a heat sink. Soon after the whimperer goes quiet, the Old Man orders the atmosphere completely recycled. Then, "Corpsman, I want the Group One sleepers given."

It's warm now but I shiver anyway. Sleepers. Knockouts. The last ditch effort to extend Climb endurance by reducing metabolic rates and making the least critical men insensitive to their environment. A desperation measure. Usually applied much later than this.

"Voss, why don't you just hand out capsules?" I ask the Pharmacist's Mate as he comes through Weapons with his injection gun. It looks like a heavy laser with a shower-head snout.

"Some guys would palm them."

I roll up a tattered sleeve. Vossbrink ignores me. He turns to Chief Bath, whom I consider more important to the ship's survival. The Chief looks like a man expecting never to waken.

"Why not me? How do you choose, anyway?"

"Psych profile, endurance profile, Commander's direction, critical ratings. You can almost always find somebody to do a job. Can't always find somebody who can take the heat and pressure."

"What about when we go down?"

He shrugs. "They'll be gone. Or they won't. If not, it won't matter."

I lean his way, offering my arm. The sleeper looks like an easy out. No more worries. If I wake up, I'll know we made it.

"No. Not you, sir."

"There's nobody more useless than me."

"Commander's directive, sir."

"Damn!" Right now I want nothing more than total absolution of any responsibility for my own fate.

Fourteen hours. Feeling feverish. Unable to sit still. Soaked with perspiration. Breathing quick and shallow because of heat, stench, and the low oxygen content of the air. Pure oxygen. It's supposed to be pure oxygen.

What the hell is the Climb endurance record? I can't remember. How close are we? Looks like the Old Man means to break it. And stretch it with every trick ever tried, including predicting his heat curves with the discounts of the men we lost.

Don't look at the bulkheads. Mold blankets them now. I can almost see it spreading, sporulating, filling the air with its dry, stale smell. Jesus! There's a patch of it on Chief Bath's shirt. I'm coughing almost continuously. The spores irritate my throat. Thank heaven they don't give me an allergic reaction.

The last of our juice is gone. We're down to water and bouillon and pills. Yo-ho-ho. Famine in the Climbers.

Where's that fearless old spacedog who jollied the boys on the beacon? Ho! The life-takers have whisked away his disguise.

Vossbrink came round an hour ago. He bypassed me again. I cursed him mercilessly. He gave me a tablet I'm to swallow only on the Old Man's orders.

Those of us still conscious are a little insane. I want out, but... I don't have enough residual defiance to take the tablet. Been thinking about it, but can't get my hand to my mouth.

Christ, it's gloomy in here!

Maintaining a tenuous touch with reality by hating the Old Man. My old friend. My old classmate. Doing this to me. I could cut his throat and smile.

And those bastards out there. Why the hell don't they go away? Enough is enough.

Westhause and the Commander are the only watchstanders left in Ops. I can't hear anything from Engineering, but somebody is holding out. Only Bradley is active in Ship's Services. The Ensign is stubborn. Here in Weapons I have two open-eyed companions, Kuyrath and Piniaz.

Kuyrath suddenly throws himself toward the Ops hatch. Muttering, he tries to claw his way through. What the hell?

Aha. Another reason for the sedations. This could be contagious. The madness howls along the frontiers of my mind. I force myself to rise, to stalk Kuyrath with a hypo Vossbrink left for this contingency.

Kuyrath sees me coming. He leaps at me. His eyes are wild, his teeth bare. I punch the hypo into his stomach, yank its trigger.

For a dozen seconds I shield my testicles and eyes, writhe away from champing teeth, evade clawing fingers, and wonder what went wrong. Why doesn't he fold?

He collapses.

"What's going on back there?"

I stagger to a comm, mumble. Somehow, the Commander understands. I stare at Piniaz. Why didn't he help me?

His eyes are open but he isn't seeing anything. He's out. The bastard. What the hell did he do?

"All right." The Commander sounds like he's talking from the next galaxy. "Take Alewel's board."

"Huh?" I'm getting foggy. Want to give up. The exertion drained me. I can't get the drift.

"Take over on Alewel's board. I've got to have somebody on Missiles. Where's Piniaz?"

"On Missiles. Somebody on Missiles." I stagger to Alewel's seat. The Missileman is curled on the deck grates. His breathing is strained and ragged. He's in bad trouble. "Tired. Going to take capsule now. Sleep."

"No. No. Come on. Hang in there. We're almost home. All you have to do is activate the missile board."

"Activate missile board." My fingers act of their own accord. My hands look like thin brown spiders as they dance over the slimy, mold-green board, caressing a wakening galaxy of key-lights. I giggle incessantly.

"Where's Piniaz?"

This time the message gets through. "Sleeping. Gone to sleep." Alewel is making a thin, whining sound.

"Damn. Be ready to launch when we go norm."

"Ready… Launch missiles." One spider starts dancing the arming sequence. The other explores the mysteries of the safeties.

"Negative. Negative. Get your hands away from that board. Waldo, I'm going to have to go back there."

A semblance of reason returns. I draw my hands back slowly, stare at them. Finally, I say, "Missiles prepared for launch. Launch Control standing by."

"Good. Good. I knew I could count on you. It'll be a while yet. Just hang on."

Hang on. Hang on. Only five men conscious in the whole damned ship and one of them is hollering hang on. Till when? Till the Commander and I are the only ones left? Suppose the party is still going on when we go down? It won't matter to the others, but what am I supposed to do? Bend over and kiss my ass good-bye?

Alewel has stopped making noises. He's even stopped breathing. Mostly I feel puzzled when I look at him.

I don't think he's the only one. It's that bad in here.

I drive myself back into rituals of hatred and anger, thinking up tortures to inflict on the Old Man. Curses and threats rip themselves from my throat in an evil imitation of a Gregorian chant.

It passes the time. It keeps me going.

Skulking on the borderlands of lunacy, I find myself victimized by one of time's relativistic pranks. Before it seems possible, another two hours have fled.

"Hey down there. Stand by. Going down in five." Westhause. He sounds choky.

I glance at the time. A new endurance record, no doubt about it. Hurray.

"Uhn." The Commander. "Damn it, Waldo. Not now. Wake up. We're almost there. Shit." He sounds as if speech is pure torment.

Reluctance to leave the ghost world inundates me. Even hell gives one a sense of security, I suppose.

What happens if the whole crew passes out before a Climber goes down? I guess she'd keep heating till her superconductors failed, her magnetics went, and she destroyed herself in a sudden annihilation.

Why do I feel less uncomfortable now than I did two hours ago? Internal temperature is higher than ever before. Literally, we're cooking.

Haltingly, the Commander says, "All I want is for you to be faster on the trigger than anybody waiting for us. Quick enough to keep them from getting out an instel."

"I'll try."

"Ten seconds. Nine… Eight…"

It's a savage plunge to zero Bev. The concretization of my surroundings stuns my conscious mind.

The frightened old tree ape in the back of my mind is on survival watch. I finish the launch sequence before the venting machinery begins humming. In fact, I start before the ship is all the way down, and launch before any instrument has anything to say about targets.

The way Tannian fusses about wasting missiles, this could earn me a Board of Inquiry....

Except there is a target. The Old Man and Mr. Westhause made an astute guess.

We break cover less than ten thousand kilometers from the bones of the murdered moon. Fate does us a favor. She puts the watcher in the gap, not a hundred kilometers from our drop point. I can see her on gun camera. So. They thought we were gone, but left somebody just in case. They always do.

"About damned time it went our way," I mutter.

The missile is on its way. The Fire Control system barely has time to lock it on target.

The Commander holds norm for just four seconds. Hardly long enough to make a microdegree's difference in internal temperature. We run.

The missile, accelerating at one hundred gravities, strikes home before the gentlemen of the other firm get their thumbs out of their ears.

In essence, a classic Climber strike. With a lot of luck thrown in.

The Commander goes down again five light-seconds away. He vents heat and watches.

The destroyer dies. And neither the radio nor tachyon detectors react with anything but blast noise. No messages out. The Commander played the right card. He outwaited the hunt. The Executioner has gone looking elsewhere.

The glare of the fireball fades. I check the temperature. It's falling slowly. Maybe a degree a minute. The minutes tramp away on the feet of snails.

The destroyer got no message out, but that treacherous probe remains.

The first hunter hypers in an hour later.

A dozen men have recovered sufficiently to resume work. Several more are gone forever....The Commander commences a new ploy. He calls me, says, "Program the Eleven bird for maximum straight-line hyper fly." Piniaz hasn't recovered. For the moment I'm in charge.

The new arrival is moving away from us, into the nether reaches of the system. Westhause hits hyper and runs.

Five minutes pass. Fisherman reports, "She's turning, Commander."

"Very well. Weapons, stand by to launch. Mr. Westhause, stand by to Climb."

The minutes roll away. The hunter gains slowly. "She's close enough, Commander," Canzoneri says.

"Thank you. Weapons? Ready?"

"Aye, Commander." I quickly hammer orders to the missile. The destroyer will recognize the fake if the weapon tears away too fast.

"Ready, Mr. Westhause? Go, then."

I launch. My surroundings ghost. The Commander directs Westhause onto a new course. This should work. It's a new trick.

The missiles can run for hours in hyper. I programmed its translation ratio high. Hopefully, we'll get a good start before the destroyer gets close enough to unravel the deception.

Fearless Fred will roar like a wounded bull when he hears about this.

The Commander no longer gives a damn what Command thinks. He wants to bring his people home alive.

We drop back to norm as soon as the destroyer has time to pass the limits of detection. We drift for hours, on minimum power, still venting heat. That's a laborious process. We can't use the energy weapons for fear of giving ourselves away. The hunt should be gathering again.

Normal cruising temperature feels incredibly cold. I'm in pain when it hits a pre-Climb level.

We have twenty-three men effective when, after three hours, the Commander takes us up again.

We leave three men behind, buried in space, eulogized and mourned only after the vessel is safely in Climb. Picraux and Brown from Ops, and Alewel. They were luckier down below.

"It's criminal," Fisherman mutters. "Out the garbage lock. It's criminal."

"You maybe want to keep them aboard?" Yanevich demands.

Fisherman doesn't answer. Heat and bacteria would work horrors during an extended Climb. The bodies got a gross enough start as it was.

I remember that story about the Commander who insisted on coming home with his dead.

Funny. My threshold for smell seems to adjust as the ship grows more fetid. Our atmosphere is only mildly annoying, though it would gag somebody plucked off a ranch on Canaan.

Lieutenant Diekereide has been running Engineering while his boss is indisposed. Varese recovers suddenly. With a howl. "Get out of the fucking way, Diekereide. Goddamnit, Commander, what the fuck did you do to my CT stores? You jackass…"

"Shut your mouth, Varese. Thank me for the chance to bitch."

Varese succumbed early. The more thoughtful Diekereide kept himself in action by donning our one remaining suit and using its cooling capability.

The squabble goes on. Pure stress talking. Will the Old Man press it? He'll have the evidence on the Mission Recorder. Varese is insubordinate. I take no notes, wanting nothing on paper that might be subpoenaed.

"We're down to a cunt hair over four hours of Climb time," Varese rages. "With that and some luck, we'll only get our asses blown off, not baked."

Yanevich takes over for the Old Man. "Be glad you're alive. Now tend to your knitting. Don't give *me* any of your shit. Understood, mister?"

Varese has sense enough to shut his mouth. He sulks instead.

Time to get some sleep.

I waken with a heightened sense of fatalism. I'm not alone. The CT is practically gone. The missiles have flown. The graser could be one shot from failing. The other energy weapons are unreliable. Only the magnetic cannon can be used for any length of time. We won't show much in a fight.

I paid my dues. I hung in there. I did my job while the others fell. I can be proud of myself. Maybe they'll give me a medal.

We're still a long way from home. It'll be a tough, hungry trip. Then we'll have to run the steel curtain around Canaan. Do we have enough CT?

In Weapons everyone is at war with the mold. "Looks like a victory for mold," I say to a slightly shy Kuyrath.

"Got a good hold this time, sir. The paint's ruined. Some of the plastic, too." He tears the protective wrapping off a roll of electrician's tape. Two empty cores lie beside him already. "Had to let it ride, though."

"Yeah. What can you do?"

"Wouldn't it be the shits if this crap did us in? I mean, they gave it their best shot. The Executioner. But the Old Man pulled us through. So we got mold. What do you do about fucking mold? You can't out-think it."

"It would be an ironic end," I agree. And don't count the other team out. They're still looking, my friend.

Piniaz drifts over. "Understand you did some first class shooting, Lieutenant."

"Uhm." His attitude has mellowed. "It really happened? Seems like a dream."

"You took notes the whole time. Interesting. I put them in Bath's hammock for now."

"Don't remember any notes. Be like reading somebody else's report." I snort. "Gunners. No respect for anybody but the fastest draw."

Piniaz frowns, perplexed. "I was offering the olive branch, Lieutenant. I didn't figure you'd bite my hand."

"Sorry. Thanks. Just lucky, I guess. What's happening?"

"We lost them. Or they let go. Something funny about it, if you ask me. Shouldn't have been this easy."

"Maybe it wasn't."

"They had to know our CT was about gone. That gets them excited." He shrugs. "The Old Man will take what they give him."

"For instance?"

"First we make an instelled beacon. Let Command know we're alive."

"Uhm. Think Tannian will be disappointed?" Sometimes I think he wants us dead.

Piniaz is capable of his own paranoid reasoning. "I'd guess the Old Man is gambling. People will hear we're alive before the news reaches the top."

Could it be true?… No. Not even Tannian… Crazy thinking. I've been out too long. "You figure Fred will have to pull all the stops to bring his heroes in?"

"Exactly."

Ito's strained, dark little face reveals a truth. *He* believes there's a plot. The upcoming leave best be long. These men are all out of their minds. I wouldn't want to space with them again.

I won't have to. I smile to myself. One patrol is all I have to survive.

Get me home, Commander. Get me home.

We've made our beacon. The Commander reported yesterday. After putzing around for hours, Command told us to come on home, following normal patrol routine, beacon to beacon. They showed no inclination to gossip.

We've scrounged a little water and food. Pity we can't get any CT. Going to be rough if we hit unfriendly territory.

Lunch with the Commander. He's near the end of his tether, yet remains as inaccessible as ever. How do I reach the man? How do I reassure him? I don't think it can be done now.

He speaks of the pursuit as though it were normal patrol routine.

Six days gone. Six days closer to home. The Old Man is avoiding routine, rather than pursuing it. He doesn't want to give potential watchers anything they can use. We're proceeding in short hyper flies separated by extended periods in norm. We do a lot of listening. Paranoia has become a norm. The computer people winnow every bit of information gathered from the beacons, hunting a clue, believing Command an enemy more deadly than the other firm. I can unearth no rational reason for the attitude. I occasionally succumb myself.

This is dangerous. Too much time wasted on speculation. We could get so spooky we turn into our own worst enemies. This could create a self-fulfilling prophecy.

More time gone. I've lost track of the days. We're close. I'm not sure how close, but near enough that Canaan seems real again. Here, there, men are talking like there's a human universe outside the Climber.

Space here is crowded. We have frequent contacts. Hardly a watch slides by without Fisherman's being startled into a croaking panic. Curiously, none of the contacts are interested in us.

We've been lucky, maybe. Every contact has been remote, while we were in norm. Chances are we've just not been spotted. A ship in norm is harder to detect from hyper than vice versa.

A tongue-in-cheek theory goes the rounds. It says we're dead already. We're really a ghost ship. We're going on because the gods haven't given us the message yet.

Lieutenant Diekereide half-seriously postulates that our record Climb rendered us permanently invisible. We'd all like to believe that.

I have my own thoughts on why we're having no trouble. They terrify me.

"Contact, Commander," Fisherman says. He's said it so often, now, that he no longer gets upset. He gives bearing and range and elevation, and, "Unfriendly."

This one's coming right at us. Fast. A destroyer. What the hell can we do? Where the hell can we run?

The Old Man powers down, plays possum.

The terror is over. She's gone. She passed within a few hundred thousand kilometers of us. Is it possible she didn't see us? What the hell is happening?

The Commander knows. I can see that now. He becomes shifty and evasive when I try to talk to him. All the men have their suspicions. The other firm just doesn't ignore crippled Climbers. Not without a damned good reason. Somehow, our importance has declined dramatically.

As I say, I have my thoughts. I don't want to think them. Sufficient unto each watch that I waken and find myself alive. Later, maybe, I'll want more.

Later, we all will. We'll want Tannian as guest of honor at a cannibal feast.

10

HOMEWARD BOUND

The insecurity has bottomed. Shoots of optimism are sprouting in an infertile soil of pessimism and cynicism so old it's almost religion. Like the robins coming north on Old Earth, there are signs of spring. Rose and Throdahl are laying formal plans for predations upon any female not stoutly haremed. Others are harkening to their ritual. We haven't heard this stuff for over a month.

I've begun to realize there may be women out there myself. I get hard just visualizing an hourglass. I'll make an ass of myself first time I run into a female.

All part of the Climber game. I understand they have Shore Patrol on hand when a Climber disembarks. Just to keep order.

The Chief remains convinced of our impending doom. His despair retards the growth of optimism. The ship is, he claims, in the hands of an infantile, cat-mannered fate. These glimpses of escape are being allowed us only to make our torment more exquisite.

He may be right.

I'm sure the Commander secretly holds the same view. And Lieutenant Varese would agree if he and the Commander were speaking.

The Engineering Officer is behaving like a five-year-old. How did such a petty man get cleared for Climber duty?

Headed home. Man and machine, everything falling apart. Enemy intervention may not be necessary to our destruction. Home is still a long fly, to be made alone.

Command turned down our request for a mother rendezvous. No explanation. Our request for a CT tanker was denied, too. Again, no explanation. That's scary. Hard to believe that somebody in Command wants us dead.

Throdahl says, "It stinks like a ten-day corpse at high noon. They could at least give us excuses. Some pudsucker just doesn't want us to make it." He sings the same song every few hours, like a protective cantrip.

He doesn't stop making plans. They all continue. They have faith in the Old Man.

"Here it is, Commander." Throdahl has been hunched over his board for half an hour, awaiting the response to our latest plea. The Commander asked for a rendezvous with a stores ship—or anyone willing to share their victuals. Is that an unreasonable request? Meals are pretty bleak these days.

"Request denied," the Commander says softly. He takes a deep breath, obviously controlling his temper. I meander over and read the full text. Its tone says we should shut up and leave Command alone.

I smack fist into palm. What the hell is with those people? We're in a bad way.

Fisherman blurts, "It doesn't make sense!" We've had two days of silence from Command. "They always *try...* now they don't even say, 'Sorry.'" Even he lusts for a solid planet beneath his feet.

The Commander has commenced gravity drills despite the fuel shortage. Regular exercise is mandatory.

I catch Yanevich alone. "Steve, I have an idea. Next instelled beacon, report me dead. See how the dominoes fall."

"Sheer genius!" He roars. "Yeah. Probably a ton of stuff published that they wouldn't want you to recant. But shit..."

He pauses thoughtfully. "It won't do. You aren't the reason. Too late for that anyway. They know you're the healthiest son of a bitch aboard." At a hair above a whisper, he adds, "Don't pin tails on devils. Not yet. It's an act the Admiral does. Got to hate somebody in this goddamned war."

"Uhm." Actually, Tannian's system is due only a few complaints. The Admiral is playing on a big chessboard, for stakes more important than any one Climber. How can you fault him? He's managing admirably for a man who started with nothing.

"But how long will I stay healthy?" I'm in my hammock, talking it over with Fearless. Other hammock space is available, but I'll stay where I am. I don't have to share.

Fred seems none the worse for wear, though he's lost weight. Poor Fearless. He doesn't know any better. The Climber is his whole damned universe.

Gaunt he is, but he's not going hungry. He makes out like a bandit. He's the ship's most talented moocher. This is just a diet for him. A dozen soft-hearts slip him nibbles from their rations.

Were it not for the generosity of manned beacons, we'd be subsisting on Kriegshauser's famed water soup.

Hungry days. Hungry days. But we're getting closer to home. Distance can be a balm as soothing as time. Even Throdahl no longer mentions Johnson's Climber.

Can there be a more powerful indictment of the Climber experience? A year ago these boys would've been stricken by any violent death.

What are we making of ourselves?

Sometimes there's a niggling fear. What will become of the survivors?

There will be survivors. And, no matter how bad it looks from here, the fighting won't last forever.

What becomes of those whose entire adult lives have been devoted to war? I've met a few who came in right at the beginning. They know no peacetime service past, can foresee no other future. War is their whole life.

I adapted to civilian life—barely. I didn't have to endure years of life-and-death pressure before I went outside. I think that will be an important factor.

If, as some experts predict, the war lasts a generation, there'll be big trouble when this ends. A generation will see warfare as the norm.

Kriegshauser draws me back from an imaginary era where whole fleets turn on the worlds they've been defending. "This isn't the fourteenth century," I mutter.

"Found something for Fearless," the cook says. He massages a tube of protein paste with thin, pale fingers.

"Something you had squirreled away?"

Kriegshauser grins. "The cook knows where to look for the overlooked."

"You traitor, Fred." The cat has deserted me. He's purring around Kriegshauser's ankles. "Judas."

"His only allegiance is to his stomach, sir."

"Only loyalty any of us have when you get to the narrow passage."

"Laramie says we might be home day after tomorrow, sir."

"Haven't heard anything that definite. The Old Man is playing them close to his chest."

"But Laramie would know, sir."

"Maybe. I think it'll be longer than that." I can't raise the subject that brought him to me. He's let it slide a long time. I forgot about it. I have no answers.

Eight men died. I sort of hoped one would be his nemesis.

Like most young men, I've experimented. I find homosexual relationships too alien, too sterile.... I can't picture Kriegshauser being attractive to man or woman. Beyond being unwashed, he's the ugliest man I've ever met. His pursuer must get off on the bizarre.

Beauty is in the eye, and so forth. And the cook has personality, as they say. He's a likable rogue.

"My problem... Have you thought about it?"

"A great deal," I lie. "Have you? You know where the leak was?" Kriegshauser is an insecure, dependent-type personality. He wants decisions made for him. He will, if he survives the Climbers and the war, make Navy his career. The Ship's Services assignments draw people who need secure, changeless niches.

While in the bombards I encountered a nonrated laundryman who hadn't been off ship for thirty years. Approaching compulsory retirement, he was a bundle of anxieties. He committed suicide when his waiver request was denied.

Navy was his family, his life. He had nowhere to go and nothing to do when he got there.

Kriegshauser shrugs. He doesn't want the burden of decision.

Why help a man who won't help himself? "You don't seem that interested in getting off. Any special reason you won't tell me who it is?"

"I'd just rather not, sir."

"Don't want to make him mad?"

"I guess."

"What did you expect me to do?"

"I don't know, sir. I just thought..."

"This way I can't do anything. You'll have to work it out yourself. You can cut his throat, give in, or call his bluff."

"But..."

"I'm not a magician. I can't push a button and give you three wishes."

I've had no luck identifying the culprit, though I admit I haven't looked hard. The obvious bisexuals aren't the blackmailing type. (Homosexuals are screened into segregated crews.) Their dalliances are matters of convenience. Eliminating them, the dead, and myself leaves a lot of possibilities.

Not that I care, but it's got to be somebody who wants to stay in the closet. An officer? Piniaz or Varese, maybe?

The first- and second-mission men are out. And anyone who maintains an obvious friendship with the cook. Reasoning the possibilities down to a half-dozen is easy. But the exercise is pointless.

"Look. This guy has something to lose. Everybody does."

"We've been so busy...."

I control my temper. "See me tomorrow. After you've thought it over. You have to do more than wish."

"Okay." Kriegshauser's disenchanted. He does want magic.

"Come on, Fearless. Back up here. Where'd we leave off? Yeah. How do I stay healthy in Tannian territory?"

Command wouldn't really get physical. But messengers of exposé have vanished into Psych detention before. That happened to the man who tried breaking the Munitions Scandal, didn't it?

I've developed a certifiable paranoia. Comes of being an outsider. "Know what I should be doing, Fred? Instead of playing pillow? Duplicating my notes."

Fearless is used to my maunderings. He ignores them. Pushing his head against my hand, he demands another ear-scratching.

I wander into Ops. They're busy, busy, busy. Especially Fisherman. Heavy traffic outside.

We're in norm. Carmon has the display tank active. Four blips inhabit it. Three are red. He's singing bogey designator numbers in the middle thirties.

The Commander hasn't ordered general quarters. Pointless. I'm the only man who missed the first whiff of danger. I'll never make a Climber man.

Our neighbors aren't interested in us. In norm, coasting, powered down to minimum, we're hard to see.

"Doubt they'd bother us if they did spot us," Yanevich says "They're after bigger game."

"How long to make it, this way?"

"Our inherent is high." He grins. "Maybe only six or seven months."

"One hundred ninety-six days, fourteen hours," Westhause volunteers.

"A long haul when the cupboard is bare." Still, we're close as spatial distances go.

"Yeah," Yanevich says. "I'm sizing up that drumstick of yours."

"What's going on out there?" I have a notion already, don't like it.

"Shit, man, I don't know." He looks a little grim. "There's always traffic around Canaan, but not like this. They're everywhere."

"Not just a training exercise?"

Yanevich shrugs. With enough falseness to say he knows an answer he can't tell. "We'll slide in. Mini-jumps when we can get away with them. Into the inner belt first. Some emergency stations there they haven't found yet."

"It's going to take a while, then."

"Yeah." He looks bleak. He's begun to realize what it means to be Commander. "A while. Look. Tell that cat-loving cook to turn loose if he doesn't want to be on the menu himself."

It's getting to him. He's changing. "You hear that, Fearless?" The cat followed me here. "Fang him on the ankle." To Yanevich, "I really think he has. Scraped bottom, I mean. He's talking about water soup."

"He's always talking about water soup. Tell him I'm talking cat soup."

"Change the subject." I'm hungry. Generally, food is fuel to me. But there're limits. Water soup!

Throdahl and Rose—O Wonder of Wonders—have found a new subject. The feast they're going to have before cutting their swath through the splittail.

"Looks like our probability coming up, Commander," Westhause says. "Good for a program three."

I glance at the tank. Just one red blip, moving away fast. There're no dots on the sphere's boundary, indicating known enemies beyond its scope.

Program three, I assume, will bite a big chunk off the road home.

The Old Man says, "Give me one-gee acceleration. Stand by for hyper." He turns, growls, "Anything shows, I want to know yesterday. *Capiche*, Junghaus? Berberian?"

Evidently we're slipping through a picket zone.

"Steve, you going to use your seat?" Yanevich shakes his head. I seat myself. Fearless occupies my lap. The Commander arrests my attention. Amid the disrepair, stench, and slovenliness he nevertheless stands out. His apparel is dirtier, more tattered, and hangs worse than anyone else's.

He's a haggard, emaciated, aged young man. His wild shapeless beard conceals his hollow cheeks, but not the hollow eyes that make him look like a corpse of twenty-six haunted by a century-old soul.

Maybe twenty-seven. I've lost track of the date. His birthday is sometime around now.

His eighth patrol. He has to survive two more, each with Squadron Leader's added cares. Pray for him....

He won't be able to handle it. Not unless this next leave is a long one. He has to put Humpty together again. Maybe I'll stay awhile. Maybe he can talk off the ship.

I don't think he's been eating. He's more gaunt than the rest of us, more dry and sallow of skin. We all sport psoriasis-like patches. He has a splash creeping up his throat. Scurvy may turn up soon, too.

The veins in his temples stand out. His forehead is compressed in pain. His hands are shaky. He keeps them in his pockets now.

He's on the brink, going on guts alone. Because he has to. He has a family to lead safely home.

I understand him just a little better. This patrol has been the thing too much, the burden too great to bear. And still he drives himself. He's a slave to his duty.

And Yanevich? The shoulders being measured for the mantle? He knows. He sees, understands, and knows. In Weapons much of the time, I've missed many of the turning points in his growth, in his descent into a terror of his own future.

But he's young. He's fresh. He possesses a soul as yet unconsumed. He's good for a few missions. If the Commander breaks, he'll step in. He has enough left.

"Time, Commander."

"Jump, Mr. Westhause." The Old Man's voice hasn't the resonance or strength it once had, but is cool enough.

Westhause. Our infant-genius. Silent, competent, imperturbable. A few more patrols and he'll be First Watch Officer aboard some moldering, homecoming Climber, staring at a burned-out Commander, into the burning eyes of his own tomorrow. But not now. Now he sees nothing but his special task.

Throdahl has enlisted in the conspiracy of silence. At long last he has exhausted his stock of jocular denials of loneliness and fear.

Chief Nicastro clings to a structural member, his eyes closed tight. He remains convinced of his fate.

Laramie's insult bag has come up empty.

The computermen mutter on, making magic passes over their fetish, communing with the gods of technology.

Berberian, Carmon, the others—they wait.

In his gentle way, Fisherman is trying to intercede with his god, on behalf of his friends. He prays quietly but often.

Only Fearless is living up to his name and the reputation of the Climbers.

That cat is the all-time grand champion. He's done more Climber time than any other creature living. It bores him now. He wriggles onto his back, athwart my lap, thrusting his legs into the air, letting his head dangle off my leg. From his half-open mouth he trails a soft, gurgling feline snore.

A complete fatalist, Fearless Fred. *Que sera, sera.* Till it does, he'll take a nap.

What's happening below? Yanevich has sealed the hatches.

"Contact," Fisherman says. "Bearing…"

"Drop hyper. Secure drives, Mr. Varese."

I'm becoming a fatalist myself. I can do nothing to control my future. It's just a ride I have to take, hoping the luck will go my way.

What point to the Old Man's tactics? The ship has gone her limit. Soon we won't be able to take hyper for fear of not having enough fuel to make it home.

"Commander, we've gone below one percent available hydrogen," Varese reports. "It'll take a lot to fire her up again."

"Understood. Proceed as instructed, Mr. Varese."

The Engineering Officer no longer argues. He's given up. The Commander won't be swayed.

Even he has to admit that we're past the point where protecting a reserve makes sense.

What's the meaning of one percent? Fuel for two days at maximum economy? After that, what? How long till emergency and accumulator power fail? Fisherman's history suggests weeks. But his was a healthy vessel before being stricken.

The whole business has become disgusting. There has to be a limit!

The only real limit is human endurance, my friend.

Berberian and Fisherman warble contacts like songbirds in mating season. Galactic clusters of red and green blips fill the display tank.

"Goddamned!" Throdahl swears. "So goddamned close…We could

walk it from here." If they'd let us.

I glance at the tank again. There are gold pips in there now. We've reached the asteroid belt. One of the asteroid belts, I should say. Canaan's system has two. The inner belt is slightly more than one A.U. outside Canaan's orbit. The other lies in roughly the same range as that of Sol System.

Rose has to respond to his friend. "We're going to get mugged first."

"Can the chatter!" the Commander snaps. "Throdahl, signal Command. Homecoming. Idents. Status Red." He turns to Westhause. "Astrogator, into the belt. Find an emergency base."

The signal will tell Command we're here and hurting, that we need help in a hurry.

I toy with the viewscreen, locate Canaan. The camera is erratic. Hard to keep in train. The planet shows as a fingernail clipping of silver. TerVeen is invisible. Maybe it's behind its primary. The larger moon is a needle scratch near the planet's invisible limb.

A lousy 170 million klicks.

I don't think we're going to make it.

Throdahl, who has been talking with Westhause, says, "Commander, got a response on station Alpha Niner Zero. Automatic signal. Looks like they've pulled the live crew."

"Mr. Westhause?"

"It's two million klicks off our base course, Commander."

"Rose, see what it can do besides life support."

Rose has the data up already. "Emergency water and food stores, Commander. Enough till this blows over if it's fully provisioned."

"This" is my earlier and correct guess. Rathgeber or the mauling of the convoy was the last straw. The gentlemen of the other firm have halted their assault on the Inner Worlds till they carve this Canaan-cancer out of their backtrail.

The camera shows the negotiations at a fiery pitch. Canaan's moon is taking a pounding. Maybe staying out here would be smart.

In the grand view the situation represents a glorious milestone. We've stopped their inward charge at last. They'll have to commit an inordinate proportion of their power to follow through here. Tannian's *Festung Canaan* will be a hard-shelled nut. Maybe hard enough to alter the momentum of the game.

Tannian has gotten his way at last.

Knowing I'm on the fringe of a desperate and historic battle isn't comforting. I can't get excited about sacrificing myself for the Inner Worlds.

A wise man once said it's hard to concentrate on draining the swamp when you're up to your ass in alligators.

Tannian will be a hero's hero. It won't matter if he wins or dies a martyr. He'll be immune to the darts of truth. What I write won't touch him. No one will care.

"Anything from Command?" the Old Man demands. There's been ample time for a response.

Throdahl raises a hand placatingly. He's listening to something. His expression sours. "Commander... all they did was acknowledge receipt. No reply."

"Damn them." There's little heat in the Old Man's curse. He doesn't sound surprised. "Make for Rescue Alpha Niner Zero."

Thrust follows almost instantaneously, lasts only a few seconds. Westhause is taking the slow road. We don't dare leave too plain a neutrino trail.

Word filters through the ship. We'll have something to eat soon.

Eight hours gone. After one brief hyper translation, there've been but a few slight nudges with thrusters, sliding round asteroids. Now Westhause cuts loose a long burn. He has to reduce our inherent velocity.

The Commander tells me, "Keep a sharp watch for a flashing red-and-white light. We may not recognize the rock on radar."

"Range one hundred thousand, Commander," Throdahl says.

"Very well. How long, Mr. Westhause?"

"Two hours till my next burn, Commander. Maybe three altogether."

"Uhm. Proceed."

I'm salivating already. Damn, this sneaking is slow work.

Burn complete. Closing with the Rescue station. I catch occasional glimpses of its lights, activated by our signals. "Commander, that rock is tumbling."

"Damn." He leans over my shoulder. "So it is. Not too fast, though. Time it."

We ease closer. The asteroid isn't tumbling as fast as I thought. It has several lights. A rotation takes about a minute. According to Berberian it's slightly over two hundred meters in distance. It's wobbling slightly as it rolls.

Closer still, I discover the reason for its odd behavior. "Range?" I demand.

"What?" Yanevich asks.

I have my magnification set at max. "How far to the damned asteroid?"

Yanevich snaps, "Berberian. Range?"

"Nine hundred thirty kilometers, sir."

The First Watch Officer moves round behind me. "What's the matter?"

"Something wrong." I tap a big lump as it rolls into view. Yanevich frowns thoughtfully. The Commander joins us. I ask, "Can we bounce a low-power beam off that?"

The Old Man says, "Berberian. Shift to pulse. Chief Canzoneri. Link with radar. I want an albedo. Mr. Westhause, dead stop if you please." He leaves us, monkeys into the inner circle.

We're three hundred kilometers closer before Westhause gets all weigh off. The men exchange tense glances. Fisherman asks, "What is it, sir?"

"Can't tell for sure. Looks like there's a ship on the rock."

The Commander joins me. He says, "Radar albedo isn't distinct. A dead ship doesn't show much different from a nickel-iron asteroid." He stares into the screen. It shouts no answers. "Wish we had flares."

Yanevich says, "If they were going to shoot, we'd have heard from them by now."

"Maybe. Open the door." Standing in the hatchway to Weapons, he tells me, "Roll tapes."

A minute later Piniaz lays twenty seconds of low-wattage laser on the asteroid. "It's a ship," I tell Yanevich. "Not one of ours, either."

He leans over as I reverse the tape. "Not much of one."

It looks like an inverted china teacup, thirty to forty meters in diameter. The Commander rejoins us. He looks puzzled. "Never saw anything like it. Route it to Canzoneri. Chief! ID this bastard."

A minute passes. Canzoneri says. "That's an assault landing pod, Commander."

We exchange baffled looks. An assault pod? For landing troops during a planetary invasion?

"What's it doing here?" Yanevich murmurs. He turns to the Commander. "What'll we do?"

The Old Man checks Fisherman's screen and the display tank. "Throdahl. Anything from Command?"

"There's a lot of traffic, Commander, but nothing for us."

The Commander contacts Weapons. "Mr. Piniaz, put a hard beam into that lump. Mr. Westhause, be ready to haul ass."

Piniaz fires a few seconds later. Glowing fragments fly. Part of the pod turns cherry, then fades. The lander doesn't respond.

Again we exchange glances. The Old Man says, "Take her in easy, Mr. Westhause."

Two hours of increasing tension. Nothing from the pod or Rescue station. We're now twenty-five kilometers out. The pod is obviously damaged. Its underside is smashed. It came into the station hard. Canzoneri says the impact put the spin on the asteroid. But we still can't fathom what the pod was doing out here. It's a long way from Canaan.

Apparently the pod crew came for the same reason we did. Both sides use the other's Rescue facilities.

Westhause says he can match the rock's tumble. It'll be tricky work, though, till we can anchor the Climber somehow. I ask the Commander, "Why bother? Just suit across—at least till we know if it's worth our trouble."

He grunts, ambles off.

I look at Yanevich, at the Commander's back, at the First Watch Officer again. Yanevich shows me crossed fingers. He too sees the disintegration the Old Man is holding at bay.

I'm worried about the Commander. He's damned near the edge. He may go over if we fail here. He's taking our failures on his own shoulders, despite the fact that the mission's course has, largely, been beyond his control.

"Fifteen kilometers," Berberian says.

Rose and Throdahl are exchanging speculations on the treasures the Rescue station may contain. I hear something about nurses. Throdahl frequently interrupts himself to repeat something he has overheard on his radio.

The situation is obvious. The other firm is trying to kick hell out of Canaan and our bases. News from the larger moon is depressing. Enemy troops have reached its surface.

"Looks bad, sir," Chief Nicastro says. His face is pale, his voice a murmur. I can read his mind. What point surviving the mission if he goes home to die in an invasion?

How are they doing, getting at Canaan itself? Seems there'd be vast areas where they could put down virtually unopposed. Where I came in, say. All they'd have to do is crack a gap in the orbital defenses.

"Ten kilometers," Berberian says.

The Commander asks the First Watch Officer, "Who do we have EVA qualified?"

"Have to check the personnel records, Commander." Yanevich slides up to the inner circle, talks to Canzoneri. "Commander? Mr. Bradley, Mr. Piniaz, Mr. Varese, Chief Nicastro, DellaVecchia."

"Who's DellaVecchia?"

"That new Damage Control Third of Mr. Varese's."

"Who's got the most time?"

"Mr. Bradley and Chief Nicastro."

"The Chief hasn't been outside since I've known him."

"I'll go, Commander," Nicastro says. He draws a few surprised stares. The Chief volunteering? Impossible.

"I don't want to send any more married men, Chief."

"It doesn't much matter, does it? It's over for Canaan. Might as well be me. I'm used up. Mr. Bradley is just getting started."

The Chief and the Old Man trade stares. "All right. Keep your helmet camera going. Open the hatch, there."

"Five kilometers," Berberian says.

I smile at the Chief as he passes. "Luck."

"Thank you, sir."

I turn back to the screen. We're close now. The Commander has our maneuvering lights directed at the asteroid. Details stand out.

Big lump of nickel-iron, hollowed, with a carbuncle on its hip... The assault pod looks like it has gone through three wars. I still wonder what it's doing here.

The Commander leans over my shoulder, says, "Uhm. Strange things happen," and moseys toward Mr. Westhause, who is maneuvering to match the asteroid's spin.

The rock keeps sliding off camera.

Chief Nicastro floats across a fifty-meter gap, lands lightly. His magnetic soles fix his feet to the asteroid. I've been evicted from my seat. The Commander himself has it. Yanevich and I watch over his shoulders.

Nicastro's voice crackles thinly. "Lander or station first, Commander?"

"Lander. See if anybody survived. Don't want you walking into a trap." The Old Man pushes a button. He's taping.

Throdahl says, "Incoming for us, Commander. Command."

"I'll take it." Yanevich scrambles to the radioman's side, watches while Throdahl scribbles. He returns, hands the message to me.

Command wants us to make a mother rendezvous at Fuel Point. In his wisdom the Admiral has declared that homecoming Climbers gather there and stay out of sight. If necessary, the mothers will carry us to Second Fleet's base.

I pass the message to the Old Man. He glances, nods.

"Any reply?" Yanevich asks.

"Later. Depends on what happens here."

He faces a split screen. On top we see the Chief from here. Underneath, we have what the Chief himself is seeing.

Nicastro circles the pod. It's in bad shape. He peeks inside. The troop bay is jammed with torn bodies. She came in hard.

"Can't tell if anybody got through it," the Commander mutters. "Coxswains would've had better luck…. Guess he has to go inside. Maybe they've been picked up already. Find an entry lock, Chief."

Nicastro locates one a few meters from the pod. "What now, Commander?" His voice is taut and shaky.

"Go on in."

"He should have backup," I say. "We won't be able to see what's happening after he's inside."

"How are you at breathing vacuum?" Yanevich asks. His tone is hard, irritated. "We'll give you the Commander's pistol." He wears a sneer. Maybe I should keep my stupid mouth shut.

The Chief cycles the lock and disappears. Half the screen gets snowy, vague. The Old Man mutters imprecations upon the ship's designers. They could've given us a broader range of frequencies.

Tension builds. Five minutes. Ten. Where is the Chief? Fifteen. Why doesn't he get on the station's comm gear? Twenty minutes. They must've gotten him. Can we bluff them with our energy weapons? We can't leave him here….

"Here he is, Commander," Throdahl shouts.

"Put it over here."

Nicastro's voice croaks from a small speaker below the viewscreen.

"… you read?"

"Got you, Chief. This's the Commander. Go ahead."

"Nobody home, Commander. Somebody cleaned the place out. Fuel stores zilch. Medical supplies, zip. Ten cases of emergency rations. That's it."

I'm still recalling the inside of the pod. Almost as bad as the drop-ship at Turbeyville.

"Damn!" the Old Man says. "Bring what you can to the lock, Chief." He turns. "First Watch Officer. Tell Command we can't rendezvous. Insufficient fuel." Back to Nicastro. "Any spare suits down there, Chief?"

"Negative, Commander. I can manage. Cases don't weigh much. Gravity system is off."

"Take care, Chief. Out."

Yanevich returns with a note he passes to the Commander. Command says to stand by here. The Old Man looks disgusted.

Yanevich leans forward, whispers, "We're not alone, Commander. There's a weak neutrino source two hundred thousand klicks out at two seven seven, twelve nadir. I had Berberian bounce a pulse. Corvette. No IFF."

"Relative motion?"

"Almost zero."

"And powered down?"

"Yes sir."

Of the air, softly, the Commander demands, "Why is she hiding?" He stares at the display tank. Nothing unusual happening there. "Chief? Can you hear me?"

No response. "Must be moving the rations," I say.

"Brilliant. Here. Sit. Tell him what's happening." He slides out, moves toward Westhause. "Put us behind this turd relative to this new bogey. No need attracting too much attention."

My gut feeling is we've been seen already.

Berberian calls down, "Commander, she's powering up."

I tell Yanevich, "Here's a guess about where the pod came from. Our boys hit a transport on its way in, then shot up the pods when the troops bailed out."

Yanevich isn't interested. His gaze is fixed on the display tank. "Fits the known facts. A Climber attack, probably."

I glance at the tank, can't tell if anything is happening.

"She's accelerating, Commander," Berberian says. "Slowly."

"Where's she headed?"

"Angling across the belt, sir. Inward. She might've been headed here, then noticed us."

"Getting any closer?"

After a pause, Berberian says, "Yes sir. CPA about eighty thousand klicks. Be a long time, though. Looks like she's sneaking away."

By getting closer? Well, maybe. If that's what she's got to do to reach her friends.

The Commander snaps, "Mr. Yanevich, go twist Mr. Varese's neck till he gives you some accurate figures. Absolutely accurate figures, not what he wants us to believe."

Nicastro reaches the lock with the first case of rations. I explain the situation. "It'll be a long time before anything has to be decided, Chief. Up to you."

"Be less efficient, sir, but I'll bring the cases over one at a time. You'll be sure to get something if you have to haul ass."

"Right." I relay his plan to the Commander, who merely nods. He's preoccupied with the corvette. He's worried. She isn't behaving right.

After a time, he comes to peer over my shoulder. "What's she doing?" I ask.

"Sneaking. Probably figures we're a Climber. Must guess we've seen her. She should be crawling all over us."

"Berberian thought she was headed here when she spotted us. Maybe she's hurt."

"Why didn't she yell for help and stay put?"

She hasn't yelled. Neither Fisherman nor Throdahl have detected a signal. "Maybe she's hurt bad."

"Maybe. I don't trust them." He stalks toward Westhause.

He has his second wind. His shoulders no longer slump. His face is less sallow, more determined. He has the antsyness of a man eager to act. Were we in better shape he'd jump the corvette just to see what happened.

Next time past he says, "Eighty thousand klicks is close enough for energy weapons." He rolls away again, reminds Mr. Westhause to keep the asteroid between us and the sneak.

Chief Nicastro appears with a second case of rations. Glancing at the compartment clock, I'm surprised to see how long he's taken. Time is zipping.

The First Watch Officer comes through the Weapons hatch. He

has a metal case in his arms, a sheet of paper in one hand. The Commander peers into the case. "Pass them around." He snatches the tattered sheet.

Yanevich hands me a ration packet. I laugh softly.

"Something wrong with it?" the Old Man asks.

"Emergency rations! This's better stuff than we've been eating for three months." I pull the heat tab. A minute later, I peel the foil and—lo!—a steaming meal.

It's no gourmet delight. Something like potato hash including gristly gray chopped meat, a couple of unidentifiable vegetables, and a dessert that might be chocolate cake in disguise. The frosting on the cake has melted into the hash. I polish the tray, belch. "Damn, that was good!"

Yanevich gives each man a meal, then hands me another pack. They come forty-two to a case. He sets the last aside for the Chief. To my questioning frown, he says, "That's for your buddy."

Out of nowhere, out of the secret jungles of metal, comes Fearless Fred, rubbing my shins and purring. I heat his pack, thieve the cake, place the tray on the deckplates. Fred polishes his tray in less time than I did mine.

The Commander hasn't quit staring at the sheet Yanevich brought. Now he passes it to me, heats his own ration pack.

Just a list of figures. Water, so much. Cracked hydrogen, so much. CT, fourteen minutes available Climb time…

I'll be damned. That Varese is a classic. He swore we had no CT. And there's twice the hydrogen he admitted was available. I look up. Through a mouthful, Yanevich says, "I twisted Diekereide, not Varese. Varese wouldn't have admitted it."

I raise an eyebrow. "Gets a little carried away, doesn't he?"

"I feel better now," the Old Man says. He tosses his tray into the empty ration case. Yanevich makes the rounds, cleaning up. We're all doing our share of odd jobs. We have to take up the slack left by the departures of Picraux and Brown.

I can't imagine how Varese is managing.

I seldom visit Engineering. Afraid Varese and I will get into it. We barely tolerate each other in the wardroom. I don't understand it. We've no real cause.

Yanevich shakes me awake. He wears a pale grin. "Sleeping on station, eh?"

Of course. We all have for weeks. "I don't think I could find my hammock anymore. Foreign territory. What's up?"

"Corvette changed course. CPA fifty-five thousand klicks. Commander figures it means trouble."

"Jesus. What'd we ever do to those guys?"

He grins. "They probably said the same thing at Rathgeber."

"Yeah."

"You'd better figure this scow is number one on their shit list. The Executioner is back…." He pauses. Then, "Sometimes I think he's a renegade."

"What?"

"His style. He gets involved."

"Uhm. How's the Chief doing?"

"One more trip."

I punch a few keys, pan camera across Canaan's end of the sky. The big show is still smoking. "How?"

"The Old Man will think of something."

Come on, Steve. Not you too. You're a big boy. You'll be the Old Man yourself your next time around.

The Commander joins us. He looks washed out again. "Real skyshow, eh? Berberian says the 'vette acts shot-up. Canzoneri agrees. Hyper generators and comm out. No missiles. Else they'd be climbing our backs. This's a popular station."

"Think they'll leave us alone?"

"We look too easy to take."

"She'll be in best fire configuration in five minutes, Commander," Berberian announces.

"Very well." The Old Man visits Westhause, then Canzoneri. "Battle stations." We're on station already. He tells me, "Get the Chief back inside."

Yanevich watches over Throdahl's shoulder. The radioman has started logging the traffic he copies. The First Watch Officer selects some notes and brings them to me. Reading them is like painting by the numbers. A picture slowly appears.

The squadrons which attacked the convoy back when were very successful. So were two more which made a follow-up strike after the first three broke off. One note is especially interesting. "Commander, the *Eight Ball* did it again."

"How so?" He seems only mildly intrigued.

"Brought home another six stars. Two red and four white." Meaning she took out two warships and four logistic hulls.

"Uhm. Henderson is a good man."

Down toward the Inner Worlds they're trying something unique. Second Fleet is raiding Thompson's System. The heavies are laying back, guarding a flotilla of mothers, tankers, and tenders from which the Climbers are jumping off. They're even rearming in space. Interesting.

Wonder if we'll have any Climbers left when the dust settles.

Nicastro is on. "Get your butt in here, Chief. Looks like trouble." I watch him float over, steering the last carton of rations.

Damn, but I feel better. Amazing how a few cases can boost a man's morale.

"Coming up to optimum, Commander," Berberian says.

"Very well. Stand by, Mr. Westhause. Is the Chief in yet?"

"He's at the lock, Commander."

"Mr. Varese, get Nicastro inside."

"Oh, damn!" Berberian snarls. "Commander, they faked us. Missiles launching. Flight of four."

"Velocity to compute. Time till arrival, Canzoneri."

"Aye, sir."

"Feed to astrogation."

Westhause surveys the compartment. His gaze meets mine. He smiles, returns to work.

I watch the four red darts streak through the tank. At one hundred gees they won't be long arriving.

"Chief's inside," Varese announces.

"Ready, Mr. Westhause?"

"Ready, Commander."

"Engineering, shift to annihilation."

"Engineering, aye."

We're going to Climb?…That's right. They 'fessed up to having some CT. But how much good can it do?

Canzoneri does the counting down. "Missiles arrive in thirty seconds." Where did the time go?

"Can we do it, Mr. Westhause?"

"I have enough data, sir. If she doesn't go hyper."

"I don't think she was lying about that. There're enough drive anomalies to indicate bad generators."

"Ten seconds," the Chief computerman says. "Five…"

Alarms hoot. I hear his three and two, then we're going up.

Six minutes later we're down again, so close the corvette fills my screen as the gun cameras lock. Lightning bolts span the gap separating us. At this range it won't matter if her screens are up.

The Old Man laughs. "We lied to you, too, hunter-man We had CT left."

Red sores appear on the corvette's flank. One, near her fly-eye bows, bulges outward, erupts. A shower of junk sprays through the gap.

Alarm. Ghost world again. The Commander is beside me. "Down to Weapons, boy. We got nothing but your toy now. Ito has to cool his beamers. Go for her drives. Come on! Up now. Go along."

I hear him arguing with Westhause as I push through the Weapons hatch. Sounds like Westhause wants to run while we have Climb time left.

I fling myself into the seat at the cannon board. Piniaz has it warmed already. The target data is flowing. I break the arming locks, scan the compartment. Only Piniaz seems unperturbed. I flip to manual. I'll do this myself.

Alarm.

Damn! I'm not ready!

There she is. The stars beyond her say we're down opposite the flank we hit before. Targeting rings amidships. Fire and try to drag my point of aim aft. Holes on the moth's wings. "Too high!" I shout. "Got to get under the wing."

A beam licks out from the corvette. It passes between can and torus. The ship rocks. A stay member glows and parts. I send a burst into the beam mount. "Down, damn it!" We're moving, but too slowly.

This is mad. We're two pit bulls with broken backs trying to sink our teeth in one another's throats.

More sewing machine holes along the side of the corvette. Gas escaping through some. Wing apparently rising. We're actually dropping. Fierce glow round the corvette's drive vents as she puts on power.

Stitching moving aft fast. Targeting rings traversing the heat vents, swinging back. Christ! I could reach out and touch her, we're so close.

Red lights across my board. "Ammunition gone!" I shout. "Get out of here."

Hyper alarm. Another beam from the corvette. Wham! Launch Three ripped off the torus in a hail of echoing fragments. Launch Three, that caused so much trouble after Rathgeber. Hope the accelerator path wasn't breached. We wouldn't be able to Climb.

Ghosting.

It lasts only a few minutes. Down we go. Cameras searching, hunting the corvette. What's she doing? Coming after us? There she is. Two thousand-some klicks. Accelerating... nova!

Damn! Must've gotten a few marbles into her fusor room. A weak, ragged victory growl runs through Ops.

I pile out of my chair, only now realizing that I didn't strap in. No one closed the Ops hatch either. I scramble through, slam it.

Yanevich is waiting, grinning. "Damned fine sniping for a one-legged intellectual."

I grin, myself. "Yeah. Hey. Another red star for the Old Man."

The Commander is hanging over Westhause's shoulder again looking gloomy. Berberian and Carmon are talking at once. Fisherman shouts something. "Enjoy," Yanevich says. "The party's just beginning."

11

END GAME

There's a stir in the display tank. They know a Climber has struck. They don't know we're harmless now. Their reaction seems to be a controlled panic.

Carmon goes to his broadest scale. Red and green blips swirl everywhere.

The Old Man is grumbling at Throdahl. Must be arguing with Command. There's no way we can make a rendezvous at Fuel Point. TerVeen is our only hope.

"Stand by to take hyper," the Old Man says.

We have to jump. Have to get as close as we can. Maybe there's a shred of Planetary Defense umbrella left. Long shot.

We could do a few zigzags and power down completely, go on emergency power, and drift in, but the men aren't up to a norm crossing. The best we could hope for, Canzoneri says, is a nine-day passage. Through the heat and heart of battle.

No thank you. That's a suicide run.

Do we have enough hydrogen to jump and make adjustments in inherent velocity when we get close?… Why worry? Command may not send tugs into the crucible for a lone, beat-up Climber they don't want there anyway.

The Commander appears only mildly concerned. He's started another up cycle. Telling weak jokes. Asking Throdahl and Rose for the addresses of those girls they're always bragging about. "Jump, Mr. Westhause. Maximum translation ratio."

Oh-oh. We have company. Nuclear greetings are headed our way.

Our chances look longer all the time. I don't think we'll make it.

It's been one hell of an interesting mission….

The Commander is beside me. "Go get your notes."

"Sir?"

"Get your stuff together. Stow it in a ration case under your seat."

I move down to Ship's Services, strip my hammock in seconds. "What's going on out there?" Bradley asks. He doesn't know we've just shot it out with a corvette, and that a missile flight is closing in.

Kriegshauser is right behind him. "Give it to us straight," he pleads.

I sketch it. "It doesn't look good. But you can count on the Old Man."

That seems assurance enough. The Ship's Services people are unshakable. Maybe they were selected for that.

I pause as I pass through Weapons. Piniaz looks grim. He forces a smile. One hand drifts to my shoulder. "Been all right, Lieutenant. Good luck. Just write it the way it was."

A hell of a gesture for the little man. "I will, Ito. I promise."

I settle my things under the First Watch Officer's seat. Pity I can't make peace with Varese, too.

"What's happened?" I ask Fisherman. The mausoleum silence of Ops demands a soft voice.

"Getting worse." His screen is a-crawl with hyper wakes. The pencil strokes characteristic of high-translation ratio missiles spaghetti through the mess. We're cruising the middle of a barn-burner. Both sides have gone kill-crazy.

Chung!

Chung!

"What the hell is that?"

Chung!

Sounds like some mischievous child-deity is hammering the hull with a god-sized gong-beater.

"We're hyper skipping," Fisherman says. "Randomed."

I figured as much. It's one way to rattle a missile's moron brain. But that doesn't have anything to do with the noise.

Chung!

"What's the noise?" It's pounding the can about ninety degrees round the circle.

"Mr. Westhause said he was having trouble with inertial rectification."

"That wouldn't..."

"Commander, Engineering. There's a chunk of water-ice bouncing around in the Six Reserve Tank. Can we have a constant vector and acceleration while we melt and drain?"

"Negative. We can live with the racket. But go ahead and melt."

"Engineering, aye."

That was Diekereide. I haven't seen him for a while. Have to buy him a beer if we get out of this.

"Weapons. Gunnery status?"

"Energy all go, Commander. Got them cooled and tuned enough for a couple shots." We nearly lost them while dueling with the corvette. "They won't last, though."

"We won't shoot unless a Christmas present falls in our lap."

The Old Man has reached back and found one more reservoir of whatever it is that makes him go. He jitters from station to station, restless as a whore in church, almost eager for the squeeze to get tighter. Poisonous clouds belch from his pipe. We take turns coughing and scowling and rubbing our eyes. And grinning at the Commander's back when he moves on.

He's alive. He'll bring us through again.

That faith, the thing that the Commander so fears, resents, and loves, helps me understand both him and Fisherman a bit better.

Fisherman has surrendered his life and soul to a universal Ship's Commander. He just keeps plugging while he waits for that heaven-bound ride.

The others yield only to faith in snatches, in hard times, to a man, when they fear their own competence is insufficient. It's a pity the Commander can find no fit object for faith himself.

He's too cynical to accept any religion, and the Admiral's circus antics have alienated him from any demigod role. What's left? The Service? That's what we were taught all those years in Academy.

Tannian is Command's strength and weakness. For all his strategic genius, he can't inspire his captains.

The gong-beating fades, but not before the plug-ups rush to a tiny crack in our bulkhead.

The Climber is dying slowly, like a man with a nasty cancer.

A chunk of water-ice. Not a completely unpleasant surprise. It means a little extra energy, a little extra mobility. Or a long, cool drink for the crew. Lord, I'm thirsty. I've got nothing left to sweat.

"Stand by, Weapons. We have a possible Target One. Designation vectors coming down now."

What the hell?

One especially intense streak stands out on Fisherman's screen. That the one? Only an advanced tactical computer could make sense of that mess. The mix has grown too dense, the changes too rapid.

We've drawn a lot of attention. The tank shows a lot of green blips. Maybe Command is lending a hand.

The whole mess is probably an ad lib.

"Commander, Engineering." That's Diekereide again. Where's Varese? "I'm getting an erratic flow through Hydrolysis. I don't think we can process enough hydrogen to meet your present translation demand."

"Auxiliary?"

"On the line."

"Reserve hydrogen?"

"Down to fifteen minutes available. We lost the main pressure gauge sometime…. Don't know how long we've been drawing. Had to read it by…"

"Notify me when you're down to five minutes. Mr. Piniaz? We've got a missile coming. Got to skrag it."

"Targeted and tracking. Commander."

"On my mark, then." The Commander exchanges whispers with Westhause.

Rose says, "Commander, we've got another unavoidable coming up." He's insanely calm. They all are. Weird.

The walls are closing in. The tank makes some sense now, on a local scale. Missile coming in. We'll have to dance with it, confuse it, take it in norm, with our energy weapons. And the delay will let the other team lock us into a lethal groove.

Alarm. We go norm. "Now, Mr. Piniaz."

The result is unspectacular. The missile vaporizes, but I can't catch its death on screen.

"Commander, Weapons. We've lost the graser for good."

This junk pile is falling apart.

The dream dance on the borders of death continues another half-hour. We knock out four pursuing missiles, lose another laser. Westhause squanders fuel tinkering with our inherent velocity. As always, the Commander keeps his own counsel. I haven't the foggiest what he's planning. I try to lose myself in my troubles.

A change. More excitement. I look around. Three missiles have us zeroed. How do we duck this time? We don't have a time margin to fool with anymore. If we stop to take one, the others will get us.

"Commander, Engineering." Varese is back. "Five minutes available hydrogen."

"Thank you, Mr. Varese. Max power. Shunt as much into storage as you can."

I pan to Canaan. Getting close now. Walking distance.

"Sir?" Varese asks.

"Wait one. Mr. Westhause, proceed. Lieutenant, just give me all the stored power you can."

The Commander loses himself in thought. I look at the tank, at Westhause. He's stopped dancing. Canaan is expanding like a child's balloon blowing up. We're running straight in.

The Commander switches on shipwide comm. "Men, this's the last hurdle, and the last trick in our sack. This's been a good ship. She's had good crews, and this one was the best. But now she's done. She can't run and she can't fight."

What's this defeatist talk? The Old Man never gives up.

"We're going to assume a cislunar orbit and separate compartments. That should satisfy the other firm. Rescue will round us up. During our leave I'll have you all out to Kent for a party in the ship's memory."

I can smell the pines, hear the breeze in their boughs. Is Marie really gone? Sharon… did you bring your Climber through, honey? At least a dozen were lost against that convoy….

The crew answers the Old Man with silence. It's the most compelling stillness I've ever experienced.

What's to say? Name another option.

"Men, we made history. I'm proud to have served with you." For the first time ever, the Old Man sits down while he has the conn.

He's done. He's shot his last round. But restless banks of smoke still brew around him. In a weary voice, he asks, "How long, Mr. Westhause?"

We're making a final, brief hyper fly. Skipping in millisecond jumps. Keeping the missiles confused.

"Two minutes thirty… five seconds. Commander."

Strange, that Westhause. Unshakable. Still as professional as the day we boarded. Someday he'll command a Climber with the cool of the Old Man.

"Chief Nicastro, give us a separation countdown. Throdahl, give Command another squirt on our intentions. Mr. Westhause will give you the orbital data. Use Emergency Two."

What will the missiles do when their target splits five ways? Three missiles. Somebody is going to make it.

Give me a break, ye gods of war.

There's a chance. Not a good one, but a chance. One small point going our way. Those three doom-stalkers can't be controlled by their masters. They're dependent on their own dull-witted brains. Which is why we've stayed ahead this long.

My stomach constricts ever more tightly. Fear. The moment of truth is roaring toward us.

We've passed some barrier the enemy won't yet hazard. Maybe Planetary Defense has maintained a tight death pocket round TerVeen. Only those three killer imbeciles continue dogging our trail.

On camera. There's TerVeen. Battered all to hell, but still in business, a spider spinning webs of fire.

The Climber zigzags. Westhause and Varese exchange curses. Final seconds before orbit.

I'll say this. When you're scared shitless it's hard to concentrate on anything else.

Write. Keep your hands busy. Anything for a distraction.

Nicastro's soft voice drones, "… nine… eight… seven…" Six-five-four-three-two-one-ZERO!

Bang!

You're dead.

No. I'm not. Not yet.

Barrages of sound rip through the hull as the explosive bolts go. Perfectly. God bless. Something is working right. The force slams me from the side. Our rocket pack blasts us away from the rest of the ship.

"We have separation and ignition on Ops and Engineering, Commander." How very perceptive.

Head twist. Glare at the tank. Where are those missiles? Can't tell. The antennae were mounted on the torus. We're flying blind….

Thrust ends. The plug-ups break it up around the Weapons bulkhead. I feel lightheaded…. Free-fall. No artificial gravity. The Commander drifts out of his seat.

The serials are continuing in the rest of the ship. Ship's Services will be last to separate. The din there must be murderous. Charlie, I hope you make it. Kriegshauser, you never did get back with that name.

"We have separation on Weapons, Commander."

I still have one outside camera. I watch the rockets flame. Jump the magnification. There's the torus, wobbling, spinning, dwindling rapidly, illuminated by the rockets. It shows silvery patches where beams licked it.

The Climber slides out of view. A crescent of Canaan appears. We're tumbling toward the dawn. I hope Rescue can handle the end-over-end.

The sun rises. It's brilliant, majestic, as it crawls over the curve of the world we've lusted after so long.

Where are those missiles?

There's something special about a mother star materializing from behind a daughter planet. It fills me with the awe of creation. I feel it now, even though death bays at my heels. This, and perhaps clouds, are the supreme arguments for the existence of a Creator.

Time to check the torus again.

My God! A new sun!…

Berberian says, "The torus. First missile took the torus." His voice is a toad's croak.

Well, naturally. The torus is the biggest target. It'll be over in seconds…. Sighs all through the compartment. A diminution in tension. We have a fifty-fifty chance now.

"Hey! Torus again!" Berberian shouts. "Goddamned second fucking missile took the torus, too!"

"Let's have proper reports," the Commander admonishes.

I could howl for joy.

And yet… there's that third bird, lagging the other two. Big black monster with my name engraved on its teeth.

Got to get Canaan on screen. I want a world in my eyes when I go.

What a sweet world it is. What a beautiful world. I've never wanted any woman, not even Sharon, as badly as I want that world.

"Three won't target on the torus," Laramie says.

"Shut your cocksucker, will you?" Rose snarls.

Piniaz will try with his one laser, but it won't be enough. He's failed twice already, hasn't he?

Nevertheless, the Old Man has won. There will be survivors.

If Fisherman's Devil exists, his favorite torture must be guilt. Three more compartments out there, and me here hoping the hammer falls on one of them. Part of me is utterly without shame.

A flash brightens my screen. "Gone." I stammer getting the word out.

"Who?" a voice demands.

"Berberian? Throdahl?" the Commander asks.

Seconds pass. I scribble frantically, then wait, pencil poised. Throdahl says, "Commander, I can't get a response from Ship's Services."

"Ah, Charlie. Shit."

"That's it, men," the Commander says. "Secure. Mr. Yanevich, take charge." He pauses to knock ashes from his pipe. "Emergency watch bill."

Kriegshauser. Vossbrink. Charlie Bradley. Light. Shingledecker. Tahtaburun. All gone? No. Some were in Engineering.

Poor Charlie. He had a future. Crapped out first patrol. Welcome to the Climbers, kid.

I'll mourn him. I liked him.

Wonder if Kriegshauser made it. He hated being away from his little galley.

Well, if he didn't, he doesn't have a problem anymore. Too bad I couldn't help him.

Look on the positive side. They didn't hurt. They never knew what hit them.

Nothing to do now but wait for Rescue. Wait and wonder if we'll ever hear their approach signal.

Going to find an empty hammock. Probably won't sleep, but I need a change. Need to get away.

Chatter down below. "Think they'll throw anything else?" That's Carmon. "We're sitting ducks."

"Don't worry your pointy head, Patriot," Nicastro says. "We won't know it when it hits us." The Chief refuses to believe there's a tomorrow.

"How long we got to wait?" Berberian asks.

"Throdahl? Anything?"

"Sorry, Chief."

"As long as we have to, Berberian."

Berberian says, "Thro, get on the horn and tell them to get their asses out here."

"I did, Berberian. What the fuck more you want?"

"Pussy. Pussy and more pussy. Whole platoons of pussy. Just line them up and I'll lay them down."

I was right. Can't sleep. I roll, peer down through the tangle. The Commander is seated near Westhause, writing something. He rises, struggles up to his cabin. Even in free-fall he finds the climb hard work. He's burned out. Nothing left.

You got us home, old friend. Hang on to that.

"Let's get on it here," the First Watch Officer snaps. "We're supposed to conserve power." His tone is relaxed, confident. The tone of a Commander. He's come along. "Carmon, secure the tank. Mr. Westhause, Chief Canzoneri, lock your memory banks and close up shop. You too, Junghaus. Berberian, Throdahl, stay warm. Might need to help Rescue. Laramie, secure the cooler and atmosphere scrubber. Going to get cold anyway. Give us a spritz of oxygen while you're at it. Chief Nicastro, secure some lights. If you don't have something to do, crap out."

Men lying still use fewer calories and perspire less. The First Watch Officer is gentling us into the starvation leg of our journey.

"Hope to fuck they hurry," Throdahl grumbles. He keeps tinkering, trying to find something on the Rescue band. "I'm hungry, thirsty, horny, and filthy. Not necessarily in that order."

"I'll buy that," Rose says.

"What the hell does that mean?"

"That you're filthy, Thro. Right down to the stinking core."

The pace picks up. Laramie joins in. Berberian contributes the occasional quip. They're feeling better.

For me the waiting is intolerable. We're too near home.

Laramie moans something about he's going to perish if he don't get some pussy in the next twenty-four hours.

"You'll last," Fisherman snarls. The men look at him, mouths open. No. He's not joining the game. The cut-low session recesses. Junghaus's shipmates aren't insensitive.

"At least you had water," the usually silent Scarlatella grumbles. I roll slightly, peer through the tangled piping. Lubomir Scarlatella is a strange one. He's Electronic Technician for Chief Canzoneri. I don't think he's said a hundred words all patrol. Silent, proficient, imperturbable. You hardly notice him. Now hysteria edges his voice.

"Until it was a choice between using power to recycle it or to heat the ship." A sublime calm visibly overtakes Junghaus. In a gentle voice he begins quoting scripture. Nobody shuts him up.

I slept. I don't believe it. Twelve hours. Might have gone longer if Zia hadn't wanted the hammock. Clambered down to my old seat. Listened to the halfhearted murmur of the men. Mostly it was speculation about what's happened to our friends in the other compartments.

Hour fourteen. Thro lets out a whoop. "Here they are!"

"Here who are?" Mr. Westhause asks. He has the watch, such as it is.

"Rescue… goddamned. They're going after Weapons. The bastards." He slugs his console angrily.

"Take it easy. We'll get our turn."

The sons of bitches!

You don't know how selfish you can be till you're in a survival situation seeing someone else being saved first. Forty-two minutes, every one spent hating and cursing Piniaz's cutthroats.

Now our turn. With Rescue cursing us as heartily as we cursed Weapons. It takes them three hours to get the spin off the compartment.

"Not going to tow us," Throdahl announces. "They're going to take us out right here. Going to scab a tube to the top hatch."

A *chung* echoes through the compartment. More delicate sounds follow it. Someone is walking around on the roof.

Yanevich waves me over, beckons Mr. Westhause. "Let's get up by that hatch. We'll have to keep order."

"What do you mean?"

"You'll see."

I do. We have to threaten violence when the fresh water comes through. Some people seem willing to kill for a drink. We're lucky they're really too weak to riot.

"Take it easy!" I snap at Zia. "Drink too much and you'll make yourself sick."

Yanevich says, "Throdahl, get back to the radio. They'll tell us when to open the hatch."

The stench of bile assails my nostrils. Zia has puked his stomach empty. "I told you…." Never mind. He had to learn.

"Undog the hatch," Throdahl yells. "They've got the tube on."

Yanevich checks the telltales on our side, unlocks the hatch. Several men surge up behind him.

A pair of Marines squat outside the hatch. "Get back," one says. They're wearing combat suits. "You don't get out yet." They slither in, station themselves beside the opening.

A med team follows them. A doctor and two medical corpsmen in white plague suits. What is this? Are we carriers of the Black Death?

The men crowd round our visitors, touching, murmuring with the awe of primitives. They can't really believe they're saved.

Have these rescuers ever seen anything this bad? We're worse than a bunch of galley slaves. Unbathed for ages. Unshaved. Clothed in moldy rags. Skin masked by scab and scale. Some men losing hair.

Lucky the med team aren't female. Good way to get torn apart. These men aren't human anymore.

In a few months the process of degeneration will begin anew, aboard a new Climber. But I won't be going out. Thank god. Not again. Neither will Chief Nicastro…

The Chief. "Steve. Waldo. Where's the Chief?"

"Nicastro?" Yanevich says. "He was right… Come on."

We spread out. Not much to search. Westhause finds him immediately. "Here. DC station. Medic!"

I find him with fingers against Nicastro's jugular. He shakes his head. "Medic!" I shout. "What happened, Waldo?"

"I don't know. Heart maybe."

Yanevich mutters, "He was determined he wasn't going to make it."

The doctor goes the whole CPR route. No good. "Nothing I can do here," he says. "Under normal conditions…"

"Nothing's normal in the Climbers."

I'm so numb I couldn't mourn my best friend. Nothing but low, banked coals of rage remain.

The men are leaving. The Marines are making sure they stay civilized.

"Where's the Old Man?" Westhause asks.

"Upstairs." I point.

"I'll get him," Yanevich says. "Go ahead."

"Where's Fearless? Hey! Fred!" Suddenly, that cat is the most important thing in my universe.

The men are all out. Westhause clambers through the hatchway. "Now you," the doctor says.

"Can't. Got to find…"

The Marines make short work of me.

The long, tight tube leads to a receiving bay aboard the Rescue ship. I scramble through fast. Another med team is waiting. They're expecting animals. A barrage of water smashes me flat. I tumble across a cold, hard deck. Three times I get to my feet and go after the hose man.

He has no trouble protecting himself. The bay is under full gravity. My weary, weak muscles can't handle it. Disgusted, I surrender to the inevitable, let myself be driven into an immersion bath. They don't give me time to shed my clothing.

Takes the piss and vinegar out of you fast. I suppose that's why they do it.

Splashing and wailing, I struggle to the tank's far side. There's no fight in me anymore. A hand comes down. I grab it. In a moment I'm lying on the deck, panting. My shipmates gag and gasp around me. Throdahl, in the bath, is promising murder. The med crew don't let him out till he changes his mind.

"Can you stand up?" My helper's voice is spooky. Planetary atmosphere here, and he's wearing a mask. I grunt an affirmative. "Get your clothes off. Sir."

It's a struggle, but I manage. "What about my stuff?"

The medic scoops my rags into a basket with a little plastic pitchfork. "You'll get it back. If you want it."

"I mean my stuff from the ship. It's important." This is the critical passage. My notes and pictures could disappear without my being able to raise a finger.

A horrible caterwauling erupts from the escape tube. An orange Fury whirls out. Fearless is reluctant to leave home. He's giving a Marine all he can handle. Man, is he going to be mad when… the hose man goes to work.

I'm wrong. Old Fearless is so stunned by the indignity of it all he just goes along. He barely reacts when I drag him out of the pool. He hasn't the strength to don his usual mask of aloofness.

A hand is in my face. "Drink this." I drain a small squeeze bottle. "Now use one of the showers." The medic points. "Be thorough, but don't waste time. Your buddies are waiting. So is breakfast."

"Breakfast?"

"It's morning to us, sir."

"Come on, Fearless." I waste little time showering. That squeeze bottle contained an all-time purgative. There's little for my stomach to be rid of, but it's making a valiant effort.

Breakfast turns out to be lunch. They put us through four hours of intensive decontamination before they dump us into the ship's hospital quarters and feed us. By then I'm so dopey I don't know where I am. I fall asleep with an IV in my arm, feeling like a voodoo doll after the ceremony.

I waken much later. Pain. Gravity gnawing at my every cell. Yet I feel healthier than I have in months. My body has been flushed of accumulated poisons.

My stomach knots in hunger.

Clean! I feel clean. There's nothing more sensual than clean sheets against freshly scrubbed skin.

A male nurse helps me sit up. I survey the ward. Seems we're still aboard the Rescue ship. Westhause is in the bed to my left, Yanevich to my right. Both are awake, staring into nothing. "Where's the Old Man?" Varese, Diekereide, and Piniaz lie beyond the astrogator. We're laid out in Service pecking order.

Westhause won't meet my gaze. He hears me, I know. But he won't answer.

"Steve?"

"Psych detention," he whispers. "They brought him out in a straitjacket. Didn't realize it was over. Wanted to light off the drive. Said he had to help Johnson."

"Shit. Goddamned, shit. Wonder if I can find Marie? Maybe she can put him back together. Shit. This fucking war."

"Won't find Marie. Won't any of us see Canaan again."

I survey the ward. Everyone is here. Including Bradley and his gang. How can that be? That missile got them.... Or did it? Did Ito get in one straight shot, when it counted?

Yanevich plunges ahead. "They have troops down on the surface."

What? If Canaan is lost, everything is done for. Holy shit. I twist toward Westhause. He has family down there. There's a tear track on his cheek.

Something stirs beside me. Fearless rises, stretches, moves to a new napping place atop my chest. What are the medics doing? "At least you'll get out, you one-eyed pirate. Whether you want it or not. How long till we make TerVeen, Steve?"

Yanevich gets the same hollow look Westhause has. "We're headed outsystem. They've broken through TerVeen's defenses, too. Hand-to-hand fighting, last we heard. Rescue people say they've lost contact."

Westhause curses softly.

"He had a girl there. Under your seat, all your stuff; I made them bring it out."

Down the way Rose and Throdahl revise plans for their leaves, wherever we're going. Second Fleet's baseworld, I'd guess. Laramie and Berberian trade halfhearted insults. Fisherman is seated in the lotus position on his bed, looking more oriental than Christian as he communes with his god. Diekereide is telling Bradley a story we've heard before. Varese and Piniaz have retreated into their sullen, solitary worlds. Kriegshauser is curled in a fetal ball, facing the wall. They're all here. All but the paterfamilias.

"Shit. This fucking war."

You cheated me, my friend, you never did come in out of the bushes. You didn't shed your warpaint and reveal the man behind. Maybe now you're so well hidden no one will see you again. If so, good-bye. We loved you well. I wish you'd given us the chance to understand.

This goddamned war.

That evil-mouthed Laramie is humming the "Outward Bound." One by one, with malign grins, the others take it up.

What the hell? Here's up yours, Fred Tannian. "Hmm-hmm-de-dum…"

EPILOG

Twenty years have fled since *Clara Barton* carried the crew of 53-B from the Canaan System. The hospital was the last ship out, given safe passage by the other firm. Admiral Frederick Minh-Tannian died with weapon in hand twelve days later, as TerVeen finally fell. He lived and died the role he demanded of his command.

His death was his great triumph. Historians now mark it as the watershed of the war.

We who served him, for one mission or many, and survived, can neither forget nor forgive. Yet the man was a genius. He established a goal, and fulfilled it. One stubborn mongrel nipping at the enemy's hamstrings, he broke Ulant's inexorable stride. After that the war was won. Numbers and production were our advantages, though blunt instruments slow to hammer out the armistice.

They were heroes, the people of Climber Fleet One. They were everything Tannian claimed. In the aggregate. However, *we* were individuals, frightened men and women trapped in the crucible of war.

True heroes seldom picture themselves as heroes. True heroes just stick to their jobs in the teeth of the dragon winds of heart and hell.

Twenty years have flown. Only now has the bitterness waned enough to permit this true tale to be told. There was no effort to censor me, back when. *Civilians* decided the public was not ready for this. Even now, those who bring you this are afraid of the furor it may raise....

For all he seemed shattered and lost, my friend recovered with his confidence redeemed and renewed. Six years later he commanded the Task Group that reclaimed Canaan.

Yanevich, Westhause, and Bradley likewise prospered. The first and last are still in, and Admirals today. Westhause is a math professor on Canaan.

Piniaz perished his second mission after they gave him his own Climber. Diekereide was his Engineer. What became of Varese no one knows.

Of the enlisted men of 53-B, six survived the war. Of those, two have survived the peace. The price of the Climbers, and of victory, continues to be paid. Sometimes it seems Ulant came out better than we did.

Night Shade Books Is an Independent Publisher of Quality SF, Fantasy and Horror

ISBN 978-1-59780-063-1
Hardcover; $23.95

For three centuries the city of Shasesserre has been kept safe from harm, shielded by the wizardry of its legendary Protector, Jehrke Victorious. Those many generations of calm, however, have just come to a calamitous end: the Protector has been brutally slain by a mysterious stranger. Immediately, it falls to Rider, Jehrke's son, to take on his father's responsibilities as Protector of the City and to avenge his death. Rider and his cohorts must utilize their every resource—wits, swords, and magic—against the vile minions of the devious dwarf Kralj Odehnal and his terrifying and merciless master, the wicked eastern sorcerer Shai Khe, who conspires to conquer Shasesserre and rule the world with an iron fist.

ISBN 978-1-59780-004-4
Hardcover; $25.00

All is not well in Lamentable Moll. A sinister, diabolical killer stalks the port city's narrow, barrow-humped streets, and panic grips the citizens like a fever.

Emancipor Reese is no exception, and indeed, with his legendary ill luck, it's worse for him than for most. Not only was his previous employer the unknown killer's latest victim, but Emancipor is out of work. And, with his dearest wife terminally comfortable with the manner of life to which she asserts she has become accustomed (or at least to which she aspires) -- for her and their two whelps -- all other terrors grow limp and pale for poor Emancipor.

But perhaps his luck has finally changed, for two strangers have come to Lamentable Moll... and they have nailed to the centre post in Fishmonger's Round a note requesting the services of a manservant.

Find these Night Shade titles and many others online at http://www.nightshadebooks.com or wherever books are sold.

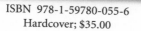

Night Shade Books Is an Independent Publisher of Quality SF, Fantasy and Horror

ISBN 978-1-59780-062-4
Tradepaper $14.95

Years ago, the last desperate hopes of Earth were crushed as corporate Orbital Blocs ruling from on high devastated the planet's face. Today, the autocratic Orbitals indulge in decadent luxury far above the mudboys, dirtgirls, zonedancers, and buttonheads who live out violent lives of electronic distraction and dependence amid the flooded, ruined cities and teeming slums of a balkanized America.

But there are heroes: those who would stand against the hegemony of the Orbital powers. From Walter Jon Williams comes Hardwired, the hard-hitting, seminal classic that feels as prescient today as when it was first published. Like a steel-guitar-fueled Damnation Alley, as directed by Sam Peckinpah, Hardwired demonstrates how Williams's singular vision helped define the cyberpunk genre.

ISBN 978-1-59780-044-0
Trade Paper; $14.95

Seconded to a military-religious order he's barely heard of—part of the baroque hierarchy of the Mercatoria, the latest galactic hegemony—Fassin Taak has to travel again amongst the Dwellers. He is in search of a secret hidden for half a billion years.

But with each day that passes a war draws closer—a war that threatens to overwhelm everything and everyone he's ever known. As complex, turbulent, flamboyant and spectacular as the gas giant on which it is set, the new science fiction novel from Iain M. Banks is space opera on a truly epic scale.

Find these Night Shade titles and many others online at http://www.nightshadebooks.com or wherever books are sold.